PRAISE FOR THE OXENBURG PRINCES SERIES

THE PRINCE WHO LOVED ME
A *Publishers Weekly* Book to Watch for 2014!

"Hawkins puts her unique stamp on Cinderella in a tale that shines with humor, sparkling dialogue, and plenty of sexual tension."

—*RT Book Reviews* (4½ stars, Top Pick)

"This is the funniest and most satisfying Hawkins book yet! A clever retelling of Cinderella complete with a handsome prince, two social-climbing stepsisters, an ambitious and ruthless stepmother, and (instead of a fairy godmother) a curse-throwing gypsy grandmother!"

—*Romance and More*

"You'll fall in love with the hero prince, want to be best friends with the bookworm heroine, and wish that the rest of the cast (including three adorable dogs) could be a part of your family. A truly warm and funny romance."

—*Cherry Picks Reviews*

PRAISE FOR THE DUCHESS DIARIES SERIES

HOW TO CAPTURE A COUNTESS

"A delightful, sprightly romp is what Hawkins does best, and when she sets her witty tale in Scotland and adds a charming castle and an engaging cast of characters, readers have the beginning of an appealing new series."

—*RT Book Reviews* (4 stars)

"A beautifully written romance filled with passion, zest, and humor."

—*Addicted to Romance*

"Spiced by a chemistry that practically leaps off the pages. Readers will be thrilled at every witty repartee between these reluctant lovers."

—*Coffee Time Romance & More*

HOW TO PURSUE A PRINCESS

"Sparking, witty repartee and heart-tugging emotions. With a wonderful romantic story, this book is pure, unadulterated Hawkins."

—*RT Book Reviews* (4½ stars, Top Pick)

"Incredibly witty and sweet with the kind of fairy-tale charm that cannot help but remind us of our own childhood dreams of handsome princes and happily ever after."

—*Novels Alive.TV*

HOW TO ENTICE AN ENCHANTRESS

"This fairy tale gone awry is just different enough, just quirky enough, and just wonderful enough to have readers sighing with pleasure."

—*RT Book Reviews* (4½ stars)

"Doesn't disappoint on any level. There's heat, humor, misunderstandings, and finally, love."

—*Tampa Bay Books Examiner* (5 stars)

"A quick, funny, and light read."

—*Literati Literature Lovers*

ALSO BY KAREN HAWKINS

Available from Pocket Books

KAREN HAWKINS

The Prince and I

Pocket Books

New York London Toronto Sydney New Delhi

Pocket Books
An Imprint of Simon & Schuster, Inc.
1230 Avenue of the Americas
New York, NY 10020

This book is a work of fiction. Any references to historical events, real people, or real places are used fictitiously. Other names, characters, places, and events are products of the author's imagination, and any resemblance to actual events or places or persons, living or dead, is entirely coincidental.

First Pocket Books paperback edition September 2015

POCKET and colophon are registered trademarks of Simon & Schuster, Inc.

For information about special discounts for bulk purchases, please contact Simon & Schuster Special Sales at 1-866-506-1949 or business@simonandschuster.com.

The Simon & Schuster Speakers Bureau can bring authors to your live event. For more information or to book an event, contact the Simon & Schuster Speakers Bureau at 1-866-248-3049 or visit our website at www.simonspeakers.com.

Interior design by Yvonne Chan

Manufactured in the United States of America

10 9 8 7 6 5 4 3 2 1

ISBN 978-1-4767-8597-4
ISBN 978-1-4767-8609-4 (ebook)

To the best author's husband in the world, aka HOT COP.
Thank you for picking up dinner/doing laundry
and dishes/walking the dogs/doing all the vacuuming
those few hundred times while I was suffering
from Deadline Dementia.
You make the difficult times easy.
I love you with all my heart.
Thou and I.

Acknowledgments

A special thanks to my fabulous proofreaders, Rachelle Wadsworth, Cail Rodgers, and Suzanne Verikios, who helped so much with their thoughtful comments, spot-on questions, and sharp eyes for detail.

From the bottom of my ink-stained heart, thank you!

The Prince and I

Chapter 1

"... the roads are wretched, this carriage is sprung like a log, and I am freezing. *Bozhy moj*, have the people of this frigid country never heard of a foot warmer?" In the dim glow of the lantern that swung on a hook in the creaking coach, Grand Duchess Natasha Nikolaevna waited for a response. She'd catalogued no fewer than fourteen complaints, yet her companion didn't look impressed. In fact, he seemed to be asleep.

Deeply asleep.

But she knew better. Her grandson might be a prince, but he was also a lifelong soldier who'd made a name for himself in many hard-won battles. A famed general and the leader of the Grand Army of Oxenburg, Prince Gregori Maksim Alexsandr Romanovin didn't sleep deeply. Ever.

His brothers and parents called him "Grisha," a nickname for Gregori, but Natasha had refused. From the day he was born, she'd called him "Max" as befitted a conqueror. The name had fit him, and to his parents' irritation—and Natasha's delight—he grew to prefer Max and eventually refused to answer to anything else.

But warrior prince or not, there was no excuse for ignoring his grandmother. She thumped her cane on the carriage floor.

His lashes shifted and she knew he'd slipped a glance her way. Though it wasn't much, it proved her point: she was being deliberately ignored.

Her hand tightened on the gold cane top and she imagined his face if she rapped the cane across his knee. *That* would make him take heed. Sadly, it would also infuriate him, and she needed to be in his good graces. At least until she found a way out of her not-so-little predicament.

She forced her tightly curled fingers to relax. There would be time to sort that out later. For now, she should focus on her grandson. To be honest, he worried her.

Like his three brothers, he was tall and broad shouldered, his hair thick and black, his eyes a deep green. Unlike his brothers, he bore a scar on his forehead, caused by the graze of a bullet during some battle. Other scars marked his chin and jaw, and doubtless other parts of his body. The scars she could see did not concern her, though.

Lately she'd come to think that her grandson bore much deeper wounds. If what his companions reported was true, the death of Max's childhood friend and one of his top aides, Dimitri Fedorovich, had strongly affected him.

Not that Max would admit such a thing, no matter how many opportunities she gave him. He hadn't become the best general and the most brilliant tactician in all of Europe by admitting weakness, and he wasn't about to start now.

Damn it. She scowled as she regarded his handsome profile. Even scarred, with an oft-broken nose, he still looked princely. *As befits a prince of the blood of stately Oxe—*

The coach jerked to one side, tilting crazily as if lifting onto two wheels. Natasha grabbed the edge of her seat but was tossed forward. With the grace of a lion, Max caught her midair and set her back into her seat, just as the coach slammed back onto all four wheels and continued on at a much faster pace.

Huffing, Natasha collected her shawl, tugging it back over her shoulders in the light of the wildly swinging lantern. "That was nearly a dangerous accident— no surprise, considering the way this coachman has driven, hitting every bump and hole in the road."

No longer pretending to be asleep, Max flicked back the curtain and looked outside, his brow lowered.

Shouts mingled with the wild neighing of horses and the coach suddenly lurched to a dramatic halt, sliding to one side of the road. There was a thud and then a drop, as one wheel seemed to slip into a ditch. Once again Natasha flew forward, a rag doll tossed by the wild ride. She would have hit the edge of the opposite seat had Max not once again caught her.

He deposited her on the coach floor and blew out the lantern, casting them into darkness.

She scrambled to return to her seat, but he placed a hand on her shoulder. "Stay."

"I will not sit on the floor—"

"Shh! I must listen." Max peered through a small crack in the curtain, a sliver of light from the lantern outside making a white slash across his face. "The luggage coaches have stopped as well."

Discordant voices rose in the dark; yelling, followed by anxious shouts.

Natasha noticed the suddenly firm line of his mouth, the intentness of his expression.

A voice bellowed through the night, harsh and astonishingly loud, asking the coachmen to step down.

Natasha gripped her cane tighter. "Highwaymen?" She'd heard there were none, but she'd told Max that they preyed constantly on this isolated road in order to convince him to escort her. "I *told* you there would be—"

"Silence," he hissed. Another bellow rang out, this time an oddly polite but firm request to the two outriders to dismount. At the sound of a scuffle, Max's face grew harsher as he closed the leather curtain, leaving them in blackness. She heard a rustling movement, and then a blanket was tossed over her. "Stay here."

"*Nyet!*" She yanked the blanket from her head, smoothing her mussed hair. "I will not hide."

"You will do as I tell you." The soft words brooked no argument, and she realized she was hearing the general, not her grandson.

"Whatever happens," he said calmly, "do *not* let them know you are here. If they open the door, make yourself as small as possible and do not move. If we are lucky, they will not see you in the dark."

"You don't need to tell me what to do; I am not a fool."

"What you *are* is a stubborn old woman far too used to getting your way."

"Pah!"

He lifted one corner of the curtain to provide a faint ray of light as he adjusted his sword, and then quickly examined his pistol. Satisfied, he returned it to its hiding place in the back of his belt, and closed the curtain. In the dark, she heard the click of the door handle.

She lunged for his arm, grabbing it with both hands. "You cannot go out there!"

There was a chilled silence, and she could imagine the hardness of his expression. With a wince, she released him. "You cannot protect me outside. That is your job: to protect me and no one else. If someone opens the door you may shoot them, but you will not place yourself in danger—"

"Stay down." With that he threw open the door, the dim light outlining his broad figure. The last thing she saw before he was enveloped by darkness was his black fur-lined cape swinging from his broad shoulders, his boots agleam in the lantern light.

Shutting the door behind him, Max gave quick thanks for the low mist that allowed him to make his way unseen behind a trunk that had fallen off one of the other coaches. It laid on its side, broken open, several of Tata Natasha's expensive fur-lined cloaks spilled across the mud.

Crouching behind the trunk, he surveyed the scene before him. Two men wearing kerchiefs over their lower faces had collected the coachmen into a small knot. Two more masked highwaymen guarded the other coaches' doors to prevent the inhabitants from exiting. As Max peered over the trunk, a third masked highwayman was sent to watch Tata Natasha's coach. Max had been fortunate to get out when he had.

Where are my men? He leaned to the side of the trunk, keeping low. Piotr Orlov, his large, gruff sergeant at arms, the youngest son of a minor noble from Oxenburg, and Max's most trusted man, leaned against a tree at the side of the road, holding his arm against his chest, a smear of blood on his forehead. A few paces back, Ivan Golovin, a tough four-campaign veteran, was unconscious on the ground, his nose bloodied. The rest of his men were nowhere to be seen, probably sent ahead by Orlov to scout for just such an ambush. *Which I suggested he do, dammit. The thieves were fortunate in choosing their time of attack. Or have they been watching us as we travel?*

Max bit back a growl. The security of the entire trip had been marred by Tata Natasha's demands that they stop at every inn they passed, a practice he'd allowed to continue for far too long. The delays had forced them to travel at night, which was much more dangerous, but he'd been swayed in his decision by her age and obvious exhaustion. Despite her hard words and harder glares, Tata Natasha was old and frail. *And as unpleasant as soured wine. That old woman will be the death of me.*

A movement in the bushes drew Max's gaze. *Ah. More of you hide among the trees.* He counted four shadowy figures flitting in the mist. It was impossible to tell if the men were armed, but it would be foolish to assume they weren't.

As if this number of ruffians weren't enough, sitting astride a steed at the head of the whole was a lone man. The mist swirled about the legs of his steed while a lantern shone behind him, casting light on those before him and highlighting the barrel of a long rifle. *A sharpshooter, and in the same position I'd have placed him, too.*

Which was it, a rifle or a blunderbuss? The uncertain light glinted on the barrel but hid the rest of the weapon. Rifles were harder to load than blunderbusses, and had to be cleaned between shots as the barrels were easily fouled by black powder residue. But they were extremely accurate; one shot could be deadly. *Whoever planned this little encounter has done a damn fine job.*

As Max watched, a slender figure appeared at the edge of the road. The newcomer held back, away from the action, yet all of the thieves instantly focused on the slight man. *So, the leader has shown himself.*

The man spoke quietly to the largest of the thieves watching over the coachmen, a veritable giant who turned toward where Max was hidden behind the fallen trunk.

The large man's hand moved to the curved butt of what appeared to be a pistol stuck into his thick leather belt as he bellowed, "Pray come oot, Yer Highness. We know ye're hidin' there. We can see ye, we can."

So they know my title. Interesting. There was little profit in continuing to hide if the thieves knew where he was, and much profit to be had in facing them, so Max rose and stepped forward.

"Hold!" the giant barked. "Dinna come any closer."

Max eyed his opponent narrowly. The brute was larger than any man he'd ever seen, his face broad, a red beard showing beneath the kerchief on his lower face. The man possessed an impossibly thick neck and had arms the size of most men's thighs.

"I will speak with your leader." Icy puffs of breath punctuated every word.

The man's eyes narrowed. "Ye've an odd accent."

"Do not pretend that surprises you. You know who I am, so you must also know I'm from Oxenburg."

"I know many things, bu' I've ne'er heard of this Oxenburg."

"That's quite all right. I only recently learned of Scotland, and I'm beginning to dislike it."

The man's brows snapped together. "If ye dinna like it, then ye can go home where ye belong."

Another man snorted, this one a slim youth with flowing brown hair, his mocking blue eyes bold over the top of his mask. A jaunty but worn hat adorned his head, a scarlet cape swinging from his narrow shoulders. "A prince, eh? Lord Loudan is gettin' fancy."

They also know whose guests we are. How did they get such complete information?

As if aware of the slip, the large highwayman cut a warning glare at the second man, who shrugged, not the least remorseful.

Loud of mouth and brash of person are weaknesses, my young friend. The giant has the right of it. Max addressed the bolder highwayman. "You know I'm a guest of the earl's."

"Tha' is the reason we're here." The highwayman's voice dripped with barely contained fury. "We only bother the low scum as come to visit his lordship, the Earl of Louse."

The giant hissed a warning, but the lad was roused and continued, "The earl has done naught bu' thieve his whole life, and we're here to see to it tha' he stops."

"If what you say is true—which I doubt . . ." Max paused to let that sink in, watching the lad stiffen in outrage. ". . . then look at you. You are no better than he: a low-life thief."

The youth's blue eyes blazed, but before the fool could open his mouth and blurt out more information, the giant snapped, "Whist, now! Dinna say nobut wha' needs to be known—which isna much." The giant returned his attention to Max, his breath puffing white like that of a huge dragon getting ready to spit fire. "Throw yer pistol on the ground."

Max wished he could draw and engage; except for the lone highwayman positioned at the head, not a single man had his weapon drawn. While not having their guns ready was a good strategy to keep rowdy troops from unnecessarily firing and perhaps raising an alarm, it left them open to surprises.

It was sorely tempting to answer this lack of foresight, but the realization that his grandmother was in the coach behind him and thus directly in the line of fire, kept Max from pursuing the risky course.

Instead, he shrugged. "As you wish." He withdrew his sword and dropped it at his feet, yet close enough to reach should the opportunity arise.

"And yer pistol." The giant's eyes narrowed. "Dinna say there's none, fer we know ye've one, and mayhap two."

Max resignedly removed his pistol and dropped it to the frozen ground beside his sword.

The giant nodded at the youth, who loped forward to pick up the weapons. Ignoring the sword, he fell upon the pistol, examining it in an expert way. "Silver engravin'. Italian?"

"And a hair trigger," Max said in a dry tone. "Don't point it in a direction you don't wish to shoot."

The young highwayman's jaw tightened. "I know pistols, I do. I've no need fer yer advice." He emptied the chamber, pocketed the bullets, and dropped the pistol back onto the road beside the sword.

Why didn't he take the—

"Dinna get any wild ideas, Prince," the giant warned.

"The only idea I have is to find a warm fire and some ale, and there's none to be had here."

The giant grunted agreement. "'Tis possible a small donation might see ye sooner on yer way to a wee dram and a warm fire."

"A donation?"

"Aye. A thanks, ye could call it, fer safe passage." The giant's eyes gleamed with humor. "The woods are filled wi' bandits."

"So I've heard," Max returned drily. He'd never met such polite highwaymen, and in his wide travels he'd met quite a few. *What is this? There must be a reason. Perhaps I should test them.* He rocked back on his heels. "I'm in no mood to pay a donation. If you wish for hand-outs, go see your parish church."

The giant didn't move, but his brows lowered.

Max added, "In fact, I am tired of standing in the cold and believe I shall go." He bent and retrieved his sword.

"Stop there!" The huge man moved toward Max, his beefy hand rising to the pistol stuck in his belt. "Drop yer sword!"

"*Nyet,*" Max said softly. He slid the sword back into its scabbard, using the side of his foot to surreptitiously nudge away his pistol so it wouldn't be underfoot if he had to use the blade. "If you want it, then come and get it." He readied himself, but the leader, who still held himself from the group, murmured a word that made the giant's brow blacken yet more, though his hand moved away from the pistol in his belt.

Obviously every bit as disappointed as Max, the huge man growled, "I suppose ye can keep it. *If* ye'll find yer way to makin' a small donation to our cause, oot of sheer happiness of havin' a safe way ahead of ye."

"How do I know it's safe from here on out?"

"Because we made it so, dinna we, men?"

"Aye!" replied the men, several of them oddly gruff in tone.

The giant nodded his shaggy head. "There ye go; a guarantee. If ye like, ye can toss yer gold where ye threw yer pistol."

If Tata Natasha weren't here, the outcome of this would be vastly different. Even as he had the thought, Max caught a movement where Orlov stood. In Oxenburgian, Max said quietly to his sergeant, "We cannot. The duchess is with us."

Orlov, whose hand had been slowly moving toward his hidden pistol, grimaced and then gave a regretful nod. "Aye, General."

"Here now," the giant called gruffly. "Dinna be talkin' tha' gibberish. If ye've somethin' to say, then say it in proper language."

"I was telling my sergeant we should cooperate so that we might soon be enjoying a beverage near a warm fire."

"If he'd really like to help quicken yer departure, he can donate to the cause, too." The giant looked at Orlov. "Would ye like to gi' a bit to the effort, lad?"

Orlov scowled, but with a regretful glance at the duchess's coach, pulled some coins from his pocket and tossed them where Max's pistol lay.

Max cast a hard glance at the slender man still standing in the shadows. No doubt he was silently laughing at their helplessness. *Ehta prosta nivazmozhna. I will enjoy bringing you to justice, my fine friend.* But for now, there was no more to be done. "Here." Max withdrew a few coins from his pocket and tossed them to the icy mud.

The giant's smile slipped. "Surely tha' isna all ye ha'."

"It's all you'll get."

The giant's thick red brows knit over his nose, but he gestured to the caped highwayman, who hurried forward to collect the gold.

Max tried to get a look at the handle of the pistol sticking out from the youth's waistband, but the knotted belt rope prevented a clear view. Still, the belt told its own story. *A flamboyant cape but only a frayed rope for a belt. The cape is fine indeed, but the belt indicates the true state of affairs.*

Max flicked a glance over each of the men within the faint light cast by the lanterns on the sides of the coaches. Though he could see none of their faces, their barely adequate coats, boots with holes in the toes, and the rest of their worn attire were plainly visible.

He noted then the thinness of the caped lad's hands, the deep lines around his eyes. *They look as if they're hungry.*

Max's jaw tightened and he sent a look at Orlov to see if he'd noticed the same thing, receiving a faint nod in return.

Max turned his attention back to the young man, who was now tucking the coins into a worn leather bag. As he did so, he bit each one. "Ian, they're all real!"

The giant stiffened, while the leader shifted in the shadows.

"Sorry," the lad mumbled as he pulled out a small bag and secreted the coins away and then hurried out of sight.

Max eyed the giant with a grin. "Ian, is it?"

Ian's thick brows couldn't have been knit tighter. "Ferget ye heard tha'. Now open the door to yer coach an' ask the grand duchess if she wishes to donate to our cause, too. I daresay she has a brooch or two she's tired of, and would like to see used fer worthier reasons."

"*Nyet.* There's nothing of value in that coach other

than a cranky old woman. Well . . . except a basket of food I'm willing to 'donate,' as you call it."

"Food?"

"*Da.* Some spit-roasted chickens, fresh bread, jams, boiled eggs, cheeses. You may have it only if you will leave the grand duchess in peace and let us leave quickly."

The giant's eyes glistened and he placed a hand on his stomach as if already tasting the contents of the basket. His gaze flickered to their leader.

A faint nod answered him.

"Fine!" Ian rocked back on his heels, looking well pleased. "We accept yer donation. A chicken or two would no' be amiss."

Max returned to the coach and opened the door, his body blocking the view of the interior. A slat of light fell across Tata Natasha's furious face.

"What are you doing?" she hissed.

He picked up the basket, whispering sternly, "I told you to stay hidden."

"*Nyet!*" Her gnarled hands grabbed the basket handle. "I won't give good chickens to a group of dirty thieves!"

Max lowered his voice. "They are hungry, Tata Natasha."

She stopped tugging on the basket, her gaze locked on his face. "How do you know?"

"I can see it in their eyes."

"Oh." She released the basket, adding in a sullen tone, "I suppose they can have it, then. We can stop at the next inn—"

"*Nyet.* We go straight to Rowallen Castle. We will be safer there than in these woods."

She scowled. "I will starve by the time we—"

He threw the blanket back over her head, took the basket, and slammed the door behind him.

Ian had moved closer, the light from the lone remaining lantern now slanting across his face, and Max could see the man's blue eyes were now crinkled with good humor. "The grand duchess sounds like a woman of spirit."

"That's one word for it. I call it stubbornness." Max placed the basket on the ground and pushed it forward with his foot.

The giant jerked his head, and the scarlet-cloaked youth came to take the basket. He peered inside, his eyes wide. "Och, Ian, there's a ham hock the size o' yer heed! An' bread, an' pots of jam, an'— Bloody 'ell, there's one, two, three . . . four chickens!" He tilted the basket so his comrades could see.

The men stirred, some of them closer now and several steps away from their original posts, their gazes locked on the food.

The leader called out, his husky voice hushed but commanding.

The men returned to their posts, reluctantly tearing their gazes from the basket.

Hopefully a group of thieves so obviously happy to have procured a basket of food would now be in a hurry to send them on their way. But Max still had to tread carefully, for there were weapons all around him and— He frowned. Were they even loaded? Men who couldn't afford food could not afford powder. *If Tata Natasha weren't here, I'd test that theory.*

The scarlet-clad thief carried the heavy basket into the mist-thickened woods. One of the shadowy figures came out from behind a tree to take it from him, lantern light catching the thief's hands—far too delicate and slender for a man's.

A woman? Max's frown deepened. *Perhaps the shadowy figures are all women, trying to create the imager of a larger force—*

"The basket and the coins are a guid start," the giant said, obviously emboldened by his success. "But I noticed ye've a pretty bauble upon yer hand. One last donation, Prince, and we'll leave ye to a smooth, safe journey."

Max looked down at his gold ring, a gift from his mother when he'd turned sixteen. He curled his hand closed. "While you are more than welcome to the gold and the basket, the ring is personal property. You'll get no more."

Ian's brow lowered as he rested his hand on the butt of his pistol. "Ye're a greedy one. I've a mind to—"

The leader coughed softly, and Ian removed his hand from his pistol.

You have them under tight control, my friend. Max couldn't help but grudgingly admit some respect for the brigand leader.

But only a little. "Our business is done, and—"

The leather curtain on the coach lifted and Tata Natasha's hand appeared, no longer be-ringed as she tossed some rings upon the ground, a few gold coins rolling with them.

Damn it, you were told to stay hidden! Will you never listen?

Ian blinked in astonishment at the unexpected bounty, and his eyes crinkled with delight. "Och, Her Grace is generous, unlike her grandson." He raised his voice, "Thank ye, Yer Grace!" He squinted at the reply, which wasn't in English. "Wha' did she say?"

"It had to do with goats and your parentage."

The giant chuckled. "Full of vinegar, is she?"

"You have no idea. But be that as it may, I am done with this, so I will leave you." Max turned and walked toward the coach.

"Hold!" the giant bellowed. "Wha' of tha' ring?"

Max turned, resting his hand on one hip. It was a showy pose, but it put his hand in easy reach of his sword. "If you wish to attack me, you with your entire retinue of fools and thieves, all so brave behind your pistols and muskets, then do so now. I grow tired of this game."

Ian puffed out his cheeks, his face red. "I'll show ye brave—"

"Stand doon, Ian. I ha' this." The leader stepped forward, walking into the edge of the light that pooled from the lantern. Tallish and slender, he was dressed far more dapperly than the others in a green coat with silver buttons.

Max hid his pleasure at this new development. *Finally, you join in the fun. Perhaps this little encounter will be enjoyable after all.*

Chapter 2

Almost as one, the thieves moved back for their leader. Not that the man needed much room. Judging from the thief's lanky movements and his narrow build, he was more child than man.

It was a pity Max couldn't see the youth's face to confirm his age, for a kerchief covered most of it, leaving naught but bright eyes shining in the shadow of his hat brim.

And that hat! It was splendid, if old, in fashion a half century ago. As green as the youth's coat, it was decorated with a bold white feather. It was just the sort of hat a youth might think made one look dashing. *A rather vain youth.*

"Wha' seems to be the problem?" The lantern touched the leader's velvet coat with a shimmering light as he swaggered forward, one hand resting on the elaborate hilt of his sword.

Ian grunted. "'Tis the prince, sir. He dinna wish to donate more to our cause."

"A pity, fer 'tis such a just one."

Max flicked a curious glance over the leader's

weapons, which were boldly on display. A bow and arrows hung in a quiver over one shoulder, while a thin sword hung from the wide leather belt that tightened the lad's too-large coat around his waist.

The sword held Max's attention. It was a rapier, one of exceptional quality, if the style and ornate work on the hilt were any indication. *In the wilds of Scotland? Wherever you stole that, you're out if you think to use it. Commoners do not know how to fence, my finely feathered friend.*

The leader eyed him now, a boldness to his stance. "I'm pleased to make yer acquaintance, Yer Highness."

"You have the advantage of me; I don't know your name." Max raised his brows. "Unless you're afraid to share it?"

"Tryin' to tease me into revealin' more than I wish, are ye?"

Max bowed. "Why not?"

"Why no', indeed." Humor clear in his light-colored eyes, the leader said in a husky voice, "If ye must ha' a name, then ye may call me 'Robin.' Robin of the Hood."

Max wished he could see the expression in the lad's eyes better under that damnable hat. They were astonishingly pale, though, making the lashes that framed them seem thick and dark.

"I know the story of Robin Hood." Max moved a bit, hoping to make the lad turn more toward the lantern. "We have a similar story in my own country, of a thief who steals from the rich and gives to the poor. Of course, in our story, he is caught and hanged, as is only proper for a thief."

Though the lad shrugged, Max had the impression that 'Robin' had lost his smile, though the kerchief covered the evidence. "Och, time will tell, will it no', my fine foreign prince? Meanwhile, if ye wish to speak wi' me, ye may call me Robin. *Master* Robin."

Once Max had subdued this pack of mangy thieves, he'd take great pleasure in schooling some manners into this youth. "So, boy . . ." Max waited for a protest to the term "boy," but none came. *Odd. I don't know many young men who wouldn't chafe at that.* "As I told your giant, I've given all I'll give."

Ian grumbled, "There's more our prince here can give. Fer one, he has a ring on his hand."

The thief tilted his head, regarding Max for a long moment. Whatever he saw, the thief shook his head. "Nay, Ian. I think His Highness ha' already donated weel and guid. He may ha' more, but there's no reason fer greed." He waved a hand at Max. "Off wi' ye. And thank ye fer yer donation toward keepin' yer travels safe in our fair forest."

The youth's insolent tone boiled Max's blood. *"Your* fair forest? You have it wrong: this forest belongs to the Earl of Loudan. I owe *him* for my safe passage, not you."

Something flashed in the pale eyes, something icy and quick. "You know the earl well, do you?" The lad's voice crackled with fire.

"I know Loudan quite well," Max lied. *An angry opponent makes mistakes. And this seems to make you quite angry.* "In fact," he added ruthlessly, "the earl is one of my closest friends. I admire and like him." Max met the lad's gaze. "I think Loudan the finest human being I've ever known."

The youth's eyes burned, his entire body rigid. "If that is true, then you dinna know many people."

Such passion. I once had that. Passion that saw me through the hardest of times. He'd had that until the last war had dashed it from his soul. Though to be honest, it wasn't the war itself that sat on his shoulders late at night and weighed down the brightness of the morning, but the aftermath of that war.

Over the years he'd had to deliver last words to too many tragic-eyed widows, had been forced to look into the hopeless gazes of too many freshly orphaned children grieving for fathers who would never return. It had never been easy, and the taste of those encounters had been bitter upon his soul.

But in the last war, Max had lost one of his own. Dimitri Fedorovich had been as close to Max as his own brothers, perhaps closer. Fedorovich had died from a sniper's bullet during a heated battle with the French, and had been standing so close to Max that the bullet's zing rang in his ears for days after. Max had felt the death keenly, but worse was to come—on his return home he'd had to tell Fedorovich's young wife of her loss. Henrietta had screamed hysterically and could not be comforted, and then, sobbing wildly, had thrown herself from the window of her home. She'd survived but had been horribly injured.

The entire incident had left Max with a burning hole where his soul had once been. Hot coals of fury at the loss still remained, and the slightest breath of air fanned them into life.

And right now those flames had been stirred by an insolent youth with a flair for the dramatic. Max's good humor was no more.

"I've had enough of this, and enough of you," he snapped. "You are a fool, and a thief, and a paltry want-to-be outlaw."

Robin stiffened, his cocksureness turning into outrage. "How dare you!"

"How dare I? How dare *you*, a thief who hides behind a kerchief? You are a coward and nothing more."

"You have gone too far, Prince," Robin snarled through clenched teeth. "But I am not surprised; all of Loudan's so-called friends are as despicable as he."

Max showed his teeth in a smile he didn't feel. "Oddly, your dislike of the earl has chased away much of your accent." The lad's accent had gone from rustic to refined; his speech was quite similar to what Max had heard at the Edinburgh court not three days ago. This thief had once been fed with a silver spoon. "You, sir, are a lie."

The lad grasped the hilt of the rapier.

"Easy, there," Ian rumbled. "Dinna lose tha' temper of yers."

So young Robin can be intemperate. I can use that. Max reached into his pocket.

Instantly, the air about him charged, every eye upon him.

"Halt!" Robin said. "Take your hand from your pocket."

Max lifted his hand free, turning it to reveal a small gold box in his palm. "My snuff box."

"So you wish to donate more bounty to our worthy cause." Robin gestured to the mud. "Throw it at your feet."

The giant grunted in agreement.

"I am not 'donating' anything else." Max flicked open the lid and helped himself to a small pinch of snuff. He didn't normally partake of it, but since it irritated Tata Natasha, he'd made an exception this trip.

Robin's eyes blazed with irritation, but Ian's gaze remained locked upon the box.

"It is fine, *nyet*?" Max held it so that the gold sparkled in the torchlight. "It was given to me by my cousin Alexandr."

Ian's heavy brows lifted, wonder on his craggy face. "Is tha' a real diamond in the center?"

"*Da.* It is a very large, very expensive diamond." Max ran his thumb over it. "Worth more than this entire forest."

The giant moved closer.

Max shifted so that his weight was on the heel of one foot. As soon as the fool came within reach, Max would—

"Ian." Robin's voice was quiet, but held a distinct warning. "He's baiting you, just as he was baiting me. Look at him."

The giant paused, looking from the glittering snuff box to Max.

Max froze, trying not to give anything away by so much as a twich of an eyelash.

"*Look* at him," Robin repeated.

Ian's gaze flickered over Max's face and then, with a grimace, the giant moved back into position.

Dammit. The thirsty flames in Max's soul flickered in disappointment.

He snapped the box closed. "I won't give a band of lazy thieves anything but the end of my sword."

Beneath the wide-brimmed hat, the pale eyes narrowed on Max. "You wish to fight, but not today, auld man."

Old man? Max's simmering blood rose and bubbled—perhaps because since Fedorovich's death, he had begun to feel . . . yes, old. And perhaps because he was irked at being forced by his grandmother's presence to stand passively in the icy cold, instead of summarily taking care of this situation in a satisfactory manner. And perhaps because he was furious life had been so bloody unfair lately. Whatever it was, he snapped, "I repeat: you are a coward. A lowborn, dirty coward."

Robin's eyes blazed, Ian muttered a warning, but it was too late.

The rapier flashed in the lantern light. With a *whip-whip-whip*, it danced through the cold air.

Stunned, Max looked down. His coat was ruined, the letter "R" clearly carved into its heavy wool.

Orlov cursed under his breath.

Max gritted his teeth. "Why you little . . ." He drew his sword. "Try that again and see what it will earn you, whelp!"

He expected Robin to realize his mistake. Instead the fool's eyes blazed and, to everyone's astonishment, Robin saluted with his blade. *"En garde, mon général!"*

The rapier danced once again, but this time Max was ready, his sword neatly catching the thin blade.

Had Robin taken the hit directly the blow would have broken his blade, but instead he deflected Max's sword with a twist of his wrist.

The whelp knows how to fight. Still, Max had the advantage in experience, the weight of his sword, and the power of his arm. He rolled his weight to the ball of his foot and spun, twisting in an attempt to catch the youth's blade and send it flying, but Robin was too fast, and the fight began in earnest.

The rapier danced in again and again with barely contained fury, keeping Max on the defensive. He found himself moving back, trying to find good footing on the frozen ground.

Amid the attack, he realized the lad wasn't trying to deliver a deathblow—he aimed for exposed skin, not the heart or neck. Nay, the lad was after a quick blooding, administering a lesson to his elder.

Impudent whelp! I'll be damned if I let that happen. Blow after blow, Max's sword deflected the rapier. It slid away before swishing back to meet him like a scorpion's tail, ready to bite at first chance.

Max blocked each bite, watching his opponent for an opening. He would break that rapier if it were the last thing he did.

Steel met steel over and over, and finally Max was able to move the lad back. Though every blow was dodged or deflected, ultimately Max's strength began to turn the battle.

The lad was tiring; Max could feel it. The thief's

movements had lost some of their former grace. Though his attacks were just as ferocious, they were less frequent now.

Max increased his efforts, aware of Ian's muttered outrage. But the giant knew better than to interfere in the fight; he might easily distract Robin at a crucial moment.

But then it happened. After an especially adroit parry, Robin slipped on the icy ground and fell backward.

Ian cried out a warning as Max closed in, his blade true. But instead of piercing the thief's chest, as was his right, he used his blade to flick the kerchief from the youth's face.

The lad jerked back, catching the tip of his ear on Max's blade. And as the kerchief drifted to the ground, Max saw his opponent's face for the first time. His face was oval, his lips full, and his eyes silver gray, like coins in the bottom of a still pool. Large and thickly fringed with curled lashes, they were set under flyaway red eyebrows. *Those eyes—if I didn't know better, I'd think you were a—*

"Yer ear is bleedin'!" the giant snapped. "I'll kill tha' mon fer—" He took a step toward Max.

"Nay!" Robin scrambled to his feet, tying the kerchief back in place with hasty hands. "Leave him. 'Tis but a nick."

"A nick? I'll nick tha' lout—"

"Ian."

The quiet word made the giant pause.

"Leave him. 'Twas fairly won."

Ian said between clenched teeth, "Ye could ha' bloodied him when ye cut his coat, but ye dinna." He cast a furious glare at Max. "There was no need to continue thus."

"There was." Robin dusted his breeches and sighed. "I forced that fight, and you know it. 'Twas my own fault."

Behind Max, the coach door flew open and Tata Natasha stood on the top step, every eye locked upon her. The wind swirled her black cloak dramatically, the coach lantern cast long shadows over her face, and her hair was wild from where she'd been shoved under the blanket.

Ian sputtered, "Bloody 'ell, wha' is tha'?"

"It's a w-w-witch!" another brigand said.

Max couldn't disagree. "Damn it, Tata Natasha, you were told to stay inside."

"Pah!" She drew her cloak closer. "I am tired of these games you play. It is time to go."

Max ignored her and addressed the thief. "Your giant has the right of it: while I drew first blood, you could easily have done so earlier when you left your initial." He tapped his shredded overcoat.

Unexpectedly, humor shone in Robin's silver eyes. "I thought aboot it."

"I'm glad that's all you did," Max said honestly. "I did not give your toothpick blade the credit it deserved."

Robin crossed his arms over his chest, his feet planted wide. "You dinna ask that your donations be returned. 'Tis your right, as you won."

Max shrugged. "You may keep what's already been given. But there will be no more."

Robin bowed. "As you wish. And thank you; that is unexpectedly generous."

"It is foolish!" Tata Natasha snapped.

"*Tikha!*" Max snapped over his shoulder.

She muttered under her breath, only the words "foolish boy" and "lost chickens" audible.

Robin chuckled. "We will go and let you tend to your grandmother."

"I'd rather you stabbed me with that toothpick of yours," Max muttered.

Robin choked back what was surely a laugh, the silver eyes lively. "Och, I'm sure you would. Family can be costly, both in money and pride." He bowed once again, as graceful as any courtier. "'Til we meet again, oh scarred and frowny one."

Max returned the bow, a stirring of interest in his soul that he hadn't felt in a long, long time. "Oh, we *will* meet again, young and cheeky one. I vow it."

Robin's eyes twinkled. "So be it." With that, he turned and walked into the woods, his slender form melting into the shadows.

The world was instantly drearier without an impudent highwayman waving a rapier like a scorpion tail. Oddly disappointed, Max reached into his pocket, pulled out his kerchief, and tossed it to the giant. "I only nicked Robin's ear, but you may need to apply some pressure to stop the blood."

Looking surprised at the gesture, Ian pocketed the kerchief, though he kept a careful eye on Tata Natasha. "Thank ye, I'll take care of Robin, but who will take care of *tha'*?"

Max turned to see his grandmother making odd gestures in the air. "What are you doing?"

"I'm putting a curse on these *chor*."

"A curse?" squeaked the long-haired highwayman, peering around Ian's wide form.

"What's a *chor*?" Ian asked.

"A thief," Max answered. "My grandmother is Romany. She oft uses their language."

"Bloody 'ell, she's a Gypsy!" Ian backed up, his eyes wide.

"She is harmless." *More or less.* He turned to the coach. "Tata, stop casting curses; there's no need. I won the fight and we are unscathed."

"But I'm almost done!"

"We are leaving. Allow me to assist you back into the coach." He handed her inside, leaving the door open. He watched out of the corner of his eyes as Robin's men melted one by one into the dark, misty forest. Two of the thieves carried off the lanterns, extinguishing them before they disappeared, until only the lantern hanging from Tata Natasha's coach remained.

The sharpshooter stayed at the head of the road, his rifle barrel glinting in the lamplight. Soon only his form and Ian's broad one were left, outlined in the shadows of a large tree.

Whist! An arrow whizzed past Max's head and struck the lone lantern, the sound of breaking glass startling in the night.

They were plunged into darkness while Tata Natasha released a string of Romany curses.

"Shush, woman!" Max told her. "Orlov, we need a functioning lantern."

"*Da*, General." It took a moment, but Orlov found a lantern near a baggage coach that had fallen in the mud at the onset of their encounter and lit it. He held it up, a golden orb of light spilling across the leafy woods. "They are gone."

"Pah! You are cowards, all!" Tata shook her fist in the air. "Come back, for I'm not done turning the lot of you into goats!"

"Leave it, Tata." Max turned to where Orlov was now helping an obviously dizzy Golovin to his feet, a trickle of blood running down his chin. "Was anyone else injured?" Max asked.

Orlov slipped his good arm about Golovin to steady him. "One of the coachmen fell scrambling from the coach, but it does not seem serious, and two footmen have banged heads from falling from the backs of the coaches—but that is all."

"Fools, the coachmen," Golovin said in a surly tone. "They didn't even try to fight."

Max grimaced. "We were the fools, to send the rest of our troops ahead to scout for a danger that was here. That was my fault. Golovin, come to my carriage. Her Grace will see to your wounds."

Orlov helped Golovin to the coach steps. Golovin sat down on the top one, his hand to his head. With an encouraging pat on the shoulder, Orlov left to see to the coachmen and outriders.

"Tilt your head back," Tata ordered. She pulled a kerchief from her pocket and pressed it to Golovin's bloody nose. "Hold this while I fetch my medicines."

Golovin did as requested while Tata Natasha pulled

a leather bag from under the seat and set to work, her face tight with irritation. "Pah! What fools, to think they could attack the royal entourage of Oxenburg. And you, Max, giving them your gold and our basket of food!" She used a cup to mix a powder from a small ivory vial with a drop of liquid from a dark brown bottle.

Golovin watched with growing fear in his eyes.

Tata Natasha's shrewd dark gaze locked on Max. "You said they were hungry."

He nodded.

Her frown softened, and after a moment she said in a magnanimous voice, "Then I do not mind giving up a few chickens. This time." She dipped a small cloth into the mixture and pressed it to Golovin's nose.

He gagged at the smell.

She waited only a moment and then removed the cloth. "There. The blood has stopped."

Golovin touched his nose gingerly, looking surprised. "Good!" He stood. "I will help Orlov and—"

"*Nyet*. You will come with me." Tata Natasha pointed to the coach. "No riding; it could start the bleeding again."

Golovin cast a wild look at Max. "General, you will want me to—"

"I'll want you safe, inside the coach. And do not worry about your horse. I will ride it."

"But—"

Max lifted his brows and Golovin gulped. "Aye, General." With obvious reluctance, he climbed into the coach, casting an uneasy glance at Tata Natasha as he did. Tata followed, scolding loudly.

Max shut the door.

Orlov approached, leading Golovin's horse. "The coachmen are readying the vehicles now."

"Excellent. Did you find my pistol?"

Orlov pulled it from his pocket.

"Thank you." Max checked it and then tucked it away. "We will leave as soon as the coachmen are ready. We are vulnerable here." Max mounted the horse and waited for Orlov to do the same.

As Max waited, the wind shifted and a hole opened in the thick mist. To Max's surprise, the masked sharp-shooter was in plain view on his horse, but this time the coach lantern illuminated his rifle barrel . . . only it was no rifle. Instead, he held a long pipe.

Seeing Max, the man lifted the pipe in a cheerful salute, then kicked his horse and disappeared into the mist. Max let fly a row of colorful curses.

Orlov turned his horse. "I'll get him."

"*Nyet*," Max ordered. "We don't know the woods, and will harm ourselves and our horses. We must let him go."

Orlov cursed long and loud. "I've never met more insolent thieves."

"Neither have I. I'm far from finished with this inci-dent." Max looked grimly down at the large "R" carved into his coat. "A Romanovin never forgets a debt."

We will meet again, Robin.

And soon.

Chapter 3

"Bloody hell, Ian! Do you have to bounce us so?" Lady Murian MacDonald Muir grabbed onto the side rail of the cart as a hard jolt threatened to unseat her.

"Whisht, watch yer language, lass." Ian Beagin wished he could slow down, but they not only had to reach the village and trade their wares, they also had to return home before dark, which would take at least two hours. Such was the price of living deep in the woods, hidden from every easily accessible road. "Yer mither would roll in her grave to hear ye use sich language."

"My mother would complain even louder if she were being trundled in a cart with square wheels."

Widow Reeves, clinging onto the seat beside Murian, added, "At this rate, I'll no' ha' any teeth left by the time we arrive." A tall, angular woman with iron-gray hair and a deeply lined face, Widow Reeves was once the cook at Rowallen Castle and had—like Ian—watched Murian's late husband, Master Robert, grow from a babe into a man. "Who will bargain fer our wares if I canna speak?"

Ian snorted. "Och, I'd like to see ye hold yer tongue,

teeth or no. 'Tis no' in yer nature." While Widow Reeves huffed, Ian hied the farm horses to go a little faster.

Murian grumbled something under her breath. Ian was fairly certain it wasn't anything a lady should say, so he added, "Bear wi' me, lass. 'Tis only another ten or fifteen minutes—ye can see the smoke from the chimneys."

Lady Murian turned her head to look, the wind teasing her bonnet. It pressed on the wide brim and folded it over her bandaged ear. She grimaced and tugged the brim back into place.

"Hurts, eh?"

"Nary a bit." She threw him a jaunty, only slightly strained grin. "I forgot it was there."

Which was a lie, and he knew it. She was young, this leader of theirs—barely twenty-one, with wild red hair, silver eyes, cream skin dusted with freckles, and entirely feminine from her curls to her toes—yet as plucky as anyone he'd ever met.

When Lord Robert, at the cocksure age of twenty, had agreed to wed sight unseen the ward of his cousin, the powerful Duke of Spencer, Ian and the other servants at Rowallen Castle had been concerned. They'd loved Lord Robert in spite of his impetuous nature. Fortunately, their concerns had proven unfounded: Lady Murian turned out to be a strong, lively, beautiful young woman, and to the happiness of all, she'd quickly fallen in love with Lord Robert, and he with her.

Sadly, their happiness had been short-lived. A scant year and a few months later, Lord Robert had been killed and Lady Murian left alone. Ian had found himself Lady Murian's protector, when she'd let him, which wasn't often. God love her, but she was a spirited lass.

Too spirited. Someone needs to tame this one, and soon.

"I hope we sell all of our wares," she said now, her pains already dismissed from her mind.

Widow Reeves patted the large basket of lace, jams, and cheeses. "Aye, fer we've shoes to buy from the cobbler. Widow Brodie's five boys are nigh wi'oot them now. The soles ha' more holes than leather."

A shadow crossed Lady Murian's face, and Ian knew she was concerned about the coming winter. They all were. The weather had not been kind to their village this season, bringing no rain during the summer months and reducing their plentiful fields to withering vines. When the rains had finally arrived, it was so late in the season that they had brought nothing but icy winds, leaking roofs, and muddy paths. They were already growing short on stores, and there were many long, cold months ahead.

He fought the urge to sigh. Times were hard; that was all there was to it. Besides himself, young Will Scarlae, and Lady Murian, their small village was home to seven widows and their children, for a total of twenty-one hungry mouths to feed.

Beside him, Lady Murian impatiently brushed a red curl from her cheek. She was forever having to do that, for her hair was thick and unruly, as untamed as the lass herself.

Ian glanced her way and remembered when she'd

first arrived at Rowallen. In her silk gowns, jeweled pins sparkling in her hair, she'd been more beautiful than any princess. Lord Robert had been so proud.

Ian's throat tightened. It seemed forever since that day. Now Lord Robert was cold in his grave, the castle lost to tragedy, and the gowns and pins sold to provide for those of them who'd stayed. Now, instead of silk or lawn, Lady Murian's gown was made of coarse wool, her feet shod in heavy brown boots, her hands chapped and red.

She swayed as the cart hit a rut, and Ian realized her brows were knit. "Ye look a bit miffed, lass. Still angry at tha' prince?"

A smile flickered over her face. "You know me too well. Aye, I was thinking of the prince. I could have bested him, had I not slipped."

"He was guid wi' his sword, lass. Tha' is all there is to it." Ian scowled. "We dinna know what sort of man we were dealin' wi'. Unluckily for us, he was no' a usual sort of prince, but a warrior prince."

She shot him a surprised look. "There's more than one kind of prince?"

"Aye. Sad fer us, we got the sort as likes a fight."

The cart lurched to one side and she grabbed the edge of her seat. "He was interesting, this prince."

"And handsome," Widow Reeves chimed in.

Lady Murian sent the older woman an amused glance. "So he was. Though you shouldna have teased him by showing him you werena holding a rifle, but a pipe."

"Ha! 'Tis guid fer a mon to know when he's been made a fool."

"He was arrogant. But as irritated as I am at the prince, I'm much angrier at the earl. Loudan put us in this mess, so that we're forced to the highway to try and clear the guards from my own castle."

Ian sighed. "I canna believe 'tis been a year and more. . . ."

"In two days 'twill be a year and a half," she said softly, her gaze darkening.

Ian wished he could give the lass a hug, but she was a prickly thing. So he settled for a gruff, "Master Robert was a guid mon, he was."

"Aye," Widow Reeves agreed as the cart trundled on. "And he loved ye more than the earth loves the sun."

Lady Murian smiled, a genuine one this time, one that crinkled her eyes and revealed a charming dimple. "Spencer chose well for me; Robert and I were well suited."

Widow Reeves tugged her cloak more tightly about her. "How is it the Duke of Spencer came to be yer guardian? I've always wondered tha'."

Ian waited to see if Murian would answer. She rarely spoke of her parents, but to his surprise, she did. "My parents died from a horrible ague when I was a child. My father was a soldier and had fought alongside the duke. When Father realized he wasna' going to live, he wrote to the duke and asked him to watch over me. Spencer did more than that; he raised me as his own."

"Like his own son," Ian said sourly. "He shouldna' ha' taught ye to fight wi' a rapier. 'Tis unseemly."

"Nonsense. It's been verrah handy."

Ian couldn't argue with that, but he still didn't like the way it put the lass in harm's way. "The duke should ha' seen to it tha' you were taught wha' most ladies know: paintin' wi' watercolors, readin' poetry, and embroidery and such."

"Embroidery? Me?" She chuckled. "I'd die of boredom!"

"*And* he should ha' taught ye proper language," Ian said sternly. He'd been in service at Rowallen Castle since he'd been a lad, and he knew ladies from landed gentry did not curse, nor did they still have a brogue—even a soft one—when they went off to London for their season. But the Duke of Spencer had little interest in polite society, so he hadn't bothered to provide his charge with such lady-like training. Murian had been raised as if she were the son of a warlike house, and while she could point out every country on a map, speak Greek, fight with a sword, and discuss war treatises and political stratagems with ease, she still had a trace of a highborn brogue, and could perform none of the duties a properly raised lady should.

The cart dipped into an especially deep rut, and Lady Murian scowled as she bumped upon the seat. "Blast Loudan. We'd all still be warm and toasty in Rowallen Castle if not for him."

"Demmed thievin' horse's arse," Ian agreed. The earl was the bastard half-brother of the Duke of Spencer, although the two were opposites in every way. Where Spencer proved his bravery and mettle in the war, donating much of his wealth and time to protecting his country, Loudan hid in the Scottish countryside, spending his half-brother's funds as if they were his own, and planning a grand return to society once the war was over.

Ian guided the cart around a corner in the road, the smoke from the village now plainly visible over the treetops.

"Odd to see such smoke this late in the afternoon," Lady Murian said.

Ian followed her gaze. "The smithy must have the anvil fires goin'."

She watched the smoke curl overhead into the bright, frosty afternoon, and then disappear into the cold sky. After a moment, she said, "Ian?"

"Aye, lassie?"

"I was thinking of Robert's journal."

Widow Reeves shook her head while Ian bit back a groan. "No' again."

Murian's jaw firmed. "There's proof against Lord Loudan in that journal. I'm sure of it."

Ian had heard those same words a thousand times. "I know, lass. But we've looked for it and found naught."

"We haven't searched the master bedchamber," Lady Murian said.

"And how would we do tha'? Lord Loudan sleeps in tha' chamber now."

Widow Reeves shook her head. "'Tisn't possible. Besides, ye took all the furniture when ye left, so the room was empty. If it ha' been there, surely ye'd ha' found it then."

"Perhaps Robert hid it in a secret place. Under a stone in the hearth, or behind a loose panel."

Ian didn't hesitate. "Nay. We canna take such a chance."

"But we know Robert's journal exists, and that Loudan hasn't found it. If he had, he wouldn't go to such lengths to keep us oot of the castle. And now that we've searched most of the castle except that one room, it must be there."

"Lass, 'tis one thing to sneak into the castle when the earl and his men were oot, and peek aboot the lower levels in the study and sittin' room. Bu' to invade the earl's own bedchamber, especially now tha' the castle is so heavily guarded— Nay. Just nay."

"Ian is right," Widow Reeves said. "And e'ery month the earl hires more thugs to guard the castle. 'Tis too dangerous now."

"We'd get caught, we would, especially now tha' Will botched things oop."

Two weeks ago, when the earl was out hunting with some of his men, Will Scarlae had been sent to search the study desk for the lost journal. It was one of the few pieces of furniture they'd left behind.

Sadly, the lad had been caught, returning home two days later beaten and bloody, having been held in the dungeon until a chambermaid had helped him escape. He'd sworn he hadn't revealed their secreted village, and as no one came to chase them from their homes, Murian believed him.

Ian scowled now. "'Tis suspicious, I am, tha' the lad returned at all."

Widow Reeves sent him a condemning glance. "Will would ne'er tell the earl aboot us. He's a guid lad."

"He's a sullen lad, is wha' he is, wi' a chip on his shoulder the size of Edinburgh. And now Loudan ha' the castle locked oop as if 'twere a bank filled wi' gold. We canna chance sneakin' into the castle anymore."

"But—" Murian began.

"Nay! Besides, ye've been spittin' in the earl's eye these last few weeks by holding oop his guests. Surely tha' is satisfaction enou'."

"I dinna do it for satisfaction, and you know it. It draws the guards from the castle so we can search."

"It *used* to draw the guards from the castle, but no more. An entire squadron surrounds the place now. The last time we went, we couldna get past the drive, there were so many soldiers wanderin' aboot."

Her shoulders slumped, but she refused to agree with him.

Widow Reeves patted Lady Murian's hand. "Just be glad Loudan dinna ha' the sense to hire locals, or we'd ha' been caught already." The earl's men were hired thugs from the streets of London, so they were neither trusted nor liked by the locals, who refused to give away Murian and her little village.

Lady Murian sniffed her disdain. "No real Scot would work for the earl."

"I dinna know," Widow Reeves answered thoughtfully. "He pays well, I hear. Verrah well. And it has been a hard year fer e'eryone."

Murian sent Widow Reeves a black look, and Ian knew the truth of the widow's words troubled the lass.

"Ha' some patience," Ian said. "There's naught we can do until the earl loosens his grip."

"If only Spencer knew what a horrid man his half-brother has become." Murian fidgeted with the edge of her shawl. "I've written the duke time and again, but he never answers. My letters are not reaching him." She sighed. "If I wish his help, I'll have to wait for his return."

"*If* he returns," Ian said, refusing to soften his words even when Murian sent him a horrified look. "Surely ye realize Loudan hopes his half-brother will get killed. It could happen, fer the duke's a brae one, always in the thick of things."

"'Twould be to our benefit were Spencer less brave and would come home. I need him more every day." She caught Ian's concerned look and forced a smile. "But I'd be better served wishing for the sun to stop shining than to wish he would stop rushing to the front of every war. 'Tis in his blood."

"And yers, too, lass." They rounded the final bend, the village slowly coming into view. "I've ne'er met a more— Bloody hell!"

Murian's heart sank into her heels.

"Och no!" Widow Reeves's voice cracked in shock.

The smoke they'd seen had come from the inn. The entire front of the building was blackened, the door half burned from the hinges, the windows broken. A large black hole in the center of the roof over the main taproom trailed smoke into the air, thick black smudges outlining the windows.

Ian's heavy brows knit, his mouth a slash of bitterness. "I hope no one was injured."

"Aye," Widow Reeves agreed fervently.

"We were here just last week, too." Murian looked at

the other buildings—some cottages, a blacksmith shop, a small stable. The village was tiny, far from the main roads, which was why they traded here. They'd thought they were safe from Loudan's men this far from Rowallen. And that the villagers would be safe, too.

Is this because of us? Please, God, don't let it be so.

They pulled up before the inn, and Murian noticed curtains flickering in a few of the houses. "No one is coming oot to greet us." Her throat was tight, as pained as her thoughts.

Ian said in a grim tone, "I know, lass. It dinna look guid."

Widow Reeves placed her hand over Murian's and squeezed. "Perhaps 'twas just a kitchen fire."

"Nay. It started in the main taproom. You can see it from the hole in the roof." Ian stopped the cart and jumped down to tie the horse. "Wait here." He went to the inn and stuck his head into the half-charred doorway, calling out a greeting before disappearing inside.

Murian gathered her cloak and hopped down from the cart.

"Lass, ye shouldna—" the widow began, but Murian was already hurrying inside the inn.

The walls were blackened with soot, the floors a mess of ash and water, and a ceiling beam lay tilted across the hallway. She paused at the door to the taproom. Ian stood in the center, kicking at a broken, half-burned chair. He scowled on seeing her. "Ye should ha' stayed in the cart."

"I must know what happened."

His bushy red brows locked over his nose, but with a grimace, he yelled, "MacPhee!"

No one answered.

"MacPhee!" Ian bellowed.

From the back of the inn came a testy reply. "Hold yer horses, will ye? I was in the pantry!" There was a noise from the hallway and then the landlord appeared, stepping gingerly through the mess.

MacPhee was a huge, bald man, his face red on a normal day, and doubly so today. He looked slightly sunburned, one cheek redder than the other, his clothes soot-streaked, his britches and sleeves bearing holes from where hot ash had landed upon him.

He came to a sudden stop on seeing Ian, his gaze flickering to Murian and then away.

Murian saw the answer in the innkeeper's eyes. "Loudan."

The innkeeper rubbed his neck, suddenly looking far older than his years. "I suppose ye'll find oot whether I tell ye or no'. His men arrived yesterday afternoon. They knew ye'd been here before, and tha' we'd bought some goods fra' ye. They demanded to know where ye were. I told them I dinna know—though I wouldna ha' told the bastards e'en if I did."

"The louts," Ian growled.

"Aye. Anyway, they tol' us we were no' to trade wi' ye anymore, and I refused—as did e'eryone else in the village."

Murian could only shake her head, her heart heavy. "You shouldna have risked so much for me."

"No offense, Lady Murian, but 'twas no' just fer ye.

We willna ha' a bloody Sassenach telling us wha' we can and canna do, especially after wha' he did to Lord Robert." MacPhee cast a quick glance at Murian and then said, "'Twas all o'er in a moment. The earl's guards forced their way inside my inn, threw chairs into a pile, set them afire, and left, sayin' they'd be back. We tried to put oot the flames, but it flared oop somethin' awful." He looked around the room, disbelief on his face. "This inn belonged to me father, and me father's father before him. And now . . ." He pressed his lips together, his eyes watering.

Murian took a step forward. "MacPhee, I'm so sorry. I—"

"Lass, please!" He forced a smile. "'Tis no' yer fault, but the earl's, damn his black soul."

"Aye," Ian agreed in a heavy voice. "He's a blight on the land, he is."

The innkeeper's red-rimmed gaze flickered to the road and then back, his voice quavering as he said, "I'm sorry to say it, me lady, but I dinna think ye should be here. They said they'd come back, and if they find ye . . ." MacPhee's face grew grim.

"Lady Murian!" Widow Reeves stood in the doorway. Her wide gaze took in the blackened, charred room as she said, "Men are comin'. Ye can see them through the trees."

Loudan's men! Heart in her throat, Murian hurried to the charred hole of the window. Still at a distance, flashing through the forest, she could just make out a stream of red uniforms. "'Tis not Loudan, but the prince and his men."

"The prince?" Ian came to look over her shoulder. "Bloody hell, wha' is he doin' here?"

"Wha' prince?" MacPhee asked, looking confused.

As Ian answered him, Murian watched the progress of their visitors. Their pace was leisurely, so they didn't seem to be on a mission. Why were they here, this far from Rowallen?

She bit her lip, trying to ignore the flicker of excitement that hummed through her. He fascinated her, this prince with green eyes and a master's arm with a sword. But why he was visiting Loudan—for she didn't believe his tale of admiring the earl. The earl had high societal aspirations, and she strongly suspected that was why he'd gone to such lengths to possess Rowallen: to gain a suitable perch to lord it over the countryside. It hadn't worked, because once word had spread of how the earl had come to possess the castle, the local gentry had refused to attend any of the earl's events. But having a prince as a guest could well change that.

She scowled, though she couldn't blame the locals. There was something about a real-life prince that stirred one's curiosity, especially when the prince looked so . . . princely. There was no other word for it, and it irritated her how often she'd thought about him since their encounter.

Widow Reeves came to stand with Murian. "We should go."

Murian nodded and followed Widow Reeves outside to the cart, Ian following behind.

He untied the horses. "Lass, we'll never make it oot

of town in this slow cart before the prince and his men reach us. We canna let the prince see ye."

"Why no'?" Widow Reeves asked.

Ian climbed into his seat, the cart tilting as his weight settled. "The prince has seen the lass's face. He thinks our Robin is a 'he,' but if he sees her again, he might realize his mistake. Tha' is no' information I'd want him to pass on to Loudan."

"Aye." Murian tugged her hood over her bonnet. "I'll leave the two of you to drive the cart oot of town, while I cut through the woods."

"Hold!" MacPhee hurried from his inn. "Ye had something ye wished to sell, did ye no'?"

Widow Reeves pointed to the basket on the seat of the cart. "Some jams and wha' no', bu' we'll find somewhere else to sell them. The earl's men—"

"I'll no' let those miserable spalpeens tell me wha' to do! I'll buy it all, the whole basket."

Widow Reeves turned pink with pleasure. "All of it? Are ye sure—"

"Of course he's sure," Ian said testily. "If ye're goin' to sell yer wares, do it. We've no' much time." He turned to Murian. "Go whilst ye can."

"I'll take the path behind the barn. It runs into the cart path after the bend near the stream."

"I'll meet ye there." Ian scowled. "I dinna like this, but we've no choice. Stay hidden, lass. Take no chances, ye hear?"

She nodded and, with a wave of her hand, hurried toward the barn, glad to make her escape. Still, a small part of her wished she might see the prince and that he would recognize her. It would be sweet to see his expression when he realized he'd been bested by a woman.

One day, Prince. One day.

$\mathcal{M}$ax raised his hand as he turned his horse into the small village, and the line of men behind him immediately came to a halt. For the last few days, he and his men had systematically searched for the highwaymen who'd held them up, but to no avail.

Yet.

Orlov pulled up his horse beside Max. "It looks as if there has been a mishap to this village, much like the other three villages we've visited over the last few days."

"I wonder if they'll have the same story to tell?"

"That nothing happened? That one of the few buildings they use for commerce has been razed, but for no reason anyone knows?" Concern darkened Orlov's face. "They lie. While our search for this thief has not been successful, it has brought us another mystery."

"A big one. Someone has gone through this forest and systematically reduced the local villages to ashes, and at Loudan's orders, or so it seems to me. His guards ride out each day, and each day there is a new fire."

"As we are Loudan's guests, no one will tell us anything. They fear retribution." Orlov looked disgusted. "Why would he do this to his own people?"

"I don't know—yet. There is a large man by the inn. You, Demidor, and I will speak with him. Have Pahlen and Golovin catch up to that cart that just pulled away and see what those people might know. Have the rest of the men knock on doors and try to find out what happened. Offer coins, and leave a few even if the villagers offer no help. Everyone we've seen thus far appears to be in need. It is the least we can do."

"*Da*, General."

Max urged his mount down the path into the village. As he reached the smoldering inn, the woman in the cart seat turned and looked over her shoulder toward the woods. She only looked for a second, her face creased as if in worry, and then just as quickly, she turned back around, hunkering down. Max's gaze moved from her to the man at her side. *Such a large man, too, like a giant—*

His gaze narrowed. He turned in the direction the woman had looked. For a moment, he saw nothing but large trees, half-withered shrubbery, and a swath of brown leaves. Nothing of interest.

But as he started to turn back, a flicker of movement caught his attention. He stood up in his stirrups and just caught sight of a figure disappearing into the woods, a greenish cloak blending with the late-fall foliage.

"What is it?" Orlov asked, dismounting beside Max.

"I don't yet know." Max climbed down and handed Orlov his reins. "Talk to the innkeeper, and do not let those two in the cart get away. I'll be back."

Orlov nodded and called out orders to the other soldiers.

Max headed toward the woods, catching sight of a faint path that wasn't evident from the main road. As he entered the trees he slowed his gait, walking softly and avoiding crisp leaves and noisy branches that might alert his prey.

It took him only a moment to catch up to her, for she'd not had much of a head start. She hurried down the path, apparently confident she'd made good her escape, as each step crunched on dead leaves and fallen sticks. As the path bent around a large oak, the sunshine lit the hood and shoulders of her cloak and he caught sight of a thick red curl that clung to her shoulder. *Red hair, tall, slender, strides as if every step had a purpose— Finally, I have found you.*

Chapter 4

Murian shivered as a chilly breeze ruffled her hood and tugged at her skirts, her mind on the prince. He intrigued her—it was rare that she'd been bested in a sword fight, but then, not many men still adhered to what was now considered an antiquated way of fighting. Spencer had often lamented that improvements in the accuracy of pistols and rifles had turned many men from the older and, to him, more honorable ways of warfare. She had to agree that a person's true mettle showed during a fight by blade. And judging from the prince's performance, he was a foe to be respected.

She glanced back over her shoulder, wondering if Ian and Widow Reeves had made it out of town before the prince and his men arrived. Hearing nothing but the rustle of the trees and her own footfalls, and hurried on.

She had much more to think about than a visiting prince. Besides the worrying issue of supplies, the crofter's cottages were far from ready for bad weather. Her people had the skills to make repairs—Widow Brodie was good with a hammer and saw and had made chests for each of her five boys, while Widow MacCrae, who wove the loveliest of lace, had also replaced the crumbling chinking on one wall of her cottage using a recipe she'd gotten from a groom at Rowallen. And while helping Ian build a stone fence for their animals when they'd first moved to the village, Murian had learned enough to help repair some of the chimneys.

A low branch hung over the path, and she ducked to avoid it. As she straightened, her hood was yanked from her head. She turned to untangle it from the branch—and found herself facing a wall of red wool.

And not just any wool, but fine red wool adorned with large gold buttons.

Oh no. She gulped, her heart thudding hard as she slowly, ever so slowly, looked up. Her gaze traveled over a broad chest, to a firm chin, and then to eyes the deepest of green.

The prince had the cold, clipped beauty of a hawk, his jawline sharp, his nose aquiline, his gaze piercing— every line masculine and commanding, including his scars.

The moonlight had softened them, but in the brightness of the late afternoon sun, they were plainly visible. An angry red scar cut one eyebrow in half, skipping his lid only to catch the bold cheek beneath it. Another scar, older and white, marked his upper lip, and there were two more on his chin and jaw. But his scars didn't alter the masculine line of his mouth, nor did they soften the firmness of his jaw, nor detract from the long lashes that framed his green eyes.

He was extraordinarily beautiful.

A shiver traveled over her, an instant, heated reaction that weakened her knees and tripped her heart. *It's fear,* she told herself. *Fear that he will reveal me to Loudan.*

Besides, she wasn't even certain he recognized her. She could tell little from his expression, which was politely inquisitive, and little else.

"You seem to be in a hurry." His voice was like dark, creamy honey.

Surely if he'd recognized me, he'd have said something. She forced herself to smile politely. "I am walking home, and it is growing late."

He glanced at the sinking sun. "I hope your home is close. Sadly, I am lost and do not know my way. Do you think you might help me?"

She examined his expression more closely and saw no spark of recognition. *It was dark that night, and there was only one lantern.* She relaxed a bit. "Where are you staying, that you are lost?"

"Rowallen Castle. My men and I were hunting. We stopped at a village, and I saw a hare. I followed him into the woods and now—" He shook his head and laughed a little. "That is what I get for not paying attention."

That seemed possible. She rapidly reviewed her options. She supposed she could run off and leave him here. Though he might be faster, she knew these woods well, and with some planning and a dash of luck, she could get away. But what would that achieve?

A better plan would be to allow him to accompany

her at least a small way, and—if she were subtle—find out what he knew. *Perhaps I will discover what is happening at Rowallen.*

She nodded at the path ahead. "This runs into a trail. If you find it and go north, it will take you to the main road that leads to Rowallen. It will be much quicker than the road you were upon."

"Ah. Problem solved."

"Yes, but the trail isna well marked. Perhaps I should walk with you a bit, and show you the way. Once you see where it joins the main trail, you can return and show your men."

"Very good. Show me this trail."

She turned and walked on, the prince falling into step beside her. For a few moments, they walked in silence. He held back branches that barred their path, and placed a hand on her elbow when they had to scramble over some rocks.

All in all, it was rather pleasant having a companion near her own age. She snuck a glance at his profile. He was far too handsome for his own good. And for hers.

"I hope your home is close," he said. "It is not safe after dark. There are brigands in the woods."

She fought a grin. "Och, yes. Everyone is talking aboot them."

"They are evil creatures. Dirty, malodorous—you would not wish to meet them in the middle of the night."

Her smile disappeared. "I'm sorry . . . did you say they were *malodorous*?"

He curled his nose. "I had an encounter with them a

few days ago and cannot get the stench from my nostrils."

What a ridiculous accusation! But she couldn't say anything without admitting she was one of them. She said through tight lips, "I doubt the brigands will pay any attention to me. They willna expect me to have anything worth taking, so I'll be safe."

"That, I cannot believe." His gaze flickered over her. "You're an attractive woman, and these men were the lowest forms of thieves I've ever met—brutal, barbaric, and vicious."

She ducked under a low branch, fighting to keep the outrage from her voice. "They canna be too vicious. They've harmed no one."

"They are animals. Despite my grandmother's pleading, they demanded her basket of food." He scowled, his expression stern. "What sort of person takes food from a hungry, frail old woman?"

When he put it that way, it did sound rather horrible. She felt guilty for having enjoyed the roasted chicken quite so much. "Perhaps they were hungry themselves. It is coming onto winter, and a longer, colder fall we've never had."

"I doubt it. They were all very fat."

She came to a complete halt. "*Fat?*"

"*Da.* With huge bellies and dirty hands." He bent to remove a burr from the side of his boot. "They were incompetent, too. Obviously very new at their profession. Amateurs, really."

Amateurs? Murian's back could get no stiffer.

The prince straightened, dropping the burr to the

ground. "But that's no surprise, considering the leader of this band. He was—how you say . . . ?" He patted his arm. "No strength. Like a sick kitten."

Bloody hell, I'll show him how strong I am! She wished she had her rapier with her now. "I heard a verrah different story aboot this thief. I heard he was quite the fighter and handled his rapier like a master." Because she *had*, damn it.

"Hardly. I beat him well and good." He smirked, making her want to box his ears. "I barely nicked him, and he squealed like a stuck pig."

I didn't squeal! Not once! She fisted her hands in a futile effort to keep her temper.

The prince continued, "It was over quickly, of course. Battles with such lackwits usually are. After flashing his tiny sword, he begged for mercy."

"*Begged*?" Her voice cracked on the word.

"*Da*. He almost wept in happiness when I allowed him to leave unscathed. Well, except for his ear. I cut it off, you know."

"You dinna," she said firmly.

"*Da*, I did. One cut and . . ." He waved his hand, slicing through the air. "Gone."

"I'm surprised you didn't keep this ear and make a purse of it," she said furiously, failing to keep the sarcasm from her voice.

The prince looked surprised. "Who would want a purse made from the ear of a malodorous coward?"

She didn't trust herself to speak.

The prince seemed unaware of her fury, pursing his lips for a moment before saying, "But perhaps you are right, and it is safe for you to travel at night. Such a thief is not to be feared."

She couldn't believe she was listening to such— *drivel*! *Damn it, I planned that raid and it went very well! Well . . . it did until* he *complicated things.* She sniffed. "I dare say you've experience in those things—holding up coaches and such, so that your opinion has merit."

"Experience? As a common thief? *Nyet.* Of course not."

"Well, there you have it. You canna judge them, then." She turned on her heel and marched down the path.

He was beside her in a second. "I may have never planned a paltry holdup, but I have planned many battles and faced many adversaries—and all successfully, too."

"Those are not the same."

"They are more similar than you might think." His gaze narrowed and he added in an arrogantly certain voice, "But as you've had experience in neither, you would not know."

Words burned behind her lips, and she walked faster to channel her anger away from her tongue. Her feet hitting the earth harder with each step, she said in a polite, frosty tone, "And yet even an inexperienced person such as myself canna help but notice that these— what did you call them?—inexperienced and amateur thieves won the day. They say you handed over a fortune in gold."

"They did not win the day. I took pity on them and gave them a few paltry baubles, and sent them on their way."

Braggart! Liar! Arrogant pig prince! She had to count to ten before she could speak. "The tales being passed about the villages are quite different. They say the thieves gained a significant amount of coins, as well as Her Grace's rings."

"And my grandmother's supper," he added. "My Tata Natasha missed the food more than her rings, for she was very hungry, and it was hours before we reached Rowallen."

"Hours?"

"*Da.* We had to calm the horses, find the lost lanterns—such things as that. And waiting for supper is not easy for an old woman."

Muriel's heart sank, her anger dissipating. They'd never meant anyone to suffer. Perhaps they shouldn't have taken the basket of food, but she'd been thinking how welcome it would be to the children, who were tired of stew and turnips—

The prince captured her elbow and pulled her to a stop.

Surprised, she looked up at him.

He brushed her cheek with his fingertips, and in his eyes she saw understanding. This man knew responsibility. How decisions could have repercussions one couldn't expect. How the weight of one's decisions could press down, making it difficult to breathe.

"Ah, *dorogaya moya*, do not look like that. If you'd known my grandmother was hungry, you would have left the basket. I know it."

The sympathy in his voice soothed the ache of

uncertainty in her heart. "Truly, I dinna know, or I'd have—"

His eyes glinted.

She clamped her lips together and yanked her hand free. "You knew! You knew all along!"

"*Da.* The other night, I saw your face quite clearly." He brushed a finger across her cheek, sending waves of shivers up her back, his eyes darkening. "I would never forget it."

She found it hard to swallow. "And now, you will tell Loudan."

The prince's hand dropped back to his side. "Never. I only said he was a friend of mine to irritate you."

Aha! When he'd spoken so highly of the earl during the fight, she'd thought then that the prince had been shamming; it was gratifying to be proven right. "The earl dinna have friends. Only sycophants."

"So I've noticed. I'd never met him before I reached Rowallen." The prince's gaze brushed over her face. "By the bye, you and your band light up like firepots whenever the earl is mentioned. It is a weakness."

She inclined her head. "We will work on that. So, Prince, if you're not a friend of the earl's, then why are you here?"

The prince's eyes warmed and though he didn't move, he seemed closer. "You wish for information, do you?"

"Why not? You dinna seem to have anything better to do."

His lips twitched. "All in good time. First, you owe me

an apology for slicing up my best coat." Before she could do more than flash him a disbelieving look, he added, "But do not worry; I will accept a simple gesture—a kiss—as a token of your remorse."

A kiss. The mere thought made her fight a shiver. But she could not capitulate quite so easily. She had the distinct impression the prince didn't normally suffer from a lack of kisses, and she had no desire to be just one of many. She lifted one shoulder in a bored shrug. "I dinna give away kisses."

"You owe me something for my ruined coat," he pointed out. "In addition, I won our little skirmish."

"Only because I slipped."

He looked amused. "I will say this: you have talent with that sword. I was caught unaware."

Well. It was surprising he would admit that. She rather enjoyed hearing it.

He glanced at her ear, which was hidden beneath her hair. "How is your wound? Is it healing?"

"It hurts, but not much."

"I didn't mean to cut you. You moved as I moved, and the result . . ." He spread his hands. "I am sorry."

"As am I. I dinna wish anyone harmed, nor did I wish to inconvenience your grandmother." She hesitated. "You will want your possessions returned."

"Nay. You may keep them."

Surprised, she tilted her head to one side. "Are you certain?"

"I did not allow anything to be taken that I cared about."

"Ah. Thank you, then." She shared a small smile. "It

would have been difficult to reclaim the chickens from Ian."

The prince grinned in return, his eyes crinkling. "I would never come between that giant and his food."

"You're a smart man."

He chuckled and captured her hand. "I should spank you for your arrogance, my little thief, but I have too much admiration for your skills." He lifted her hand and brushed his lips over her knuckles, lingering on her bare skin.

Her fingers trembled, a flurry of wild sparks cascading through her. She should yank her hand free or distract him with a swift kick to his shin—something other than stare at him, wondering what he might do if she leaned forward and pressed her lips to his and— *No! What am I thinking?*

As if unaware of her turmoil, the prince ran his thumb over her palm, his gaze dropping to her hand as he traced the calluses there. A faint crease appeared between his eyes. "Life has not been easy for you."

Her face burned and she tugged her hand free, wishing she'd thought to rub in the peppermint liniment Widow Brodie made for such. "We do our own farming, and there is wood to cut, and stones to move." There was no shame in that; she was proud of her people, of their progress. She lifted her chin and met his gaze dead-on. "We dinna live in luxury, but we live well enough."

A flicker of regret crossed his face. "I did not mean that as a criticism. Indeed, I applaud your resourcefulness." He shook his head. "I am—how do you say—pushing over the cart?"

She had to smile a bit. "Upsetting the apple cart."

"Perhaps we should begin again, you and I. We have not been properly introduced, and I have been told such things are important in this country—so allow me." He stepped back and swept an elegant bow, looking up at her through his lashes. "It is a pleasure to make your acquaintance. I am Maksim Alexsandr Romanovin." He straightened. "Please call me Max."

"I should call you Your Highness."

"I would not answer. In my country, we do not stand on such formality as you do here. I have been informed that you are only informal when in private." He gestured to the woods around them. "It does not get more private than this. Besides, the next time you wish to cut an initial in my coat, I would like it to be the correct one."

She had to laugh. Besides, she wanted to taste that name, to let it roll over her lips, and see his reaction as she did so. "Max it is, then. I make a very neat M, by the way, in case I need to mark another coat."

Max grinned. It was a tiny victory; asking a highwayman to break societal customs wasn't a very big challenge. But still, this one was prickly with pride. Every concession counted, and he felt as if he'd won something substantial. Something valuable. "So, my thief, I have told you my name. Now you must tell me yours."

She started to speak, but then her expression closed.

"You still worry I will tell the earl. I promise I will not. I have several very real reasons of my own to distrust the man."

"Such as?"

He hesitated, but then shrugged. "The earl has some hold over my grandmother, but I do not know what. She is the reason we came, and her behavior has been odd, to say the least. The earl, too, has been very dismissive in the way he speaks to her. She would not normally allow that, but . . ." Max spread his hands.

"She willna tell you what's happened?"

He grimaced. "My grandmother is of a stubbornness rarely seen upon this earth."

Murian chuckled, her eyes crinkling.

God, what a delicious laugh. Husky and low, it curled around him and made him want to scoop her up and hold her tight.

He pushed his wandering thoughts aside. "In addition, I just rode from a village where the earl has left his destructive mark, and I have seen far too many like it over the last few days. What little I know of the earl has made me despise him."

The smile left her, her voice breathless. "He has done the same elsewhere? Burned buildings? Frightened the people?"

Max nodded.

A spasm crossed her face, as if the thought pained her like the brush of fire. "I canna allow that to continue. I . . ." She took a steadying breath.

"You did not set a single building on fire. The earl's men did."

"I am still responsible if my presence causes harm. But that is my concern, not yours." She gave him a tight smile. "I believe I owe you a name, dinna I? That, I'll give you, but no more." She curtsied. "I am Lady Murian, wife of the late Lord Robert Muir."

Bozhy moj, she is too young to be a widow. He looked for tragedy in her gaze and found a flash of sadness she hid deep within, though it only added to her loveliness. Hers was a vibrant beauty, one never forgotten. Her face was a delicate oval, but with a strong jaw, her thickly lashed eyes flashing with passion and intelligence. He could make out a faint sprinkle of freckles across her pale skin, a dimple flickering in one cheek, her pulse visible in the graceful line of her neck.

A pang hit him, and he found himself thinking of Dimitri's widow, who was a lovely woman too, and who held the same tragedy in her eyes. But Henrietta's pain had never been hidden. She'd lived in it, expressed it over and over until there was nothing but the sadness. Meanwhile, Murian stood with her back straight, her jaw set. *She fights back. That is how she mourns.*

A flicker of admiration warmed him. Here was a worthy woman. *A strong woman.* "I take it Loudan was somehow involved in the death of your husband? You say the earl's name as if you burned for vengeance. There must be a reason."

She regarded him with caution, her gaze flickering to his mouth and then back. It was like a touch, that glance, and it sent his searching gaze to her mouth. That was an error, for instantly his thoughts fled and all he could think about was her lips, so plump and ripe, so ready for a kiss.

His body hummed in response and he had to fight the desire to grasp her waist and drag her to him. Her gaze locked with his, and it was as if they shared the same thoughts, the same desires. *She wants me, too.*

The realization urged him on, and he stepped toward her—just as she rose on her tiptoes and pressed her lips to his.

It was a delicate kiss, almost cautious in the way she did it, leaning forward, her body still separated from his. He fought the urge to pull her to him, wanting her to take that last step into his arms herself. It almost killed him, for her touch set him afire.

Just as he was beginning to give up hope, she stepped forward and placed her hands on his chest. *Finally.* He rocked back on his heels, lifting his arms to encircle her—

She shoved with all her might. He fell over a log. One moment he was kissing an intriguing, mysterious, fair maiden, and the next he was lying upon the ground, looking up at the tree canopy.

Cursing, he scrambled to his feet . . . but it was too late. She was gone.

Chapter 5

Two nights later, a knock came on Murian's cottage door. She put down her quill pen, wrapped her shawl about her, and went to answer it. As she opened the door an icy wind roared past Ian, who hurried inside and shoved the door closed.

He pulled off his cap, his face red. "'Tis bitter oot-side."

"I know. Every time the wind blows, it snuffs my candle." She nodded to where she'd made a small barrier about her candle using two books and a cloth.

"It dinna gi' ye much light like tha'."

"'Tis the best I can do." She walked back to the desk. "I'm making a list of supplies we need to fix the worst issues with our cottages. We can make wattle for chinking, and there's plenty of rock by the river to fix the chimneys. What we dinna have is planked wood."

"There's wood enou' in the forest, but we'd dinna ha' the tools to plane it into boards."

"I know." She sighed. "We canna purchase it, not after seeing what Loudan's men have been doing to the local villages just for trading with us."

Ian muttered darkly under his breath as he went to hold his hands to the snapping fire. "We'll find a way, lassie. We must."

"I hope so." She sank onto the settee before the fireplace, then held her feet toward the fire and wiggled her toes. They were snug inside her bulky knitted slippers, a gift from Widow MacDonald.

A crackling heat came from the fire, and Ian sighed. "If Loudan keeps harrassin' the locals, we may ha' to move where his long arms canna reach."

"Nay. That would make it more difficult to reach Rowallen and win the castle back. Besides, Loudan isna the sort of man to let a small thing like distance stop him. He would only send his men after us, and we'd be worse off than we are now. At least here, we have friends, though we must protect them when we can."

If she truly thought moving away would help, she'd do it in a second despite the distance from Rowallen. These were her people, and she was responsible for each and every one of them—Ian, Will, seven widows, and twelve children. Counting herself, there were twenty-two heads to shelter and feed, day in and day out. It was a lot. More than she'd ever thought to carry on her own.

"I suppose ye ha' the right of it, lassie. The earl is determined to smite us all." Ian picked up the fire iron and adjusted the logs, the scent of smoky pine rising through the small cottage. The fire stirred to a respectable height; he returned the iron to the stand. "Fer some reason, I keep thinkin' of the prince."

So had Murian, although she was certain she and Ian

had different reasons. She picked up the blanket from the back of the settee and tugged it about her shoulders, resting her feet upon a small, silk-covered footstool she'd fished from close by. "What have you been thinking aboot the prince?"

"In the village the other day, the prince's men seemed genuinely shocked by the actions of Loudan's guards." Ian stared into the fire, a thoughtful expression on his face. "'Tis a known fact the men of an army reflect their leader. If tha' is true, then the prince may be a guid mon."

Murian snuggled deeper into the blanket, oddly cheered to hear Ian's rare approbation. For a moment, she was tempted to tell Ian of her encounter with the prince in the woods. She hadn't mentioned it because the grizzled groom tended to be overprotective at times.

Besides, keeping it secret meant the memory of that too-brief but oh-so-sweet kiss was hers and hers alone. Though she doubted Max thought of it as a memory worth treasuring, she most certainly did.

She sighed restlessly and wished she'd dared explain to Max how things really were because of Loudan. Perhaps she'd get that chance one day, though she doubted it. Max had admitted he already disliked his host, which meant the prince and his men would leave as soon as they could. She wouldn't blame him one bit.

It was a pity, really. She'd have liked showing him her village, too. She looked about her with satisfaction. Though the cottage had been built by goat herders and the mud-daubed walls and broken slate roof were as plain as could be, the luxurious furnishings comforted her ragged spirits. All taken from Rowallen, they made the dirt floor and cracked plaster walls palatable.

She had taken more than a few items from Rowallen during their mad flight, too. Beneath the footstool was a heavy Aubusson carpet, while two red tufted chairs flanked the fireplace. The thickly cushioned settee shone with gilded wood and was framed on each side by small marble-topped tables. In one corner of the cottage, near a red Chinese silk screen, stood the magnificent mahogany bed that had once graced the bedchamber she'd shared with Robert. Hung with purple velvet curtains and piled high with pillows and thick down counterpanes, it was a jewel in a very small, plain box.

The Earl of Loudan might have killed her husband and stolen their castle; he might have kicked their retainers from the land and tried to starve them when they fought back—but he hadn't been able to keep Murian from taking everything not nailed down with her when she'd left her home.

When things were bleak, she imagined Loudan's fury on returning to Rowallen after filing his claim in Edinburgh and finding the castle nearly empty, devoid of almost everything but a few stray pieces of furniture too large to fit on the carts.

What was even better was that not just her cottage was so decorated, but every crofter's cottage in their small village. Though the wind might whistle through the cracks in the walls, they had soft rugs under their feet and good mattresses upon which to rest.

In the beginning, when things had gotten desperate, she'd thought to sell some of the items, but had quickly realized the earl was watching for such transactions. So, with nowhere else to put them, she'd stored the rest of the furnishings in the barn, covered in heavy tarps to protect them from the weather. One day she'd see them all returned to Rowallen. *One day soon.*

She hoped. A deep restlessness flickered through her. Her patience was close to an end. "Ian, I canna—"

A brisk knock sounded at the door before it was thrown open and Widow Reeves stomped in. She turned to close the door, but was unable to hold it against the wind, so Ian hurried to help her.

Murian rose to greet the older woman. "Widow Reeves, what are you doing oot in this weather?"

"I've come to share some news. Return to yer seat, me lady. There's no need to stand. 'Tis no' as if I dinna know ye as well as me own elbow."

Murian laughed and sat down while Widow Reeves hurried to the fire, her iron-gray curls puffed about her red cheeks and forehead. The widow tucked her mittens in her pocket before holding her hands to the flames. "Och, tha' is better. I miss bein' the cook at Rowallen. I was ne'er cold then."

"Nay, ye were always complainin' of the heat," Ian said.

She shot him a hard look. "Aye, and ye were always complainin' aboot havin' so much to do, wha' with so many horses bein' kept in Lord Robert's stables. I suppose neither of us were as grateful as we should ha' been."

He grunted an agreement.

"Widow Reeves, what is this news?" Murian waited expectantly. "Shall I put on some tea?"

"Och, I canna. As soon as I'm through here, I'm off to Widow Brodie's to lend her a hand in puttin' her lads to bed."

Ian grimaced. "Five lusty lads, they are."

"Aye, and Iona's too soft wi' them, as I've told her fer years." Widow Reeves rubbed her hands together. "Ah, this is nice. 'Tis warmer here than in me own cottage."

Murian frowned. "Dinna you have wood for your fire?"

"Aye. 'Tis no' lack of wood, bu' the hole in my roof, which lets in the wind and rain." She caught Murian's expression. "Och, lassie, dinna look so. Ye canna fix e'ery leak in e'ery roof."

Murian managed a smile. "I wish I could."

"Ye do enou' as 'tis. Master Robert found a gem when he found ye, and we say a blessin' fer ye e'ery day. All of us."

At the kind words, Murian's face heated. "If anyone had a large heart, it was Robert. Long before I came to Rowallen, he took in every widow and orphan he stumbled across."

"Ye are both angels, which is why I'm pleased to bring ye some guid news." Widow Reeves came to sit on the settee, an air of barely suppressed excitement lighting her face. "As ye know, me sister Lara is a cook fer Lord and Lady MacLure. Lara brought some of her scones this morning, and while she was here, she mentioned tha' her lord and lady were invited to a dinner party at Rowallen Castle this coming Friday to welcome the prince."

Murian leaned forward. "Lord and Lady MacLure are attending?"

"Aye. From wha' Lara has heard, all the local gentry will be attendin'."

"Loudan will be beside himself."

"Aye. Fer the last year, the MacLures and the other gentry ha' refused e'ery invitation fra' Lord Loudan—but they canna say no to meetin' a real prince."

"I wonder if that is why the earl wanted the prince to visit him in the first place. I suspected as much."

"Aye. My sister heard Lady MacLure say tha' Loudan canna convince anyone fra' Edinburgh to join him at Rowallen, so 'tis the local gentry or no one. So now he must make his amends for all the times he's slighted them, or there will be no one to entertain in his new castle."

"I dinna see why this is guid news," Ian said.

"Ian! How can ye be so daft?" Widow Reeves scoffed. "On Friday night, the castle will be filled wit' the local gentry. *None of whom Loudan knows.*"

Murian couldn't contain her smile. "This may be the chance we've been waiting for. The castle will be filled with strangers. We'll get into the castle and search the master bedchamber before the earl even realizes w—"

"Nay, lass." Ian shook his head like a shaggy bear. "'Twill still be heavily guarded. Besides, Loudan may no' know the local gentry, bu' he knows wha' *ye* look like. He saw ye when he came to chase us fra' the castle, wavin' his papers under yer nose."

"True." She pursed her lips. "I'll need a disguise—"

"Nay, nay, *nay!*" Ian's face was dark as thunder. "Ye canna go into tha' castle, and tha' is tha'." He turned to Widow Reeves. "Tell her she canna go. She'll listen to ye."

Widow Reeves looked surprised. "I dinna think she will—will ye, lass?"

It was clear Murian might have to do this without Ian's help, so she said brightly, "I'm willna think aboot anything tonight. I'm too tired." But she would think about it, and by all that was holy, she'd get into that castle and find Robert's journal.

"See, Ian Beagin? She's no' e'en thinkin' on it this evenin'." Widow Reeves held her hands toward the fire. "But e'en if she were thinkin' on it, and e'en if she went, she'd be safe. Loudan couldna touch her, no' in front of a castle filled wit' local lairds and ladies."

"Loudan is evil but he isn't stupid," Murian added. Which was sad, indeed.

"We willna be takin' tha' chance to find oot, will we?" Ian grumbled.

Widow Reeves exchanged a glance with Murian and then said, "No' to change the topic, but the other widows and I thought we might visit one of the villages tha' the earl's men burned and offer our help. 'Tis a tragedy, and we feel partially responsible."

"That's an excellent idea," Murian said. "I'll join you."

"Damn the earl's black soul fer harmin' the locals fer tradin' wi' us," Ian said. "We'd ha' starved if they paid him as much heed as he wished."

"We're in a difficult position," Murian admitted. "But look at the talent and skills that thus far have saved us. You and Will keep our woodstoves filled, and often bring deer and rabbits for roasts and stews."

Ian snorted. "A lad of twelve could do tha'."

"No lad of twelve tha' I know." Widow Reeves eyed him up and down. "Ye've brought us more fresh game than any other mon could."

Ian's face turned red. "I'm a fair shot, bu' no more."

"You can also make metal do your bidding," Murian said. "You smith like one born to it, while Will has a way with greens that, before the drought, has kept us in carrots, turnips, and cabbage."

"'Tis true," Widow Reeves said. "And Widow Mac-Donald sews better than the dressmaker in the village."

"And yer cookin' is no' to be ignored, either," Ian added. "'Tis magic wha' ye can do wi' the most paltry of items."

"I do wha' I can. Thank the heavens fer Widow Atchison's cheeses. Those ha' helped mightily."

"The inns clamor for more," Murian said, "and will pay, too. A shop in Inverness has asked Widows Mac-Thune and MacCrae for more of the lace they've been making, if they'll come after dark so Loudan's men dinna get wind of it."

"Lady MacLure asked my sister to fetch more of the baskets Widow Grier makes, too," Widow Reeves said, looking pleased.

"I'm lucky you all threw your fortunes in with mine." Murian was proud of her merry band of widows and two braw men. Had Loudan left them alone, they would have done quite well. But he'd vowed to bring them to ruin. He wanted to run her off, away from Row-allen. *And the only reason he could possibly have for keeping me away from the castle is because he knows there might be proof of his perfidy. If he'd already found Robert's journal, then the earl wouldn't care if I'm nearby, for he'd have already destroyed it.* It was the only hope she had.

The wind rustled mightily, puffing wind down the chimney and sending a poof of black soot into the room. Widow Reeves shivered. "Och, I must be goin'. Master Beagin, why dinna ye come, too? The lass looks tired, and we could use yer help gettin' Widow Brodie's wild lads to bed."

"Aye. I'll walk wi' ye."

"Thank ye." She stood. "Lud, five lads. 'Tis too much fer any mither." She tugged her mittens back in place and walked to the door.

Ian followed, taking his cloak from a peg. As he tied it about his neck, he told Murian, "Lass, get to bed and forget aboot visitin' the castle whilst Loudan's still on alert. The time will come to make another move, bu' we'd be fools to rush things."

Widow Reeves blew out her breath in exasperation. "Lor' love ye, Ian, leave the lass be. She looks whipped nigh to death. Ye can berate her in the mornin', when she's no' so tired."

Ian looked chagrined as he pulled up his hood. "I'm sorry, lass. I'll wish ye guid night."

"You too, Ian. Sleep well, both of you."

Widow Reeves opened the door, and the icy wind swirled into the room. She hurried out, Ian following. "Lock the door," he ordered over his shoulder, then closed the door behind him.

Murian rose and dropped the wooden bar across the door. She cast a final look over the list she'd been making before Ian's visit and then tucked it away. Finally, more tired than she thought possible, she dressed for bed, put out the lamps, took off her slippers, and crawled between the cold sheets. She hugged the thick blankets as she waited for her body to warm the bed, her mind wandering to the prince, as it had every night since they'd met. She thought of their kiss, regretting that she'd had to use it to set him off balance so she could escape. She wished she'd been able to stay long enough to kiss him in earnest. *What would that have been like?*

He was probably angry with her, and who would blame him? She bit back a sigh and rolled to her side, hugging a pillow, shivering as her legs slid over the chilly sheets. The big bed felt lonelier and colder than usual.

Ah, to have a bed warmer. Before Loudan's perfidy, Murian had never gone to sleep between cold sheets. She doubted the prince had ever done so, either. In fact, she'd wager that his sheets were silk rather than linen. She wondered what it felt like to have so much wealth that one could toss gold coins onto the ground as if they were pence? She couldn't fathom it.

The prince was probably being entertained by Loudan right now. Or perhaps not. It was late and Max had said he didn't care for his host's company. More than likely he was already in his bed, pampered and placated, stroked and complimented, his every need attended to. Yet Murian wouldn't have traded places with him for the world. She was here where she belonged, with her people. For some reason, she had the impression the prince wasn't so fortunate. There'd been something in his eyes when they'd been talking in the woods, something lost. *What happened to you that you look so? Was it when you got those scars? Or was it something else?*

She sighed and snuggled deeper into her pillow. Whatever tragedy the prince had withstood, she had her own worries. Soon—finally—she'd be in Rowallen, and this time she'd find Robert's journal.

She *had* to. Her people counted on her.

She closed her eyes and slipped into a dream-filled sleep where she once again lived in Rowallen with Robert, their people all healthy and smiling.

The Grand Duchess Natasha paused inside the wide doors of the ballroom. The room glittered and glowed, the orchestra playing to the swoosh of silk gowns as the dancers swirled by, augmented by the constant murmur of gossiping voices. Bedecked with boughs of greenery, softened by the flicker of hundreds of candles, and decorated with the neighboring lords and ladies in their finest silks and satins, Rowallen Castle was adorned for a ball.

Natasha sniffed. "Preening peacocks."

Max, on whose arm she was leaning, sent her a faintly irritated glance. "It's a ball, Tata. They must dress accordingly."

"That's no reason to expose one's bosom to all of society. And these breeches the men are wearing are so tight, they show everything. It's scandalous! The fashions in Oxenburg are much more seemly." She eyed his uniform. The coat was blood-red with gold epaulets and braiding. Tailored, it clung to his broad shoulders before tapering down to fasten with brass buttons at his waist. His black breeches were comfortably loose, tucking into his black Hessians, as was proper for a man, she thought with pride.

Some of his men stood behind him, well out of earshot, and similarly attired. With their uniforms and beards, they looked larger and far more manly than the other men in the room, though her grandson outshone them all, as was only proper. Even beardless, he was taller, bigger, and more powerful.

Max glanced over her head. "Are you hungry, Tata Natasha?"

"*Nyet*. We just had dinner."

"It looks as if the earl fears we did not partake enough." He nodded to a row of tables.

A blinding array of serving dishes sat between numerous heavy silver candelabras. Gold and brass platters flanked crystal-tiered cake holders, where French rolls, bonbons, sugared walnuts, wafers, almonds, rum-soaked cakes, trifles, and other delicacies beckoned. Other tables held sherry, punches, and wines, as well as lemonade and tea. To the other side, a huge ornate buffet held an assortment of ices.

"The earl is trying to impress us." She sniffed disdainfully. "As he should. We are royalty, while he is a bastard son, given a title in an attempt to pull him up in the world. Not that it's helped." She couldn't keep a sour note from her voice.

It had been more than a week since they'd arrived— ten days, in fact, and every day she'd requested to speak to the earl about their little matter. And every time he'd refused, citing a number of reasons—he was busy, it was too close to supper, he had to dress to ride with his guests.

Her jaw ached with fury at his insolence. Did he not know who she was?

But of course he did, the *mool*. In public, he paid her every attention, but it was a show and nothing else.

She muttered under her breath. She would teach that fool a lesson if it were the last thing she did. *I will cast a spell on him that makes hair grow in his ears. Long, coarse black hair, like a goat's. That'll teach him not to—*

"Tata, you will break your teeth if you keep grinding them so."

She forced her jaw to relax. "I am cold."

Max's brows knit. "Shall I have a shawl brought from your rooms?"

"I'm fine. Just old. Too old to stay in such a damp castle."

"Loudan's castle is not so bad. It is far more pleasant than our host."

She had to agree. To be honest, Rowallen was the best part of her trip thus far. The castle was large, had more amenities than most castles she'd visited, and was surprisingly well appointed. The woodwork was ancient but superbly preserved, the windows new, the floors fairly even, and every bedchamber had a water closet.

Everything was more pleasant than she'd hoped for . . . except their host. She glanced about the room and found the earl standing near the doors. Ian Prinnas, the Earl of Loudan, was a tall man with brown hair and well-set shoulders. He might have been considered handsome if one did not notice how close set his eyes were, and the almost feral way he habitually glanced about him every few seconds, as if fearful a mongoose might leap from behind a chair and attack him. He had a weak chin, too. *So many signs, yet I ignored them all.* She released an angry sigh.

"For the love of— Tata, why so much sighing and teeth grinding? What has happened?"

"Nothing. I was thinking, that is all."

"You were glaring at Loudan as if you wished him to the devil." Max eyed their host. "Not that I blame you, for I can barely stand the man." Max turned his cool, hard gaze her way. "I must ask you yet again—why did you drag me to the wilds of Scotland to visit a low-bred *dunahk*?"

Hearing Max call the earl a fool dissipated some of her anger, and yet she did not answer. She couldn't quite give up the hope that she might find a way out of her difficulties without directly involving her grandson.

Max watched as his grandmother's expression shuttered once again. "Just tell me! If what I hear is true, Loudan's a heartless overlord, a thief, and worse. He's wronged many people."

Tata merely sniffed.

Stifling the urge to throw the entire matter to the winds, Max turned to watch the earl as he greeted the guests. It had been a long week. After collecting his pride when Murian had bested him (again, though he didn't like to think of it that way), he'd returned to Rowallen and ordered his men to find out what they could about the previous owner of Rowallen and his death.

It hadn't taken long before Demidor, ever the flirt, had found a chambermaid willing to tell between breathless kisses everything she knew. According to the maid, Lord Robert had lost the castle and lands to Loudan after a bloody duel over a questionable game of chance. Rumors throughout the countryside hinted that it had been murder and not a duel, but as only Lord Loudan and his friends were present, no one could naysay his version of the events.

The maid, who been hired after Loudan arrived, had gotten most of her information from the butcher in the nearby village. Having fought many wars, Max knew there were truths to be found in the gossip of the common people, and he was inclined to believe all the maid had to say.

No wonder Lady Murian was bitter. She'd lost her husband within a remarkably short time of her marriage too.

Max watched Loudan as he greeted a late guest, an elderly woman who appeared uneasy just standing close to the man. "These people do not like him."

"I don't care how these people feel about the earl. What I care about is what he's done to m—" Tata Natasha clamped her lips closed, sending him a harassed look. "He is beneath us."

"Then why don't we leave?"

She clamped her lips together tighter.

Max eyed her closely. "Tata, what has he done that you traveled all the way here to face him? You must tell me."

Her gaze flickered to him and for a moment, he thought she'd finally tell him, but then her expression hardened. "There is nothing to tell. I thought it would do me good to come to the countryside for fresh air."

"Fine. Do not tell me. I will address Loudan directly. I'll ask him why you are here, how you two came to meet, why—"

"*Nyet!* I forbid you to ask him anything that has to do with me!" She sniffed in outrage. "Perhaps if you did not disappear for the better part of every day, you could help me deal with the earl."

"Help? How? I don't even know what's happened!"

"You can help by being here, and showing that foolish earl that I am not alone and unsupported."

"He already knows that. Besides, there are things I must do, too." Like search for the home base of a cheeky wench who had twice now left him feeling like a fool.

Max supposed he should be angry with Murian, but other thoughts kept creeping in, pushing aside his outrage. At the oddest times he remembered how her soft lips had felt against his, or how she'd stared at his mouth when he'd talked, as if hungry for far more than food, or—more tantalizing still—how her voice had trembled slightly when he'd pressed his lips to her fingers.

She wanted him. He knew it, and that saved his pride.

Tata Natasha's snort interrupted his thoughts. "You have things to do, eh? Like what? Search the woods for a thief who bettered you at swordplay?"

"Swordplay is what actors do upon the stage. There is nothing playful when one fights."

She cocked her eyebrow. "I do not understand; you

and your men have looked for these thieves every day, yet you cannot find them. Why?"

"The woods go for miles and miles and are very dense. There are few roads, or even pathways. We've searched near every village, but it seems the bandits have not set up their camp near one, as we expected. We will keep looking; I know we will find them."

Tata Natasha snorted. "You have become obsessed with these bandits."

"I do not obsess, Tata Natasha," he corrected her gently. "I inquire. I search."

"For thieves."

"For interesting thieves." Far more interesting than the earl's sycophants, who shared his dinner table night after night.

"You should be here at the castle, keeping me company," Tata repeated in a stubborn tone.

"What am I to do, hold your knitting? If you truly needed me here, you'd explain yourself."

She made a disgusted sound. "Why do my grandsons refuse to do as they are told? None of you listen to a thing I or your parents say. You do not behave as princes should."

"And how should princes behave?"

"They should do as they are asked, and marry and settle down."

"Wulf and Alexsey have married. That's half of us."

"*You* have not married."

"Nor will I. Soldiers should not marry."

"Pah. That is nonsense."

He didn't answer.

She looked up at him, and for a moment she stopped being an imperious grand duchess and became his grandmother, her face softening slightly. "Oh, my Maksim, what have these wars done to you?"

"They have made me grow up. Soldiers are married to their causes. They should not forget that." He never would. He was a soldier, as were his closest companions, Orlov and poor Fedorovich.

The sons of nobility, they were distant cousins of Max's. The two had been present at almost every court function where—enticing Max away—they'd slip out of the castle for games of hide-and-seek, running wild through the sedate gardens and cultured park land. Later, as headstrong youths, the three had attended the same military school. Then, as young adults, they'd joined the Oxenburg military as adjutants to famous General Zhukov where, when not performing their duties, they'd hunted wolves and women. Max had thought of them as brothers.

But over time, things changed—General Zhukov's health failed and Max was named as the new general; Orlov inherited his father's lands and title; and after a long and tumultuous courtship, Fedorovich married Orlov's youngest sister.

Lively and pretty, Henrietta had become a welcome part of their little group. When she'd had a son, both Orlov and Max had been deemed "uncles" to the baby. And over the years, Fedorovich and Henrietta's house became the center of their visits. To the amusement of all, Max and Orlov fell into a growing competition to see who could buy the boy the more extravagant gift.

Thus Max had bought the boy his first rocking horse, his first play sword, and his first pony.

And it had been Max who, after a terrible battle won only through dogged perseverance and the blood of many, many men, had ridden to the house that held so much laughter and wonderful memories, to tell Henrietta that her beloved Fedorovich wasn't coming home.

He'd told her the news in private, but her cries had brought her son running. Only eight, he'd burst into tears upon realizing what had caused his mother such distress, and the two of them had fallen into each other's arms, inconsolable and lost. Max, suddenly an outsider, could do nothing to stem the tears; all he could do was watch.

That moment had seared his soul. And matters had turned even worse when, a week later, an inconsolable Henrietta attempted to take her own life, throwing herself from the top window of the house. She'd lived but the damage had been severe, and she was confined to her bed, never to rise again. Orlov, newly married, had moved her into his home and was now raising Artur as his own son.

The events had devastated Max. He'd been well aware of the tragic costs of a soldier's death, but he'd never felt one so deeply, and it had taught him well. "Soldiers should never wed. It isn't fair to their families."

"Pah!" Tata said. "Soldiers may wed if they wish. Your father was once the leader of the armies of Oxenburg, and he wed."

"If my father knew what I know, he would never have done so."

She scowled. "You are stubborn, and will not listen to reas—" Her gaze locked on something behind Max.

Max followed her gaze to the refreshment table, where a woman stood, her hand hovering over a silver tray filled with delicacies. As he watched, she picked up a tart, looked around, and then slipped it into her pocket.

"That's the third one," Tata said. "She also took some pears and wrapped her kerchief about some sweet biscuits and stuffed them away, as well."

Max watched as the woman casually wandered to a tray of pastries, glancing about the room as she did so. She was round, her body stuffed into a puce-colored gown until she looked like a sausage. She was older, with frown lines at the sides of her mouth. Her dyed brown hair hung in fat, heavy ringlets at each side of her face, an old-fashioned style he'd only seen in portraits.

She reached for some sugared walnuts and he noted her face was heavily rouged, her eyebrows darkened to match her falsely colored hair, a trick used by elderly women the world over. While he watched, she slipped a handful of the sugared walnuts into her pocket and then glanced about to see if anyone had witnessed her theft, her eyes plainly in view for the barest of seconds.

Max stiffened. "We must go." He tucked Tata Natasha's hand into the crook of his arm and firmly led her toward the corner where three of his men stood watching the young ladies swirl past in the dance.

"What are you doing?" Tata Natasha asked, huffing with each step.

"I must speak to this woman."

"Why?"

"I will tell you if you will share why we are here visiting a man neither of us like."

"We are not talking about Loudan; we are talking about that woman stealing food." Tata's voice grew hard. "She is a nobody. You can see it just by looking at her."

Ah, Tata, if only you knew. Max reached his men, nodding to Orlov, Demidor, and Pahlen, who'd come to share the burden of the night's activities. He placed Tata Natasha's hand in Orlov's. "Take care of Her Grace."

Orlov bowed over the grand duchess's hand. "Your Grace. Allow me to—"

She jerked her hand free and scowled at Max. "Let Loudan keep watch over his own refreshment table. You are a prince. You cannot—"

Max was already crossing the floor. As he approached the refreshment table, his quarry paused before a tray of cream pastries.

He walked behind her and bent close to her ear, the scent of vanilla and lavender tickling his nose. "Not those. They will stain your pockets."

The lady stiffened and then turned his way, astonishment on her face. Thickly lashed eyes met his, as silver as the tray near her graceful hand.

He smiled. Murian had done an excellent job at disguising herself. In addition to the heavy rouge, someone had expertly shaded her nose to make it more prominent. Faint circles had been added under her eyes, and perfectly drawn lines ran between her nose and the corner of her mouth, giving her a permanently displeased look.

Had he not been looking to see how the differences in her appearance had been wrought, he wouldn't have noticed them, even close. Such was the magic of dim candlelight and well-applied greasepaint. The question now was—should he tell her he recognized her? It would be practical to do so, but not nearly as much fun.

Besides, he owed her some uneasy moments. Max inclined his head. "I'm sorry, did I startle you?"

Murian couldn't move, couldn't think. All she could do was soak in the rich sound of that deep voice, her body tightening head to toe, her heart thudding in her throat. *Can he see through my disguise?*

The silence was growing awkward, so she cleared the uncertainty from her throat and bobbed the sort of heavy, perfunctory curtsy she imagined a middle-aged spinster might make. "How do you do? I dinna believe we've been introduced." She kept her voice flat and toneless, hoping to keep from stirring his memory.

His gaze flickered over her. "I don't believe we've met."

"Nay, we havena." Her mind, usually agile when taxed, froze yet again. There was something about this man, something forbidden, something that tugged at her. Though he'd made no move to touch her, she was intensely aware of everything around her—the linen tablecloth under her fingertips, the weight of the padding tied about her waist to disguise her figure, the fullness of her pockets stuffed with treats for the children.

What would an awkward spinster say to a handsome prince

at a country dance? "Och, 'tis hot in here," she blurted out, trying to sound as if she'd recited those exact words a thousand times before.

"So it is." His eyes glimmered. "I see you are enjoying the refreshments. They are good, *nyet*?"

She nodded, unable to look away from him. She was a tall woman, but she still had to tilt her head back to meet his gaze. She realized she should respond to his comment, and she managed to say, "Aye, the refreshments are excellent. I've never seen so many."

He glanced with unconcern at the table. "Neither have I, but then, I do not attend many dances."

Because he was no ordinary prince, but a warrior prince. Her gaze locked on his face. *He looks like an angel. A warrior angel.*

He chuckled, the sound rumbling in his broad chest. "A warrior, *da*. But I am no angel."

No! I didn't mean to say that aloud. She bit back a groan, and could have gladly sunk into the floor if she'd thought it might save her from this moment.

Her chagrin must have shown on her face, for he moved a bit closer. "Do not run. I will tell your secret to no one."

Her heart slammed to a stop. "My . . . secret?"

His lazy half-smile made her gulp. "That you are carrying ten people's worth of delicacies in your pockets."

"Och, that! 'Tis not for me." She forced herself to smile. "It would be verrah kind if you dinna mention this to anyone."

His green eyes glinted with humor. "It is how we angels are."

Her cheeks heated. "I dinna say 'angel.'"

"I distinctly heard the word 'angel.' But perhaps I am wrong. What did you say, then?"

She desperately cast about for a suitable replacement. *Good lord, doesn't* anything *rhyme with "angel"?* As the seconds ticked on, the silence became more awkward.

Finally, she said in a tight voice, "It doesna matter, but that's not what I said."

His lips twitched, but otherwise he maintained his grave expression. "I see." He tilted his head to one side and regarded her with a narrow gaze. "Forgive me, but you weren't at dinner, were you? I examined every face present, and I am certain I did not see yours."

Why did you do that? "I wasna at dinner. My mother grew ill as we were leaving. In getting her back to bed and a doctor to her side, I was late arriving and missed dinner." She silently thanked Widow Reeves for deciding they should have a story ready in case someone wondered why she hadn't been at dinner. It would have been too chancy to attend dinner in her disguise, for the lights would have been bright and she'd have been seated close to her fellow guests. But here, at the dance afterward, where the lights were dimmer and everyone was either dancing to Scottish reels or gossiping in small groups, it was much easier to remain unnoticed.

"If you didn't come to dinner, then you must be starving. No wonder you are raiding the sweets."

"They're for my mother. I thought they might cheer her oop a wee bit." She peeped at him through her lashes to see if he believed her. She shouldn't have taken the chance of drawing attention to herself, but the children so rarely had sweets, and seeing the table groaning with such bounty had been too tempting.

"I hope your mother will appreciate your efforts." His gaze flickered over her and he inclined his head. "But introductions are in order, *nyet*?" Before she knew what he was about, he'd taken her hand in his large, warm one and bowed, his lips brushing the back of her sugar-coated fingers. "I am Max."

At the touch of his hand on hers, waves of weakness washed through her, and she had to swallow twice before she could speak. "Verrah nice to meet you." She dipped an awkward curtsy, the wadding around her waist making her feel off balance. As she rose from the curtsy, she freed her hand from his grasp.

"And your name?" he asked.

"Miss MacDonald." There were as many MacDonalds in Scotland as there were blades of grass.

"MacDonald. Of course." His gaze raked her face once more.

He was so close, his foot brushing hers, and so large, filling up the space about them until she felt encompassed, warm . . . and breathlessly excited. Such feelings meant nothing, of course. The mere thought of a possible flirtation was heady stuff after so many months alone with her small group of widows in the woods. She wished she could act upon that longing, if only for a few moments. Of course, dressed as she was, she doubted he felt the same—and she had to smile, thinking of how he might react if plain, dowdy Miss MacDonald pulled him into a corner for a passionate kiss.

A quick glance around the room told her she wasn't the only one thinking such a thing. Every gaze in the room seemed to find the prince, dart away, and then return to linger. And why wouldn't they stare? He looked masculine, deadly, and . . . something else. Something that made every woman in the room watch him with longing, and every man send concerned looks his way. *It's as if he entices the women, and the men—seeing his effect—are threatened, but dare not confront him.*

She didn't blame them. A raw, restless power sat on his broad shoulders, shimmered in his green eyes, and rippled through his muscled arms.

He smiled faintly, and she realized she hadn't said a word in response to his question. "I'm sorry, but I was distracted by your uniform. Are you a guard?" Perhaps that would get him to admit to his birthright.

"I am a soldier, Miss MacDonald." He spoke simply, with a quiet, firm pride.

"What kind of soldier are you?"

"A busy one." He gave her an impatient look. "I have answered your questions, so now you will answer mine."

She stiffened at his preemptory tone. He might not admit to being a prince, but she was beginning to suspect he never stopped acting like one.

He glanced past her to the refreshment table. "What other sweets would your mother like?"

"Oh. I'm sure I have enough." She patted her heavy pockets.

"But you were admiring these pastries when I arrived, so I'm determined you shall have them." He pulled a kerchief from his pocket and placed several almond pastries in it. Then he wrapped them up and handed them to her, a smile in his green eyes. "Now they will not stain your pocket."

She looked at him with surprise, unable to frame a coherent thought. "That is verrah kind of you."

"It is nothing—but you should tuck them away before someone sees." He bent closer, his voice low and intimate, tracing over her like warm hands. "Not everyone is as understanding of thievery as I am."

She blinked up at him, and in that instant, she realized he knew exactly who she was. "*Oh!* You've been teasing me this entire time!"

"*Da*. But do not worry, *dorogaya moya*. You are safe. I will tell no one you are not this Miss MacDonald."

Her relief was quickly followed by a flash of irritation. "How did you know?"

"Who else would sneak into the earl's household and steal food rather than priceless treasures? Only you." He captured her hand, turned it palm up in his, and dusted the remaining sugar from her fingertips.

She tried to still her heart and snuck a glance at the large ornate clock against one wall. *Almost ten.* "Thank you for your kindness, but I must go."

"Not yet." He tucked her hand into the crook of his arm. "Wherever you need to go, I will go with you."

She looked down where her fingers rested on his

coat sleeve. The brushed wool was soft and fine, yet it did little to disguise the powerful arm under it. Never had she touched a more muscular, rock-hard arm. Even more surprising was the heat that radiated through the cloth. His warmth made her yearn to move closer, within the circle of his arms, her body pressed to his. She shivered at the thought.

He gave her a questioning look. "You are cold."

"Nay, a goose walked over my grave," she lied.

His brows lowered. "But you are not dead, and so do not have a grave."

She laughed. "It is an old saying. Supposedly when you shiver for no reason, it's because someone has walked over the place you are to be buried."

"That sounds most unpleasant. I do not like this saying." Max looked down at her, reveling in having her close once again and, in a way, under his control. She'd fled from him twice already. He would not permit her to do so again. "Where do we go from here? I will take you."

Her lips thinned, and she looked far from pleased. He'd seen her glance at the clock, an impatient set to her chin. *Ah, she wishes to be rid of me. She is planning something, this intriguing woman.*

"So many odd sayings you English have. My grandmother is Romany. They have much better sayings than this one of yours about the grave and goose."

"Oh?" she answered absently, her gaze on one of the doors leading into the ballroom.

"*Da. May mishto les o thud katar I gurumni kai.* It means

something like . . . it is easier to milk a cow that does not move."

She shot him an amused look, her mouth quirking with humor. "That's certainly practical."

I like seeing that smile. Her mouth, full and lush, teased him and made him think of kissing her. *Which I shall do again*, dorogaya moya. *And soon.*

She looked once again toward the door, so he asked, "Are you expecting someone?"

She turned a wide, innocent gaze on him. "Och no. I was merely looking at all the beautiful gowns."

More beautiful lips had never lied so much. Max traced a lazy circle on the back of her hand where it rested on his arm. "I find I am thirsty. Would you like a beverage, as well? A sherry or some lemonade?"

A flicker of irritation crossed her face, but she quickly hid it. "I would like some lemonade, please. In fact"— she withdrew her hand from his arm—"I'll wait here while you fetch it."

"There is no need." He nodded to Orlov, who stood across the room. Orlov said something to Demidor, who glanced to where Tata Natasha sat in a large chair, scowling at everyone, looking like a disgruntled queen trying to decide which of her court deserved to die first. Though Demidor was a rugged soldier, there was unease in his glance as he left Orlov and moved closer to the grand duchess.

His responsibility reassigned, Orlov made his way through the crowd to Max.

"One of my men comes. He will fetch refreshments

so we can continue our conversation uninterrupted. Ah, here he is now. Orlov, her ladyship will have a lemonade."

"*Da*, General. Would you like something, as well?"

"Some of Lord Loudan's whiskey will do. According to him, there is none better in all of Scotland. For some reason he has forgotten to place a decanter on the refreshment table, but I suspect you will find some in his private library."

"I shall fetch it." Orlov grinned, his teeth gleaming in his black beard. "And I daresay Demidor and Pahlen will wish for a glass or two, themselves."

"It is a party and the earl wishes to impress us, so we shall let him, *da*?"

"Very good, General." Chuckling, Orlov left.

"Well done, Your Highness." Murian was smiling.

"It is Max to you. Only Max." He bent closer to her ear. "Murian, why are you here? I can see you are—"

A noise arose from the door, a woman's raised voice, another joining it. The voices were shrill, excited, and even frightened.

Guests turned and merged on the newcomers, so Max couldn't see what was happening, but like the wind, people nearby began to exclaim, repeating what they'd heard, and soon phrases swept their way.

It was robbery . . . the thieves stole her jewels . . . the jewels of both . . . a handsome youth with a bow and arrow . . . but polite . . . with a band of men . . . like Robin Hood—

Max blinked. *Like Robin Hood*? He turned to Murian,

a question on his lips . . . but she was no longer at his side.

And there was not a trace of her to be seen, not in the emptying room behind him, nor in the press of the crowd hurrying forward.

Once again, she was gone.

Chapter 6

Ian took a seat beside Murian at Widow Grier's table. Outside, clouds rumbled uneasily, a bitter wind shaking the trees until the trembling leaves crashed overhead like the waves of the ocean.

Murian rested her chin in her hand, her spirits as dark and restless as the weather. Upon returning home from the dinner party, she'd bathed and scrubbed the paint from her face until her skin burned pink, yet it was nothing to the deep burn of disappointment that stung her soul. "Damn Lord Loudan for posting guards in every hall of the castle."

Widow Grier looked up from the pot she'd been stirring. Tall and thin, with light brown hair and fair skin decorated with a spattering of freckles, she was the youngest widow in their small band. She had one child, a round, chubby-cheeked lad who was even now sleeping in a crib by the fire and whose three-toothed grin won the hearts of all who saw him. "There were guards in *e'ery* hall?"

"All nine. The four floors in each wing, plus the main hall." Ian looked as despondent as Murian felt.

"E'ery last bloody hall ha' guards, and there were four stationed ootside his bedchamber. There was no way past them."

From where she sat across from Murian, Widow Reeves asked, "Did the guards see ye?"

Murian nodded. "Aye, but your sister did a fine job with my disguise. No one knew me at all."

"She was pleased to help. No' many know this, but Lara was an actress fer a short time when she was young."

"Was she now?" Widow Grier looked impressed. "When I was younger, I wanted to do the same."

"Aye, at seventeen, she ran away to Edinburgh determined to become an actress. It near broke our mither's heart, it did, but Lara was determined and she e'en met wi' some success, too. She made her living tha' way fer several years, and was quite guid, but then she met her Daffyd. He was a carpenter as worked upon the sets. Eventually they returned here, and she was hired into the kitchens at the MacLures' and Daffyd given a job helpin' aboot the estate."

"And now she's their head cook." Widow Grier placed the wooden spoon to one side and put a lid on the pot. "Yer sister seems quite close to Lady MacLure."

"Her ladyship likes food, especially sweets. She's always plotting wi' my sister aboot the newest dishes. They're closer than most servants and mistresses, I think. 'Tis why my sister stays where she is, even though the MacLures canna pay well."

"I owe your sister a debt of gratitude," Murian said. "She knew exactly what we needed for my disguise."

She managed a smile, though her shoulders sagged. Such an excellent disguise, and yet still no journal. *All that work for nothing.*

The most difficult part had been planning a believable distraction. It had taken a lot of convincing to get the vicar's sister to make a grand entrance and pretend she'd been held up on the way to Loudan's dinner party. The ploy had worked like a charm and had sent the guards running to try and catch the thieves. Two entire squadrons had ridden away from Rowallen and into the woods, but it hadn't been enough. They'd known Loudan had hired more guards, but no one knew how many.

Too many.

She sighed, placed her elbow on the table, and rested her chin in her hand. It had been nice of Miss MacLeod to help them. The older woman had been spurred on by the fact that the earl rarely bothered to attend Sunday services. And when he did, he slept through them, snoring rudely.

Even worse, the man hadn't donated so much as a penny to the parish, a grievous error that had lit the fires of wrath in the heart of the vicar's protective older sister. So Miss MacLeod had been very glad to help Murian for the opportunity to "stab Loudan in his overblown pride." She'd been even more eager to help when Murian had explained about Robert's journal, which could unseat Loudan completely.

"Miss MacLeod did a fine job, too," Ian said.

"Aye," Murian agreed. "Even I believed her when she came in and threw herself into Mrs. Whitcomb's arms as if too overcome to walk. And then she babbled on and on aboot her 'horrifying' experience. 'Twas the perfect distraction."

Murian had been able to escape the prince, slip into the library, and open the window for Ian. Had the two squadrons been all of the earl's guard, things would have been merry for them from then on.

She couldn't hold back a sigh. Nothing had worked as she'd hoped. She should have just stayed with the prince. A distinct pang of disappointment sank through her. He was interesting, this warrior prince. *Interesting and devastatingly attractive.*

Sadly, they were destined to run into one another only at the worst times, and in the worst possible ways. What would it have been like if things had been different—if they'd met in a ballroom as men and women normally did, with no secrets between them? It was a silly thought. Life had given her this challenge, and that was that. She had to give Max credit, though; her disguise hadn't fooled him one bit. And it seemed as if he'd been as good as his word and hadn't revealed her to Loudan.

In some way, she was now in his debt.

Ian patted her shoulder. "Dinna look so dour. Ye tried, and tha' is all ye can do."

"Ye tried too hard, if ye ask me." Widow Grier lifted the pot from the flames and carried it to the rough plank table, where she carefully poured cider into four tin cups, the sweet scent wafting through the air.

Widow Reeves took a cup and wrapped her chapped hands about it. "I'm just glad ye made it oot of the castle.

If the earl had caught ye, it would ha' been a nightmare fer us all."

"Aye," Widow Grier agreed. "Ye went right into the lion's den, ye did. We were frightened fer ye."

"And it was all for naught." Murian breathed in the aroma of the cider and let the steam curl over her cold lips. The scent of the cider, flavored with a precious bit of cinnamon, soothed her depressed spirits. "There must be a way to call off all of Loudan's guards, not just the ones stationed ootside. I just need to think it through, and plan something larger."

Ian groaned. "Lassie, nay. Ye canna—"

Someone knocked on the door.

Widow Grier hurried to open it, and a blast of wind accompanied Will Scarlae inside, swirling his red cloak.

"Come," she ordered, shutting the door behind him. "We're just havin' some cider to try and chase off the cold. Would ye like some?"

"Och, thank ye, Widow Grier." He pushed his long brown hair from his eyes. "Indeed, I would."

Murian had always thought Will a handsome youth, but, over the last year, she'd come to decry his penchant for fine clothes he couldn't afford, women he should avoid, and too much whiskey.

He looked at Murian and the others, suspicion on his narrow face. "I heard ye talkin' and thought I'd come and see wha' ye were aboot."

Poor Will. He was always so ill at ease, though it had been worse when Robert had been alive. From what Murian had been able to glean from chance comments Robert had made, the two men had grown up together and had been playmates, but had grown estranged as they'd gotten older. She didn't know what had caused the final break, but Robert had been quite cold to Will.

It was a pity, for the men had much in common, both in their pride and in their love of Rowallen. But Will was the son of a kitchen maid and an unnamed father who'd never claimed him, while Robert was the son of a lady from a great house and the lord of the castle. Such differences in station had caused a strain when Robert had assumed his responsibilities as the lord of the castle upon his father's death. Her husband had never really spoken about it to her, which made her believe the split between the two men had been painful.

She smiled at Will now. "The cider is quite lovely. Come and sit with us and have a cup."

He looked both pleased and uncertain. "I believe I will, thank ye."

Ian cocked a brow at the young man. "Are ye certain ye've nowhere better to be? On guard, perhaps?"

Will flushed. "Nay. 'Tis Widow Atchison's turn now. I'm to relieve her in an hour and walk the night." He undid his cloak.

Widow Grier nodded to a peg by the door. "Hang it oop and ha' a seat, lad. I'll fetch ye some cider."

"Thank ye." He sat at the table, appearing happy. "So, wha' are we talkin' aboot?"

"Lady Murian's latest scheme." Widow Reeves took a sip of the cider, sighing with pleasure. "Och, Ailsa, ye make the best cider."

Widow Grier blushed. "Thank ye, Fiona. I'd make it e'er day if it would tempt our lassie fra' danger." She handed Will his cup of cider, sat down on the bench, and pulled her own cup forward.

"Danger? Wha' danger is tha'?" Will asked.

"Lady Murian visited Rowallen this e'ening," Widow Reeves said.

Will's gaze jerked to Murian. "Ye went to Rowallen?"

"I thought Robert's journal might be hidden in our old bedchamber." She sighed. "But I couldna reach it. There were too many guards."

Ian muttered, "We all know why tha' is, too. Because some fool got hisself caught sneakin' into the earl's study no' so long ago, so the earl decided to increase his guard."

Will grimaced. "Ye mean me, Ian, and I know it. 'Twas ill luck, bu' it is wha' it is. Wha' I wish to know is why no one tol' me aboot Lady Murian's adventure."

Murian said, "We didn't tell anyone who dinna need to know. 'Tis safer that way."

Will's scowl deepened and he said sullenly, "Ye could ha' trusted me, Lady Murian. Ye know ye could."

"Now why are ye so ootraged, I wonder." Ian cocked a bushy brow at the lad. "Is it because ye dinna ha' a chance to run and tell someone, and earn a bit of blunt?"

Widow Grier murmured her disapproval.

"Tha' is enough of tha', Ian," Widow Reeves said firmly.

Ian shrugged and retired to his cup.

Will's face was tight with anger. "Ye've ne'er trusted me since I was caught by the earl's guards, which was weel o'er a month ago."

"Aye, and ye just walked oot of the castle wi'oot a scratch on ye."

"My eye was blackened!"

Ian scoffed, "Ye could ha' given yerself such a wee bruise. The only way ye could ha' escaped was by givin' the earl wha' he wanted."

"If tha' is true, then why isna the earl here now? Raidin' our homes and stealin' our livestock? He'd do tha' if he knew where we were. But he dinna know—and he ne'er weel if I ha' anything to do with it."

Ian didn't look impressed. "Mayhap he's waitin' on somethin'—timin' his arrival so tha' he finds us at our worst."

Murian put down her cup. "Ian, that's enough."

"Nay," Will said, his face red. "Let 'im mock. He always has. If he wants to know how I escaped, I'll tell 'im wha' I've told him a hundred times now: I escaped because I know tha' castle better than anyone. I was born there, raised here, and I ran through her halls as a wee lad until the day Robert threw it away bein' a bloody fool!"

Murian's smile disappeared. "Watch what you say aboot the dead. Whatever Robert did or didn't do, he was a man of honor."

Will's flush deepened.

"Weel now," Widow Reeves said, breaking the tense silence. "Mayhap we shouldna talk so much aboot the past. 'Tis done and we canna undo it." She looked at

Murian. "I was wonderin', did ye see the prince? Ye havena mentioned him."

"Aye, he was there." She sipped her cider, hoping that would be the end of it.

"And?" Widow Reeves urged.

Widow Grier scooted closer to Murian. "Oot wi' it. We want details, we do."

Murian put down her cup. "There aren't many. He saw me sneaking food from the refreshment table, and when I told him 'twas for my sick mother, he wrapped up some tarts so they wouldna stain my pockets."

"Och, the tarts! I almost fergot them." Widow Grier stood and went to a tin that rested on a shelf over the oven. "There are a few left after we shared them wi' the children." She found a small plate, arranged the tarts on it, and then carried it to the table.

Will took one from the plate and moaned with pleasure at the first bite.

Ian made an exasperated noise, but Widow Grier chuckled. She nodded toward the wooden crib that held her sleeping son. "Ye should ha' seen my wee one's face when I put a dab of almond pastry on his tongue. He looked as if he'd seen Peter standin' at the pearly gates."

"I can see why," Will said, chewing slowly.

So could Murian. She'd never tasted anything so lovely. The delicate buttery almond flavor rolled over her tongue in a blissful manner.

Will took another bite. "I bet Lord Loudan and his like eat this way e'er day."

"Of course they do," Widow Reeves said.

Ian finished his pastry with a look of regret. "Widow Reeves, do ye think ye could make such a pastry as this? If ye had the ingredients?"

The conversation digressed into what Widow Reeves could and could not cook without a proper stove, which left Murian to reflect on this evening's adventures. Though it had been a failure in finding Robert's journal, it had been a success in proving she could gain access to Rowallen without the earl knowing. That was worth a lot, since they'd been afraid to search the castle after Will had been captured.

In a few weeks' time, she would try it again. *A few weeks . . . I wonder how long the prince and his grandmother will stay at Rowallen? Not that long, surely.* Nay, it was best to face the fact that she'd never see the prince again. Which was quite fine with her, she told herself firmly. He disturbed her, made her feel . . . uneasy. And the last thing she needed was a distraction— especially one who could send her senses reeling and make her shiver from head to toe with a mere look.

She absently traced her finger around the rim of her cup as she decided to keep her attention where it belonged: away from the prince and on her duties here. *Which is how it should be,* she told herself firmly.

Aware her silence was causing Widow Reeves to send curious glances her way, Murian pushed the troublesome thoughts away, and joined in the conversation.

Chapter 7

The next morning, Max stood on the front portico of the castle and looked up at the sky. The thunder and clouds of the night before had blown away. Today the sun shone brightly, and though the breeze carried the scent of winter, the air seemed slightly warmer than the days before.

Tugging on his riding gloves, Orlov came outside. On seeing Max, the sergeant came to stand with him. "I have some information for you."

Conscious of the footmen at each side of the door, Max led Orlov further out on the portico. "About Murian Muir?"

"*Da*. Pahlen found a groom who has lived in this area his whole life and discovered there's a bit more to the story than Demidor's chambermaid knew. Murian and Robert Muir were the last owners of this castle. Robert lost the castle and lands to Loudan in a card game. According to the earl, desperate to get them back, Robert offered to play another hand and was caught cheating. Loudan confronted him, and there was a duel."

"Which the earl claimed to win."

"So he says."

Max raised his brows. "But this groom believe otherwise?"

"There are many rumors that perhaps there was no duel, just a pistol shot and a dead lord."

"No witnesses, I take it."

"Only friends of the earl. But it gets worse. Before Lord Robert was even cold, Loudan raced to Edinburgh to file his claim. While he was gone, he sent word to Robert's widow that she and all the retainers were to be gone when he returned, or he would have them arrested."

"Bloody hell." No wonder there was so much fury in Murian's eyes.

Orlov nodded. "According to this groom and everyone else we've talked to, Loudan is vile. There are other uncomplimentary stories, but none as blatantly evil."

Max rubbed his jaw, thinking about the information Orlov had just shared. "So our thief broke into her own home last night. I wonder what she's looking for?"

"I do not know, General. Do we look for the thieves today?"

"Aye, but . . . this time, let's narrow our search a bit. We assumed Murian and her band would wish to be away from Rowallen in order to avoid the earl's men. What if, instead, they are closer? I begin to sense a wiliness to our thief, and a brashness, as well."

"That would make sense. That way they can keep an eye on the castle and who comes and goes."

"Exactly. And it is the home they never wished to leave. Their pride may outpace their fear."

Orlov nodded slowly. "We will comb the woods closer to the castle, then."

"Good. Have the horses readied. And do not—"

"Ah, Your Highness." The earl's oily voice broke into their conversation. "There you are."

Max and Orlov turned to find Loudan standing nearby.

Dressed in fine riding clothes, his boots as shiny as a mirror, the earl bowed to Max, ignoring Orlov completely. "Your Highness, I assume you received my message this morning?"

"Aye."

The earl's lips thinned. "I wondered, for there was no reply. And here you are, leaving yet again."

Orlov spoke up. "We are hunting, as are other members of your party."

Loudan didn't even glance in Orlov's direction. "Tell me, Your Highness, what do you hunt for, that you are gone every day, all day?"

Irritated that the man would ignore Orlov in such a way, Max crossed his arms and said shortly, "Wolves."

The earl chuckled. "There are no wolves in this area. I fear you won't catch anything."

"Perhaps. And perhaps not." Max turned to Orlov. "If you are bored, do not feel you must stay. I will join you soon."

A flicker of scorn crossed Orlov's face. He bowed to Max, and—ignoring the earl as the earl had ignored him—turned on his heel and left.

Max turned back to the earl. "My aides-de-camp are

men of honor, all of them sons of the great families of my country. They deserve at least a greeting."

The earl's gaze narrowed. "I would have offered one. Eventually."

Max had to force himself to hold his temper. *I have reason to be here. I cannot forget that.* "You sent a missive this morning. Something about a constable?"

"I have been trying to convince Constable Ruddock to pursue this highwayman and his band more seriously."

"And he will not?"

Loudan curled his lip. "He is incompetent, but he is still the constable. He has the authority to put out warrants for these miscreants, but he refuses. If you will tell him what you know, it will force him in that direction."

"I assume Miss MacLeod will be coming as well, to tell her story?"

"No. She has romanticized the entire incident and would be a useless witness. She says the thieves never demanded her jewels, but merely asked her to donate to their cause."

Max had been tugging on his glove, but at this, he looked up. *Donate? Bloody hell.* "They said the same to us." *And I didn't catch it, either.* He had to laugh.

Loudan's expression soured. "Did they? Even if—"

"Good morning!" Tata Natasha swept through the door, a black lace shawl over her shoulders. "I am surprised to see the two of you up so early."

Max inclined his head. "Good morning, Tata Natasha. I was just about to explain to the earl that I cannot be of help to him."

The earl mouth thinned. "Why not?"

"Because my testimony would be no different from Miss MacLeod's."

"You never said a thing about 'donations' until I told you what Miss MacLeod said."

"Because I hadn't thought about it, but it is exactly the wording they used."

The earl could not have looked more furious.

Tata looked from one of them to the other. "Max, surely you can—"

"I cannot. He wishes me to convince the constable to pursue the highwayman who held us up, but—sadly—I just realized we were never robbed."

"What?" Tata gaped.

Loudan's jaw tightened. "You were, too, robbed."

"Our coaches were stopped, yes. But the thieves—I hesitate to even call them that now, because, as Miss MacLeod so succinctly noted, they did not demand anything, but merely asked. That is not illegal."

"But your coat was slashed," the earl said.

"Only because I drew upon the leader. He retaliated, as well he should have."

Loudan's expression never changed, but Max could feel the ill will radiating from the man. "I cannot accept that. These thieves have been preying upon my guests for months. I *will* have them captured, and I require your testimony to do so."

"Fine. I will testify."

"Good. And let us have no more nonsense about 'donations.'"

"My testimony will be the truth. I will tell the constable that they had no weapons trained upon us, and all they requested were donations to their cause."

Loudan's eyes blazed, but to Max's surprise, the man didn't say another word to him. Instead, the earl turned to Tata Natasha and said in a clipped, arrogant voice, "The constable will arrive within the hour. Bring your grandson to the study at eleven and make sure he knows what to say."

He didn't add an "or else," but Max heard it as surely as if the man had shouted. Fury burned through Max. "Loudan, you will remember you speak to a grand duchess."

"I know exactly whom I speak to." The earl gave Tata Natasha a hard look and then turned on his heel and left.

Max reached for his sword and started after the earl.

Tata grabbed his sleeve. "*Nyet!*"

"No one speaks to the house of Romanovin in such a way."

"Leave him! He—he is just abrupt. He means nothing." Tata Natasha's knuckles shone whitely where she held Max's sleeve.

"Why do you protect him?" Max demanded. "What does he hold over your head?"

"Nothing! I—I . . ." She wet her lips, and concern, uncertainty, and worry all flickered over her face.

In that instant, he saw her face as it truly was: not that of his beloved if troublesome grandmother, but that of an old woman wracked with fear. He sighed and removed his hand from his hilt. "In all the years

I've known you, you've never allowed a *gadjo* to order you about like a servant. Whatever has happened, you must tell me."

She hunched her shoulders and said in a sullen tone, "You won't like it."

"Probably not."

She sighed, her shoulders dropping. "I suppose you are right. Very well. I will tell you. I brought you here because I have lost something."

"Lost?"

"In a manner of speaking. And Loudan has it."

"You lost this item . . . as in, you put it down and he found it and took it? Or you lost it in a game of chance?"

A dull color flooded her cheeks. "I held three queens."

"*Ty shto shoytish!*"

"It was a sign. Or so I thought."

"*Bozhy moj*, Tata!" Max turned from her and paced away and then back. "Why were you gambling with a man like that? One look and you can see he has no principles, no honor."

"I know, I know," she replied testily. "I was at a table; he joined after the game started. I did not choose to play with him, and I definitely did not choose to lose to him."

"I must know what this object is that you have lost."

"It doesn't matter. I requested he return it. He is considering it."

"At a cost, I presume."

"Of course at a cost!"

"I fear he is toying with you. Men like that are more interested in power than in money."

Her expression said she'd had the same thought.

"Max, can't you fight him, or just let him know you will kill him outright? It would be quicker."

"Tata, I cannot do that. If I were to threaten a nobleman, it could involve our country in many difficulties. Surely you know that."

She sighed, her face etched deeply with worry. "Fine. Then that leaves us no options. Until he agrees to sell it back to me, our hands are tied and we must do whatever he suggests."

"You are joking, *da*?"

"Would I joke about something like this?"

"You may do as you wish, but I will not capitulate." *Not to a weaselly creature like Loudan.*

"But—"

"You brought me here as a threat. I cannot be both a threat and compliant. If you wish me to convince him that I will not bargain with him for this thing you've lost, then I must let him know I do not play his games."

"What will you do?"

"Ignore him, and pretend I do not care if he has this item or not. It will infuriate him. And angry men do not bargain well."

"He will ask why you are not meeting the constable."

"And you will tell him I was too busy hunting."

Her lips twitched. "He will be angry."

"I am counting on it."

"Fine—irk the man. What am I to do in the meantime?"

"Stop acting as if you are desperate to have this item back. Pretend you are reconsidering whether you even want it."

"I can do that. I have to admit, though, that I was at a loss as to how to proceed. He keeps raising the price and I . . ." She shook her head, shivering a little. In the sunlight she looked older than her years, the lines by her mouth deeper than usual.

"From now on, Tata, you will let me speak to Loudan about this object. Tell him I am in charge of the negotiations now."

Relief brightened her face. "Very well." Her gaze met his. "We must get it back, Max. We *must.*"

"We will. One way or another. But I must know what it is. I cannot bargain if I do not know what it is."

She glanced back at the footmen. "I will tell you later. Now off with you; you have an earl to enrage, and some hunting to do."

He bowed. "Good day, Tata." He left the portico and walked to the stables. Sunshine traced the lush slopes and played upon the sparkling waters of a small loch that stretched before the castle.

Orlov stood near the stables with Demidor, Raeff, Pushkin, and Golovin, their horses saddled and ready. As Max approached, a groom brought out Max's large black gelding.

Orlov left the others and came to meet him. "You escaped, I see."

"Aye. By the bye, it appears our brigands are cleverer than we realized."

"How so?"

"Last night, the lady who was robbed said she would not call it a robbery, as they never demanded anything— they politely requested donations."

Orlov's eyes widened; then he smiled. "As they did with us. I must give them credit for that."

"*Da*. The earl was not happy when I realized I'd come to view our meeting with the brigands in the same light as Miss MacLeod did hers—a donation request gone awry. He wanted—nay, he *demanded*—I lie to the local constable so that charges could be pressed."

Orlov whistled silently. "Loudan is determined to capture these thieves."

"Indeed. And I will not help him; I said no."

Orlov grinned. "The earl won't like that."

"I'm counting on it. I tire of the man's attitude."

"As do I. By the way, speaking of the brigands, I may have found something to aid us in our search." The sergeant pulled a paper from his pocket and unfolded it. "This was in the earl's library. It is a plat of all the lands held by the Rowallen estate."

Max took the map and scanned it. "Does the earl know you took this?"

"I left a note, as is only polite, though I did not write it in English. I'm sure he will figure it out in time."

Amused, Max traced their location on the plat. "We've covered here, here, and most of here." He shook his head. "So much, and yet it's only a small amount of the forest."

"Even with a reduced area, we are searching for a needle in a haystack. The woods are thick, the trails few and seemingly unused, and the locals have done nothing but mislead us. They are determined to hide these thieves, whoever they are. I dislike our chances."

"*Da*, but I am convinced they are closer than they

want anyone to know. It is a good strategy, to be close enough to watch your enemy, yet hidden well enough that he doesn't even know he is watched."

"True, General." Orlov regarded the map for another moment, then refolded it and slipped it back into his pocket. "Has the grand duchess shared why she allows the earl's atrocious behavior? It is most unlike her."

"She lost something to Loudan in a game of chance. Whatever it is, she is desperate to have it returned."

"And he refuses."

"More than that, he holds it over her head like a sword." Max crossed his arms and gazed at the castle, gray and stern, set in a manicured park so meticulously groomed that the grass appeared to have been combed blade by blade. "I could forgive the earl for winning over an old woman at a game of chance, even though that shows a weak character." Max's jaw tightened. "I will *not* forgive him for causing her such worry."

"This situation complicates our mission."

"It can, yes. If we let it." Max shook his head. "I should be angry with her, but then we, too, have secrets."

Orlov glanced at Max. "You received word?"

"A packet arrived this morning by special courier. I would have said something earlier, but the earl interrupted us."

"I don't suppose there were any other letters in that packet?"

"There were. And yes, one is from your beloved wife, and yet another from your sister."

Orlov beamed. "I shall read them as soon as—" His

gaze locked on something beyond Max's shoulder. "Ah. The earl's constable has arrived."

Max turned to follow the sergeant's gaze. A large, heavily built coach rumbled up the long, picturesque drive toward Rowallen's arched door. The coach pulled around the fountain decorating the looped drive and stopped. A liveried footman raced from the castle, opened the coach door, and put down the steps. The constable stepped out of the coach.

At the sight of the constable, Max froze. *"Ty shto shoytish."*

"What is it?" Orlov asked.

"The constable—you see him? He is the second giant we've seen since we arrived in Scotland."

"The second? When did we see— Ah!" Orlov's brows rose in comprehension. "The giant with the brigands. Ian, *nyet*?"

"And our Ian has the same reddish hair, and the same shape of face."

Orlov watched a moment. "They even walk the same."

"Now we know why Loudan's constable is reluctant to pursue these brigands."

"Da, the man is related to one of them."

Max nodded. "I think I will speak to the constable after all. Stay here. I'll return shortly."

"Aye, General."

Max walked toward the castle, his gaze locked on the huge man strolling toward the front door.

Max smiled. *Ah*, dorogaya moya, *I will find you yet.*

•   •   •

An hour later, Max pulled his horse to a halt on a small, almost invisible path deep in the woods about an hour's ride north of Rowallen, and held up his hand.

Behind him, his men went still and silent.

From somewhere in the woods, beneath the rustle of the trees playing in the breeze, and over the rush of a nearby creek, came a melody that faded in and out of hearing with the direction of the breeze. It was a woman's voice, singing a Gaelic tune. Max knew that voice, knew it well.

As they listened, other sounds lifted now and then, blown their way—the sound of a door closing, the occasional moo of a cow.

"We have found them," Orlov said, faint surprise in his voice.

"So it would seem," Max said. "A mere two miles from the village of Kilmarnock, where Constable Ruddock's family hails from."

"And less than three miles from Rowallen Castle," Orlov added. "We were looking much too far away."

"The earl has been making the same mistake, for every village he set afire was twelve miles away or more. He has no idea they are under his very nose."

Orlov nodded. "What do we do now?"

"*We* don't do anything. It is best if I go into the village alone."

Demidor's horse shifted as if conveying his rider's unease. "I don't like that," the younger soldier said. "We should go with you."

"Which would make it look like an attack. *Nyet.* I will go first and speak to their leader. Then I will call you in. Demidor, take Raeff and Pahlen back the way we came and guard the path. If we need to leave quickly, we'll want the way open. If we need you, we will call."

Looking unhappy, the young soldier nodded and, collecting the others, he turned his horse and left.

"Orlov, you will stay here with Golovin and Pushkin. I will get as close as I can and see if I can find the leader. After ten minutes, circle around and move closer."

"And then?"

"Wait for my signal. Be very careful you are not spotted. I don't wish to startle anyone or they might think their village is under attack." The wind shifted yet again, and the singing grew a touch louder. Max winced as the singer lingered on an off-key note.

Pushkin, large and barrel-chested, with a long black beard that made him look a bit like a wild pirate, exchanged an uneasy look with Golovin. "I don't know about this, General."

A tough, grizzled veteran with a grumpy demeanor, Golovin agreed. "We're away from civilization *and* near water. And now there's a female singing."

Max's brows knit. "What's that have to do with anything?"

"Whilst I was assisting Her Grace into the carriage last week, she told me about creatures who sang songs in the wild. Evil women, they were, luring a man to the water with their singing and then . . ." He made a slashing gesture across his throat.

"Sirens," Max said in a dry tone.

Pushkin brightened. "*Da!* You know of them."

"I know they are imaginary. My grandmother was doing what she does best: spinning tales and causing problems. I will wager my finest sword the woman you hear singing now is just that—a woman. She is not magic, and she's certainly not drawing us closer with that atrocious singing." She was, however, dangerously intelligent, and held the answers to his growing list of questions. "Orlov, I leave you in charge. If you do not hear from me in twenty minutes, you may come for me."

With that, he turned his horse and headed toward the distant voice.

Chapter 8

The late-morning sun slanted through the shutters as Murian sank deeper into the tub, warm water sloshing over her shoulders. The large brass tub was another prize she'd stolen from Rowallen, and she still took great delight in thinking of the earl having to use one of the small tubs she'd left behind. He'd barely be able to sit in one, his legs folded in front of him, which would be most uncomfortable.

Grinning, she slid farther down in the water so that it encircled her face and her hair fanned around her. She'd been singing her favorite song, one her mother had taught her when she was a child, about maidens and knights. With her ears underwater, her voice was muffled and—to be honest—much improved.

The warm water felt heavenly, her cares dissolving into the thick curls of lavender-scented steam that rose from the tub. It had been a long few weeks and she'd needed some time to let her cares go.

Yet try as she would, she hadn't been able to stop thinking about the prince, wondering why he'd taken such an interest in her. Was it mere pride, because she'd bested him at a sword fight? She didn't think so, seeing as how he'd turned the tables at the end. Though if she hadn't slipped— No, it was better not to dwell on might-haves. Life had taught her that lesson far too well.

At one time, she'd had a new, adoring husband, a beautiful castle for a home, and a future that had seemed endless. In one day, she'd lost it all. The only way she'd been able to come to terms with such devastation was to move forward and keep moving. She missed Robert dearly and knew that a part of her always would. But as time passed and she heard stories from the widows who'd been wed for years before being parted from their husbands, she'd realized her and Robert's relationship had only just begun to grow roots. She was certain it would have become a towering tree, had they been allowed the luxury of time. As it was, she was left with an empty heart and many sweet memories, which had been enough until now. Somehow, meeting the prince had awakened her imagination and made her wonder *what if?*

She shouldn't even be thinking about the prince; she'd only met him three times, anyway. Which was three times too many.

Still . . . there was something about him that stirred her curiosity. She felt as if she knew him in some way, which made no sense, for they had nothing in common. She should just forget him.

And she would, for she had many things that needed her attention far more. Like how to get the supplies to repair their cottages, and when Loudan might ease his guard and she could slip back into Rowallen.

She reached up and grasped the high sides of the tub, pulling herself into a sitting position. The water lapped at her shoulders as she leaned back against the elegant slant of the tub, her hair clinging to her neck and shoulders before floating around her in the water in red silken waves.

She sighed happily and closed her eyes. Life was always surprising. Who would have ever thought she'd meet a prince? "Prince Max," she said aloud. "Mighty, oh-so-sure-of-himself Prince Max."

"You called, *dorogaya moya*?" came a deep voice.

Her eyes flew open. Surely . . . that couldn't have been . . .

Heart pounding, she lifted her head and peered over the edge of the tub.

The prince stood just inside her window, re-closing the shutters. When he finished, he faced her and said in a polite voice, "Good morning, Murian."

"How did you get in here?"

"I climbed through the window."

"But . . . how did you find me?"

He smiled, and her heart fluttered. "Ah, I cannot give you all of my secrets. Not all at once, anyway."

"I dinna— You shouldna be here!"

"But I have some questions for you."

She could call for help and Ian would come running, but then there would be yelling and very little talking. From the prince's demeanor and the fact that he hadn't moved from the window, perhaps he wished for just what he said—answers to his questions.

Well, she had questions, too. Besides, there were two

loaded pistols and a rapier in her cottage, so she was plenty safe.

His green eyes warmed with amusement, a lopsided smile curving his chiseled mouth. "Do not look so surprised. Surely you knew I would find you."

Her heart, already beating irregularly, gave a sick thud. "Does the earl know?"

"*Nyet*. The earl and I, we do not—how do you say?—chat."

Murian liked the way he said "chat," as if he thought the word might bite him back. "Why did you climb through the window?"

"If I had walked down the street and politely knocked upon your door, your giant might have come off his leash."

Her lips quirked despite herself.

His gaze flickered over her, his eyes darkening. "I did not expect to find you so . . . exposed, *dorogaya moya*."

Bloody hell, I'm naked! She'd been so shocked by his arrival, it hadn't registered. Thankfully, all he could see were her bare shoulders and arms due to the tub's high lip. "Turn around!"

"Of course." There was a distinct note of regret in his smoky voice, but he turned his back, his feet planted firmly as if to prove he wouldn't whip about and peer at her.

She rinsed the last bit of soap from her arms and, with a glance to make certain he was still facing away, she climbed from the tub. She snatched up her towel and dried quickly, then reached for her robe. She struggled to put on the thin lawn garment, which clung to her damp skin in a most revealing way. "Dinna turn around. My clothes are beside the screen near the bed, so I must go there to dress."

"I will not move from this spot." He turned his head slightly so that she saw the barest glimpse of his profile. "I vow it on my honor."

He spoke simply, with quiet strength.

She believed him, which surprised her. "Thank you." She wrung her dripping hair over the tub, twisting the water from the heavy strands.

Behind her, Max fought the urge to turn and watch her.

Into the quiet, she said, "You said you have questions?"

"Many. The most pressing one is why you run from me every time we meet."

"I dinna run from you last night at the castle. It was just time to leave."

"You did not say good-bye."

"I had things to do."

"Like what?"

"Perhaps I wished for a quiet corner where I could eat all the pastry I'd stolen."

He sighed. "You are not making this easy."

"I dinna believe I'm supposed to," she pointed out. "You have other questions?"

"Last night, did you use Miss MacLeod as a diversion, to send the guards from the castle?"

"I don't know a Miss MacLeod."

He let his silence tell her of his disbelief.

She sighed. "Fine. I may know Miss MacLeod."

"You do know her. You disguised yourself and snuck into the castle, and had Miss MacLeod appear at exactly ten and claim she'd been held up. The earl sent some of his men after the thieves, who had been described by Miss MacLeod to sound exactly like you and your men."

"Aye, he sent some men," she replied, her voice sharp with irritation. "But not enough. The halls were still heavily guarded."

"So you *were* looking for something. I suspected as much. But what?"

"Something of my late husband's. Something hidden."

"Even from you?"

"Aye." Her voice was muffled through the towel as she dried her hair.

He let his gaze wander over the part of the room within his line of vision, noting the furnishings for the first time. Bozhy moj, *such luxury for a cottage.* Damask- and velvet-clad chairs and a matching settee sat near the fireplace, while thick Turkish rugs covered the dirt floor. Here and there were mahogany side tables, one holding a heavy silver tea set. Even the huge tub was fitting for a palace, for the beaten copper gleamed with polish, the handles on each side exquisitely wrought.

But still more surprising was the woman herself. He would recognize her anywhere, but in the bright morning light, he saw things he'd missed before—how long her red hair was, how her eyes sparkled when she was irritated, how delicate her features were when her hair was slicked back from her face. *And this is the thief who almost bested me with a sword.*

He remembered her bared shoulders and arms; she was far more feminine than he'd expected. When she'd first peered over the edge of the tub, her wet hair clinging to her, her shoulders glistening with water, he'd been hit with a shockingly strong urge to stride across the room and hold her, naked and wet. It hadn't been mere passion, though he'd felt that as well; it was more a desire to save her from the dirt floor peering between the rugs, the leaky water stains that flanked the fireplace, and even the rapier standing against the wall.

He knew one thing for certain: Murian Muir was not meant for this sort of life. She was a conundrum, this woman warrior. The line of her chin and jaw showed strength, while her beauty had an untrammeled wildness that called to him—a lack of discipline in the way her thick lashes spiked about her wide, silver eyes that boldly examined him, a refusal by her dark red hair to yield as it curled even when dripping wet.

Behind him he heard a faint rustle, and he caught Murian's reflection in the silver teapot by the fireplace. The angle of the teapot gave him a full view behind the screen where she dressed.

He watched her bent reflection as she removed her robe, a towel wrapped about her head. The robe slid off her, revealing her spectacular shoulders, tall, trim form, and gracefully long legs. She threw her robe over the edge of the screen, her arms smooth and lightly muscled. Her breasts, high and small, perfect for a man's hands, were adorned with pink nipples that made his mouth water in anticipation. She was angelic, this woman, a veritable—

Her gaze met his in the reflection.

With a frantic movement, she yanked her robe from where she'd hung it and held it in front of her. "You said you wouldna look!"

"I said I wouldn't move, and I haven't." Cursing his inability to look away once the reflection had presented itself, he turned so that he could no longer see her. "There. Now dress. I haven't all day."

"Och, if you wish to twist words into lies, then return to Rowallen and the earl. He excels at such games."

Max was struck by her bitter tone. "Put on some clothes," he ordered, his voice unexpectedly harsh. "I am no eunuch."

A stiff silence met this. A second later, she said in a firm voice, "Stir the fire while you're waiting. I'll need the heat to dry my hair."

He found himself faintly amused that this slender girl should order him about without the least hesitation. People never ordered princes to bank fires, but as it was growing cold in the cottage, he was more than willing to do the task.

He undid his cloak and hung it on a peg on the wall by the door, pausing to inspect the rapier that sat nearby. It was a superior blade, Italian made, with a hilt set with intricate carving. He wondered where she'd found it, and how she'd been trained to such mastery. *I have so many questions for you, little one.*

He replaced the blade and then crossed to the fireplace. After adding some wood from a nearby stack, he found the fire iron and stirred the flames to life.

As the flames leapt in response, Murian walked

across the cottage floor to join him. She was dressed simply, her gray gown nondescript and plain. Sturdy boots peeped out from her skirts, while a heavy wool shawl had been pinned about her shoulders. She carried an ivory comb, her damp hair curling wildly about her shoulders.

Max put down the fire iron as she sat close to the fire in a decadently stuffed chair covered in the finest damask.

She gestured to the settee opposite and, pulling her wet hair over one shoulder, began to comb it. "Pray have a seat, Your Highness."

"Thank you." He sat down, leaning back and admiring the reds and golds of her hair as the fire played across it.

She fastened her direct gaze on him. "Perhaps you should begin by telling me why you are here."

"To be honest, at first I was determined to seek you out so that we could finish our swordplay."

She grinned. "Och, I would have enjoyed that."

Her grin was so instant and spontaneous that he found himself returning it. "*Da*, I would have, too. But since then, I've come to learn several things about you and your little band here, and now I'm not sure why I was so determined to find you. Perhaps it is because I, too, have no love for the earl."

"So we are together in our dislike of Loudan."

"Dislike, distrust—he concerns me." Max wondered how much he should tell her. Not much—some secrets weren't his to tell. But it would not hurt to share Tata Natasha's predicament. "Loudan won something from my grandmother in a game of chance and will not return it."

Her brows lowered. "So . . . history repeats itself."

"What history?"

At his question, her lashes lowered to conceal her expression. "It is a long story. Too long."

Max found himself wishing she'd trust him. To ease the moment, he traced a hand over the cushion of his chair. "I must say, you have excellent taste in décor. Did you take all of this from Loudan?"

"No. And yes." Her lips quirked. "I dinna steal them, if that is what you mean; they were mine to take. I was lady of Rowallen Castle until my husband's death." She ran the comb through her hair yet again, the wild curls fighting the ivory teeth. "There is no harm in telling you why we are hiding in the woods. Robert Muir was my husband. Rowallen was—is—his. It has been in the Muir family for centuries."

"How did the earl end up with the castle?" he asked, though he already knew. For some reason he wished to hear the tale from her lips.

"My guardian, the Duke of Spencer, arranged my marriage to Lord Robert Muir."

He raised his brows. "I know the duke. He is a brave soldier."

"He would be honored you think so. After I married Robert, Spencer left for the war. A year and a half ago, while I was visiting my parents' graves in Edinburgh, Robert had some unexpected visitors at the castle— Loudan and two of his so-called friends."

"So you husband did not invite him?"

"I dinna think so. As far as I know, they'd never met. Besides, had he expected guests, Robert would have asked me to stay. I know he would have." The comb lay still in her hand, a faraway expression on her face. "The housekeeper was present when Loudan and his men arrived unexpectedly. She said Robert was most unhappy to see them, for he'd planned on spending the next few days with his man of business. But he was a gracious host and invited them to spend the night. He had the housekeeper ready three rooms, and ordered a grand dinner. That night there was much whiskey served, and someone suggested a card game."

"The servants saw all of that?"

"Yes, but very little else. Something happened during that card game. The earl claims Robert got caught up in the excitement and wagered Rowallen and her lands."

"You don't believe he would do that."

"Nay. He would never have done such a thing. After the game Loudan offered to allow Robert to play one more hand in an attempt to win back all he'd lost. According to the earl, Robert cheated and was caught. Harsh words were exchanged and a challenge was issued." She looked at the ivory comb in her hand. "The servants heard raised voices, so there was definitely an argument of some sort. But Robert told them nothing. He stormed off to bed and refused to speak to anyone. The next morning, as the servants were riding, they heard gunshots in the garden. Loudan was standing over Robert's body. There were two guns, one in the earl's hand, and one on the ground near Robert."

"A duel."

"So Loudan would have everyone believe. He told the servants the castle was now his, his friends corroborated his story, and off he went to Edinburgh to file his claim."

"You fought him on this, I assume."

"Every way I could. As soon as I returned home and found out all that had happened, I visited the local justice of the peace. He went to Edinburgh but could do nothing. Loudan is too well connected, his story confirmed by his handpicked witnesses. . . ." She shrugged. "There was nothing I could do."

"So he took the castle." He watched her face. "And the people with you here are all from Rowallen?"

She nodded. "Loudan ordered everyone to leave. Some had families they could go to, or other employment opportunities. I wrote dozens of letters of reference. But some had nowhere to go—like me. Ian knew of these cottages. They're forgotten; I don't think even Robert knew of them, and he kept meticulous records." She sighed and lifted the comb to her hair once more. "And so we are here."

"When did this happen?"

"A little over a year ago."

Only a year. And yet she has managed to pull herself together enough to become a nuisance to the earl. "So that is what you mean by history repeating itself—my grandmother lost something in a card game, and so did your husband."

"Aye." Her gaze was thoughtful. "Loudan has a pattern. After Robert's death I made inquiries; our relatives are not the only ones to lose prized possessions to the earl. In Edinburgh last year, he played the Earl of Argyll and won the man's best stallion. Later, the cards were found to have been marked. Loudan accused the earl of perfidy."

"But Argyll lost the game."

"Exactly. And I know Argyll; he's an honorable man and would never cheat. I think Loudan accused Argyll as a way to keep attention off himself. There are other instances, too, where Loudan won prestigious items in card games. What's odd is that he rarely plays. But when he does . . ." She lifted her brows.

"So the earl cheated my grandmother."

"I'd wager my last piece of silver. He never plays unless there is something valuable to be won. And he never loses when he plays."

Just listening to Murian's story infuriated him. *Damn that man. Who could be so heartless?*

"And he has done more than take possession of the castle," Murian continued. "The Muirs had been in possession of Rowallen since the thirteenth century. Now, Loudan refuses to allow anyone to say the family name, even the servants. He removed the family crest from the castle wall, a crest that had been there since the fifteenth century. He was going to destroy the castle ledgers, but the vicar took them and stored with the parish records." She scowled darkly. "The blackguard is trying to purge the family's ties with the castle entirely."

"Is it working?"

A satisfied smile curved her lips and made him think of a cat with a bowl of cream. "Nay, 'tis not so easy as he wishes. The people know Rowallen; they remember and love Robert and his family. The locals willna' forget he was cheated of his birthright and shot like a dog in his own garden." Her voice quavered and she snapped her lips closed.

He could feel her pain, see it in the flash of her eyes. "I'm sorry."

She managed a tight, quick shrug. "It is what it is." She pulled the comb through her hair, her movements jerky with fury.

Max found himself fascinated with the stubbornness of her curls. With each stroke, the curls would straighten, but the second the comb was free, her hair sprang back into a wild morass of gold and red. He wondered what it would feel like to sink his hands into such glorious thickness and—

Silver eyes locked on him. "I have answered your questions, but you havena explained why you are here."

Her lilting voice made him yearn to hear more. "I came to get my chickens back."

She laughed, low and husky, her sadness dissipating like the mist before the sun. "You'll have to talk to Ian aboot that." Her smile faded a bit. "'Tis sometimes a challenge, feeding so many people."

"How many are you?"

"Twenty-two. We were doing well enough, trading with the local villages for what we canna produce. Then the earl began threatening everyone who did so."

He'd seen evidence of that himself. *Damn Loudan's black heart.* "The earl has much to answer for."

"Aye. When Spencer returns from the war, Loudan will be dethroned. All we have to do is survive until then."

"You'll make it. You're plenty strong enough to win over a weak-kneed weasel like Loudan."

Their eyes met, and the air about them swirled with the flickering heat from the fire, scented with her lavender soap, and lay between them, heavy with questions and curiosity.

He was here, and now he knew her full story. He'd accomplished what he'd wanted—but he found himself loath to leave. She intrigued him, so bold and unbowed despite having lost a husband and her way of life, banished from a sumptuous castle to a lowly crofter's hut in the thick of the woods. Any one of those blows would be devastating to many, yet she sat with her head up, so vibrant he felt he could warm his hands on the heat of her soul. "It seems we have a common enemy, we two. We should help one another."

Her gaze narrowed. "How so?"

"You know the castle well."

"Aye. Many of us here do."

"If I cannot make the earl see reason about the item my grandmother lost to him, I may need to find it myself."

"I see." Her gaze flickered to his mouth.

It was like a touch, that glance, and sent his searching gaze to her mouth, so plump and ripe, ready for a kiss. His body hummed in response and he had to fight back the desire to drag her into his lap.

"What did your grandmother lose?"

He dragged his mind back to the present. "I do not know. I think she is too embarrassed to tell me. My grandmother is much older and frailer than she'd have the world believe. But whatever she lost, the earl is holding it for ransom. I believe what he really wants is not money, but an elderly grand duchess forced to dance to his tune."

Murian scowled. "Blackguard! To torment an old lady so."

"Indeed. It weighs upon her."

"I'm surprised you dinna just challenge him."

He hesitated. "I will if I must, but there must be less violent ways to retrieve this object."

She wondered at his hesitation. But so far, she thought he'd been telling her the truth. He was chivalrous, and he obviously cared deeply for his grandmother. Behind the handsome charm, behind the scars and the lines etched by life, she saw purpose, determination, and character.

She didn't know if Max had shared the whole truth of his purpose here, but her instincts told her that his intentions were pure. "If I can help you with my knowledge of the castle, I will."

"Thank you." He leaned back, his broad shoulders eclipsing most of the settee. "Perhaps I can do the same. What are you searching for that you must sneak inside Rowallen dressed as a plump spinster with a sweet tooth?"

"My husband's journal. In it, I believe he wrote the truth about the card game and the duel. If I find it, and present it to the courts in Edinburgh, Rowallen willna longer belong to the earl. I can return her to the people who love her."

The prince nodded thoughtfully. "I would like to see Loudan's face when you reclaim your castle. I take it you looked for this journal during Miss MacLeod's spectacular diversion?"

She grimaced. "I couldna; Loudan now has guards in every hall, and several posted outside his bedchamber. But I *know* that blasted thing must be there. That room is the only one we haven't searched."

"How do you know the earl has not already found this journal and destroyed it?"

"Because he does everything he can to keep us oot. Why would he bother, unless he fears I'll find what he canna?"

The prince nodded thoughtfully. "You have thought this through."

"I've had a lot of time to do so. You should know that neither of our objectives will be easy. Some of the earl's guards dress like footmen, some as grooms. It is difficult to know who is truly a servant and who is more dangerous."

"They bother me not. You will need another social event in order to slip in and search, *nyet*?"

"It would make things much easier."

"I will find out what the earl has planned." Max hesitated, and then said, "He's mentioned he's trying to schedule an opera singer, and that he will once again open the doors of the castle to the locals. But I don't know when."

"Once we find out, we will plan our search." She held out her hand. "We have a deal, then. We are partners."

He took her hand in his. The women he normally met had pale, soft, white hands. Colorless hands, he decided, admiring the strength in hers. He ran his thumb over the callus on one of her fingers. "From drawing your bow, I think?"

She flushed, but nodded.

"And this one . . ." He traced a finger over her palm, where another callus rested. "A shovel?"

"An ax." She curled her hand closed. "I am verrah good at splitting firewood."

He'd wager she was. She was also good at heating his blood until all he could think about was how her lips would feel under his. He lifted her hand, uncurled her fingers, and pressed a kiss to each callus.

She watched him, her eyes smoky and dark, her lips parted. Each press of his lips to her skin made her take in a small, sharp breath. She wet her lips and tugged at her hand. "You shouldna be doing that."

"*Da*. I should be doing this, instead." He slid his hand under her long silken hair, pulled her closer, and kissed her. He'd wanted to do this ever since the day he'd cut the kerchief off her face and realized she was a beautiful, bold woman.

The second their lips met, it was as if a fire had exploded into flames. They kissed, consumed, and devoured as they wildly embraced.

Max plundered her mouth with all of the passion she'd ignited in him time and again. He pulled her into his lap and let his hands roam over her, up her back and shoulders, feeling the firmness of her curves, the sheer femininity of her form. She arched against him, her mouth opening to his seeking tongue, her legs parting as she did so, unconsciously echoing his own thoughts. She was lush and sensual, her hands as active as his own, his passion matched stroke for stroke. He slipped a hand from her waist to—

Suddenly, dogs started barking.

She broke the kiss and looked toward the door.

There was a loud shout, and then another. A bell started clanging insistently.

Murian pushed herself out of Max's lap just as he heard Ian bellow a warning.

A piercing whistle broke through the melee, and Max groaned. "I'm sorry; those are my men." He stood, his cock tenting his breeches uncomfortably. *Damn it!* "I forgot to give them the signal."

"What signal?"

"One letting them know I was not strung up for the wild animals to eat by that giant of yours. I was to give a whistle and let them know all was well, but I became . . . distracted."

Her lips quirked as she braided her hair with quick, practiced movements. "We must go out there or there will be a fight."

"Aye."

She pulled a ribbon from her pocket and tied off her braid, then grabbed her cloak and slung it over her shoulders. "Come."

Feeling as sulky as a boy whose toy has been stolen, Max removed his cloak from the peg where he'd hung it. At least his arousal was starting to deflate.

Already striding past him. Murian caught up her rapier and opened the cottage door, the cool air swirling her cloak and blowing his.

Max unsheathed his sword. "I will—"

"Follow me," she ordered over her shoulder, and charged outside.

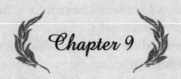

Chapter 9

The next morning, well before the earl or his guests had awakened, Max walked down Rowallen's grand staircase. He'd had a hell of a night, tossing and turning, his mind unable to stop thinking about the small village in the woods where the lovely red-haired, rapier-wielding thief lived.

Yesterday had been filled with surprises. When his men had arrived in the village, Murian's giant had roared through the small street, a blacksmith's hammer in his meaty fist as he threatened to kill anyone who dared come any closer. The other inhabitants had soon appeared, too, racing out of their cottages and stables and into the street, all holding weapons—axes, planks, thick sticks, and one very old, very unsteady blunderbuss.

Max had been startled. Not at the weapons, but at who carried them. With the exception of the giant and a sullen youth, all of them had been women and children. Murian had told him as much, but she didn't do this. Seeing it, the full evil of the earl's actions had hit him like a hard punch.

After Murian had calmed Ian and the villagers, and

explained that their visitors hadn't come to murder them or turn them over to Loudan, she'd introduced Max and his men to the members of her band. He remembered each and every face. Seven widows, twelve small children, an angry giant, a sullen lad, all of them with hauntingly suspicious eyes and dressed in worn, ragged clothing. While none were starving, they had the look of people pushed to their utmost to survive.

But in the midst of them all was red-haired, creamy-skinned, fiery-spirited Murian, a light in a very dark world. These were the people Murian fought to protect. The people she hoped to save Rowallen for.

So many cares and worries, all resting on such delicate shoulders. He shook his head as he thought of the fear he'd seen in the women's faces when they'd first seen Max's men, yet they'd overcome that fear to race into the lane, makeshift weapons raised, ready to protect each other. It took a great leader to inspire a soldier to overcome his innate fear. It would take an even greater one to inspire an entire village.

Thoughts of Murian and her small band had stirred Max's thoughts until he could not sleep. He knew he hadn't been the only one affected; those of his men who'd visited the village had peppered him with questions on the ride home. He'd told them what he could without breaking Murian's confidence, and he sensed that, like him, they were unwilling to leave things as they were.

What a remarkable woman. She has her guardian's spirit, that's for certain. It is from him Murian gets her bravery. Max didn't know the Duke of Spencer well, for they represented different countries, but they'd met, talked, and had liked one another. The Golden Lion was a great warrior, bold and disciplined.

Max reached the bottom of the staircase and threw a critical glance around the foyer. While he liked the exposed timber rafters from the Elizabethan era, some fool had later paneled the entire foyer in dark wood and then, to add insult to injury, had hung ancient weaponry on the walls in fancy designs. It was offensive to see valuable pikes and pistols used as decorations.

As he walked toward the breakfast room, he silently counted the footmen standing in attendance in the foyer. Most households would have one, perhaps two stationed in this section of the house. A much larger establishment might have four. Loudan had twelve. *Just enough for a troop. Interesting. And there are so many "footmen" stationed throughout the castle that no one can have a private conversation.* Unless they spoke a lesser-known foreign language.

He supposed it was remotely possible one of them might know Oxenburgian, but he doubted it. It was not a language much in use except in his own country. Someone who knew Russian might be able to pick out a few words that were similar, but that was all.

He reached the breakfast room just as Orlov and Pahlen stepped out.

"Do you eat, General?" Pahlen asked. At twenty-two years of age, he was the youngest of Max's men. Blond and tall, with piercing blue eyes and a faint scar on one cheek, he was the one most likely to be found with a chambermaid. Sometimes two.

"I ate a full hour ago, you lazy slugabed."

"Did they have food ready at that hour? Other than

our men, I've yet to see anyone rise before noon in this place."

"I arrived before the eggs. Someone rousted the chef, and that was soon corrected."

"Lazy chef," Orlov said, clearly amused at the thought of a sleepy chef cooking their breakfast.

"Indeed." Max withdrew two missives from his vest pocket, then spoke in Oxenburgian. "These must be placed on the mail coach in Inverness."

"You do not trust our host's frank?" Orlov replied in the same language.

"*Nyet*," Max said baldly. "Whoever takes them must return immediately. I don't want the earl to know I've been circumventing his post."

"Very well, General." Orlov took the missives. "I will send Golovin. His horse is the best at long distances."

"Very good. I will visit the village this morning." Max looked past his man into the breakfast room. "Where are the others?"

"They wait with the horses," Orlov replied.

"They wait? For what?"

Orlov cleared his throat. "General, those of us who saw the village yesterday noticed they were poorly prepared for winter, and yet it comes."

"We would help them," Pahlen said.

Pleased, Max said, "You are more than welcome to join me, but I warn you, it will be hard work and there will be many challenges."

Orlov shrugged. "We are ready."

A mischievous glint lit Pahlen's eyes. "Already we have obtained a wagon."

"Obtained?"

"That is one word for it," Pahlen said, grinning.

Max laughed. "Very good. We will need many items; the wagon will be most useful."

Orlov nodded. "I've made inquiries, and unfortunately there are no lumber mills nearby other than the private mill the earl uses."

"We dare not use his mill; he will know we're doing something and grow suspicious."

"So I thought, too. If we need wood, we'll have to travel two days each way to fetch it."

"That could be a problem." Max considered this. It was a pity they couldn't use the earl's mill; it was only fair that Loudan bear some of the expense himself. "Hmm. I may have a solution for the wood. What else will we need?"

"Nails, saws, hammers—we have those."

"*Da*," Pahlen said. "We found many tools in an old, unused barn in the back of the earl's property. He will never miss them."

"Then we are set. Let's join the others." They walked toward the wide doors and went back out into the foyer. "We will hunt along the way. We will leave the fresh meat in the village, but bring back the pelts. That way it will appear we are hunting rather than—"

"Hold!" Tata Natasha's voice rang out, sharp enough to cut ice.

Max grimaced.

She made her way downstairs, one hand firmly grasped about the railing, the other holding up her skirts. "I have been looking for you. Where have you been?"

Max turned to his men. "Go on without me. I won't be more than a minute or two."

As soon as Orlov and Pahlen were out the door, Max crossed the foyer to his grandmother, who'd just reached the bottom stair. Dressed in her usual black, a gold and emerald comb in her hair, she looked every bit the witch she wished others to think her.

To Max's amusement, the liveried footmen looked uneasy whenever her gaze fell their way. *So there is a benefit to be had.*

She marched up to Max. "Where are you going?"

"Out."

Her mouth thinned. "That is no answer."

"It is the only one you will get. I have things to do, Tata Natasha. Things that will help us both."

Her gaze sharpened and she took his arm and said quietly in Oxenburgian, "You have found a way to get Loudan to release what I've lost?"

He merely looked at her.

She flushed and released his arm. "I cannot tell you." She waved a hand. "Just go. Do this thing you wish—whatever it is. While you are out hunting, or drinking in a tavern, or whatever it is you do, I will be here, doing what I must to save our country from embarrassment."

"Save our country?" A flicker of unease rose through Max. "What could you have lost that could embarrass our entire country?"

Twin spots of dull red rose in her parchment cheeks. "You know enough of my foolishness. I cannot tell you more. I was such a fool, but the cards—Max, you must know, I thought I could not lose."

He noted a faint quiver in her hands as she clutched her shawl closer about her. "That is no surprise. I have heard from a knowledgeable source that our host is an inveterate cheat."

"What? Who told you that?"

"It does not matter. But you stand in a castle he won in a game of cards. He rides a stallion he won in a game of cards. From what I've been able to discover, he's living off the fortune he's won at cards. He is very careful and only plays when there are large sums to be won. I see a pattern that has very little to do with luck."

"*Ty shto shoytish!*" Her eyes widened and she pressed a hand to her mouth, her fingers heavy with rings that winked in the light. "During the game, I won many hands in a row. That should have made me suspicious. But I started thinking the fates were with me, that I was blessed. So I played more and more recklessly until . . ." Her shoulders slumped. "I was a fool."

"*Nyet.* He is very good at cheating, however he does it. And you are one of the smartest women, and the cleverest Gypsy queen, I know."

She flashed an annoyed look at him. "I am the *only* Gypsy queen you know."

"*Da.* Do not worry so. I am forming a plan. But for now, I must go."

He gave her a quick kiss on her cheek and turned to the door. As a footman sprang to open it, she called, "Max?"

He looked back.

"Do not let this man get away with this. He must pay."

"He shall, Tata Natasha. He shall."

• • •

Sleep sifted through Murian, soft as silk, deep as down. Somehow she was no longer in her village, but on a horse, riding across a moor dotted with purple thistles. At the far end of the field sat a white tent. She needed to reach that tent. Needed to find out who was there, what they wanted.

Faster and faster she galloped, the ground passing beneath her horse's hooves, yet the tent stayed elusively out of reach. She rode harder, urging the horse on, but the moor stretched longer and longer, now crisscrossed with streams and rock ledges that grew wider, deeper, more dangerous. Yet on she rode, jumping this ledge, fording that stream, her gaze locked on the white tent.

As she grew closer, she could see tent pennants flapping in the wind. On them, a deep purple background surrounded a large black bear with ferocious teeth, one eyebrow split by a silver scar. *Like the prince.*

As soon as she had the thought, the tent opened and he walked out holding the bridle of a magnificent black steed with a silver and gold mane. The prince swung into the saddle and watched her approach. Though he didn't speak, she could hear his voice deep in her mind, deeply accented and rich as chocolate, urging her to join him, to stay with him.

His urgency became hers, and she pushed her mare to leap over wider and wider rivers, the last one a seeming ocean.

She should have been afraid, but neither she nor the horse paused. With a mighty launch, they flew . . . up and up and up. The wind blew her hair over her face, obscuring her vision. He was closer now. Though she couldn't see, she could feel his presence, his desire.

And just as suddenly, her mare had wings, large and white. Exulted, she leaned forward, anxious to—

BAM!

Gasping, she sat bolt upright, shoving her hair from her eyes and found herself in her own bed. All looked the same as the night before. "It was just a dream," she murmured, her heart still pounding. Oddly disappointed, she fell back against her pillows, the morning light streaming between the cracks of the shutters. As her heartbeat returned to a normal pace, she had to laugh at herself. "Such a fool, dreaming of a prince. It's daft, you are."

She should get up; there was much to do today. She and Ian were to—

Bam! Bam! BAM!

She sat up again. What *was* that? It sounded like—

BAM! BAM! BAM! BAM! BAM!

She threw back the covers and arose, aware of a growing number of voices outside her cottage. *What is going on?* Muttering to herself, she yanked off her night rail and grabbed a chemise and gown from where they hung over the screen. Moments later, her feet shoved stockingless into her boots and still tying her gown into place, she threw open the door to her cottage.

The little lane bustled with activity. Everywhere she looked, there were men. Big men. Men with broad shoulders, white-toothed smiles flashing from their beards, and deep voices. Some were climbing up on roofs, hammers in hand, while others removed broken shutters and carried them to a wagon filled with lumber and other materials.

In the center of this organized madness stood Max. Like the others, he'd discarded his coat, his shirtsleeves rolled up to reveal powerful forearms. His black hair was mussed by the wind, there was a smudge of dirt on his cheek, and his collar was torn as if it had caught on something carried on his shoulder.

He crossed his arms and rocked back on his heels, his gaze everywhere as he watched his men work. He said a few words to a man by his side, who instantly repeated them to someone else in a booming voice. Whatever Max wished corrected must have been fixed, for after a moment, he gave a satisfied nod, and sent the man to assist someone in removing a broken shutter. Then he went to the wagon and started unloading buckets of nails.

Widow Grier saw Murian and hurried up, her small son wrapped in blankets and resting on her hip. "Och, 'tis a miracle, me lady!" The deep boom of a man's laughter rose over the hammering, and she sighed. "I've missed the sound of a mon's laugh—the sort he makes when he's hard at work, makin' life a bit easier fer e'erone . . . I dinna think there's any finer sound."

"Indeed. Where's Ian? I assume he's helping with all of this."

"Nay, yer ladyship. He left wi' Will to hunt hours ago. They've no' come back yet."

"Then who did the prince talk to, before he began this work?"

"Why . . . I dinna think he spoke to anyone. He and

his men arrived here no' five minutes ago and went straight to work."

Murian's jaw tightened. She was deeply thankful for the help, but this was *their* village, damn it. For the prince to take over without so much as a by-your-leave . . . She swallowed the curse on her lips. "That was certainly bold of them."

Widows MacThune and MacDonald walked past, carrying large iron pots. The wind tugged their skirts, over which they wore heavy aprons.

"We're making stew fer a luncheon," Widow Mac-Donald informed Murian. The plump widow's face was red from carrying the heavy pot, though her brown eyes twinkled with excitement.

Widow MacThune grinned, her two boys carrying baskets overflowing with potatoes and turnips behind her. "Look wha' the prince and his men brought us! All this and fresh venison!"

"*And* a brace of rabbits," the other woman added over her shoulder as they moved on. "We're to ha' meat again, me lady!"

Eyes sparkling, Widow Grier turned to Murian. "I'll fetch some water in case anyone gets thirsty."

"That's an excellent idea," Murian agreed, the sight of the food deflating her growing irritation.

With a wave, Widow Grier hurried to fill a pail with water and carry it from work site to work site.

Murian returned to her cottage and fetched her cloak. When she returned, Widow Reeves was hurrying up the middle of the street, a basket of wet laundry on her hip. She scowled at the men who were climbing on her roof, tearing off broken slate pieces, and tossing them to the ground.

Murian joined the widow. "'Tis surprising, is it not?"

"I'm deeply appreciative that ye picked me cottage fer a repair, lassie, but they'll crack the plaster and the whole house will be filled wi' it. Had I known they were comin', I could ha' put sheets o'er the furnishings."

"I didn't give them permission. They just showed up and did it."

"I'll ask them to stop until I can get the house ready." The widow hurried up the street. Once she arrived, she yelled to the men on the roof and then ducked into her house. A moment later, she came out, holding the pieces of a teacup in her hand.

Murian saw the tremble of Widow Reeves's mouth as she looked at the broken teacup and took a step toward her, but Widow Grier was closer. In a moment, they were arm in arm, looking at the damage.

That did it. Murian whirled on her heels and found Max on the other side of the street, talking to some of his men.

She marched up. "Max!"

He turned and his expression warmed as he excused himself from his men.

"Well," he said with a smile as he joined her. "Did I not surprise you?"

"Och, I was surprised all right. Too surprised for words."

His smile faded a tiny bit. "That does not sound like a good surprise."

"It's not."

Max followed Murian's gaze to where Widow Reeves stood clutching what appeared to be broken pottery. The widow wiped a tear from her cheek.

"What's happened?" Max asked.

"Someone barged into the village and began working on her roof without letting her know. These are old cottages, Max. When you stomp aboot on the roof, it cracks the plaster and showers the place with debris."

"Oh." He hadn't thought of that.

"Apparently, one of Widow Reeves's teacups were knocked over and one was broken."

"I will buy her a new one," he said immediately.

"The set is from her mother. You canna buy her a new one."

Max watched as she pressed her lips into a straight line, struggling to find the words.

"This is *our* village, Max. And while I truly appreciate your help, you should have asked first."

"You do not want your—"

"Widow Reeves's precious tea set, the only thing she has from her mother, was ruined by a few moments of needless haste." She caught his expression and said less heatedly, "Your heart is in the right place, but we should have talked aboot this, and let everyone prepare. They have so few precious things, the loss of even one is difficult. And this place, ragged as it may seem to you, has been our home for the last year and a half. We deserve a say in what happens here."

Max looked past her to the village where his men worked, and suddenly he saw it through her eyes. Who was he to ride into her village like some arrogant knight on a white horse and, without consulting her or anyone else, "fix" everything in sight? *Damn it, I am as high-handed as Tata Natasha.* "I should have asked. I'm sorry."

Surprise crossed her face, followed by a quick smile. "Thank you. And I'm sorry if I dinna appear grateful, but you should have talked to me first. I was sound asleep and awakened to find my village invaded by Cossacks."

"Cossacks? *Nyet!* Our uniforms are *much* handsomer than theirs."

Murian hid a grin at his outraged look. The Oxenburg uniforms *were* quite striking, with their red coats and gold braid. But she liked what he wore now even better, a simple white shirt tucked into black pants and boots. She rather liked how the pants clung to his thighs and—

He muttered something under his breath, grasping her elbow and leading her toward the stables.

"Where are we going?"

"I would ask you a question one for your ears and no one else's."

They reached the stables and stepped into its dimness, the morning sun blocked by the large door. Max released her then, his expression serious.

"Aye?" Murian asked, aware they were now very much alone. They'd been alone yesterday and, except for a few awkward moments, she hadn't minded. But now, things seemed . . . different.

Max placed his hand under her chin and gently tilted her face to his. "You have very expressive eyes. They tell me everything. They tell me when you are upset. They tell me when you are worried. And"—his gaze dropped to her mouth—"they tell me when you want a kiss."

She gaped up at him. "When I— Nay, I dinna want a kiss." But the second the words left her lips, she knew she lied.

She *did* want a kiss.

And facing him here, his broad chest so close to hers, his warm hand still cupped under her chin, she wanted it badly.

"Already this day, I have been in trouble for not asking permission. To keep from being in trouble yet again, I will not kiss you unless you say I may. So, I ask. May I kiss you?"

"What if I say no?" Her voice sounded husky.

He slipped an arm around her waist, pulling her to him. The instant her body melted against his, her skin prickled to life, every bit of her alive in an unmistakable wave of desire.

She couldn't look away from his green eyes, framed so seductively by his thick black lashes, and she wanted to kiss him not once, but over and over. She wanted to taste his mouth, to capture his breath, to feel his hands over her body— She bit back a moan. It had been so long since she'd felt such desire, so long since she'd wanted someone so much.

His lips hovered a mere breath from hers. "Say it," he whispered. "Say you wish for me to kiss you."

"Yes," she breathed. "Please—"

Max captured her mouth with his, lifting her to him. This was a woman worth tasting, worth fighting for, worth fixing roofs for, worth risking his life for. And God help him, she kissed with the same fiery passion that she fought with, her tongue pressing past his lips, teasing him, promising more delights, her hands clutching, tugging, stroking— He felt as if he would explode from the sensations she caused.

A kiss wasn't enough for either of them, and for a wild second he feared that with her, it would never be enough. Unable to stop, he clutched her firm ass and lifted her, still kissing her as he carried her to a stall filled with fresh hay. There he pushed her against the door, holding her tight. Her arms entwined about his neck, she lifted her legs and clamped them about his waist, drawing him closer. Through the layers of clothing he pressed his desire to her, his body afire for her. Kiss by kiss, fire to fire, they writhed against one another, held apart only by their clothing.

Just as he thought he could bear no more, she broke the kiss, throwing back her head, panting wildly. He couldn't resist the graceful line of her neck, so he trailed kisses up and down it, pressing his engorged cock against her.

"Max," she moaned, her hands sinking into his hair. "We canna . . . not here. They will— Someone will see us."

She'd barely whispered the words, lament in each one. But he heard her, and knew she was right. It took every ounce of self-possession he had, but he stopped kissing her and slowly, ever so slowly, allowed her feet to slip to the floor.

For a long moment they stood there, his forehead

against hers, their breaths still mingling, their heart-beats racing in time.

Finally he took a deep, long breath and pulled her to him once more, burying his face in the wild silk of her hair. Much of her braid had come loose and the curls clung to him, as if to hold him there.

His groin ached now, but he forced himself to ignore it. When he could speak, he lifted his head. "*Dorogaya moya*, that kiss . . ." He could find no words.

She chuckled, the sound husky and surprising. "That was more than a kiss. I . . . I'm sorry if I shocked you. It's been a long time since—" Her cheeks were as red as her hair.

He cupped her warm cheeks and kissed her nose. "For me, too. You did not shock me. You excited me very, very much."

"Well . . . good, then." She wet her lips, which stirred him again. "I'm glad you were so enthusiastic, too."

"I am still enthusiastic."

She glanced down. "So I see."

He chuckled. "I shall have to stay here for a while before I return to work." His smile slid. "*If* you wish me to go back to work. Murian, I did not intend to run roughshod over you and your villagers. I saw a need, and I thought to please you by addressing it. I suppose I was being too much a general."

"Hmm. I hear they can be very abrupt."

His lips quirked. "You heard right. But I should have spoken to you and the others first."

She brushed her hand over his chin, smiling when he caught her hand and kissed her fingers. "You're very kind, and I canna thank you enough for wanting to help."

"So we should continue with Widow Reeves's cottage?"

"Of course. But you should help her move her things somewhere safe. I would suggest you next address Widow Brodie's cottage. Whenever it rains, buckets of water leak down the chimney."

"That is good to know. Anything else?"

She told him the condition of the various cottages, and what repairs needed to be done on which. He offered suggestions as to which should be done first, and how to best make each cottage snug for the winter.

"You know a lot about repairs," Murian observed.

"An army travels from town to town, village to village, and you must make the best of whatever housing you are given. Sometimes you are given a home, sometimes a barn, and sometimes a tent in a field. If you do not know how to make basic repairs, you might awaken to water dripping on your forehead."

"Ah. I hadn't thought of that." She leaned against him, toying with one of the buttons on his shirt, soaking in his warmth. "I've been wondering about something."

"Aye?" He brushed a curl from her cheek, his fingers warm on her skin.

"Where did you get the lumber? The wagon is filled with it, but there's no mill for miles except Loudan's." A sinking feeling hit her stomach. "You dinna get it from there, did you? If you did, he'll be told, and it willna take him long to realize—"

"It is from Loudan, *da*, but not his mill. Now you

can have better roofs, better doors, and—" He frowned. "What do you call them? On the windows?"

"Shutters."

"Shutters," he repeated. "Many were broken and would not close."

"But the lumber," she repeated. "How can it be from Loudan if it's not from his mill?"

"You will not rest until I say, eh?"

She raised her brows.

"Stubborn, like a Romany. Fine, I will tell you. It is from the earl's barn."

A confused look crossed her face. "Why did Loudan have so much lumber in his barn?"

"No, no. It was not inside the barn. This wood, it was *from* the barn."

She gaped, and then gasped on a laugh. "You took the earl's barn apart? *All* of it?"

"*Nyet.* Just a portion of the back. But as we need more boards, we will take more."

"He willna notice?"

"Loudan has many barns and will never miss the back wall of this one, which is set far from the castle. It is very old and used for storage of forgotten things."

She could only shake her head.

"One groom noticed us, and it was when we took tools, for those are stored in the main barns and sheds. He started to say something, but Orlov growled at him."

"Growled? Like a dog?"

Max frowned. "*Nyet!* Orlov has a good growl. Like a bear."

She laughed, soft and merry, and it was all Max could do not to sweep her into his arms for another kiss.

"Oh, Max. Thank you. Thank you for coming today, for helping repair the cottages."

He couldn't have been more pleased than if he'd won an entire war. "It will take more than one day, of course, but we have more time, and we are glad to do it. This work is good for my men. They are used to a more physical existence than the castle offers."

"You dinna like to ride to the hunt?"

"In Oxenburg, we do not hunt foxes. We hunt wolves. They are much more cunning, and stronger and far more dangerous. My men are used to being challenged, and I fear they grow fat and lazy at Rowallen Castle." He eyed her with a considering gaze. "We are happy now, *nyet*?"

"*Da*," she replied, teasing.

He reached over and captured a strand of her hair, tugging it gently. "You remind me of my grandmother."

"Is that a good thing?"

"Oh yes. She is a strong woman. She never gives up, and she never hesitates to tell a man when he is wrong."

Murian's face heated, and she turned her face toward his hand, where his warm fingers brushed her cheek. What was it about this man that made her feel so— She didn't know *what* this feeling was. It was desire, curiosity . . . and something more.

Max tilted her face until her eyes met his. "So? You accept this gift from the earl?"

"If it will irk Loudan, of course I will accept. But if he ever finds out, he will be so angry."

"He deserves that and more. I consider it a payment for having to put up with his intolerable person. Every night at the dinner table, I must listen to that arse congratulate himself for his false accomplishments." Max swept a hot glance over her before taking a reluctant step back. "I suppose I should get back to work—unless you wish for another kiss."

She wet her lips, fighting a wild impulse to demand more—several more. But they had to remember where they were. "Not now."

Her voice was huskier than she'd intended, and his gaze instantly darkened. He took a step toward her, but she quickly moved away, stepping out of the barn and back into the sun. "There are too many people aboot." That, and she wasn't certain she'd be able to stop next time. She thought of them in the stall, of how she'd wrapped her legs about him, and how she'd felt his hardness through her chemise. She'd been wanton, yet she couldn't be sorry for a second of it; she'd enjoyed it all very much.

Max came to stand beside her in the sunshine. "You are right, there are too many people about." He lowered his voice, "But know this: I *will* kiss you again."

She fought a shiver, her throat so tight she couldn't swallow. "I hope so."

The words had been so easy to say, but now they hung between them, strong with meaning.

Max bent forward, his expression intent. "*Dorogaya moya*, you and I—"

"General!" One of the prince's men hurried up.

Max closed his eyes, taking a deep breath before he turned to his man. "*Da*, Orlov?"

Seemingly unaware he'd interrupted anything, the man bowed to Murian and then rattled off several sentences to the prince.

Max answered shortly. As soon as the man left, Max turned to Murian. "I'm sorry for the interruption. Orlov found some slate by the stream that will make good stepping-stones around the well. It is wet there, and very muddy."

"That's a good idea. We should rejoin the others. We've a busy day ahead of us."

He smiled, and for a moment, she thought he might say something more . . . but then with a warm smile that promised much, he left. Murian watched him go toward Widow Reeves's cottage. With nothing left to do, she went to find Widow MacDonald to help prepare their luncheon.

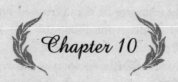

Chapter 10

Murian stacked two more broken shutters onto a pile. The thick woolen mittens she wore made the work slower than she liked, but the icy wind kept her from taking them off. As she bent to pick up more shutters the wind tugged at her hood, making her shiver. It was a cold, dreary morning, with gray clouds rolling overhead and the taste of snow in the air.

A heavy, wet snow, if one went by Widow Reeves's aching knee. Murian straightened and rubbed her stiff back, looking around the village with satisfaction. The small lane bustled with energy, everyone hurrying to do as much as they could before the weather arrived. Everyone but Max, who'd been forced to remain at the castle this morning to attend to his grandmother. Orlov said the prince walked a thin line, helping with the repairs while also being visible enough at the castle each day to keep the earl from becoming suspicious. Loudan apparently considered Max's men unimportant socially, and never inquired after them, no matter how many meals they missed.

She collected more broken shutters and carried them

to the pile, grateful her people would be warmer during this snow. A lot had been accomplished over the past five days, thanks to the prince and his men. Every morning a wagon filled with planks and assorted lengths of wood pulled into the village, and every afternoon an empty wagon pulled out. More often than not, the prince's men hunted along their way, so fresh meat was now so plentiful that Murian planned to smoke some for their winter stores.

As a glad shout arose, she looked up to see Max riding into the village, dressed in his jaunty red uniform and looking so comfortable on his horse that he seemed part of it.

His men grinned and waved. Orlov and Golovin put down their tools and hurried to Max, both of them talking at once.

So many demands for his attention—yet as he swung down from his horse, he looked around until he found her. Their gazes locked and Max smiled, a quiet, only-for-her smile that made her heart quicken.

She found herself smiling back. She was just wondering if she should go to meet him when Orlov drew Max's attention to Widow Brodie's roof. Moments later, Max took off his heavy overcoat and joined the men working there.

She watched for a while longer, but then realized how silly she must look, staring at Max while everyone else worked. She glanced around furtively and was glad no one seemed to have noticed, then turned back to the shutters. It would be a while before Max was free to talk with her, or anyone else.

This week had been very frustrating. She and Max had seen each other every day, but they had been able to speak only infrequently, rarely for very long, and never without interruption. If it wasn't his men coming to ask questions or to tell him of some accomplishment, it was her villagers doing the same to her.

It is ridiculous, she thought, throwing some shutters into the pile with more force than necessary. *It's as if we have thirty-some children, and they won't give us a moment alone.*

Still, even with so many unknowing chaperones, she and Max had managed to sneak off for a few moments by themselves, moments that had left her shivering with desire and aching with unanswered passion. If he were half as good a lover as he was a kisser—

A flush warmed her from head to toe. *I must stop thinking like this, or steam will rise from my skin.*

But the more kisses one had, the more one wanted. Especially deep, wild, barely contained passionate kisses that left a woman panting and weak-kneed. She hadn't felt this way since . . . well, ever, really. She wondered if she were being unfair to her memory of Robert, but she couldn't compare the extremely young and innocent girl who'd arrived at Rowallen Castle and married an equally young and innocent Robert Muir to the woman she was today.

Life had cut short her time with Robert, throwing her to the ground and saddling her with the responsibility of an entire village. She couldn't be distracted by a few kisses from a handsome stranger.

"Guid mornin', me lady!" Widow MacCrae and her

daughter walked past, puffing frosty breaths as they carried a heavy bucket of nails together. They grinned at her, their cheeks red from the cold.

"Good morning." Murian smiled in return. "I hope your cottage will be warmer with the repairs that have been made."

"I hope so, too," Widow MacCrae replied. "Widow Reeves's knee has been achin' somethin' fierce this mornin', so 'twill be a deep snow."

"Aye, 'tis a dreich day," Murian agreed. "Be careful on the path. 'Tis slick."

"We will, me lady," Widow MacCrae called over her shoulder.

Murian watched them carry the bucket to their cottage. There, one of Max's men—she thought his name was Pahlen—stood on the roof. A large, burly man, he was dressed in a fur-lined coat, hat, and boots. It must be colder in Oxenburg than here, for all of the soldiers had such garments. Certainly, none of them seemed to feel the cold the way the rest of them did.

Pahlen removed a piece of broken slate from the roof and threw it off the back of the house onto a growing pile. Will would come by later with a cart and carry the debris to the stables, where they'd crush the pieces into gravel to pave the yard in front of the stalls.

As Widow MacCrae and her daughter set down the bucket of nails, Pahlen hung his hammer on his belt and climbed down the ladder. He greeted Leslie and her girl with a teasing remark that left them both smiling shyly. Still talking, he scooped out a handful of nails and dropped them into a leather pouch hanging from his waist. Then, with what looked like the greatest of ease, he picked up four heavy boards and, balancing without effort on the narrow ladder, climbed back onto the roof. He set the boards down, placing them against the chimney, and then leaned over to say something to Widow MacCrae. A moment later, Murian heard the widow's laughter as it floated on the wind, her daughter's following.

"'Tis guid to hear tha'," Ian said from where he'd paused at her side. He rested his wheelbarrow of sand, his gaze on the MacCraes. "I've heard more laughter these last five days than in the last three months."

"I think the women have been missing a manly presence." She hastily added, "Not that you and Will are not—"

"Whist, lass." Ian chuckled. "I know wha' ye meant. I think of ye all as me dauwters."

"And is Will like a son to you, then?"

His smile faded as he regarded Will, who was leaning against the barn, arms crossed, sullenly regarding the work being done on Widow MacThune's roof. "He'd no' want me to call him 'son,' lassie. But I will say he'd be much better off if he'd been walloped more often when he was a bairn."

"Robert said he used to be close to Will, but by the time I reached Rowallen, they couldna speak without arguing."

"Aye, they were like brothers once. The old laird treated them equal, he did. But after his death, Robert decided 'twas best fer them both to remember their places. Will dinna like tha'."

"I'm not sure I blame him," Murian replied. "I half expected Robert to banish the lad, for he seemed determined to poke at Robert at every turn, while Robert never missed the chance to belittle Will. But why is Will angry now?"

"He wished to climb the roofs, bu' the prince tol' him no—tha' 'twould be better left to his men, as they ha' boots with soles made to grip slick surfaces. Ha' ye seen their boots? There's wee studs in the soles. I've ne'er seen the like."

"That explains why they walk so easily on the rooftops."

"Aye. So now the lad's poutin'." Ian watched Will kick at a stone near his foot. "He ha' no business bein' on the roof, anyway. He's clumsy, and can barely walk across a floor wi'oot fallin'."

Murian briefly closed her eyes. "And I suppose you told Will that?"

"Aye, which is no' wha' he wanted to hear."

"Poor Will." Since Robert had never had any patience with Will, she'd gone out of her way to be kind to him, and had perhaps spoiled him a bit. She wondered now if she'd made things worse. "He's an adult, and we should give him more responsibilities. Let him be the man of his own house, at least."

Ian slanted her a glance, looking suddenly uneasy. "He may be growing in age, bu' no' in wisdom."

"He deserves a chance, Ian."

"Life's no' always fair, lass. But mayhap ye're right. If it'll make him less moody, it canna be a bad idea." He grasped wheelbarrow handles. "I'd best get this sand to the well. We're puttin' in some slabs of rock to shore oop the wall where 'twas crumblin'." As he spoke, someone called his name, and he went on his way.

Murian watched him go, her gaze passing on to other cottages where work was being done, some by the prince's men, some by her widows, the older children joining in. Shutters were being attached to new window frames, solid wood doors replacing rotting ones, mud chinking smeared into open seams.

They'd made a good start, and she took pride in how well everyone worked together. When Max had asked her to make a list of their most pressing needs, she, Ian, and Widow Reeves had put their heads together and done so. And now those cottages were being seen to.

Murian found herself watching Max again, where he stood by Widow Brodie's cottage. Of all the cottages, hers needed the most work. It was the largest, and with five boisterous boys, she'd needed the space. But the roof was steeper and more given to leaks, the chimney had been made too shallow and belched smoke, the windows were horridly crooked, and the door was so small that even the widow had to duck to go inside—and she was a short woman, rounder than she was tall.

Now, Piotr Orlov stood on a barrel beside the cottage. Dressed head to toe in wool and fur, he held up two long boards. On the roof stood Max, his feet planted on the slanted surface. Murian watched as he bent down, grasped the boards, and hauled them onto the roof.

He said something to Orlov, and the sergeant turned

to hand up a small pouch of nails. Two more of the prince's men brought a heavy load of planks, which they placed on the ground near the wall, and then they stood back, watching the work. After a moment one of them called up to Max, pointing as if making a suggestion about the chimney.

Other leaders might not heed the advice of those they outranked, but Max listened, and even asked several questions. Finally, he nodded and then picked up one of the boards Orlov had handed him earlier, and walked up the steep roof, careful to put his weight on the rafters and not between. Murian had to admire his sure-footedness, for he didn't hesitate once, his movements purposeful.

Everything Max did, he did with calm decisiveness, as if he knew the answers everyone else only guessed at. It might annoy her, but she realized that Spencer would like him; they were two of a kind.

Max reached the fireplace, placed the board, and then braced himself against the chimney to hammer the piece into place. When he was done, he bent down to view his handiwork. Then, apparently satisfied, he made his way back to the ladder.

Orlov said something to him as he neared it, and whatever Max replied made Orlov flush, while the other men roared with laughter.

Max's eyes crinkled as he grinned. She was taken by the way he smiled. A joy in life, as if he savored each moment. Whatever it was, she responded to it, and it made her feel both warm and cold, almost as if—

"Yer eyes will fall oot of yer head from starin'."

Widow Reeves stood beside Murian, her gaze on Max as well. "No' tha' it wouldna be worth it."

Murian's face heated. "Good morning. I dinna see you there."

"That's because ye were busy gettin' an eyeful." Widow Reeves watched Max climb down the ladder. "And a nicer eyeful I canno' imagine."

"Nay, I—I thought there was a crack in Widow Brodie's window. Then I decided 'twas just the way light hit it, so there was no problem."

"O' course ye werena staring at tha' bonnie prince," Widow Reeves said soothingly, a grin breaking through. "Ye were jus' countin' the leaves in the trees. Innocent as a lamb, ye are."

"Something like that," Murian muttered.

Widow Reeves chortled. "Lass, ye'd ha' to be blind no' to notice a mon like tha'. And 'tis no' just the prince." Her gaze rested on the group of men standing at the foot of the ladder. "I dinna know wha' they drink in Oxenburg, bu' they seem to ha' more than their fair share of bonny lads."

Murian couldn't have agreed more. "So it seems."

"'Tis been a breath of fresh air to ha' the prince and his men wi' us, hasna it?"

"They've been most helpful."

"And kind." Widow Reeves glanced sideways at her. "I wouldna mind a flirtation wi' a mon like the prince."

"A—" Murian blinked. She'd been thinking the same thing. Perhaps it was a normal thing to wonder, then. "Would you, then?"

"Would I wha', me lady?"

"Would you flirt with one of the prince's men? I mean, if the opportunity arose."

"Oh, indeed I would." Widow Reeves sent a sly look at Murian. "Especially if I were younger. And perhaps a lady. And I knew a handsome prince."

Murian quirked a brow at Widow Reeves. "Are you suggesting *I* have a flirtation with *the prince*?"

"I'm sure no one would wonder at it if ye did. In fact, some of us might say ye're due some fun."

Murian's gaze found the prince and she watched him for a moment, some rather startling thoughts trickling through her mind. "I'm not sure a flirtation would be the best thing."

"And why no'?"

"I dinna need the complication."

"Wha' is so complicated aboot a flirtation? Especially when one of ye will be traipsin' away soon. Tha' makes it all the more perfect—ye already know how 'twill end, so there's no fuss and no one gets hurt." She shrugged. "I've been thinkin' of flirtin' wi' Mister Golovin, meself. He's no' much to look at, all beard and bristly brows, bu' I think he—"

"There ye are!" Widow Brodie waddled over. A round scowl of a woman, she was known for her cantankerous ways, though everyone knew her heart was gold.

"Lady Murian and I were just sayin' 'tis a fine crew ye've workin' on yer cottage," Widow Reeves said.

Widow Brodie sniffed. "Aye, if'n ye dinna need any peace and quiet. I ne'er heard such thumpin' and bangin'. 'Tis enou' to wake the dead!"

"They make oop fer it wi' the view," Widow Reeves returned. "Lovely men, all of them."

Widow Brodie didn't disagree, but still added, "They hammered on me roof until the mud began to fall fra' the chinks around me door."

"That can be fixed," Murian said. "I'll stop by later and we'll see to it."

"Humph," was all the widow would say.

"Iona," Widow Reeves said in an exasperated tone, "at least say ye noticed how they've been speakin' English, rather than their language? The prince told them 'twould be rude."

"Did he? Tha' is guid, I suppose. He also told them to remember there were ladies aboot, and no' to curse." Widow Brodie rubbed her snub nose, a twinkle in her eyes, though she didn't smile. "The prince must no' ha' met Widow MacDonald yet, or he'd ha' said there are *some* ladies present."

Widow Reeves laughed. "She's a— Och!" Her gaze locked on the street. "Who might tha' be?"

Murian followed Widow Reeves's gaze to see a rider approaching. For one horrible moment she thought perhaps they'd been discovered, but then Orlov stepped into the street and waved the man over. "It must be one of the prince's men," she said, relieved.

The man dismounted and tied his horse to the side of a cart, then made his way to the prince, who was just now climbing down from the roof.

The new arrival spoke to Max, who nodded and then spoke rapidly, as if giving orders. As soon as he finished, the new arrival saluted, leapt back into his saddle, and left.

Max handed his hammer to Orlov and pointed to the ladder, and then began to walk in Murian's direction.

A flush raced through her and she tugged her cloak closer about her. Her wind-tangled hair must look like a birds' nest, but there was little she could do about it now.

"It looks as if the prince wants a word wi' ye, me lady. Come, Iona." Widow Reeves linked arms with Widow Brodie. "I could use an opinion on the venison stew I'm makin.' It might need a bit more pepper."

Unable to resist the lure of venison stew, Widow Brodie allowed herself to be led away.

Determined not to appear too interested in the prince's approach, Murian resumed gathering more broken shutters for the growing pile.

Max watched Murian work. She was a beauty, this red-haired siren stacking broken shutters in a muddy street. He liked that she was not the hothouse variety of beauty, with pale skin and delicate hands, too fragile to enjoy life. Her hands were gracefully made but had strength. She knew hard work, this one, and she threw herself into any task before her with a dedication and passion he admired.

She tossed an armful of broken wood onto the pile, her hood lifted by the wind. Her hair, wild and stubborn, danced about her face, caressing her pink cheeks, her full lips, and tangling with her thick lashes.

She shoved her hair away, tucking it behind one ear

in a gesture so practiced that she probably didn't even realize she was doing it. In this village of black mud, worn cottages, and rotten wood, she was a fiery beacon of beauty. Just seeing her lips curve into a simple smile made Max yearn for her.

And smiled she had. When he'd first arrived in the village, he'd sought her out and she'd lit up like a flame touched to a candlewick, and he'd yearned to warm his hands on her. But after the barest second her expression had shuttered and she'd returned to her chore, buttoned tight behind hastily built walls.

He stopped at the fence that surrounded the yard where she worked, and leaned against it. "Good morning!"

She straightened and offered a polite smile. "Good morning. I see the earl dinna keep you overlong today."

"*Nyet*, he is hunting this morning with a few of his friends, none of whom I'd trust near me with a loaded rifle."

"I'm surprised the earl doesn't question where you go each day."

"I told him I was hunting." Max opened the gate and strode across the uneven ground toward her. "However, I said it in such a way that he decided I meant a woman. That, he understands."

"So he thinks you're oot chasing women six, seven hours a day." Humor warmed her eyes. "You have amazing stamina, Your Highness."

Her husky, lilting voice made him want to kiss it from her lips. "So I must." He captured her hand and tugged off her glove, turning her hand over so he could kiss her palm. "You look lovely today." She was all red-gold and pink beauty, as fresh and true as a newly minted coin.

She flushed, tugging her hand free and pulling her glove back on. "You look well, too, for someone who's chasing women all day."

"I'm only chasing one woman."

"Hmm." She eyed him for a moment, and he could see she was weighing her thoughts. Finally, she said, "Every time we try to . . . meet, we are interrupted."

"*Da*, we are challenged—but not beaten." He leaned closer. "I will never give up, *dorogaya moya*. Never."

Her lips quirked as she tried unsuccessfully to hide her smile. "Still, we've a lot of work to do here."

"We do. I am lagging a bit today, too. Last night, Loudan suggested cards after dinner, and I could not leave my grandmother alone. I did not wish to wake up and discover she'd wagered away my favorite horse, or the shoes from my feet."

Murian chuckled. "Did you ever find out what she lost to the earl?"

"*Nyet*. I will make her tell me, but I've been a bit preoccupied with all of this." He looked down the street, satisfied with the activity he saw. "We've made good progress."

"Aye, but there's so much more to be done. It seems endless, dinna it?"

"*Nyet*." He turned back to her. "It seems it will be done in far, far too short a time."

Her expression softened and, as if nervous, she wet her lips.

Bozhy moj, he burned to kiss the dewy dampness from her lips. But they were in the middle of the village, within view of every eye. *As always, dammit. Every day I come here, and I see her and I want her, and every day, we are surrounded by—*

"Guid morning, Lady Murian! Yer Highness!" A small, brown-haired woman stood at the edge of the street, a smudge of white plaster on her cheek.

Max managed a smile and a nod. "Widow Atchison."

She smiled politely, though her attention was on Murian. "Widow MacThune and I've been plasterin' Widow Reeves's cottage walls. I think the plaster is thick enou', and adding more would make it likely to crack. But Widow MacThune believes we should add another coat, mayhap two, against the cold. Can ye come and see wha' ye think?"

"Of course," Murian said instantly. "I'll be there in a moment."

"Thank ye." The widow curtsied and hurried off.

A strong hand encircled Murian's wrist. Surprised, she turned to find Max beside her, surveying the village.

"No one is looking," he said.

She frowned. "So?"

"We go." He turned and pulled her after him, walking between the cottages, then behind the one she'd been working on. "Is there anyone in this one?"

"Nay. They're all plastering, or helping your men—"

He kissed her, sweeping her to him with an abruptness that made her gasp with pleasure.

Murian melted against him, her arms slipping about his neck as she returned the kiss. He smelled of fresh winter air tinged with leather and wood, and behind that, the faintest hint of his spicy, exotic cologne.

His hands moved over her, insistent, demanding. He molded her to him, his hands cupping her bottom, pressing his hips to her.

She could feel his excitement as she pressed against him, tugging him closer. She was enveloped by him, by his scent, by his touch, by his kiss. And as overwhelming as it was, it wasn't enough. She wanted more. She was aflame, panting with longing and desire, her body aching with want.

His hands slipped from her bottom to her waist as he pressed his back to the cottage and slid to the ground, taking her with him. One moment they were standing, and the next, he was sitting with her in his lap.

Murian moaned as Max pushed open her cape and ran his hands over her gown, up her waist to her breasts. His touch was heavenly, and she writhed against him as he kneaded her breast, his thumb finding her nipple and gently flicking it. The man knew exactly what he was doing and she was glad for it, her body already aching for more.

He deepened the kiss and moved his hand from her breast to her waist, and then lower. He impatiently moved her skirts aside so he could cup her calf, and then slowly, oh so slowly, he slid his hand up her leg to her knee.

His hand was cooler than her skin, yet it burned with each inch he gained. It had been so long, *too* long, and she parted her knees. Grasping his hand, she guiding it to her thigh, desperately aware of her own aching wetness.

"*Dorogaya moya*," he whispered against her lips. "*Ti takaya krasivaya.*"

The huskiness of his voice stroked her passion further. She arched against him, gasping against his lips when his fingers brushed feather-light over her center.

She threw back her head and he kissed her neck, then moved to her ear, making her writhe as he gently stroked her, watching her, fighting to keep control over his desires. Never had he seen a more beautiful sight than Murian's face lost in passion. He increased his movements, but just as she pressed herself to his hand, someone called for Murian.

Her eyes flew open and she froze.

The call came again, this time closer, a woman's voice.

With a muffled curse, Murian shoved her skirts down and scrambled out of his lap.

His body aching, Max dropped his head back against the cottage wall and watched as she frantically adjusted her clothing and hair, managing only to muss them all the more.

She caught his gaze and flushed. "Someone calls."

"Someone always calls." He sighed. "Go. They will not rest until you arrive."

She managed a smile, her gaze meeting his. "Max, I'm sorry. But I canna ignore them when they need me."

"I know." He rose to his feet and dusted off his breeches.

She watched him, her brow creased. "But I want to share this with you. There's . . ." She took a breath and then said in a rush, "There's no harm in a mere flirtation."

He didn't know why, but the "mere" irritated him. He'd had many flirtations, and none of them had held so much promise, so much excitement, as this.

"Murian!" The voice now came from the cottage.

He managed a smile. "Go. You are needed."

She took two steps, but then stopped and looked back at him. "We will continue this later?"

There was so much hope in her eyes that his irritation disappeared. "*Da*, we will continue this later. Though it may take years, from the feel of it."

She grinned, a wide cheeky grin that made his heart tighten in an odd way. "Then it's a good thing you have stamina."

"The way this is going, I'll need all a man could possibly have."

She chuckled, a merry sound deep in her throat. And then she disappeared around the side of the cottage, leaving him alone.

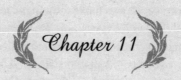

Chapter 11

Later than afternoon, Max and his men returned to Rowallen. Orlov and Pushkin rode with him down the main road to the castle, while the others took the empty wagon around the back of the estate where no one would see it.

Max dismounted in front of the castle, his men doing the same.

Orlov pulled off his gloves. "How much longer are we at Rowallen? We'll need another month, at least, if we're to finish the work in the village."

"I don't know exactly how long we will stay. If we're lucky, perhaps another two weeks." Saying it aloud made him realize how soon that was. *Two weeks is nothing.* The thought made him faintly melancholy, which surprised him.

"We will get as much done as we can." Orlov rubbed his lower back. "If we do not die before then."

Pushkin looked at his thumb, which was bruised and swollen. "*Da,* the hammers we took from the barn were poorly constructed. The head turns just as one strikes."

Orlov snorted. "They did no such turning for me."

"They worked well for me, too," Max said. "Admit it —'twas not the hammer, but the hammerer."

Pushkin flushed. "*Nyet*, 'twas the wretched hammer. It's not balanced right, and the head—"

"*Da, da.* It turns just as one strikes." Orlov laughed. "You will never convince us, brother. Best you accept the truth, that you have the coordination of a drunk, blind duck."

Pushkin sputtered.

"Or perhaps," Orlov mused, "it was the lack of attention you were giving the hammer, and were instead bestowing upon Widow Grier?"

While Pushkin muttered under his breath, Max glanced up at the gray sky, which matched the castle's ancient stone. "It may snow soon, perhaps before the night is out."

"If it is deep, we may not be able to return to the village tomorrow," Orlov said.

Max's jaw tightened. "We will still go. Our horses are used to such travel."

"Aye, but we could not take the wagon for the wood."

Max couldn't argue with that, but he wouldn't stay away from Murian come a hundred snows. *Not when there's so little time left.*

"Meanwhile, we've some scouting to do. I wish to know the habits of the footmen and guards Loudan employs. I want numbers, patterns, paths marched, evening versus day, schedules—all of it."

Orlov and Pushkin exchanged glances. "So," Pushkin said, "we go to war."

"It is more reconnaissance than war. But if all goes well, Loudan will never know he was . . . beaten . . . until we are gone."

"We plan a sneak attack?" Pushkin asked.

Max nodded. "We must regain my grandmother's lost article, whatever it is."

Orlov's brows rose. "You still do not know?"

"I will find out today. I've been much too soft on her."

"It will be good to see the earl brought low." Orlov scowled. "I do not like our host. He watches us as if he thinks we will take his silver."

"Aye," Pushkin added. "I am tempted to slip a fork into my pocket, just to see his expression."

"He deserves to be made a fool of," Orlov agreed.

"So he does," Max agreed. *More than you know.* "I must go make an appearance so our host does not get suspicious. He thinks my absence is due to my wooing a local farm girl. For now, we will let him think that."

"Good. It will make his fall all the more surprising to him." The sergeant cocked a brow at Max. "Agreed, General?"

"Agreed. He will fall hard and we will right his wrongs." Which would satisfy Max's growing need to make the lout pay for what he'd inflicted on Murian and her people.

As a prince, he should not allow her circumstances to impact his duty here in Scotland, but as a man, he couldn't ignore the deep anger that burned through him every time he thought of the earl's perfidy in getting control of Rowallen and her lands.

"Orlov, I am to receive some messages this afternoon. Be on the lookout for them. I will reply in the morning, by the same courier. If the men wish to include letters home, they may do so."

"Very good, General."

"*Spasiba.*" Max bade his men good-bye and strode up the walk to the castle.

The gray skies reminded him of Murian's eyes, which were so changeable. Silver when she was excited, darker and stormy when she was angry, light and shimmering when she was happy, gleaming and fey when she was in the throes of passion—as variable as her moods.

He looked at the stone castle and could easily imagine her here, walking up the cobblestone drive to the wide stone steps, wearing a gown befitting her station, her red hair dressed and gleaming in the sunlight. His jaw tightened when he compared that to how she'd looked when he'd left her an hour ago. She'd worn a dull brown gown with mud upon the hem, old boots on her feet, her braid loose from working outside in the wind, her hands red and chapped from the cold—the contrast between what should be and what was burned into his soul. She did not deserve the life Loudan had consigned her to.

As Max reached the steps, two liveried footmen sprang to attention and, with obviously rehearsed effort, swung the huge oak doors wide.

Max walked into the foyer and allowed two more footmen to take his hat, coat, and gloves, which they did with obsequious bows and murmurs. Max tried not to grimace, since he knew such rehearsed grandeur said a lot about what Loudan thought was owed to himself and his position.

Power was a fickle mistress. She enticed men to think of themselves as being of more value than others, when the reality was far different. Max had seen too many brave men on the battlefield who owned nothing more than the swords strapped to their ragged belts, and too many weak men bedecked in a prince's armor, to believe in such nonsense. Nobility was a joke man played on his brethren, one that set Max's teeth on edge.

Of course, some of his beliefs might have come from his mother, who'd been a commoner and a Gypsy before Max's father, the King of Oxenburg, had seen her and been instantly smitten. He'd rewritten the laws of Oxenburg to make the marriage legal, and had proudly proclaimed her his queen. As Max grew old enough to see her as more than his mother, he realized that although she hadn't been raised to it, she was an excellent queen. She worked tirelessly to help those with less, and she wasn't afraid to take on some of their country's ruling nobility in the process. And the people loved her for it.

Max admired her more than anyone else, and he'd come to agree with her view of the uselessness of some of those born into the noble class. Not all of them, of course, for some recognized the responsibility that came with their power. But some thought that merely being born into the velvet gave them rights far beyond what was intended by man or God.

Fools. He'd seen the cost of allowing individuals to ignore compassion and honor in their quest for power, and the result was bloody. And Loudan was just such a fool.

Max walked to the stairway that led to his bedchamber, pausing to examine a particularly old set of armor. Dented and scratched, it had known many fights, and he couldn't help but wonder where the owner was now. He traced the scar on his chin, thinking he, too, looked battered and worn. Yet he didn't feel so. His confidence had grown with each battle, and his determination to do what was necessary grew firmer as well. *Murian has the right of it; no matter how long it takes, one can never give in. Never stop striving. Have stamina.*

He laughed softly.

"Your Highness?"

He turned to find Loudan's butler, a short, stout man named MacGregor, standing behind him. "*Da?*"

The butler bowed. "His lordship has been looking for you. Shall I tell him you've returned?"

"I have been riding all morning and must bathe before I see him. Let him know I will join him as soon as possible."

"Yes, Your Highness. Shall I have a bath sent to your room?"

"Please."

The butler sent a sharp look at one of the footmen, who hurried off. "A bath will be drawn immediately."

"Thank you." Max started for the stairs, but then stopped. "My grandmother, the Grand Duchess Nikolaevna, do you know where she might be?"

"She may be in the west salon."

"Where is that?"

"Down the hall, Your Highness, and then to the left. It is the last set of doors on the right." The butler cast a swift glance around and then said in a low tone, "There's a fire in the west salon, and the room is quite small, so it is warmer. The older ladies sometimes gather there in the afternoons."

"And what do they do there?"

An indulgent smile flickered over MacGregor's plump face. "They sleep, Your Highness."

"Ah." That sounded very much like Tata Natasha. "I shall let her know I have returned, and will then retire to my bedchamber."

"Very good, Your Highness. The bath will be ready when you arrive."

Max made his way to the west salon. A footman was stationed at the door, which he silently opened. As soon as Max walked through, the footman closed it.

The west salon was indeed smallish, and decorated in shades of deep plum and cerulean blue. In one wall were set long, thin windows, over which hung deep-red curtains that blocked out a good bit of light. Here and there were small groupings of chairs covered in plum velvet with embroidered pillows.

Right now only one elderly lady inhabited the salon and, as MacGregor had warned, she was fast asleep in a chair by the fire, snoring loudly. Grinning, Max crossed to where Tata Natasha slept and pulled up a chair next to hers, then placed his hand on hers.

She snored away.

He patted her hand. "Tata Natasha?"

She stirred, her head dropping to one side. Almost immediately, she began to snore again.

He leaned closer. "*Tata Natasha!*"

Her eyes flew open and she sat bolt upright, staring around the room as if she'd never seen it before.

"Tata?"

Her watery gaze flickered to him. "Oh. It's you." She stifled a yawn. "I was—ah, I was just wondering about dinner."

"Were you, now?"

She cut him a hard glance. "I did not see you come in."

He hid a grin. "You were sleeping. I did not wish to awaken you, but I must speak with you."

"Sleeping? I was not sleeping."

"You were snoring."

"Pah! I never snore."

"How would you know?"

She fixed a gimlet gaze on him. "Because if I did, then one of the many men I have slept with would have mentioned it."

He sighed. "Ah, Tata. You always try to shock me."

"The truth has that effect on some people." She collected her shawl. "So, what do you want?"

"You already know."

She managed to look both furtive and put upon, and she surprised him by saying, "I am glad you are here. I have something to discuss with you, as well." She poked a finger into the hand that rested on hers. "Where have you been? Every morning after breakfast, you leave. No one sees you until dinner, and then there are so many people about that private speech is impossible."

"It is no secret where I have been. I've been hunting."

"Pah. I know better. And I am not the only one to think that an untruth. Loudan keeps asking where you are, and I do not know what to tell him."

Max raised his brows. The earl had pretended to accept Max's excuses. Was it a ploy? "What did our host say?"

"Something about never knowing a man to hunt so much."

Max considered this. "The next time he says something, you are to tell him I find the women of Scotland fascinating."

Tata Natasha's eyes narrowed. "You are not here to flirt with some nameless chit from some village. You are here to help me."

He regarded her through half-closed eyes. "I am not the sort of man to flirt with a nameless woman from any type of domicile. But that is neither here nor there. Now, we will speak of the thing you lost to Loudan. What was it?"

"You do not need to know—"

"If you want me to find it, then I do."

She fiddled with the corner of her shawl.

"Come, Tata. We know Loudan cheats at cards. Whatever you lost, it is not your fault. I have a plan to search for this thing, but I have to know what I am looking for, *nyet*?"

She said sullenly, "I suppose you will have to know sooner or later."

"Now. I would know it this minute."

She tapped her fingers on the arm of her chair. "If I tell, will you promise you will not yell at me?"

"I will not yell."

"Nor lecture me about gambling, for you can't say anything I haven't already told myself."

"I will not comment at all, except to say I will begin looking for this object immediately."

She tied the ends of her shawl into a knot, then untied them. Finally, she said, "Fine. I will tell you, but first, you should know how it happened. I met Lord Loudan at Lady MacDaniel's town house in Edinburgh, the day I arrived in this country three months ago. You were not available, so I did not see you until a few days later."

"And?"

She scowled blackly. "I was tired when I arrived, exhausted by the trip. I should never have agreed to go to Lady MacDaniel's rout, but . . ." She shrugged. "I was bored, so I went."

"And?"

"There was much food, and much to drink. And there was gaming. Loudan joined my table and he kept losing ridiculous hands. I thought he was a bad player."

"Instead of a very, very good one."

"*Da.* I got carried away. In order to match a wager, I began to throw various items onto the card table."

"What items?"

"Some rings, a bracelet, things like that." She bit her lip. After a moment, she said in a voice so quiet, he barely heard her. "I do not care if I get those back;

they can be replaced. But there is one thing that must be returned."

"*Da?*"

"A tiara."

"And?"

"That is all."

His brow cleared. "Just one tiara, then?" At her nod, he said, "That is not so bad. I'm sure it was expensive, but it can be—"

"*Nyet!* You do not yet understand. It wasn't just any tiara, it was a *specific* tiara." She took a long breath before she said in a calmer voice, "You cannot replace it, so we must get it back. I should never have brought it with me, but your mother wore it to Alexsey's wedding, and then—"

"*Izvini!* Did you say Mother wore it to Alexsey's wedding?"

Tata nodded cautiously.

"*Bozhy moj*, you're talking about the queen's crown!"

She winced. "You said you would not yell!"

"You lost the royal crown! What else could I do?" He rubbed his forehead, where a dull ache grew.

"I didn't mean to. I was certain I would win."

"I cannot believe this. You lost the queen's crown in a game of chance. The first queen of Oxenburg wore that crown over four hundred years ago and—" He scowled. "You knew this, and yet you still wagered it. How in the hell did you end up with Mother's crown, anyway?"

"She wore it to your brother's wedding and, as we were traveling together, she stored it with my jewelry. I forgot to return it to her."

"That was a year ago."

"Something like that, *da*." She shrugged. "I didn't wear it often."

"Often? You're not supposed to wear it at all! *Ever*."

"Why not? I have some earrings that are lovely with it. As if they were a set."

His jaw tightened so much, his head began to ache. "That bloody crown was not yours to wear, and it definitely wasn't yours to wager. It belongs to the people of Oxenburg."

Tata Natasha looked slightly shamefaced. "I wasn't thinking clearly that night."

He leaned back in his seat and crossed his arms. "Drinking, were you?"

Her parchment cheeks took on a dull red sheen. "Vile stuff, whiskey. But that's all they drink in this forsaken country—whiskey, whiskey, whiskey. Pah!"

Max sighed. "So, you lost the crown, Loudan will not sell it back to you, and you decided to involve me."

"I thought Loudan might agree to return it, if he feared you might get tired of his time-wasting and decide to just take it. But you do not stay in the castle long enough for him to even know you are here! You have ruined my plan."

"It's a crown, Tata. One made to rest upon a queen's brow. One that a Gypsy with no talent for cards and less head for drink should have left alone."

"I'm very good at cards," she said, clearly offended. "Usually. The drinking, not so much."

"That tiara should have been returned to the palace months ago."

"I like wearing it," she said defensively.

"But you *cannot*. It's not for—" He threw up his hands. "*Bozhy moj*, you know and you do not care. You are a stubborn woman."

Her gaze narrowed. "You said you would not berate me."

He took a deep breath and, for the first time, noticed her eyes were glistening as if with tears. Instantly, his irritation disappeared. She was a troublesome woman, his grandmother, but she was a good woman, her intentions always pure even when her actions were not. "I'm sorry, Tata Natasha. I will stop."

Silence rested upon them for a moment, both of them thinking about their predicament. Finally, she blurted out, "Will you tell your father?"

He should, he knew. His grandmother had a contentious relationship with her son-in-law, and for good reason. But Max shook his head. "If we can get it back, then there will be no need. We will find our way out of this."

"We must." She scowled. "I will turn Loudan into a newt! Or I will once I have the crown back. If I do it sooner, he cannot tell us where it is."

"Fine, you can turn him into a newt then. I shall have to think this through. Figure out the best way to set about looking for it."

"You're going to steal it back?"

"It's either that or fight him for it, and that is not acceptable."

"Why not?" she asked indignantly.

"Because I cannot fight the earl unless he challenges me first."

"Which will never happen, unless you stop gallivanting about the countryside!" She scowled. "I'd have been better off bringing along a mastiff to frighten the earl."

Max raised his brows. "So I was to intimidate Loudan like a dog?"

"Intimidate is such an ugly word. I merely wished him to know he couldn't treat the royal house of Oxenburg so. He's never threatened me, not aloud, but—" She frowned, looking pale and ancient.

Max found himself gripping the arm of his chair much tighter than necessary. "He is very careful not to confront anyone in public. This I know of him."

"He is very sly," she agreed. "But you do not have to be sly."

"I've told you I cannot—"

"—fight him, I know. I know. But you can glare at him, and scowl. Make him think you are the strongest, most ill-tempered man in all of Oxenburg. I want him to think that if you get angry enough, you will rip him apart, limb by limb, and eat the meat from his bones while spitting his liver at the full moon and—"

"Tata!" He laughed softly, holding up a hand. "I will never spit his liver, or anyone else's, anywhere." He leaned back in his chair. "You should have told me about the crown before we arrived."

"I know. But I kept thinking I could get that arse to sell it back to me."

"Why should he? He has complete control over you. I'm sure he finds having a grand duchess dance to his tune far more satisfying than some gold in his purse." Max crossed his arms, his gaze moving to the fire. *Perhaps it's more than mere satisfaction. Perhaps Loudan sees more profit in holding Tata Natasha captive than in selling her back the crown. Hmm.*

He realized his grandmother was watching him and forced a smile.

Her black gaze narrowed. "Why are you here?"

"In Scotland? Because you said you feared outlaws and needed an escort."

"*Nyet.* Now that I think on it, you agreed to accompany me rather quickly. Too quickly, if you ask me."

"So now I'm to be derided because I agreed to escort you and didn't make you beg? Tata, there is no pleasing you." He rose with a smile. "I must go; I ordered a bath before dinner. It will be waiting."

She pursed her lips, her dark eyes shrewd. "You are here for your own purposes, aren't you?" She must have seen something in his face, for she slapped her knee. "Ha! I should have known. What are you up to?"

"Nothing you need concern yourself with, so don't waste your time with conjecture. We are both here, we both have things to accomplish, and we both have the best interests of Oxenburg at heart." He took her hand and bowed over it. "That said, I promise to spend more time here, speaking with Loudan."

She appeared mollified. "Will you scowl at him? Make him fear you?"

"I rather think he already does. He is not stupid—

which is a pity for the rest of us." He kissed her fingers. "Until dinner."

She clasped his hand between hers. "Thank you, Max."

"You are most welcome, Tata." He kissed her forehead and left. *This complicates things yet more.* As he approached the door, Orlov appeared with a packet in his hand.

"Ah! Finally."

The sergeant handed the packet to Max, then glanced at the ever-present footmen before saying in his native tongue, "Several of the men have missives for the return. They are composing them now."

"Good. Tell the messenger he will be able to leave in the morning."

Orlov nodded and left, and Max entered his bedchamber. After a day of hammering and sawing, and then dealing with his grandmother, his bedchamber was gloriously quiet and warm, the fire crackling in the fireplace, a small tray with a decanter of whiskey waiting near his drawn bath.

He poured himself a glass and sat in a chair near the flames, then opened the packet. Inside were four letters. Three from his family: his father, his mother, and his brother Nikolai. Max was fairly sure he knew what was in each of them: his father would remind him of the duty before him and require an immediate return to Oxenburg; his mother would worry whether he was eating well and how he was dealing with his cantankerous grandmother; and Nik's letter would be filled with seemingly senseless gossip, but a few sentences would be subtly phrased to pass on information that couldn't be safely committed to paper.

It had been years since Max's oldest brother, the future king, had said what he really thought about anything without carefully weighing every word. Max supposed that was a good thing, as an effective king must know the art of subtlety, but he missed the carefree ways of the brother he'd grown up with. The years had changed Nik. Had changed all of them.

For some reason Max thought of Murian, alone in the woods with no family of her own, and his throat inexplicably tightened. Of course, she had Ian, Will, and her band of widows, but they were not family, and Max thought that while she took care of them, none of them had the standing to take care of her. No matter what, she was still "Lady Murian." It was sad and yet she wasn't the least bit maudlin about it.

She'd made the best of a dire situation and had made her retainers her family, so that she was now surrounded by love and respect. *It is why they mean so much to her; why she means so much to them.*

That, he decided, was bravery. Adaptation without bitterness.

The last letter rested in his hand. Stamped as a military dispatch, it came from the war front. He broke the seal, raising his brows in surprise when a small slip of paper fluttered to his lap. He picked it up and read the scrawl, which he'd seen only twice before, both times during particularly hot battles.

Max frowned as he read the note; then he opened the letter and perused it carefully from top to bottom.

When he was done, he committed the address to memory and fed the letter and the slip of paper to the flames.

The fire curled about the paper, turning the edges toasty brown before, with a flare, it began to rapidly travel over the paper, turning the scrawl to black ash. Now, in addition to finding Lord Robert's journal, they also needed to find the Oxenburg crown, and a lost piece of information. Nik believed that information was here at Rowallen, and Max was beginning to agree. The Earl of Loudan was up to something—but what?

He sat back and watched the last of the missive burn, the ashes breaking free and floating up the chimney, out of sight.

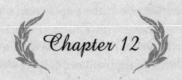

Chapter 12

The next morning, Orlov swung down from his horse, glancing at the sky. "The snow won't hold off much longer."

"*Da*," Max agreed. "We are fortunate it's held off as long as it has." Though he would have found a way to the village this morning if there'd been twenty feet of snow.

Demidor came to take the reins of Max's horse, leading the horses to the barn. Max tugged his collar higher and looked around the village. It was bitterly cold today, everyone huddled deep in their winter coats and cloaks. Widows Reeves and Atchison waved to Golovin, who was heading toward them. Widow MacCrae was standing by the well, Pahlen already hurrying to take the heavy bucket from her hand. Widow Brodie and her sons were walking into the village carrying as much firewood as they could, while Will brought a bucket of steaming milk from the barn.

There was no sight of Murian. Max walked to the well, where Widow MacCrae stood with Pahlen. "Good morning," Max said. "Where is Lady Murian this morning? I wish to speak to her about needed supplies."

"She's in Widow Atchison's house, helpin' wi' the plaster."

Ignoring Pahlen's interested look, Max made his way to Widow Atchison's small cottage. As he walked, he could hear voices mixed between the ringing of hammers. The villagers were busy working indoors today, using the new supplies to weatherproof as well as they could. *Like ants preparing for winter.*

The night before, he'd sat through an interminably boring dinner between two women who obviously thought themselves cultured and witty. As he listened to them expound on their travels, complain about minutiae, mock others sitting within hearing distance, and improperly quote authors they'd never read and discuss art they didn't understand, he'd found himself wondering how they would have reacted if their loved ones had been cruelly murdered, their positions in society lost, their fortunes gone—in a word, if they'd found themselves in Murian's situation. Would they have dried their tears, clenched their jaws against fate, pinned up their hair, and taken full responsibility for their household servants?

It had taken all of his self-control not to throw his napkin to the table and leave his empty-headed dinner companions to their empty conversation. Had his grandmother not been present he might have done just that, for he cared not one whit what such people thought.

It wasn't the first time he'd found social drivel unbearable. Before the war, as the crown princes of Oxenburg, he and his brothers had attended countless state dinners and dress balls, and had spent hours and hours engaged in inane, pointless conversations. Given his position, it had been expected, and while he'd never found them all that amusing, he hadn't minded doing his duty.

But war had changed him, just as it changed all men who engaged upon the battlefield. It made him more appreciative of small things—clean sheets, a smile, the smell of a woman's freshly washed hair, the deep beauty of the quiet. But it also made him find everyday tasks almost unbearably unimportant.

How could a man go from fighting tooth and nail for the freedom of one's country, facing mud, blood, pain, and the loss of friends and companions day after day, to sitting beside a fireplace discussing whether to ask the cook to serve roast or a duck for dinner? Max had seen many soldiers lose their way when they tried to rejoin the life they'd had before the war. War changed a man, and he had to accept those changes, and find a deeper purpose to his life than he'd had before.

Knowing Murian had made Max aware that war wasn't the only traumatic experience that could do this. She had experienced a huge upheaval, and had dealt with loses and a sudden, drastic change in circumstances that must have changed her, too. If Spencer returned and could set things to rights, would it be hard for her to return to her previous life? Would it be enough? He wasn't sure.

Behind him, he could hear Orlov ordering the men to their stations for the day, yelling for Golovin to bring more wood for the final repair of Widow Brodie's roof.

Reaching Widow Atchison's house, Max heard the murmur of female voices as he knocked on the door.

"Come in!"

He pushed the door open and stepped inside, where he found Murian and Widows Atchison and MacThune using large spoons as trowels for smoothing plaster over a newly repaired wall, the fire crackling cozily nearby.

Widow Atchison's eyes widened on seeing him. Small, brown-haired, and wren-like, she was one of the quietest of the widows. Max didn't think he'd heard her speak yet. She elbowed Widow MacThune and said with a gasp, "Och, 'tis the prince!"

Murian, who was engrossed in plastering, turned around. A pleased look flashed through her eyes, and he found himself smiling in return.

"Good morning." Murian was dressed in her usual colorless gown, sturdy boots upon her feet. Even without a single bit of finery other than her glorious red-gold hair and silver eyes, she shone like a rare jewel.

"Good morning." He pulled off his gloves and tucked them in his pocket, noting that one strand of her hair was tipped with white plaster.

The two widows dipped curtsies, as Murian pointed to a wooden bowl filled with plaster. "We're glad you came, as now you can help."

"It looks as if you're doing a very good job on your

own." He crossed the room to her side. He clasped his hands behind his back and bent to examine the plasterwork. "*Da*. Very good."

She sniffed. "Of course it's good."

"Except you missed a spot here." He pointed. "And here. And h—"

She tapped his finger with her makeshift trowel, leaving a cold dab of plaster on it. "Now you can fix those spots."

The other two tried not to laugh and failed.

"I am not afraid of a little plaster." Max fixed the spot. "There. Now, it is perfect."

"You're verrah talented at plasterwork."

"I am very talented at many things, Lady Murian. Plasterwork is only one of them."

Widow Atchison bit her lip as if to stop a grin, and busied herself stirring the plaster in the bowl, while Widow MacThune stared, waiting for Murian's response.

Murian pressed her trowel into his hand. "As you're so talented, perhaps you can fix the rest of the spots we missed? I warn you, 'tis not so easy as you might think."

"We shall see." He placed the trowel on the edge of the bowl and tugged off his coat and muffler, hanging them over a chair. The heavy mahogany chair was covered in red velvet and decorated with an unseemly amount of gold embroidery. Two matching chairs flanked the fireplace. Apparently Murian's cottage hadn't been the only one to benefit from Rowallen's loss.

He picked up the trowel and turned to the wall, touching up the few uneven spots here and there, while Murian stood at his side, her eyes dancing with humor.

"Och, now 'tis you who's missed a spot." She didn't try to disguise the satisfaction in her voice as she pointed at the wall with her trowel.

He gave her a stern look. "I haven't gotten to that portion yet."

Her lips quirked, and he couldn't look away from her mouth. No other woman had ever possessed a more kissable or bewitching mouth. Pink and plump and temptingly saucy, it deserved to be—

"Och, I almost fergot!" Widow MacThune put down her trowel and wiped her hands. "We're to help Ailsa with her bairn while she plasters Ian's cottage."

Widow Atchison looked up from loading her trowel. "We are?"

Murian looked over her shoulder, surprise clear on her face. "Why would Widow Grier need help? She told us at breakfast that her bairn'll sleep until 'tis time for him to eat. We canna help with that."

"Yes, but we promised, dinna we?" Widow Mac-Thune looked at Widow Atchison.

Widow Atchison blushed, but managed to say, "Aye."

"There! So I told ye." She tossed her makeshift trowel into the bucket, wiped her hands on a rag, and picked up her cloak.

Murian shook her head. "Could some of the older children watch Widow Grier's bairn and—"

"Och, nay." Widow MacThune shook her head firmly. "We must go."

Murian plopped her hands on her hips. "You canna stop plastering while we have an entire bowl of—"

The door closed.

Murian couldn't believe it. They'd left her alone . . . with Max.

She shot him a glance and found him still calmly smoothing the plaster with his trowel.

"It seems your friends have left." He stepped back and eyed the wall before turning to place the spoon across the bowl lip.

"They have things to do." Murian wondered if Widow Reeves had spoken to the others and suggested they leave her alone with the prince. *More than likely.*

Murian didn't know whether she was glad of this new freedom or not. It was certainly intoxicating to think of being in Max's presence without worrying about being interrupted. She hadn't been able to stop thinking about him after their last encounter, when he'd made her writhe with such need—even now, shivers traveled through her at the memory.

He came up behind her, slipped his arms about her, and gently pulled her to him. His cheek rested against her head, his breath stirring the hair at her temple. She leaned against him, soaking in his warmth, his strength.

He rubbed his cheek against her hair. "You have plaster in your hair, *milaya moya.*"

"I know. My hair willna stay in its pins. 'Tis one of the trials I must bear."

He chuckled, the sound rumbling in his chest. "I like the plaster; it shows me how you'll look when you're older and your hair is no longer red."

She winced. "I dinna want to think aboot that."

"*Nyet.*" He turned her in his arms so that she faced him. "You will be just as beautiful as you are now."

She slipped her arms about his waist. "I dinna believe a word you say, but it's still lovely to hear."

He brushed her cheek with the back of his fingers, his green eyes intent. "I meant every word."

She smiled and, savoring the heat slowly building between them, rested her cheek on his shoulder. She liked this—being held and kissed by a man she respected and admired. Passion raced through her every time their eyes met, too.

And that was enough. It would have to be. She'd come to realize over the last few weeks that she needed to preserve every bit of herself for her people. Perhaps when Spencer returned and things were back to normal . . .

She closed her eyes. There was no more normal. Robert was gone. Her old way of life was gone. And while Max had reawakened her passions, he would soon be gone, too.

Still, there was nothing wrong with this—with touching and being touched. The memories could give her strength when things again grew difficult, as they were bound to. *So what harm could it do?*

But she knew what harm. She was not a woman who gave lightly. When she cared, she cared deeply. When she loved, it was with all her body and soul. Losing

Robert had been brutal, and it had taken every ounce of strength she possessed to meet the obstacles she and her people had faced.

And they weren't done—not even close. Even if by some miracle she managed to find Robert's journal, and it proved all she thought and hoped and prayed it would, Max would still leave. And she'd be here, starting a new, and perhaps just as difficult, stage of her own life. She fought a sigh and lost.

Max tightened his hold as he heard that deep sigh. Over the last few weeks, he'd glimpsed that expression in her eyes and had recognized it for what it was—a flicker of tension, of worry. She was responsible for so many others, and he knew she felt as if she were walking atop a fence, wobbling from step to step, terrified of letting down those she loved.

But he could see she was resilient, and he knew she'd find a way to address the troubles life handed her.

She pulled back and looked up at him. "I wish we'd met some other place and time."

He didn't pretend not to understand her. "It would be easier, *nyet*? But we have what we have. It must be enough." He slipped a hand into her hair and tilted her face to his, trailing a kiss from her temple to the corner of her lips.

She closed her eyes, some of the tension leaving her face.

Perhaps this will help remove the rest. He captured her lips, gently but insistently, teasing them until she opened to him like a flower before a summer rain.

She tasted of sunshine and innocence, and his body

ached for her touch. He swept her against him, lifting her from her feet, all gentleness gone as he devoured her sweetness, kissing her until she gasped against his lips. "Max, please—"

A noise arose outside. Voices raised, the jangle of a horse's bridle.

Max ignored it, trailing kisses down her cheek, to her neck—but Murian went still.

She placed a hand on his chest. "We've a visitor. Did all of your men come with you?"

He sighed and straightened, covering her hand with his own. "*Nyet*. I left Demidor and Raeff at Rowallen to await a courier who is to arrive today."

Her gaze went to the window. "Do you think that's one of them?"

"Perhaps. But do not worry. If they need us, they will come and get us. You may not have noticed, but no one seems shy about interrupting us."

She stepped away, pulling her hand free. "I'm not teasing, Max. We are hidden in the woods for a reason. You saw what Loudan did to the villages that assisted us. He would burn our houses, cut loose our stock, dump our food stores into the stream, and leave us to starve and freeze."

"If Loudan or any of his men had arrived, you'd have heard pistol shots. All of my men are armed, and they've been told to be on the ready. But nothing will soothe your fears until you see for yourself. Come. Get your cloak." He tugged on his gloves and retrieved his coat and muffler, while she hurried to fetch her cloak.

She swung it around her shoulders and reached the door before him.

He caught her hand as she reached for the door. "When you know who has come, and are no longer concerned, may we return here? I am not finished talking to you."

"Talking, eh?" Her lips quirked, and she said with a wry smile, "Good, for I am not done talking to you, either."

He moved his hand from hers and opened the door. "After you, my lady."

She went outside, Max following. He closed the door behind him and looked down the road. "Ah, it is Demidor. The courier must have come early." Max turned to Murian. "See? We could still be talking."

Her lips quirked, but she didn't yield. "Go see what he wants."

He sighed as if much put-upon. "Fine. Wait here. I'll be right back."

Murian watched Max stride up the street. As soon as Demidor saw him, the younger man hurried forward, and the two exchanged words. At one point, Max glanced at Murian before answering a comment from his guard.

The look sparked hope. *He's had news that will help us. I'm sure of it.*

The younger man withdrew a packet from his coat and handed it to Max.

A prick of snow touched Murian's cheek. Surprised, she glanced up but could see no more. The sky, though, was solid gray. It would start within the next day or two. She could taste it.

When she looked back at Max, Demidor was leading his horse to the stable while Max was tucking the missive into his coat as he returned to her.

"What's happened?" she asked as soon as he was near enough to hear.

Max shook his head against the worry in her eyes. "*Nyet.* It is good news. Demidor overheard the earl tell some of the other guests that the singer he has been trying to bribe into visiting Rowallen has confirmed."

Her eyes flashed with instant excitement and a twinge of jealousy hit Max, an uneasy truth settling over him. He'd never thought of himself as spoiled. Though being a prince brought many benefits, he'd always kept his way of life plain, leaving behind the trappings of wealth and privilege when he could. When he camped with his men, it wasn't in a luxurious tent with gold-trimmed furnishings, which he'd seen done many times by other noblemen, including his father and brothers. Nor did Max trade on his position and name to gain favors in court, or for the attention of women.

He made his own way, based solely on his efforts on and off the battlefield. Or so he'd thought until he'd met Murian. For the last few weeks, he'd done nothing but think about kissing her again, tasting her again, touching her again. Now, after finally winning some ground from her villagers, who had a maddening tendency to protect their mistress as if she were a national treasure and they an elite troop of guards, it nipped at him that she could so quickly move her attention from him to her desire to win Rowallen.

It was maddening—and as his patience evaporated, so did his reluctance to use his title to his benefit. After days of frustration, he would have gladly issued a royal decree in order to spend some time alone with Murian.

The entire situation made him realize how rarely he had to fight for such things. When he saw a woman he thought he might enjoy, he wooed her and he won. Always. Yet this woman, her mind consumed by righting an injustice, surrounded by a small village of people who loved and needed her, seemed impervious to him.

Wooing her presented a unique challenge. If he wanted her complete attention, he would have to help her find that damned journal. Perhaps once she'd realized that objective, she would be free to enjoy what time they had left.

She brushed a curl away, leaving a plaster smudge across her cheek. "When does the singer arrive?"

"Soon." He removed his glove. "Hold still." He brushed her cheek with his fingertips.

Her eyes flew to his, surprise on her face. Puffs of icy breath rolled from her plump lips, moist and warm, her eyes shimmering with surprise and . . . excitement? God, he wished they were still in Widow Atchison's cottage, so he could capture those lips with his.

As if she could read his thoughts, her lashes dropped and she retreated behind the fortifications she was all too quick to throw up.

"Hold," he ordered.

Her gaze narrowed, but she held still. Max brushed her cheek again, this time for the mere pleasure of the touch. "You had plaster on your face. It is gone."

"Thank you." The wind whipped anew and she tugged her hood, shivering as her cloak danced about her. "We should talk aboot the singer."

"Yes, we should. Shall we retire to Widow Atchison's cottage?"

"Nay. Mine would be best."

He thought of the huge bed gracing one corner of her cottage. "Fine." He captured her elbow and walked with her toward her cottage. "We have much to plan—"

"Och, there's Ian." She stood on her tiptoes. "*Ian!*"

The giant was pushing a wheelbarrow filled with stone down the street, but at her shout, he turned their way. He came to a stop in front of Murian, red-faced and puffing. "Aye?"

"The prince has word about the singer coming to Rowallen. We must discuss how to make the best use of this opportunity."

"Here now, lassie, ye dinna need to be sneakin' back into the castle. 'Twas a disaster last time, and 'tis bound to be the same this—"

"Ian, I am cold. The wind is blowing. I'm going to discuss this in my cottage, so either come there, or do not be heard." She turned on her heel and marched up the street, leaving both Max and Ian behind.

Ian puffed out his cheeks. "She seems a bit oot of sorts."

"She's determined to find that journal. Perhaps more than is good for her."

"Aye. So I've thought fer some time. Weel, I suppose we'd best go and talk wi' her. If we dinna, she'll go on some wild ploy wi'oot tellin' us a blasted thing."

"You're right." Max sighed. "It might take the two of us to keep her out of trouble." He led the way, wistfully eyeing Widow Atchison's empty cottage as he went.

Chapter 13

Max opened the door for Ian, then followed the older man inside.

"I'll close it." Will Scarlae followed them inside, and then shut the door with a decided bang.

"Wha' are ye doin' here?" Ian hung his coat on a peg by the door. "Ye're supposed to be pickin' oop the broken boards and wha' no'."

"Widow Reeves said 'twould be best to do it at the end of the day. So I thought I'd join ye here and help." Will narrowed his gaze. "Ye are plannin' somethin', are ye no'?"

"Aye, we are." Murian tucked her mittens into her cloak pocket before she hung it on the screen at the far end of the room. "Ian, he can stay. It canna be a bad thing to have another brain thinking through our plans."

Will looked pleased as punch as he hung his coat over the back of a chair, then sat stiffly, as if ready to be presented with a daunting task.

Ian sat across from the youth, his chair creaking in protest. "We shouldna' be talkin' in front of the lad."

"Nonsense," Murian said. "Will wants the castle back as much as we do; 'twas his home."

"Humph." Ian didn't look convinced. "Will, mayhap ye should tell the prince how ye were captured by the earl's men no' a month ago."

A dull red colored the youth's face. "So I was," he said boldly. "But I know the castle weel and wi' the help of a chambermaid, I escaped."

"Ian, let the lad be." Murian sent them both a hard look as she crossed to stand before the fire. "'Tis time we expected more of him."

Ian didn't look as if he agreed the least bit, but Will sent her a grateful look. "Thank ye, me lady. I'll do ye proud, I will."

"I'm sure you will. So listen well; the prince has brought us news."

Will nodded and Max, looking at him closely, realized he wasn't as young as he'd thought. Judging from Will's slight build and sullen air, Max had thought him sixteen or seventeen. On closer inspection, Will looked to be in his mid-twenties. Max had men under his command who'd successfully led troops at Will's age, though he couldn't begin to imagine that of this weak-chinned lad.

"Will knows the castle top to bottom." Murian put another log on the fire and then took a seat nearby, holding her booted feet toward the warmth. "He grew up at Rowallen and could be of great help."

"I know the back hallways better than anyone, e'en Lady Murian."

"By all means, then, let him stay." Max crossed to the fire and leaned against the mantel. He wished for the warmth, but also the proximity of Murian, who sat not two feet from him. The log she'd added to the fire blazed, turning her hair into copper and gold.

"Wha' aboot this singer?" Ian asked, his voice rough with impatience.

Max pulled his gaze from Murian. "The famous opera singer, Madame Dufond, performs at Rowallen on Tuesday."

"In four days," Murian said.

"*Da*. There will be a dinner, followed by a performance."

Murian leaned forward. "Is he inviting the local gentry?"

"Invitations were sent this morning; one of my men saw them."

Murian was clearly pleased. "So 'tis set then." Deep in thought, she worried her bottom lip with her teeth.

A warmth rushed through Max that had nothing to do with the fire. To cover it, he asked, "What do you know of how the guards are posted?"

"A little." Murian held her hands toward the flames. "If Loudan is inviting more than a dozen or more people, he'll double the footmen in the foyer and station more at every doorway. He does that every time he has a party."

"Those are no' footmen," Will said, rubbing his cheekbone as if remembering a pain.

"Some of them are," Murian said. "You can easily tell the difference, though."

"Aye," Ian agreed. "The guards are brutes and make the footmen look like wee willies."

"So I've noticed," Max said drily. "What else do you know of the guards?"

"They're no' from around here, so they often get lost once they leave the castle." Ian stroked his chin thoughtfully. "Whene'er Loudan has guests, he adds a ring of guards ootside the castle."

"That's in addition to the guards riding the grounds," Murian said. "He's predictable, in some ways." She absently tucked an escaped strand of hair behind one ear. "Which is good for us."

Max wondered what Murian's untamed hair portended between the sheets. Would she be extra passionate? More inclined to wildness and—

Ian cleared his throat, long and loud.

Max found the giant's gaze on him, the dark red brows tightly knit. Max merely shrugged.

Murian, deep in thought, tapped her fingers on the arms of her chair. "Loudan will use the blue salon for the performance, for 'tis the nicest in the castle and holds a good number of guests. I'll don my disguise, as I did for the dance. Then, while everyone is listening—"

"Nyet!"

"Nay!"

Max and Ian snapped their no's at the same time, and Ian said, "'Tis too dangerous, lass. Ye took a chance last time. This time, let me or someone else take the risk."

"I'll do it," Will offered.

Murian shook her head. "I know what the journal looks like, and no one knows the master chamber better than I do."

"Ye'll get caught," Ian said.

"I wasna caught last time. Loudan looked straight at me and dinna know me at all."

"Your disguise was masterful," Max agreed. "But Ian is right: this event will be different than the dance, and a simple disguise won't work."

A stubborn line tightened her jaw. "Why not?"

"At a dance people mill about, moving from room to room, in dim candlelight. It's easy to disappear under such circumstances. A singer, though, will draw everyone to one room. All of the guests will be seated in one place, with many candelabras lit to brighten the performance. It will be much harder to escape notice."

Her chin firmed, and after a tense moment, she said in a tight voice. "Then what do you suggest?"

Will leaned forward eagerly. "Let me do the searchin', me lady! I can go in dressed as a footman and no one will know—"

"Where's yer haid, boy," Ian growled. "They know ye already, so one look at ye and we'd be done."

"I could wear a disguise like her ladyship did," Will said hotly. "And don a uniform like the other footmen."

"And do ye think the other footmen—who are guards—would no' notice a new face standin' there amongst them, lookin' like the biggest lump on a log?"

Will flushed, sinking into his chair. "I was just tryin' to help."

"Ye hadna thought of anything, fra' wha' I can tell." Ian sighed heavily. "So. We know there's to be an event, wi' a lot of comin' and goin' at the castle. Where does tha' leave us?"

Murian answered, "Perhaps it wouldna make sense to go in disguised. I'm not sure how else to approach it."

Max toyed with the idea of not saying anything, on the faint hope that Murian would decide it too dangerous to go near the castle, but the stubborn line of her jaw told him that such hope was in vain.

He sighed. "If you must go, my men and I will meet you inside Rowallen, clear the guards, and escort you to the bedchamber." At least then she'd be protected.

Her eyes gleamed. "Can you do that?"

"Of course. We'll need to study the layout of the grounds around Rowallen and decide which entryway would be the safest."

"We already know that," she said. "There's a rise on the west side of the castle. It's easy to hide on that ridge and then slip in under dark. Isna it, Ian?"

Ian sighed but grunted an agreement.

Max asked him, "How many times have you slipped into the castle?"

Ian stroked his beard thoughtfully. "Two dozen times. Mayhap more."

Max whistled silently.

Ian shrugged. "In the beginning, Loudan dinna have so many guards. No' like now. And it's gotten e'en worse since the earl realized we'd been in and oot of Rowallen wi'oot his knowing."

Max cut a glance at Will, who instantly flushed. "Aye," the young man agreed. "The earl doubled the guards after I was caught."

"How did you get in before there were so many guards?" Max asked.

Murian grinned. "Easy. We'd hold up the earl's guests on their way to Rowallen."

Ian said, "The earl would get furious and send his guards into the woods to find us, which they ne'er did, as none of them are fra' this area."

"I daresay you led them on a merry chase."

"Aye." Ian looked a bit smug. "We'd let them see us, ride ahead, and then hide whilst they thundered past. After they were weel gone, we'd circle behind them and ride directly to Rowallen. It worked weel, until Will was taken. After tha', there were too many guards fer us to slip past."

Max had to admire their spirit. So far, he hadn't met a single person in this small hamlet who didn't have the heart of a lion, especially their leader. He eyed Murian now. "So you must reach Loudan's bedchamber."

She nodded. "It has to be there."

He glanced past her to Ian, whose face showed doubt. *So you are not as certain as your mistress as to the whereabouts of this journal.*

Max picked up the fire iron and stirred the logs. "I'll need to walk the castle, have my men draw a layout of the grounds, do a head count of the enemy forces, test the—"

"I can tell you all you wish to know," Murian said in an impatient voice. "We dinna need your men to do more than stand guard, and, if we're discovered, keep the earl's men at bay until we escape."

"*Nyet.* That will not work."

"Why not?"

"Because neither I nor my men can be involved in a direct engagement with the earl or his men."

Three pairs of eyes bored into Max.

He explained, "Since I am a prince, everything I do is representative of Oxenburg, whether I wish it to be or not. If my men and I were to attack the earl or his men in his own castle, it could be construed as an act of aggression. It could politically embarrass my country—I cannot do it."

"I see."

He caught the deep disappointment in Murian's gaze. "But that doesn't mean I won't assist you. I've no issue with misleading Loudan or his men, or helping you reach the master bedchamber for your search." He gave her a wolfish grin. "I only have an issue with getting caught."

"As do I," Murian said, looking relieved.

"Then we're set. If you do this—"

"*When* I do this," she corrected him.

"When *we* do this, my men and I will assist you in every way possible. Loudan is hiding something that belongs to my family, too. I must recover that object, and it would be better if the earl never realized it was gone from his possession until after my men and I escort my grandmother from the castle."

"Aye. Of course." Her gaze was shadowed. "If we find the journal and your grandmother's lost item, you . . . all of you will leave?"

"*Da*. I must escort my grandmother back to Oxenburg, and then I have obligations to fulfill."

"Of course." She managed a smile, but it was every bit as tight as Max's chest felt. He'd been upset to only have a few weeks left, but now . . . *Only days?*

"Wha' part am I to take?" Will asked eagerly.

Max pursed his lips. "If Will knows the castle, then perhaps he should be the one to search—"

"Nay," Murian said.

"'Twill be easier to explain his presence than yours."

Will brightened.

"He's never seen the journal," Murian said in a firm tone. "I have. Therefore I am the only one who can do this."

"Nonsense. You can describe it to him."

"Nay." Her voice rose slightly. "'Tis mine to find, not his."

"'Twould be safer if—"

"*Nay.*" She leaned forward, her hands tight on the arms of her chair. "'Twould only be safer for *me*. Not for anyone else."

He realized that her objection wasn't that she mistrusted the lad, but that she refused to place him in harm's way.

"I see." Far better than he wanted. He pushed away from the mantel. "Fortunately, we have several days to find the safest way to do this, and the stealthiest."

Her silver gaze searched his face. Whatever she saw must have reassured her, for she nodded. "Thank you. And I vow we will find whatever the grand duchess lost to Loudan, too."

Ian's blue gaze cut in Max's direction. "Wha' did she lose?"

"A tiara. A very special tiara." Max walked to where he'd hung his coat. "I'll have my men do a survey of the castle and lands, and mark all of the guard posts. I've already had my men noting the habits of the footmen and guards. Once we have all of that information, we'll draw up a battle plan."

"How long will that take?" Murian asked.

"A few days, no more. We will be ready when the time comes. Now, if you'll excuse me, I should see if my men need assistance. We wish to finish Widow Brodie's roof before the storm hits." He took Murian's hand in his, frowning as he noted how chapped it was. "*Dorogaya moya*, wool mittens are not enough."

She tugged her hand free, her lips pressed into an unhappy line. "They do just fine, thank you." She glanced under her lashes at Ian and Will before saying to Max, "I suppose I should fetch some help to finish the plastering, then."

For a moment he was tempted—so tempted—to offer to be that "help," but he knew it was a lost cause. She was too taken with their coming raid upon Rowallen, and that same raid worried him. They had much more "talking" to do, but not now.

"I'll help with the plasterin'," Will offered.

"The lad would be guid at tha'," Ian approved. He rose from his chair and stretched. "I should finish up me chores, too. I've ten more wheelbarrows full of slate to move." He lumbered to the door. "Come along, Will. I'll show ye how to mix more plaster, fer ye'll be needin' it afore the day is oot."

Looking pleased, Will joined Ian, both of them shrugging into their coats.

Max bowed to Murian. For a moment she thought

he might say something, but all he did was murmur a good-bye before he followed Ian and Will out the door.

Left alone, Murian rubbed her arms. She'd waited and waited for her chance to return to Rowallen, and suddenly things were happening quickly. It would be much easier if she could plan the entire event herself, but she'd be a fool to not use the prince's help while she had it. *He'll be gone soon enough. Too soon.*

Her heart sank, and she resolutely told herself, *That's fine. I didn't expect anything else.* But a hollow ache grew in her chest at the thought of life after Max left. In some deep, secret part of her, she'd done that most dangerous of things . . . she'd *hoped*. What she'd hoped for, she refused to examine—because it didn't really matter. Max would leave after they'd recovered the journal and tiara. He would have to.

Fate was cruel and capricious; she gave and then she took away. Sighing, she put on her cloak and trudged back out into the cold.

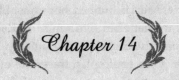

Chapter 14

The next day, the village awoke to find itself covered in a deep, heavy snow that sparkled in the sunshine. Murian loved the way the frosted trees looked like something from a fairy tale. Unable to sit still for too long despite the snow, she and Ian made their way to the barn where they worked inside, making shutters. It was good for her to do something with her hands; it would keep her too busy to overthink either the coming escapade at Rowallen or the warm green eyes of a certain black-haired, wicked-smiling man.

Yet in the lonely dark of night, oh, how she'd overthought them both.

After finishing the shutters, she and Ian had decided to brave the snow and hang them. That had been an hour ago, and she was now hammering the final hinge into place.

She squinted at her handiwork. "Well?" she called down to Ian, who held her ladder. "How does it look?"

"Grand, lassie." He pursed his lips before saying in an encouraging voice, "Only a wee bit crooked, which is nay bad at all."

"Blast it! It should be straight, for I marked it." She leaned back a bit so she could see the entire thing better. "I marked it twice; I dinna ken how it could be croo—"

Ian's guffaw made her give him a mock scowl. "Och, you're a tease, Ian Beagin."

"Jus' funnin' ye, lassie. 'Tis straight as can be. Sadly, I canna say the same fer the buildin', which leans to the right."

"I've noticed. Sadly, that, we cannot fix." She hung the hammer on the belt she'd strapped about her waist and climbed down, her boots crunching on the snow Ian had stomped into flatness for the ladder.

Murian brushed snow from her shoulder, grimacing when a sliver of it slid down her neck.

Ian guffawed again. He was much more cheerful now that so many of the repairs had been completed. He was almost giddy, knowing more would be done once the weather cleared.

The knowledge warmed her, too, though not to the extent that it did Ian. She saw their little village as a stop on the road back to Rowallen, but she was beginning to think Ian believed it to be their final destination.

Never. We will *return to Rowallen, all of us.* She'd pledged herself to this course, and she wouldn't veer from it, come what may.

She glanced down the wide path into the village. Heavy with snow, the forest seemed to swallow it up. The prince and his men might not come for a couple of days, and she felt oddly restless at the thought. She'd been that way since the snow had begun, and she'd caught herself staring out the windows when she was inside, and watching down the lane when she was out-side. She missed the bustle Max and his men had brought to their little village. But more than that, she missed Max himself, which worried her.

Perhaps it was because he didn't treat her as "Lady Murian," but simply as a woman. Even though his birth had placed him in a high position, he was quick to abandon society's rules. Of course, he'd witnessed firsthand that greatest of all levelers—war. She'd heard Spencer say time and again that there were no dukes in war, only good soldiers and bad. Perhaps that ex-plained the prince's unconventional attitudes.

Ian removed the ladder and placed it alongside the wall. "I'll fetch the shutters fer Widow Reeves's cottage, if ye're no' too tired to affix 'em."

"I'm never too tired to put up new shutters," she an-swered staunchly.

"Guid," Ian said. "Fer we've at least twenty more to do." With a firm nod, he headed to the barn.

Murian lifted her face to the cool breeze that rustled through the trees, admiring how the snow glistened on the branches. Their village was silent except for an occa-sional murmur of voices from some of the cottages, or the plop of wet snow where it fell from heavily bent tree branches.

There was no telling how long the snow would re-main. But when it did . . . Her gaze went to the path into the village. *He will return.*

Her heart leapt. It concerned her—this inexplicable excitement from just thinking about Max, a wild and wanton mixture of . . . She had no idea what it was, and she didn't want to find out. But she wished it would stop. *It's just passion. Passion and excitement. Soon I'll have Robert's journal in my hands, the prince and his men will be gone, and things will return to normal.*

Her excitement faded, a deep ache replacing it. She looked at the road into the village again and, to her horror, felt tears rising.

Thankfully the barn door opened, and Ian came out with a stack of shutters on his shoulder, a bag of fasteners tucked in his belt.

She dashed the back of her mitten over her eyes before he could notice, and soon she was helping him stack the shutters by Widow Reeves's cottage.

Done with that task, she took the bag of fasteners he handed her, and secured it to her belt. Ian stomped down the snow for the ladder.

"There. Tha' will do." Ian gave the ground a last stomp, then hoisted the ladder to the wall. "Be careful, lass. Yer boots may be slip—" His gaze focused over her shoulder, his heavy eyebrows rising. "Weel, now. I dinna expect to see tha' today."

Could it be? Her heart answered before she even turned. There, riding their horses down the snow-covered lane, were Max and his men. Snow powdered their broad, wool-clad shoulders and clung to their horses' manes. Dressed in fur-lined hats, their beards covering their thick fur collars, their riding boots shiny and wet from the snow, they seemed like exotic beings from a distant land.

Max led the way, his men laughing and talking as they followed him into the village. His gaze swept the area and found Murian, who flushed. A lopsided smile curved his firm lips and he nodded a greeting that was oddly intimate, even though he was on the other side of the village.

She wrapped her arms around herself. He looked as tasty and welcome as warm, honeyed porridge on a frosty winter morning.

As the deep rumble of the soldiers' voices grew louder, curtains flickered in windows, followed quickly by doors flying open one by one. Widow Brodie stood in her doorway, her five boys pouring out into the yard, waving and jumping and whooping. Orlov and Demidor pulled up beside their gate and leaned down to talk to the boys.

Widow MacDonald hurried to her gate and called out to Golovin as he rode past. Murian caught the phrase "venison stew," and whatever else the widow had said, Golovin's craggy face brightened and he nodded.

Widow MacCrae and her daughter hurried past Murian to wave at Pahlen, who grinned, his teeth flashing whitely in his bearded face as he directed his horse their way.

The other women and children poured from their cottages, all of them waving at the men, excited voices rippling through the once-quiet town.

"'Tis like a parade," Murian said.

"Aye," Ian replied. "While I'm glad they've been here to help, I hope e'erone realizes 'tis only temporary. The prince and his lads'll be gone soon enou'."

Max pulled his horse to a halt beside Pushkin's, which was tied to the gate, and dismounted. He handed the reins to Orlov, who took both horses and led them with his own to the stables. The other men, leaving the villagers, did the same.

Murian was suddenly aware of how she must look. Her hair, damp from the snowfall, stuck to her face and neck in wet curls, and she was certain her nose was cherry red from the cold.

Max reached them and she felt his gaze flicker over her, lingering on her face and cheeks. "Lady Murian." He bowed and glanced past her to the stack of shutters. "I didn't expect anyone to be working on such a cold morning."

"O' course we were workin'," Ian huffed. "Now tha' we've wood, there's no stoppin' us fra' wha' needs doin'."

"Excellent. Though the wagon wouldn't make it through the snow, the horses needed exercise, so we are here."

"You canna expect to work on the roofs in such weather." Murian clapped her mittened hands together to keep them warm.

Max held out his hand. "Give me your hand."

She obliged.

He peeled off her wet mittens and placed them on a ladder rung. Then he pulled a glove from his pocket and tugged it onto Murian's bare hand. The supple leather was lined with the softest fur she'd ever felt, and warmth enveloped her hand. "Thank you."

His gaze darkened. "You must have better gloves if you're to be out in such weather. Give me your other hand."

She held it out, and he pulled the matching glove from his pocket and tugged it on her hand. She held her gloved hands before her, admiring the well-stitched leatherwork. "They're beautiful."

"They were made by the Gypsies from my country. They make beautiful things with leather."

She looked at him inquiringly. "These are too small to be yours."

"They belonged to my grandmother."

"I'll thank her if I see her again."

"Pray do not."

He spoke so flatly that she cast him a suspicious glance. "I take it she dinna know she's been so generous."

"She knows. She assumed I wished the gloves for, as she put it, 'a village wench.' I would rather she did not call you that, for it would make me very angry."

Murian's lip twitched. "Your grandmother sounds very spirited. I think I would like her."

Max thought Murian would enjoy Tata Natasha's brazen ways, as well. Sadly, the two would never meet. He forced a smile. "We should discuss the mission scheduled for Rowallen. Orlov is waiting for us in the barn. The others are to join us." He looked at Ian. "We'll need you, too, and Will. The more minds we apply to this, the fewer errors there will be."

"I'll tell the lad ye need him." Ian left, leaving Murian with Max.

He proffered his arm. It was a silly, formal thing to do, but she smiled and accepted. They waded through the deep snow to the barn and went inside.

Orlov had placed a plank across two barrels, creating a table. "Good morning, Lady Murian."

She returned the greeting, removing her new gloves.

Max noted how she carefully placed them in her pocket, patting them as if to be certain they would not fall out.

Orlov removed a leather packet from the saddlebags he'd hung over a stall and brought it to the makeshift table. There, he undid the flap and pulled out some folded papers. Murian watched as he smoothed them out.

"Why, these are sketches of Rowallen." She turned through the other papers. "And schedules for the guards, too." She looked at Max, astonishment in her gaze. "Where did you get these?"

He smiled at the admiration in her voice. "We made them. This is not the first battle we've planned."

Orlov moved a piece of paper to the top of the pile. "There are fifty-six guards. Here are their names and what we know of them. Most of them are military trained."

"How did you find out?"

Orlov's teeth flashed in his black beard. "Vodka. Lots and lots of vodka."

Max explained, "It is a drink, much like your whiskey, only stronger."

"Much stronger," Orlov agreed.

"Ah," she said. "I hope the information you gleamed was accurate, and not drunken bragging. I—"

The door opened and Demidor and Golovin entered.

"Where are the others?" Max asked.

"They come," Demidor said. The two men came to stand behind Orlov.

Max turned to Murian, who was reading one of the papers. "So much information," she said, shaking her head. "You found all of this from plying the earl's men with vodka?"

"Not all. Some of our information came from Loudan's man of business."

"Aye," Demidor said. "A small man who is much given to complaining. And when he is complaining, he is also telling much information."

"The night before last, Demidor became his best friend," Max said.

"It was not difficult," Demidor said modestly. "After some vodka, the man had much to say about his employer. But it wasn't what he said that was of value, but rather what he wrote."

"I dinna understand," Murian said.

"He kept a ledger." Demidor reached over and tapped the corner of a small blue notebook that was partially hidden under the papers.

Murian picked up the notebook. "You stole it? Willna he go to the earl once he realizes it is gone?"

"Nay, he fears the earl. Besides, we will give it back later today and he will think it merely misplaced."

She flipped through the ledger. "Heavens! He wrote down everything: what he had for lunch, how his knee feels, how much sleep he had—"

"—how many guards are stationed and where, each and every day, how much those guards cost the earl, the names of every person on each squadron and their leaders—it is a complete record."

The door opened and the rest of Max's men entered, as did Ian, who hurried to Murian's side. "Will is comin'. I thought Widow Reeves might be of help, too, seein' as how she was once the cook and knows the lower floors."

"Good," Murian said. "Look at what the prince and his men have brought. Guard schedules, names of each squad commander, maps of Rowallen, and anything else we might need."

Ian looked impressed. "Then we'll be set."

Max nodded as he crossed his arms. "Here is what we think. When the entertainment begins that evening, we will allow it to continue for an hour or so—"

The barn door opened again and Widow Reeves came in, Will behind her. Widow Reeves peered at the papers on the table. "Och, bu' tha' is a guid drawin' of the castle interior! Who made it?"

Demidor jerked his thumb at Golovin, who flushed.

She eyed him with admiration. "Ye did a fine job, ye did."

Golovin didn't seem to know where to look.

"As I was saying, Murian," Max continued in a firm tone, a hint of exasperation in his voice. "Once the entertainment begins, we will throw the signal for you to approach the castle. We don't know the exact time, because you know how this sort of event can go."

"Aye. Sometimes the singer is late, or the guests linger over dinner—one never knows."

"Exactly."

"Where is the singer performing?"

He placed his finger on the map. "The blue salon, here."

Murian nodded "As we thought."

"*Da*. It is being cleaned, the rugs beaten, and chairs arranged in preparation. No other rooms but that room and the dining room are being prepared."

"How will you let me know when it's safe to approach the castle?"

Orlov pulled another paper from the stack and placed it on the top. This map was of the lands around the castle, each outbuilding sketched in. "You and Ian and Will will wait here for our signal." Orlov pointed to a ridge to the east of the castle.

"Tha' willna work," Will said.

"Why not?" Orlov asked.

"Loudan posts guards on tha' ridge from dark 'til dawn."

"The lad is right," Ian agreed. "We've seen them many times."

"True," Max said. "But *this* night, they will not be there from eight o'clock onward."

Ian's thick brows rose. "Ye can arrange tha'?"

"*Da*, which is why you, Will, and Lady Murian will arrive at eight thirty and not a moment before."

Ian's eyes gleamed. "Takin' care o' them, are ye?"

"Aye, but gently."

"Wha' are ye goin' to do?" Will asked, looking concerned.

"The guards will be convinced by two very willing

housemaids to imbibe some forbidden whiskey while working. They will wake up in the stables the next morning with no memory of how they got there. I rather doubt they'll admit to Loudan that they were derelict in their duties, but will instead pretend they were at their stations all night long."

Murian nodded thoughtfully. "So you will clear the guards on this side."

"*Da*. Once it is done, we will put a light in the small window of the yellow sitting room, which is beside the blue salon. Once you see the signal, you will come to the study window here." Max pointed again.

"The second window over." She frowned. "Why the study?"

"It is best. And come dressed as a thief, not as Maid Murian. It will make things easier, should we need to move quickly." He cut a hard look at Will and Ian. "You two must see to it that Lady Murian makes it safely to this window as quickly as possible after the signal is given. Though the guards will be gone, there is a lot of open ground here. If someone should happen to look out of the window and see her, things could go wrong very quickly."

"We will do wha' we must," Ian said firmly.

Will nodded. "Aye, bu'—no' meaning any disrespect, is tha' all we do?"

Orlov scowled. "What you will be doing is important and dangerous. You will be escorting her ladyship over open ground to the castle, and guarding her with your life."

"And while she is inside the castle?" Will asked.

"You two will move to here." Orlov pointed to the kitchen door in the back of the castle. "You will wait until we escort her out. Once we get her there, you will need to get her away from the castle as quickly as possible."

"You will have to hide while you wait," Demidor warned. "There will be many servants bustling in and out. I have watched them for the last two days, and there are only a few places to hide: here at the stone wall by the well, and—"

"—behind the icehouse," Ian finished, his voice heavy with sarcasm. "We lived there fer years; we know where to hide fra' the cook."

"I can vouch fer tha','" Widow Reeves sniffed.

"How long will we be waitin'?" Will asked.

"As long as it takes Lady Murian to do what must be done."

Will bent over the map, his gaze flickering over each room, each sketched-in window and door. "How do ye plan on gettin' Lady Murian through the castle to the master bedchamber? If she's goin' in through the study, she'll find herself facin' far too many servants to keep her presence a secret."

"Leave that to us. We have it well in hand." Max nodded and Orlov began collecting the papers. "I think that is all—"

"Nay." Murian pulled the papers out of Orlov's hands and placed them back on the table.

Orlov stopped, surprised, while Max frowned.

"We need more details, if you please," she said. "How do you expect to get from the study to the master bedchamber?"

"We've planned it well; you need have no fear of that."

"I'm sure you have, with what knowledge you have collected. But you dinna know all you need to."

"I appreciate your concern, but it's unwarranted." Max's voice was sharp with impatience. "We've thought through every contingency. My men and I have handled far more complicated details than this, and we know how best to get you where you must go. Save your worry about where you'll search once you're in the master bedchamber."

"Max, there's much you can't know aboot the castle unless you lived there day in and day oot, and had the running of it, as well. We know how things work there: what hallways are the most traveled, which rooms are never used. I'll not put myself into your care wi'oot some details, when 'tis possible we may know some things that could make your plan better."

Max stiffened, suddenly every inch the prince— stern, unsmiling, inflexible.

Her heart tumbled a little, but she refused to back down.

Will looked outraged for Murian.

After a tense moment, Ian's deep chuckle broke the silence. "Easy, now, the two of ye. Mayhap we should discuss this tomorrow, when we've ha' some time to think it through."

"I think Lady Murian ha' the right of it," Will said stubbornly. "We should be included in the plannin'."

"You have been," Max snapped.

"Nay, we havena. Ye marched in here and tossed

yer papers down, so pleased ye collected some number and wha' no'. 'Tis no' enough."

"We've been inside the castle for several weeks," Golovin pointed out. "What can you know that we do not?"

Murian asked calmly, "Which doorway does the earl use when he meets with his guards?"

"The eastern portal," Demidor answered, looking proud.

The other men murmured in approval.

"Aye, when it's dry," Murian agreed.

Demidor's smile faded. "I beg your pardon?"

"He canna use that door when it rains, for the window beside it leaks, and the stone floor becomes as slick as ice. So on those days, he goes out the main doorway and speaks with them there."

Demidor blinked. "Oh."

Max's jaw tightened, but after a moment he said to Murian, "Fine. We'll share our plans and hear what you have to say."

She met his gaze, and her expression softened. "I know you have our best interests at heart." She could see his genuine concern. His greatest fault wasn't his plaguey confidence, but an overwhelming desire to always do right.

She pointed to the castle floor plan. "What should we know first?"

As she and Ian bent over the map, Max outlined the route he and Orlov had decided on to get Murian to the master bedroom. When he finished, Murian tapped a small room almost directly across from the study. "This could be a problem."

Ian nodded. "I was just thinkin' the same thing."

Max leaned forward, his shoulder against hers. "We looked at that room. It's quite small, and is never used."

"Except during an event. Long ago, 'twas to be a butler's pantry, to stage meals for the breakfast room, which is here." She slid her finger down the hall and around the corner to a small room west of the foyer. "But as you can see, 'tis hardly convenient, so it was never used for that."

"Which was a pity," Widow Reeves agreed, "for 'twas difficult keepin' dishes warm fra' the kitchen all the way to the breakfast room." She leaned close to Golovin, who stood nearby. "We placed hot stones under the serving dishes to keep 'em warm."

"How is the room used now?" Max asked impatiently.

"'Tis used by the footmen to hold coats whenever there's a ball or a dinner or such."

"The real footmen, not the guards-pretending-to-be-footmen," Ian clarified.

"Why is that a detriment?" Orlov asked. "They will put the coats in the room before dinner, and then get them as the evening closes. I fail to see the problem."

"*Nyet*." Max sighed. "The footmen will be in and out of that room throughout the evening."

"Aye," Murian agreed. "As people arrive, the footmen will hang the coats in this room. When there is time throughout the evening, various footmen will return to brush the coats so they are clean before being returned to the guests."

"Which means," Max finished, "they'll most likely use the time during the performance to see to those duties. So the footmen will be in and oot of this room just when we most need the hallway empty."

"So the study window won't work," Orlov said wryly.

"Exactly." Murian leaned her elbows on the plank table and peered more closely at the map. "Which window should be used, then?"

Ian smacked Max's shoulder. "Sorry, lad. Ye canno' be right all the time."

Max's gaze was fixed on the map as well, his expression thoughtful. "*Nyet*, my friend. I would rather be wrong now than wrong the night of the raid." His even gaze lifted to Murian's. "We've too much to lose."

Her throat tightened unexpectedly. His voice was as steady as his gaze, and she flushed. To pass the moment without embarrassing herself, she pulled the map closer, almost bumping heads with Will, who'd leaned forward when she did.

After a moment, Will placed his finger on a small room at the corner of the back of the castle.

She looked at it and then nodded. "Aye, that will do."

"What room is that?" Max asked.

"The music room," Will answered absently, his gaze locked on the drawing. "No one has used it since Lady Murian left. They say 'tis thick wi' dust now."

"Is it?" Murian sighed. "I couldna bring the pianoforte, as much as I'd have liked to. It would have ruined in the damp."

"Yet another skill you possess," Max said.

She had to laugh. "I wouldn't call it 'skill.' The more honest word is 'peck.'"

"Whist," Widow Reeves said. "Ye played like an angel, ye did. We've all heard ye."

"You are too kind. I dinna think I could play now; it's been too long." Murian folded the map and handed it to Orlov. "The music room it is. The servants willna be walking past it, as it's well past the kitchens and the coatroom."

"Agreed," Max said.

Orlov started to reach for the rest of the papers, then hesitated. "Did ye wish to see anything else, my lady?"

Murian shook her head. "Nay, I think we've covered what we need to."

"'Tis a guid plan," Ian agreed.

"Very good." Orlov gathered the papers and replaced them in the pouch.

Max looked at his men. "We've not much time today, as the ride back will be slower than usual. But for now, we've work to do here."

"*Da.*" Demidor rubbed his hands together. "I'm ready."

Golovin turned to the men. "Since we could not bring wood today, let's fix the leaks about the windows and doors. That will be a good thing once this snow melts." He left, the other men following.

"Come, Will," Widow Reeves said. "Ye can help. I've been ripping rags fra' old skirts all mornin' to use as packin' under the doors to keep the chill oot. Ye can fetch bags of the same from Widow Brodie and Widow MacCrae and bring them to my cottage."

As he started to follow her out, Murian called, "Will?"

He looked back.

"Thank you for your help. You had a good idea, you did."

He grinned, and for the first time, she was struck with how handsome he could be. *When he smiles, he looks a lot like Robert.*

"'Twas nothin', me lady." He followed Widow Reeves to the door.

The widow stuck her head back inside. "Ian Beagin, Widow MacDonald is callin' fer ye."

"Wha' does she want?"

Widow Reeves planted her fist on her hip. "Do I look like a mind reader to ye? All I know is she's yellin' and cursin' oop a storm."

"Fine, fine," Ian grumbled. He stomped to the door and marched out.

As soon as he was gone, Widow Reeves shut the door.

Max picked up a rake, carried it to the barn door, and placed it so that the thick handle wedged the door closed. That done, he returned to Murian.

She eyed his handiwork with a smile. "Well done."

He came and pulled her into his arms. "I have many skills, *dorogaya moya*."

She tilted her head to one side. "What does that mean, *dorogaya moya*? I have wondered many times, but was hesitant to ask."

"It means 'my dear.'" Max ran the back of his hand down her cheek. "It is not a term I normally use, but for you . . . it fits."

Murian's heart thudded, her mouth suddenly dry. "Oh? What do you normally call women you kiss?"

He bent so that his lips were a scant breath from hers. "It is the oddest thing. When you are so close to me, I cannot remember any other women."

She wet her lips, his gaze darkening as she did so. "None?"

"There is only you."

Only you. How many women dreamed of a man saying that to them? Murian slipped her arms about his neck. She'd wanted to hear those words, wanted to feel the warmth of his breath on her bare skin, wanted to feel his broad shoulders under her fingertips, wanted to taste him, touch him. With an urgent gasp, she pulled his mouth to hers.

If their kisses before were wild and impetuous, this one was planned and furious. The second their lips touched she forgot where she was, forgot her concerns, forgot everything but the heat of his skin on hers, his lips moving over hers, his tongue as it slid between her lips in a way that made her writhe madly against him.

His hands slid down her waist, to her hips. He firmly cupped her, pressing his hips to hers, and she felt his erect cock pressing against her skirts. She found the buttons of his coat and then she was tugging them free, pulling his waistcoat open, tugging his shirt from his waistband as she sought the warm expanse of his skin. She splayed her hands and ran them up his bared chest, the crisp curls of hair teasing her fingers.

His hands roamed as wildly as hers. Moaning against her mouth, he slid his hands to her ass, kneading her, holding her, rocking his hips against hers.

She gasped as a shudder of heated longing raced through her. God, she wanted this. It had been so long. So very, very long.

"Murian," he breathed against her lips, trailing his warm mouth up her cheek to her forehead, creating waves of shivers as he tugged her coat from her shoulders and dropped it to the floor.

She wanted this so much, and more. "Max . . . please!" She was too caught in his touch, in his taste, for words. She kissed his cheek, his jaw, her hair silken against his cheek as she traced her tongue along his scars.

Max gasped and held her tighter, tilting his head back so she could continue her way down his powerful throat. God, but she loved the taste of him, the feel of him. He was every Greek statue she'd ever seen, every charming prince she'd ever dreamed about.

Without warning he lifted her to the makeshift table, her skirts riding up to her thighs as they caught on the wood, Max's hips between her legs.

"I want you," he whispered raggedly, and her nipples hardened instantly.

He undid the neckline of her gown and shoved it down to cup one of her breasts through her chemise, his thumb finding the sensitive nub. He flicked it— once, twice, then again and again.

It was pleasure. It was torture. It was delicious and

tempting and teasing, and she writhed against him. She held on to him and leaned back, giving him access to her breasts. He bent, his warm lips fastening on her nipples one after the other, tonguing the tight buds through the fine lawn chemise. She sank a hand into his thick hair, holding his mouth to her, pressing against him. Her body was wracked with desire, her thighs damp with longing.

With a cry that was almost a sob, she tugged at his belt in frustration.

He swiftly undid it and his breeches with one hand, holding her firmly against him with the other.

She tugged his breeches free and found his turgid cock. Her breath hissed through her teeth as she wrapped her fingers about its warm hardness.

He gasped against her breast, raising his head to meet her gaze. "*Dorogaya moya*, you are certain?"

She leaned back on her elbow, her red hair a wave of passion as it fell over her shoulders to pool on the wood behind her. He leaned forward and sank his hands into her hair, the curls clinging to him as she pulled his hips to hers. As his thick cock pressed against her, she surged forward, enveloping him fully.

"Murian!" he cried.

Her body arched, fulfilled and needy at the same time as she rocked her hips forward, driving their madness with each thrust.

He slipped his arms under her shoulders, burying his face into her neck, where he rained kisses and murmured words she'd never heard before, as he met her thrust for thrust.

Wild and untrammeled, they plundered, tasted, reveled, and sank into one another. Together, they met with each stroke, and retreated only to pull one another back, time after time.

Murian was afire, her body aching with need, desire, and longing.

Max, fighting to hold back his release, raised his head to watch her. Her head was tilted back, her eyes closed, as she held him to her, her strong legs tight about his waist. He reached down to cup her firm ass, plunging into her more deeply. She gasped, her back arching, her breasts thrust up through her wet chemise.

Never had he seen a more beautiful woman. He slowed a bit, teasing her, making her writhe, her hands clutching his shirt as she silently begged for more.

And then, as if a star exploded before his eyes, she cried his name as she arched wildly against him and gasped. She tightened about him, a grip of hot velvet, until he lost control. With deep, desperate thrusts he followed her over the edge of their passion and finally collapsed against her.

For a long, long moment, they stayed where they were—his head cradled on her chest, her hands in his hair. He could hear the steady beat of her heart, and he listened as it slowed from a wild pace to a settled, tame purr against his ear.

He slowly realized it wasn't the most comfortable of positions, and he knew the wood had to be hard under her hips, yet he was loath to move. And she must have felt the same, for she held him close.

The air about them cooled their heated skin, and he

gradually became aware of voices outside in the street. With a sigh, he lifted up on one elbow.

She slid her hands from his hair and watched him through half-open eyes. God, but he loved her eyes. He brushed a curl from her cheek. "That was the best ten minutes of my entire life."

Her full lips—looking slightly swollen now and well kissed—parted as she laughed. "I think it was more like seven."

He chuckled, his eyes twinkling warmly. "You may be right. You excite me so much—too much for control." He kissed her nose. "If we can find privacy again, I promise you much more than seven desperate minutes."

"I wasn't complaining. It was . . ." She shook her head. "There are no words. It's been so long, it's amazing that I lasted seven minutes."

He kissed her bottom lip, looking at her greedily. "Next time, we will make it last an hour."

She chuckled. "My heart couldn't take it."

He smiled. "I would make sure you rested every few minutes, *dorogaya moya*."

Heat rose in her as he cupped her breast again. "Max, can we—" A sound came from outside, too close for comfort, and she instantly sat up.

Though he hated to do it, Max moved out of her way. "I suppose it was too much to ask that we have fifteen minutes alone. Perhaps it is good it didn't last longer."

"This time, aye." She kissed his cheek. Standing, she collected her things and then slipped out of sight to the back of the barn. He heard water pouring from a bucket. He righted his clothing as he waited and soon she reappeared, looking buttoned and proper, ready to hammer shutters into place.

She picked up her cloak and shook the hay from it, then slipped it on. "Max, we should—"

The barn door rattled, as if someone tried to open it from outside. "Lady Murian?" It was Ian.

She grimaced and called back. "Yes?"

He rattled it again. "The door seems to be stuck. Should I get someone to—"

"Nay, I'll see what's wrong." She waited a moment. "Ah, a rake fell against the handle. I'll get that as soon as I finish picking up some nails I dropped. I don't want anyone to step on one." She turned to Max and whispered, "Thank you."

He caught her close. "Nay, little one. Thank *you*." He kissed her nose, her cheek, and then her mouth as he said in a low voice, "Do not think this is the end of us. We've much to accomplish, and we will do it together."

She toyed with his top button, her gaze searching. "And then?"

His heart gave an odd lurch. "And then we will see, *nyet*? You could come back with me to Oxenburg and—"

"I willna leave my people." There was no brooking the firmness of her voice.

"I cannot stay here, *dorogaya*. I must return."

Her smile didn't waver, but he saw her eyes darken with sadness. "Of course."

"Murian?" Ian called again.

"I'm almost done!" She kissed Max quickly and then stepped out of his arms. "At least we have this, hmm?"

"There will be more; I promise."

"There are only a few days—"

Ian's voice rang loudly. "Lady Murian, I can help ye find those nails."

She turned to Max with a sigh. "Would you mind ducking behind a stall door?"

"I will not hide, but I will leave." He pressed a kiss into her hand.

"What's that for?"

He curled her fingers over the kiss. "It's for now." With a quick smile, he went to the window in the tack room, undid the heavy wood shutters, and slipped out.

Murian watched him go, and tried to ignore the bitter disappointment that flickered through her. Every time she saw the prince, and then had to part with him, she always felt as if she'd found something special, something precious, only to immediately lose it once again.

"Lass?" Ian called.

"Just a minute!" She found a sack of nails, tucked them in her belt, and went to the barn door. Once there, she removed the rake and let Ian in.

He glanced at her, and then over her shoulder. "Did ye find all of the nails?"

She patted the sack. "All of them." She pulled her new gloves out of her pocket and tugged them on. "Come, we've work to do." She left the barn, Ian following behind her. "Did you fix whatever Widow MacDonald needed to have done?"

"Aye, the old—"

"Ian!"

He flushed. "Sorry. She's a temper, she does."

"I'm sure she says the same of you. Come, we've shutters to fix." With that, she sailed out of the barn, Ian hard on her heels.

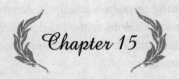

Chapter 15

"It's cold in here, like a tomb." Tata Natasha glared at everyone in the foyer as if they were all responsible for the chilly temperature.

"It will be warmer in the sitting room," Max informed her. They were gathered with the other guests, waiting to enter the sitting room.

"It had better be warmer, or I will be forced to set something on fire."

Max glanced at the shawl hanging from Tata Natasha's shoulders. As black as the rest of her clothing, it was embroidered with giant roses, which, now that he saw them up close, looked more like grinning skulls. He wondered if she were aware of it, but one glance from her sharp black eyes and he realized she knew exactly what those "roses" looked like. Refusing to comment, he instead remarked on the weather.

The line of people began to move and they passed Loudan, who was standing near the door with Lady MacLure. Her ladyship was serving as hostess for the evening's entertainment. It was a common arrangement for a bachelor to ask a friend's wife to stand in as hostess when there was none, but Lady MacLure was obviously uncomfortable with her task. Lord MacLure, who hovered nearby, appeared equally unhappy. The other guests seemed oblivious to the MacLures' distress, and laughed and talked, obviously joyous at being out after the severe weather.

Tata Natasha pursed her lips, unimpressed with the air of festivity. "What sort of singer will we be forced to listen to?"

"Surely you know; our host has mentioned it repeatedly. He's obviously very proud to have secured Madame Dufond."

"I do not like our host, so I do not listen to him." Natasha thought Loudan the worst sort of man—insipid, mean, and purposefully cruel. The kind who thought nothing of yelling at a servant, or even striking one, and for the smallest of reasons. She'd witnessed his cruelty on a number of occasions now, and her sympathies with the staff had grown daily.

Thankfully, now that Max knew about the tiara, she'd been able to stop faking politeness to Loudan, which had been a relief. The man didn't deserve such consideration. It made her head ache.

She tapped Max's forearm. "So. When do you address my problem?"

"Sometime soon. It would be better if you did not know the details."

"Soon is not soon enough. You've known the truth for days now."

"It takes time to organize such an endeavor. I won't risk our position by rushing into things."

"Humph. *I* would have already found a way to get it back." His jaw firmed, and she bit back another retort. Such was the trouble when dealing with a military man; they liked strategy. Well-planned, boring strategy.

She grimaced and looked at the other guests, deciding which gowns she liked and which were pure rubbish. "I don't suppose this singer is a Russian? I would enjoy hearing traditional singing."

"Madame Dufond sings opera."

She wrinkled her nose. "I do not like opera."

"What? You love opera."

"Only when it is sung by Italians. The French, they are too dramatic, always." She made exaggerated hand movements.

Max cut her an amused glance. "Then sleep through the performance, as you usually do. If your eyes are closed, you'll never notice her gestures."

"French." She shuddered. "Too much drama."

"This from a Romany."

"Don't be impertinent!"

He placed his hand over hers where it rested on his arm. "I'm sure you'll like this singer once you hear her. She is very well regarded in Scotland."

"So is haggis."

He chuckled. "Touché. The haggis, I do not understand."

They reached the doorway into the sitting room, but a crowd blocked their way. While they waited for the press to lessen, Orlov walked past, escorting a pretty young woman. As he passed Max, Natasha caught him exchanging a look with Max.

Aha! Natasha smacked Max's arm. "You make your move tonight, eh?"

He frowned. "There is no 'move.'"

"I saw the look you shared with Orlov. You are going to get my tiara back tonight, which is—"

"*Tikha!*" He looked around and then took her by the elbow and pulled her aside. "Keep your voice down."

"*Izvini.* I didn't think." She peeked past him and was glad to note that no one seemed to have paid them any heed. Still, she changed to Oxenburgian, saying. "It's about time you did something."

"If speed was a concern, then perhaps you should have told me immediately upon our arrival that you'd gambled away one of our country's most beloved heirlooms."

She generously decided to ignore his tone of voice. "It will be good to have it back in our possession. Once we have the tiara, we will leave." She considered this. "In fact, we could go this evening. I'll have the maids pack our bags while we are at dinner and—"

"*Nyet.* It is not that simple."

"Why not? You cannot wish to stay in this hellishly damp castle and—" Something about his expression caught her attention. A softening of his gaze, a touch of sadness about his mouth.

This grandson of hers was a difficult man to decipher, so she paid attention to even faint hints of emotion. *What has caught him so? Hmm. Could it be . . .* "This is about the woman, *nyet?*"

His gaze flickered away. "It about several things,

but—" He pressed his lips together for a moment. "*Da*, one of them is a woman."

Finally, he admits it to me! But is that a good thing, or a bad thing? She eyed him carefully. While he was as closemouthed as ever, he seemed less . . . dark. She remembered how he'd been on their ride here, lost in his thoughts and unwilling to leave them. Now he wore an air of . . . not hope, but of determination. "Who is she?"

Max's gaze grew shuttered. "You do not need to know."

"If she is so important that you must hide her, then of course I must know." When he didn't answer, she waved her hand. "Fine. I will find out on my own. Golovin will tell me everything."

"He would do no such thing."

"He fears being turned into a goat. Which I will do, if he does not tell me what I wish to know. So you can tell me of this woman yourself, or consign Golovin to many sleepless nights wondering if there is more hair on the back of his hands than there used to be."

"*Bozhy moj*, you are impossible."

"At times." She eyed him. "So? Who is this woman, and should I worry that you are about to take a thief to wife?"

"I never said anything about thieves and wives."

"You did not need to. You went in search of the thieves who robbed us, and now you've found this woman. I am not a fool. She is one of the thieves, *nyet*?"

He frowned down at her and she thought he

wouldn't answer, but after a long moment, he said, "She is a widow and her name is Lady Murian Muir."

"Muir?" Where had she heard that name befo— Ah, yes. "The previous owner of the castle." At Max's surprised look, she said, "Loudan mentioned him."

"When?"

"Last week, the week before, perhaps. It was one of the many days you were off pretending to hunt."

"I *was* hunting. Just not wild game." A faint smile touched his mouth, and for a moment he looked the way he used to—more youthful, with a sparkle in his eyes. The sight made her heart ache and gave her hope. This woman had caught Max's attention, but Natasha hoped she would not crush him, too. Some men fell in love as often as there were days of the week, while others—a special few—fell in love once, and never turned from that love.

"What did Loudan tell you about Muir?"

"I wasn't really listening. He wasn't talking to me, but to some others during breakfast." She pursed her lips, trying to remember. "He said there was a duel, but I cannot remember what it was over. Muir lost and Loudan won, so the castle became his. Then there was a duel— Pah! I cannot remember everything."

"You must remember more."

"Loudan seemed too happy with it, considering a man died. It made me angry. I understand that one has no choice in matters of honor, but his attitude was uncouth. One does not brag about having to kill someone."

"Murian believes Loudan manufactured the entire

story. That there was no card game, no accusations, and no duel, but that Lord Robert was murdered in cold blood, the act covered by Loudan and his friends."

"Does she?" *And it's not "Lady Murian Muir," but just "Murian." I must meet this woman.* "I wouldn't put it past our host. He has no morals." She looked over at where the earl was greeting the arriving guests, oozing urbane charm. True charm was worn, not leaked. She sniffed. "He is a commoner."

Max had to laugh. "It is fortunate Gypsies do not pay attention to such things as titles and noble birth."

"I am not just any Gypsy, but the *phuri dai*." She couldn't have held her chin any higher.

And she was right; she was the highest-ranking female of her band. When she spoke, her people listened—which was why she was nigh unbearable elsewhere. "You are not just any Gypsy; on that we can agree, as you are the Gypsy who lost the royal crown of Oxenburg in a card game."

"I wouldn't have done it, but Loudan kept suggesting I was afraid to wager it, saying he would have already done so if he'd had a good hand. . . ." She tugged her shawl closer. "I was a fool, I know. You don't need to say anything."

"I wasn't going to say a word. I think our friend Loudan is an expert in convincing people to throw expensive items onto his card table so that he can cheat them out of them. It's how he makes his living."

"But we will get it back—once you finish chasing this widow."

"I haven't been chasing her," he lied. And yes, it was

a lie. He couldn't seem to help himself where Murian was concerned. He couldn't be in the same room with her without wanting to touch her, taste her, *know* her in every way possible. She was as spontaneous in her lovemaking as she was in the way she approached life, and he couldn't seem to get enough. She tasted of passion, freedom, and life lust, and the more he had her, the more he wanted her.

"Ah! So *she* is chasing *you*, then."

"It's nothing like that. We have a common enemy, that is all." *And a common love of carnal pleasure, but what red-blooded male and female do not?* The crowd near the door thinned at last, and Max took his grandmother's elbow and led her forward. "Finally. Let us go."

Inside the sitting room, he noted that the sideboard near the large windows bore pitchers of lemonade and punch. A short line had formed as people reached for glasses.

Tata Natasha poked him in the chest. "You."

"*Da?*"

"Tell me about this woman. Who is she and why she is—"

"I must fetch your lemonade."

Tata Natasha blinked. "I didn't ask for any."

He left before she could do more than sputter. He took his time fetching the drink, too, for he had no interest in having a discussion about Murian. She was fascinating, damned intelligent, and far too alluring to live alone in the woods. But he had to be a realist: once this was over, they would go their own ways and to their own futures, as fate had decreed. He would return to Oxenburg, his duties set for life, while she would return to Rowallen, to eventually become a wife and mother.

His chest tightened and he rubbed it absently. He knew his grandmother wished him to find a wife, but she didn't understand the harsh sacrifice that would be required of the woman. He would *never* damn Murian, who'd already suffered so much, to a life of endless uncertainty, waiting for the day he did not return. He'd seen the darkness in her eyes when she talked about the loss of her husband, and he'd seen how that death had left her unprotected and alone, banished from everything she held dear. She deserved far better. She deserved to be a beloved wife again, mother to a number of red-haired, silver-eyed children.

An odd hollowness rustled through him. He would not think of her future life. He couldn't afford to. Yet even as he had the thought, an image of Murian with another man flashed into his mind. His chest tightened, blood roaring in his ears, as red-hot jealousy seared his being. He must have looked as furious as his thoughts made him, for the gentleman waiting beside him suddenly blanched and took a step away.

Bozhy moj, I cannot think of that. Max forced a smile, which he was sure looked as fake as it felt. "I am sorry, but the lemonade has no ice and will be warm, which will displease my grandmother."

The man gulped and nodded, still looking as if he expected Max to whip out a sword.

Max inclined his head and left. *Bloody hell, where did*

that come from? I cannot think of it again. Tonight there is only our mission. There can be nothing else.

He put his thoughts under rigid control and went through their plan once more. And then again. It took a while, but finally his thoughts settled, his body easing to calm alertness. Everything became clearer than usual, a heightened sense of awareness filling him so that he noticed everything. As he walked through the room he soaked in the fleeting scents of various perfumes, the softness of the rug under his boots, the golden glow of the beeswax candles reflecting off the chandeliers' crystals, the rustle of silk and fine wool.

He caught sight of Orlov near the doorway the servants were using to refill the pitchers on the refreshment table. *Good. He is right where he is supposed to be: ready to set the signal once we're certain all is clear.* Golovin and Pahlen were lingering in the foyer, acting as if they were arguing over whose horse was fastest, although if one knew them, one would know such a conversation would involve fists, not words. Pushkin, flirting with a young lady and her mother, both of them flushed and pleased, stood near a window where he could easily see outside. The only men not in attendance were Demidor and Raeff, who were making sure two kitchen maids were doing as they'd been paid to do in the name of a grand prank: luring the guards to the barn to partake of some forbidden—and unknown to them—drugged wine.

Max looked at the clock resting on a mantel, satisfied that everything was working as planned. Still, he couldn't ignore a growing sense of concern. Something felt . . . off. Which was totally ridiculous. They'd been careful. More than careful. And things were going well so far.

Demidor and Raeff appeared in the doorway, looking relaxed and jovial as they wandered to the refreshment table. *So, now the guards are dealt with.* The clock chimed half past eight, and a new volley of tension moved between Max's shoulders. *Murian will be approaching the ridge now. I hope she doesn't—*

"Your Highness," came an unctuous voice at Max's side. "Why so serious at our festive event? Don't you enjoy opera?"

Max turned to find Loudan standing near. The earl was alone, a faint smirk on his narrow face. Max bowed. "I enjoy opera very much."

"Good. I believe you will find this evening's entertainment especially to your liking."

"I'm sure I will. Of course, I would enjoy this evening's performance more if I did not know my grandmother suffers because of your guile."

Loudan's smile grew fixed, and he said with obvious displeasure, "You are very direct, Your Highness. I dislike that."

"I'm not a diplomat. We soldiers find direct speech more effective."

"While I find it uncivilized. But fine. If you wish it, then we will put all of our cards upon the table."

"I was under the impression that was something you never did—at least not in accordance to the rules of play."

Loudan's eyes flashed. "Are you are accusing me of something?"

"If I did, you would naturally demand satisfaction, as you did with Lord Muir."

"Lord Muir got what he deserved."

"Just as my grandmother deserved to be tricked into wagering something she did not own?"

The earl shrugged. "She had the crown in her possession and she wagered it, not I."

"She wagered it at your urging."

"I may have suggested it, but that is no crime." The earl showed his teeth in a smile that did not reach his eyes. "I'd offer to allow you to purchase it back, but it's too late. I've already sold it."

"To whom?"

"I have been working through a courier, so I don't know the true purchaser, nor do I wish to."

It was hard to believe no one had killed this fool before now. The idiot had no honor at all. "If you were going to sell it, you should have given us first right."

"But you see, I'm not really interested in you and your tiny country and your paltry heirloom. Someone else approached me about the crown before you even arrived. Someone looking for an old, respected token of authority, a crown with a history of power."

Max crossed his arms to keep from reaching out and grabbing the earl by his scrawny neck. "Only a new regime would wish for such a thing; otherwise they'd already have their own. And I can think of only one country in such a position. Napoléon has recently declared himself emperor, *nyet*?"

Loudan sent him a sour look. "You fish in a dry

pond; I do not know who bought this crown. As I said, I haven't asked and I don't intend to."

"How did this courier know you had the crown in your possession to begin with?"

"I have no idea. The man merely mentioned he knew I had it. Perhaps your grandmother told someone?"

"She told no one."

"Don't be too sure about that." A sneer entered Loudan's voice. "Everyone knows a Romany cannot keep a secret."

Max's hand curled into a fist, but he halted when he caught Orlov's concerned stare from across the room. *He is right; I must keep my mind on the objective, and not my desire to flatten this fool's face.*

Max uncurled his hand. "We will—"

The dinner gong sounded and Loudan straightened. "I must go, but . . ." He hesitated. "If I may offer a word of advice?"

Max raised his brows.

"You will wish to stay through the ending of Madame Dufond's performance. The ending is where the magic really happens, isn't it? Everything before that is . . . anticipation." The earl smiled. "Now, if you'll excuse me, I must resume my duties as host." With that, he left.

Seething, Max watched the earl make his way through the room. As he neared the wide windows, the earl paused by a footman. The man was clearly one of his guards, for no footman would have had such a thick neck and awkward physical stance.

Loudan said a word or two, and the guard nodded

and left, pausing to look out the window near where Pushkin stood flirting shamelessly. While there, the guard lifted his hand in a quick gesture, before continuing on his way.

The guards were pulled off that side of the castle, so who could he be greeting, unless— An icy hand gripped Max's heart. *They've replaced the guard. So they know. Bloody hell, they* know.

Pushkin had seen the gesture, too. Alarm in his gaze, he excused himself from the ladies and crossed to the window.

Max joined him. Moonlight dappled the ridge and the slope of lawn leading to the castle, and as he looked, the moon reflected off metal. He looked more closely, alarmed at the number of black figures moving in the darkness.

His gaze flickered to the ridge. *She does not know the danger. I promised the guards would be gone—and now this.* His heart thudded sickly, his hands damp, his skin so tight that it compressed his breath. Was this how it felt to wait for someone going into battle? To be afraid they might come to harm, to worry beyond all common sense that they would fall and you would never see them again? *This is its own hell.*

Pushkin cursed under his breath. "Someone has betrayed us."

"Indeed. We must warn Murian and the others. They are in danger."

"I'll go," Pushkin said. "You would be missed."

"There must be a way that I can—" His gaze fell

on Tata Natasha, who was still near the doorway. He turned to Pushkin. "Inform the others that we have been betrayed. I'll find a way to warn Murian."

"What do you need of us?"

"Stay here, and be a very large presence. I will be as quick as I can."

"Very well." Obviously not pleased with Max's decision, Pushkin went to inform the others of the change in plans.

Max reached Tata as quickly as he could.

She frowned on seeing him. "Where is my lemonade?"

He took her arm and pulled her aside. "We need you. Something has gone wrong."

Her gaze sharpened. "*Da?*"

"We must have a distraction, one where you need escorting from the room."

"How do—"

"My friends," Loudan announced. "It is time for dinner." He looked at Max and bowed. "Your Highness, we will follow you and the grand duchess into the dining room."

Every eye fixed on Max. There was nothing to be done but act as if everything was well, and hope and pray with every fiber of his being that he'd said enough for Tata to understand what he needed.

She placed her hand on his arm and together they walked toward the door, Loudan and Lady MacLure falling in behind them.

Max squeezed Tata's arm and she instantly cried out, and with amazing dexterity, collapsed upon the floor. One moment, she was upright, and the next, she was a black heap, the rose skulls on her shawl taking on new meaning.

Cries arose, and Lady MacLure gasped.

"Tata!" Max bent to her.

She clutched her heart. "I fear . . . I fear . . . I am . . . dying . . . the world . . . grows . . . dim. . . ."

Bloody hell, a twisted ankle would have been enough. "I'm sure you'll be fine with a little rest. I'll carry you to your room."

Loudan snapped his fingers, bringing two footmen to the fore. "Help Her Grace back to her room."

"*Nyet*," Tata said faintly. "Only a prince may carry . . . a grand duchess." She looked at Max. "Take me . . . to my room. I . . . must rest."

He scooped her up and carried her toward the staircase.

"Wait!" She threw up a hand.

All eyes rested on her.

"Send a dinner tray delivered to my bedchamber." With that, she threw her head back and pretended to faint.

Loudan's gaze narrowed.

Teeth gritted, Max hurried up the stairs, his mind, heart, and soul hanging in pained suspense over a ridge in the dark night.

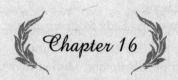

Chapter 16

Clouds passed in front of the moon, darkening the night into inky blackness.

Murian looked through a gap in the shrubs down the slope to Rowallen. The castle was aglow, its windows golden bright with hundreds of candles. "He's burning through the entire inventory of candles," Murian grumbled. "And for naught but to make it seem as if he were someone."

"He's been tryin' to impress the locals fer a while, and now he has a prince to impress, too," Ian said. "He'd do better if he'd jus' returned tha' blasted crown."

Stationed nearby, Will turned to look over his shoulder. "What crown?"

Murian sent Ian a hard look. She hadn't told anyone but him about the lost crown of Oxenburg, as Max had seemed so loath to mention it. And Will was as big a gossip as Widow Reeves.

Ian looked sheepish. "'Tis naught, lad. Just a tiara lost in a game of chance."

"Ye said 'twas a crown."

"It's bloody close to a crown if 'tis worn by a Gypsy queen, no?" Ian snapped.

"Oh. I would think so, aye." Will didn't seem to think the information warranted any more interest, thankfully, and he returned back to his duties.

The wind picked up and Murian tugged her cloak closer, glad of her warm breeches and high boots. She checked her rapier and pistol, then silently counted the arrows for her bow. She was ready. All they needed was their signal.

Will glanced up at the moon. "The clouds make it hard to see. My eyes adjust to the dark, and then 'tis light. And then they adjust to the light, and—"

"Fer the love of heaven, lad, we understood ye wi'oot the explanation. Now whist, and let us know when ye see the signal."

"Aye," Will grumbled, moving a bit farther down the ridge.

Murian said in a low tone, "Why are you so hard on the lad? You said yourself life hadna been fair to him."

"Tha' dinna mean he should get special treatment. It only means we should remember why he's such a pain so we willna strangle him when he's bein' foolish."

"And why is he—"

"The signal!" The shrubbery rustled as Will moved toward them. "'Tis time."

"Let's go, lass." Ian started to rise.

"Wait. It's wrong."

Ian stared down across the lawn at the castle. "There's a light in the window, as we were told."

"It was to be in the second window from the end. That's the third."

Will looked disappointed. "'Tis the right room, and the right signal. Mayhap the prince's men just got the wrong window."

Murian shook her head as she stared at the castle. "Nay. Hold. Ian, do you see what I see? There, on the battlements."

Ian looked, his expression impatient. "I dinna see— Och! Now I do." His face grew grim. "There're men stationed atop the castle. Tha' is new."

"Who put them there?" Will asked.

"The earl, no doubt," Murian said. "But if we choose our path carefully, we should be able to get to the castle without being seen."

She judged the angle of view the guards on the parapets would have. Finally, she nodded. "We'll go down the far left side and swing back around toward the castle. Those trees should shield us most of the way. These clouds will help, too."

Ian nodded. "Tha' will work." He arose and led the way, Murian following, Will trailing behind. They stayed low and took the slope a few moments at a time, pausing behind heavy thickets now and then before darting to a new location. They were halfway there when Murian caught a glimmer of movement to their right. She grabbed Ian's arm and stopped him, Will close behind.

They stooped, silent and watchful. As they did so, the movement she'd caught came closer, and they heard the chink of metal on metal. She peered in the direction of the noise. A guard walked past, silent and cautious, trying not to crack any branches along the way. The moonlight broke through and gleamed along the barrel of his pistol. *Guards! Bloody hell, they're supposed to be gone.*

She looked toward the castle and noticed their signal light had been extinguished. Something was wrong. Very wrong.

Suddenly the door from the study was thrown open and Max's deep voice rose loudly in the dark, singing a song in his native tongue. His words were slurred, as if he'd been drinking. *What is he doing?* She peered through the shrubbery, wondering if she should go closer.

The singing suddenly stopped. "Hold! Who goes there?" he said in a booming shout. "I'm a prince of Oxenburg and I demand you show yourself!"

There was a moment of silence, and then a man's voice answered, "Beggin' yer pardon, Yer Highness, bu' we're patrollin' the hillside."

Ian gave a muffled curse and grabbed Murian's arm, tugging her back up the hill. Will led the way, peering anxiously as they climbed.

"Are you now?" Max slurred his words yet more. "And why is that?"

"We was ordered to, Yer Highness." The guard hesitated and then added, "The earl heard there was to be a raid on the castle tonight, so 'tis no' safe ootside. May I suggest ye mi' wish to go back in?"

"A raid? Tonight? Why, it is likely to rain. Who

would plan a raid in such horrid weather? Only fools and drunkards."

As if the world agreed with him, the first drops of icy cold wetness hit Murian's cheek. She ground her teeth as she fought to keep her feet silent on their twig-covered path. *Bloody hell, how had Loudan known?*

She looked ahead to where Will's figure blended into the dark woods. *Was Ian right about Will? I can't believe 'tis him. He would never have demanded to come with us if he'd set a trap with the earl. No, it must be someone else. But who?*

They reached the top of the ridge just as Max called a drunken good night to the guard. For a moment the prince stood in the open doorway, light outlining his form. Then, with a final lift of his hand, he disappeared inside.

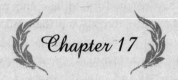

Chapter 17

The rain hit as they reached their mounts. The ride back to their village was long and miserable, as they didn't dare hurry the horses in the dark.

As they rode, head bowed against the icy rain, Murian could feel Ian's irritation with the disappointing outcome of the night's events, while Will remained sullenly silent. For her part, she was beyond frustrated, and as angry as she could be with their betrayer.

Someone had obviously shared their plan with Loudan. It had to be one of Max's men, for she knew her own people too well. Didn't she?

The hood of her cloak, now soaked beyond help, dripped water over her face. She thought of the members of her band, lingering only momentarily on Will. It couldn' be. None of them would have done such a thing; she was sure of it. Perhaps one of the prince's men had been seen while studying the layout of the castle, or had inadvertently said something in front of a servant? Neither was out of the realm of the possible.

Icy and plentiful, the rain continued to beat mercilessly upon them and pitilessly tortured the horses.

Finally, they reached the village and rode into the stables. Shivering with cold and thankful to be out of the stinging rain, Murian slid off her mount. "Bloody hell, *that* is not a ride I want to repeat." She whipped off her dripping cloak and carried it to the door to wring it out, then threw it over a hook. "I've never been so wet ootside of my own tub."

Ian sputtered at the water that dripped from his moustache and eyebrows. He looked miserable, cold, and grumpy. "'Twas a rotten way to end a foolish errand."

Her temper was quick to stir. "You think 'tis foolish to find the proof we need to win back Rowallen?"

"'Twould be best if we dinna talk aboot this now," he growled as he took off his wet coat, dropping the sopping mess on the floor before he led his horse into a stall. "I'm in no mood fer it."

"Nor am I." She unbuckled her horse's saddle and slid it off, and started to carry it to a stand by the back door.

Will tied his horse to a stall door and then took the saddle from her, ignoring her protest. "I got it, me lady." His gaze flickered to Ian before he added in a low voice, "Between the two of us, ye ha' the harder job."

"I can hear ye," Ian snapped.

"Then *talk*," Murian said. "You may not be in the mood for it, but the words are burning your lips."

Ian clamped his lips together, led his unsaddled horse into a stall, and began to dry it with handfuls of hay.

"Fine. But dinna come to me tomorrow wishing to discuss this, for I'll have nothing to say by then." She picked up fistfuls of hay and did the same with her horse.

He paused, fixing her with a glare he usually reserved for Widow MacDonald, then threw down the hay and stomped over to her. "Fine. I'll tell ye wha' I think. 'Tis time to admit we're on a fool's errand. We're no' meant to win back anything. Rowallen is gone, and she willna be comin' back."

Murian's jaw tightened. "Rowallen doesna belong to Loudan. He canna have it."

"She's right, Ian." Will unbuckled his horse's saddle. "Besides, wha' should we do, jus' sit back and let tha' no guid braggart steal it fra' us? Ye canna mean tha'."

Ian ignored Will. "Lass, ye've had yer way too long in this and 'tis time it stopped. Loudan has already stolen Rowallen and there's no gettin' it back."

"That's enough." Murian placed a horse blanket over her mount. "I refuse to believe Robert died in vain. We've pledged ourselves to this path, and we'll not leave it until we've succeeded and Rowallen is back where she belongs." Murian closed the stall door and went to collect her dripping cloak.

Ian threw down the handful of wet straw and followed her. "Ye're bein' stubborn, and someone is going to get injured! I've watched o'er ye, lass, and ha' tried to be patient, thinkin' ye might realize the truth on yer own, but ye willna'. The reality is this—the castle is gone and there is no hope. None. And e'en if there were, ye wouldna be—"

"Ian!" Will's voice cut sharply. "That is enou'!"

Murian was glad Will had spoken, for her throat was too tight to allow her to do so. Every word Ian had spoken sliced her like a shard of glass. Since Robert's death, Ian had been her rock, encouraging her, suggesting new ways to approach their problems, standing beside her in every risky venture. Except to worry about their safety, not once had he wavered in spirit or faith.

Until now. She swallowed hard. "'Tis good to know where you really stand." She couldn't keep the quaver from her voice.

Will sent Ian a hard look. "Are ye happy now, ye old bugger?"

Ian's expression softened, though his anger remained strong. "I dinna mean to hurt ye, lass, but e'en wi' the prince's help, we were in grave danger tonight. Those men had pistols and meant to use them." He sighed, his broad shoulders bowing. "It was a guid try, and ye did wha' ye could, but our luck has run oot, and we must face tha' fact."

Murian was glad her hair was dripping water over her face, for it hid the tear that leaked from her eye. "We've had a very difficult evening, we have." She took her cloak from its peg and headed toward the stable door. "We had high hopes, and promises were made but not kept. But now is not the time to think aboot it. We're tired and cold and wet. We'll discuss this tomorrow."

"I'll no' think differently then, lass."

She paused and looked back. "Did you ever really think we'd win back Rowallen, Ian? Even once?"

His gaze dropped.

A lump filled her throat. Without another word, she left the barn. Behind her Will's voice rose as he berated Ian, the older man's tones low and heavy in return.

Already wet, she merely ducked her head against the icy rain, her boots sloshing in the mud. When she reached her home she fumbled with the door, finally getting it open, and walked inside.

She closed and locked the door and then leaned against it, water dripping from her and soaking into the carpet under her feet as the rain beat the slate shingles in a noisy roar. She hung her wet cloak beside the door and used the light from the low fire to find a towel and dry her face and hands. That done, she found a candle and lit it.

A small, golden glow suffused the room, though it did little for her black mood. Trying not to think, she added wood to the fire, adjusting the flue so the flames could breathe. There, before the warmth, she took off her wet boots and undressed, peeling her soaked clothes from her skin. Naked and shivering, she toweled herself dry and then donned her robe, wrapping the towel about her wet hair.

She spread her cloak before the fire and turned her boots upside down so that the water would drain out. Before fetching her comb, she hung a kettle of water over the fire to heat. Then, comb in hand, she pulled a small stool before the fire and began to dry her hair.

When the kettle whistled, she set aside the comb and made her tea, fragrant steam lifting from her mug. Soon she was curled upon the overstuffed settee, a blanket tucked about her, her warm mug cupped between her hands, the scent of black tea and bergamot giving her comfort.

When she'd been a child, she used to watch her father make their tea, every movement as calm, unruffled, and thoughtful as he'd been. Her mother had been more impetuous and never left the tea infuser in the hot water long enough for it to have any flavor. Papa used to laugh at the faces Mama would make when drinking her weak tea.

Murian's throat tightened again as she was swept with a longing to see them both, and she had to dash her hand over her eyes to remove fresh tears. *What is wrong with me? I'm a weepy mess tonight.* But she knew what was wrong: Ian's words had cut her to the bone, and left her reeling and more alone than she'd ever been.

In the days after Robert's death, she'd leaned on Ian far more than she should have. Apparently, he'd come to feel as if he needed to support her, even if it meant lying to her, which he'd obviously done.

It hurt, though she couldn't find it in her heart to be angry with him. All she felt was a deep, overwhelming sadness.

Blinking back tears, she rested her head against the settee, realizing how very tired she was. Whether it was the cold, or getting so wet, or the near disaster of the evening, she wasn't sure. But it felt heavenly to simply sit and do nothing for a few moments.

Of course, this couldn't last. She had plans to make. With or without Ian, she would not give up on Rowallen. Too many people depended on her.

She sipped her tea, savoring the warmth as the rain clattered against the window, punctuated now and again by the low rumble of thunder, her mind flickering to Max. A faint smile touched her lips when she thought of his fakely drunken singing. It had been an inspired way to sound an alarm without the guards realizing what he was doing.

Her smile slipped and she wondered what had happened to upset their plan. Had they been betrayed? By whom? It had to be one of the prince's men. She couldn't imagine any other—

Bam! Bam! Bam! A heavy fist hit her door.

Sighing, she set her mug aside, tugged her blanket about her shoulders and hurried to the door. She unlocked it and pulled it open. "Ian, there's nothing more—"

Max strode into the room, his black cloak soaked, water streaming from his broad shoulders to the floor.

"Och, you're dripping!"

"It's a floor." He threw back his hood and raked a hand through his wet hair. "Floors are made to catch water."

"At least stand on the hearth, so the water dinna ruin my rugs." Murian closed the door and rebolted it, her body prickling awake in a heated rush. Even soaked head to toe, he exuded a sensual power that instantly reminded her of more intimate moments. She'd been feeling so alone, and now, he was here. A flutter of relief warmed her chilled spirits.

He stood on the hearth and undid his cloak, water pooling about his boots.

"Hang your cloak over that chair." She dug another towel from a trunk at the foot of her bed and brought it to him, watching as he dried off, glad to have something to think about other than Ian's defection.

Besides, whatever she thought about Max, she couldn't deny that he was a pleasure to watch. Seeing him across a ballroom, one was instantly aware of his dark, angelic beauty, augmented by his black hair, green eyes, and golden skin. But now, up close, with his hair slicked back from the rain, the sheer masculine strength of his face was in sharp relief—his stone-cut jaw, the high cheekbones, the strong nose. Frankly, it was a gift to women everywhere that he'd managed to gather those few scars, for they were the only thing that kept him from being a dangerous distraction.

He caught her gaze and his stern expression softened. "You look exhausted."

She put a hand to her cheek, hiding a desire to wince. "I am."

"It is often that way after a battle. It was a close one tonight, *dorogaya moya*. Too close." He reached over and captured one of her damp curls, sliding it between his fingers. "Your hair is like the sea, frothing and curling, like waves trying to steal the sand from beneath unsuspecting feet."

She flushed and tightened her robe, suddenly aware of the deficiencies in her dress. "So . . . what happened this evening?"

His gaze darkened. "We were betrayed. I don't know how, or by whom, but Loudan knew our plan. He allowed it to progress to a point, for we were able to remove the guards from that side of the house. What we didn't know was that as soon as we had them out of the way, he replaced them."

Her stomach tightened. "He hoped to catch us as we entered."

Max nodded. "We realized what was happening and didn't set the signal."

"Someone did. There was a candle, but in the wrong window." She sighed, pushing her hair from her neck and rubbing it. "It bothered me, that detail, but it was cold and we were so close—" She sighed. "I should have stopped right there."

"Yes, you should have." His mouth was white, his expression stern. "I knew you were on that ridge and might come down it at any moment—" He snapped his mouth closed, as if the words were bitter.

She toyed with one of the wide cuffs on her robe. "Your singing is atrocious. It probably frightened the earl's men to death."

His brows lowered. "This is not a matter for levity."

"I know. But it's all I have right now."

Their gazes met. She could see he longed to say more, that the danger of their plan was heavy on his shoulders, but she was too overwhelmed to deal with it this evening. She shook her head, saying in a tired voice, "I canna handle more tonight."

He nodded, his expression softening. "You need something to drink and some rest. You will feel better then." A faint grin tilted one corner of his mouth. "Hopefully, with some sleep, you will realize my singing was not so bad after all."

She had to laugh, which soothed her in some way. "There is not enough sleep for *that* to happen."

He sighed as if put upon. "And here I thought I did rather well, given the circumstances." He unbuttoned his coat, pausing for a moment. "Do you mind? It is wet, and while the fire warms me, it is still cold."

As steam was softly rising from his broad shoulders, she didn't doubt it. "Of course." She tried not to look as he pulled off his coat and then his waistcoat, his white shirt as soaked as the rest of him. It clung lovingly to his shoulders, his narrow waist, his flat stomach—

She realized he was watching her, smiling smugly, and she hurried to turn elsewhere. "Would you like some tea?"

"*Nyet*. Not now." He was quiet a moment. "This adventure will end soon, one way or another."

"I know." She crossed her arms, rubbing them to bring some warmth.

"But not tonight."

Not tonight. The simple words lifted her heart, which had been so downtrodden this evening. She found herself smiling. "No. Not tonight."

"Let us pretend, for form's sake, that tonight I'm merely visiting. That there is no Rowallen, and no people who rely upon us. There is only you, and me, and this visit."

"No one visits in the rain, which is why I'm not dressed for company."

His gaze flickered over her again, his mouth curving into a faint smile. "In that robe, you look like a—" He struggled to find the word, then pressed his hands together and placed them beside his cheek. "That thing you sleep on. Under your head. It is made of feathers and—"

"A *pillow*?" She looked down. The robe had been Robert's and was huge on her. It puffed both above and below the belt; she supposed she did look rather like a pillow.

Damn it, I look like a plump pillow while he looks like that. She eyed his stomach once more, noting that each ripple was perfectly spaced. Life was not fair. She tugged at her sash. "It's my favorite robe."

"It seems very comfortable and modest. You are more covered in that robe than in any two of your gowns."

Before he'd told her she looked like a poofy pillow, she'd felt exposed. Now she just felt irritated and was glad there was no mirror nearby. For surely in addition to being enveloped in a thick, fat robe, her nose must be red and her hair beginning to crackle into seaweed, which it did if she didn't comb it enough while it dried.

Max, watching her emotions play across her face, hid a grin. "A pillow," he amended, "but a much treasured pillow."

Even though she was exhausted, the humor still warmed her. "A treasured pillow, then. That's better. Somewhat."

He laughed softly and took a step toward her. His wet breeches pulled and he grimaced, losing his smile. "I should remove these." He waited to see if she'd argue.

Instead, her gaze flickered down, over his hips and legs. "Those must be uncomfortable." Her voice, always husky and enticing, had deepened.

His body reacted so instantly, he paused in reaching for his buttons.

She saw it and, realization dawning, grinned. "Dinna tell me you've suddenly become shy."

He loved her lilting, honey-soaked voice, the way some words ended with an up note, as if they begged for a quick kiss to smooth them on their way.

He found the Scottish accent intriguing, the cadence reminding him of his grandmother's people. They sang when they talked, and it reminded him of sleepy summers under a starlit sky.

"Hold a moment." She went to the bed and pulled off one of the blankets and brought it to him. "In case your shyness returns and catches you in a blush."

He couldn't stop watching her mouth. She wasn't a conventional beauty, this red-haired, fiercely independent temptress. She was a real-life, flesh-and-bone woman, with hair that rarely stayed within its pins, and skin that flushed when she grew angry. While he could see that she'd shed a few tears over tonight, she'd neither had histrionics nor downplayed the dangers, but had accepted them without a flinch. Her pragmatic nature was every bit as appealing as the full lips that made him think of carnal pleasures every time she spoke.

She intrigued him as no other. She carried herself with assuredness, as if she knew her value better than any one else. But it was more than just confidence. Without any of the artifices most women employed— rustling silks and exotic perfumes, batting eyelashes and senseless giggles—she was one of the most feminine women he'd ever met. He couldn't see her without his hands itching to touch her, his tongue wishing to tangle with hers, his body wanting to take her, over and over.

His mind latched upon her every expression, every movement, and he understood them, understood her. It was as if his body was already attuned with hers, his thoughts already entwined with hers.

And yet it still wasn't enough. He wanted more. More kisses. More touches. More laughter. More everything. There was no such thing as "enough"—not with Murian.

He threw the blanket onto the settee and strode to her side. Without a word, he lifted her into his arms, her robe parting to reveal slender, shapely legs. She slipped her arms about his neck, resting her head against his shoulder.

With a smile, he paused to blow out the candle, and then he carried her to the huge bed.

Chapter 18

Max lowered her onto the bed, consuming her with his gaze. The firelight glistened in her red hair, tracing her curls, even as it caressed the pure line of her cheek and full lips. He bent to kiss her, tugging her sash free. He opened her robe, gazing at her hungrily. Her legs were long and pale, with perfectly formed calves just made for a man's palm. He admired the strength in her thighs, and, above them, the small, crisp curls that covered her womanhood, hiding and teasing.

He slid his hands up her calves, to her thighs, and hovered over her nether curls.

She gasped, her gaze never leaving him, a question in her eyes.

"I must have you," he whispered as he moved on to her hips, cupping them and curling his fingers into her flesh, his body aching with desire.

"Nay, 'tis I who must have you." She pulled her arms free from the robe and slid into the center of the bed, nude and boldly ready for him. "I need this tonight."

She hadn't said she needed *him*, and for some reason that bothered him. But not enough to stop. He couldn't undress fast enough, peeling off his breeches and tugging his shirt over his head while she held out her arms.

And then he was there, skin to skin, nothing between them but heat and passion, desire and want. He ran his hands over her body, from calf to hip, hip to waist, waist to breast, pausing to touch and stroke and tease her. She moaned his name, her breath short and hot, her hands seeking, stroking, too.

God, but he loved to touch her. His fingertips couldn't rest, but must move. And where his fingers went, so did his mouth. He traced a line from her neck to her breast, pausing to torment her nipples into hardness, moving back and forth until she arched against him, restless with desire.

Then he went lower, kissing his way down her gently rounded stomach, her fingers in his hair as he brushed his chin over her mound—once, and then twice.

She gasped and lifted to him, balling the sheets into her fists.

He teased her again, blowing on her damp curls, sending shudders through her.

"More," she gasped and, to his surprise, entwined her hands in his hand and pressed him where she wished him to be, opening her legs and lifting her womanhood to him.

More aroused than he'd ever been, he slipped his hands beneath her bottom and lifted her to his lips, delicately parting her slick folds with his tongue. She tasted of sweetness and rainwater, his cock hardening with each movement she made against his mouth. He slipped his tongue up, over the hard nub of her pleasure, and then back to her wetness. Over and over, he traced the path.

She tugged him closer. Urged on, he slipped his tongue into her and then out, thrusting now, mimicking the movement of his hips. Over and over, he thrust, soaking in her gasps of excitement. Her hands tightened in his hair as he took her with his mouth. Suddenly, she planted her feet on the bed and arched against him, crying out his name. As she shook with pleasure, he slipped his fingers into her, stroking deeply until she clutched the sheets again and begged him to stop.

Laughing, he moved up her body, raining kisses over her creamy skin while she fought lingering shudders beneath him, her breaths ragged and short.

Finally, he lay atop her, his face even with hers, one of her legs over his hip. "That," he whispered against her neck, "was for you."

Murian slipped her arms about him, her breathing finally slowing. "Then this, my love, will be for you." She'd never been so well pleasured. She couldn't stop trembling, her body aching with fulfillment and desire.

Every trail of his fingertips, roughened from his life, made her quiver and her heart thunder in her ears. It was as if her body, so long asleep, had been awakened by his kisses, his touch, his warmth. She could no more think than breathe.

She ran her hands over his powerful arms, his broad shoulders, his muscular chest, seeking and exploring, wondering how she'd gone for so long without touching and being touched. She'd been achingly lonely, a fact she only now allowed herself to admit.

And this, here and now, felt right. She was safe within Max's arms, safe to forget who she was and where she was, when she was within his embrace. Safe to be as wanton or deliciously sinful as the moment allowed. Her body still ached from his tongue, still yearned for more. But now was his turn.

She opened her legs and lifted to meet him. She gasped as his hard cock filled her, sending new shivers through her. She wrapped one of her legs about him and then raised up on one arm, turning him over so that she was now atop him, his cock buried deeply. It was heavenly, and she watched as he closed his eyes, biting his lip as he tried to maintain control.

She pulled her knees up alongside of his hips, flattened her hands on his chest, lifted herself up the length of his cock, and then slowly, ever so slowly, sank back down.

His eyes flew open in surprise. She immediately lifted again, only to slide back onto him. Beneath her, Max gasped in pleasured agony. She went up and slowly down again, feeling his cock growing even harder, pushing more deeply inside.

And then she was rocking upon him faster and faster. His hands closed about her waist as he thrust up, meeting her.

Max gritted his teeth, his cock begging for release. He wanted nothing more than to flip her over and take her with all of the pent-up passion she'd raised. Yet he couldn't look away from the picture she made as she rocked on him, her breasts bouncing, her hair clinging to her bare shoulders, her skin glistening with exertion.

He tightened his hold on her waist, meeting her stroke for stroke. Her breath came rapidly, and then her back arched. He felt the wave of her joy before she did, slipping his hands to her ass so he could hold her firmly to him as, with a surprised cry, she bucked wildly on his cock, unleashed and crazed with desire. No longer able to control himself, he thrust into her and released himself deep inside as she collapsed upon him.

*M*uch later, when the fire had burned down low, and they'd enjoyed each other until they could no longer move, Max lifted Murian's hand and pressed a kiss into her palm. He traced his lips up her finger, bit softly on her fingertip, then pressed kisses back to the palm and lower, finding her pulse on her wrist, and capturing it with his lips.

She smiled sleepily, her silver eyes barely visible between her thick lashes. "I canna . . . I just canna."

He chuckled. "I don't think I can, either."

She settled her head in the crook of his shoulder, her lips curled in a smile replete with lovemaking.

God, how he loved those lips, dusky in color and perfectly formed. They were as intriguing as she was. He bent to taste them with one soft kiss. She kissed him back, and then she curled around him, her arm over his chest, her leg over his, her head neatly tucked under his chin, and fell almost instantly asleep.

Though tired, Max found sleep more elusive. He brushed her curls from where they tickled his chin, and smoothed his hand down her shoulder and arm. She sighed in her sleep but didn't wake, and he knew she felt safe. Protected. And he took pride in that. He'd never wanted anything more than to hold her when she needed it, to kiss the sadness from her eyes and watch her lips curl into a smile. *With that, I am happy.*

And in that moment, lying awake in the dark, Murian wrapped about him, Max realized he'd made a mistake he could never undo. At some point, he'd fallen in love with this woman. A woman he would soon have to leave.

A pain like he'd never known filled his heart. He wrapped his arms about her and buried his face in her hair, closing his eyes to time and circumstances, and everything else that damned them.

Chapter 19

Max blinked awake, wondering for a moment where he was. Memories of the night before slowly filtered to him, and he turned to find early-morning sunlight limning the very feminine arm that was draped over his chest.

Lifting his head, he followed the line of that arm to a graceful shoulder and on to an elegant neck, and a firm chin barely visible in a wave of red curls. Through the tangle of red silken hair, her breath stirred the strands with each soft puff.

After years of battle Max had become a rise-with-the-sun sort of man, but this morning, he was reluctant to stir. The bed was warm, the sheets scented with the vanilla and lavender he'd come to associate with Murian, and she fitted so perfectly against him.

He rested his cheek against her forehead, listening to her steady breath, his loins stirring. It was a testament to Murian that his cock could rise so quickly after such a night, and rise it did.

But perhaps that wasn't the best idea. Perhaps the best idea was to get up, leave, and never again see her alone.

He knew what his duty was; knew what he needed to do, why, and when. The same could be said for Murian; she was as tied here as he was tied to Oxenburg, neither of them free to follow their hearts.

But was he truly in her heart? As much as he wished to know, he knew he couldn't ask. She was fond of him, and she'd welcomed him to her bed, too. But then again, she was an independent woman, so why shouldn't she? Her desire bespoke nothing more than a healthy regard for her own sensuality.

Under normal circumstances, he'd simply ask what her feelings might be. But in asking, there was the promise of fulfillment. Unless he was willing to answer her feelings with his own, he had no right to even bring up the subject.

There was nothing to be said. As soon as his mission was done, he'd leave while she remained to continue her fight for Rowallen. There was nothing left for either of them.

The realization made him ache as if someone had hit his breastplate with a two-handed sword. He rubbed his chest, wondering that it felt so real.

A loud knock rang through the quiet. Max lifted his head.

Murian stirred at his side.

Outside, Ian called, "Lassie? Are ye oop?"

Murian blinked awake and sat up, her gaze finding Max. She shoved her hair from her face and called out, "Aye. Is something wrong?"

"We've much to talk aboot, ye and I." There was a silence. "I owe ye an apology."

Max caught the downturn of Murian's mouth and he raised his brows.

She shook her head before she raised her voice to Ian. "Go on to breakfast. I'll meet you once I'm dressed."

"Are ye sure, lassie?" They heard a sound, like a boot scuffing the ground. "I dinna mean to bother ye, but I am sorry. I had time to think things through, and I was wrong. I was just angry aboot how the raid went and . . . I'm angry wi' tha' dammed prince."

A sparkle of humor warmed Murian's eyes. "Oh? And why are you mad at the prince?"

"Because he put ye in danger." Ian adopted an odd German accent. "'Oh, there's nothin' to be worried aboot, me and my perfect soldiers will clear oot the guards.'"

Max opened his mouth to retaliate, but Murian pressed her finger to his lips.

Ian continued, "If tha' was clearing the guards, then I'm an elephant."

"He's as big as one," Max muttered.

Murian grinned, but told Ian, "Go eat; I'll speak with you soon. And dinna worry, Ian, I'm not mad. Not at all."

"Verrah weel."

They listened as he left.

Max stretched. "I suppose I must go, so you can embark upon my character assassination over your breakfast."

Murian's smile faded. "Last night Ian had a lot of bad things to say aboot everyone. He's a bit of a nay-sayer at times. We Scots are a dour lot."

Max rolled over to kiss her nose. "Never say it."

Her smile returned, though a shadow remained in her eyes.

He felt the same way, but there was nothing more to be said. Unwillingly, he arose, though it felt as if he were leaving a piece of his heart in the bed with her. He grimaced at his own thoughts.

He washed in the cold water on the small dresser by the fire, then dressed, trying not to watch her as she did the same and failing miserably. He loved the line of her long legs, her high waist, and her breasts, which just filled the palm of his hands.

She tugged on her chemise, catching his gaze as she did so.

Face heated, he gestured toward the embers. "I'll stir the fire back to life."

"Thank you."

He reluctantly turned away. The fire had long since died down, only a few embers remaining, so he added wood, and then blew on the embers until flames rose to lick hungrily at the wood. Satisfied, he put the fire iron back in the rack and checked his boots. As they were still damp, he left them by the warm fire.

Murian came to stand beside him. She was dressed, her hair unbound, her boots upon her feet. She held a comb and sent him a shy look as she sank onto the settee. "Thank you. Last night was . . . well, I feel much better."

"Thank *you*. I will never forget last night." *Never.*

The words hung between them and her shy smile faded.

She dropped her gaze to her comb. "You . . . you seem unhappy."

"I was thinking that I must leave soon."

"When you find the tiara, of course." She seemed to say it aloud as much for herself as for him.

"Aye, but not just yet." He would stay as long as he possibly could. It wouldn't be enough, he already knew that. But it was all he could do. "Before I leave, I'd like to see all of the cottages fixed."

"There's not much left to be done that we canna do ourselves." She ran the comb through her hair, pausing when she hit a tangle.

He'd thought the same thing on waking up, yet somehow the words stung coming from Murian. "I still must recover the Oxenburg crown, and . . . there are other things, too."

Murian paused in untangling her hair. "What other things?"

"Matters of state. Nothing that would interest you. Besides, you have enough to do with your villagers and finding the journal."

Her gaze narrowed on him, and it was as if, for a second, she could see right through him. "You are involved in some sort of political intrigue."

Bloody hell, could she see into his soul? "I am no politician."

She flashed him a look of disbelief. "Max, do you remember last night? I am not a patient woman. I've already proven that."

He had to smile. "You have. And very well, too. But I must point out that we've a spy somewhere, so it's better to keep any information on an as-needed basis."

To his surprise, she hesitated and then nodded. "We must find that spy before our next foray. Perhaps—"

"*Nyet.* There will be no more attempts at breaking into the castle."

She frowned.

"You were almost caught last night. They would have shot you." Even now, he could taste his fear on seeing the guards with their pistols drawn, pointing in the direction he'd known Murian to be hiding.

Her jaw firmed. "No matter what either you or Ian say, I willna give up hunting for the journal."

Ah, so that was what they'd argued about. For once, Max found himself in agreement with the grumpy old Scot. "We care for you. And of course you shouldn't give up. But perhaps you should focus on something else until Spencer returns from war. Let him handle this."

"*If* he returns from war. Loudan has someone in Spencer's employ who keeps my letters from him. What's to keep that person from doing more?"

"You believe Loudan might have his own brother killed?"

"He's killed before."

"That only proves my point. You'll have to find another way to recover the journal."

Her lips tightened, but she didn't answer, though she combed her hair with faster, more furious strokes.

An uneasy feeling arose in him. "You agree, then? To hold off on trying to find the journal until Spencer arrives?"

She put down her comb and quickly braided her hair. As soon as she finished, she fished a ribbon from her pocket, tied the thick braid, and then stood. "I appreciate your concern." Her eyes were steely, her voice cool.

And that was that. They were at a complete impasse. Max, feeling more upset and unsettled by the moment, sighed. Perhaps it would be best if he gave her some time to think about the dangers she'd faced last night. There was nothing she could do in the cold light of day, anyway.

He picked up his damp cloak. "I must go before I am discovered missing. My men and I will be back later today. We will talk more when I return."

She went to the door and took her cloak from the peg.

He watched her, rubbing the back of his neck where an ache was beginning to form. She was so brittle, so distant. This wasn't how he wanted this to end, how he needed it to end.

But before he could say another word she said, "Good-bye, Max." And with those two cool, impersonal words, she left, closing the door behind her with a decided bang.

Max went after her. As he stepped into the cold mist-covered street, his foot sank into an icy puddle. He looked down at his stockinged feet and yanked his foot from the water.

Cursing up a storm, and swearing no one could deal with such a prickly Scottish woman including God himself, Max limped back inside Murian's cottage, shoved his boots on his wet feet, and left.

Chapter 20

"Looking out the window will not help."

Max turned to where Tata Natasha sat beside the fireplace. She opened one eye to peep at him, and—apparently satisfied she had his attention—closed it again.

It was midafternoon, and after a light luncheon the earl's guests had dispersed: some to play cards, some to play billiards, some to read or write letters, while the more energetic rode out into the misty day and escaped the afternoon quiet of the castle.

After a desultory game of billiards with some fellow guests, Max had gone in search of his grandmother and found her here, sound asleep in her favorite sitting room.

"I will not consider it a visit if you do not sit." Her eyes still closed, she kicked in the direction of the seat opposite hers.

With a final look at the gray day, which matched his mood far too well, he took the suggested chair. "I'm glad to see you have awakened."

"I was not sleeping." She opened one eye to glare at him. "If I'd wished to sleep, I'd have gone to my bed."

"You were snoring when I entered."

"That was deep breathing. It helps when I am solving a riddle." She opened her eyes, hiding a yawn behind her hand. "I am trying to fathom why my grandson is moping about as if his favorite dog had died."

"I haven't been moping."

"Pah! I know moping when I see it, and you've been moping." Tata sent him a hard look. "You did not disappear this morning, as you usually do."

"Which should have made you happy." He'd spent yesterday in the village working with his men, while Murian sent him cool, unconcerned looks as if she neither knew him nor cared.

He knew what she wanted: his blessing and assistance in getting back into Rowallen, but he could not offer them. He was no longer willing to accept such a risk. He could have so easily lost her. . . . He clenched his jaw against the swell of emotion the memory brought him.

This morning he'd sent the men on to the village without him, hoping to regain his usual logical perspective. Unfortunately, he found Murian's absence as distracting as her presence. He couldn't stop thinking about her, reliving each touch, each smile—

He stirred restlessly, impatient with every damn thing.

"What's wrong, Maksim? And do not tell me 'nothing,' for I will not believe it."

What was wrong? Every second he spent in Murian's company complicated both of their lives, yet he greedily wanted more and more of those seconds, hours and days. He wanted *all* of them, damn it. And he wanted her safe, away from harm. *Is this what it's like to see a loved one ride off to war? Bloody hell, I can never do that to anyone.* His soul sank a bit more.

"Max?"

Aware of his grandmother's gaze, he forced himself to say in a calm tone, "I stayed because I am expecting missives. I'm being a good guest, which you've wanted me to do since we arrived. But"—he shrugged—"no missives. I wasted the day." He couldn't keep the bitterness out of his voice.

"There is daylight left; they could still come."

"They'd better. Our host is trying my patience." Max tapped the arm of his chair impatiently. "Loudan knows that grand fit you staged was an effort to assist me. He's been most annoying, asking after your health every time we meet."

Tata smirked. "He asked me, too. Once. I made up so many bloody fluxes and swollen cysts that he looked rather ill and left abruptly."

Max had to chuckle. "Next time, I will try the same."

"Just say the words 'female humors.' He will grow red and excuse himself." Tata's shrewd gaze narrowed. "I don't suppose he also asked how, that same night, you ended up outside, singing like a drunken sailor?"

"Who told you about that?"

"It does not matter. I know. You should not face armed men without a weapon. It is foolish."

"I was there to distract, nothing more. When Loudan mentioned it, I suggested it was one of my men who'd had too much to drink. He didn't believe me, of course, but what can he say? He will not call me a liar. Not to my face."

"I wish he would," Tata Natasha said sourly. "Then you could challenge him to a duel and we'd be done with this."

Max agreed. "He is very careful not to cross that line." Which made it curious that the earl had done so with Robert. Perhaps the difference was that now the earl was surrounded by guests who would whisper about everything they saw and heard. Loudan had confronted Robert alone, with no witness but the earl's own supporters. *He wishes to keep society's good opinion.*

Max rested his elbows on his knees and looked past his grandmother to the window, where the cold, heavy mist swirled over lush green treetops. He wondered what his men were doing in Murian's village right now. Today, they were to address the muddied path that linked the cottages. After the snow and then the rain, the village appeared to be built in the middle of a large puddle. This morning, he, Orlov, and Raeff had decided the best way to approach the issue was to line the paths with as many stones as possible, which would take some work, but would be effective. He wondered if Murian would appreciate their efforts, or if she was still fuming about—

"Are you going to tell me about her?"

Max frowned, but didn't answer.

"Only two things make you sigh in such a way. One

is food. The other, a woman. I know you've eaten today, so . . ." She shrugged.

"I wasn't sighing."

"Ha!" Her expression softened, and she placed her hand on his arm. "Maksim, tell me what is bothering you. It is not like you to sit about sighing and not *doing*."

"I *am* doing. I await missives."

"Pah! You are the general. Generals do not await common couriers."

"We have many concerns that require my attention," he said pointedly. "A lost crown, for instance."

A faint blush colored Tata Natasha's cheeks. "Oh, that."

"There are other things that need my attention as well." Several other things, and none of them were going the way he wished. In his time at Rowallen, all he'd accomplished was repairing a few leaky roofs and finding himself uncomfortably entangled with an outspoken, red-haired temptress.

On top of it all, he'd wounded her somehow. He'd stated a cold, blunt fact, something she already knew, that her quest for the journal was too dangerous to continue—but after thinking about it, he realized he'd been demanding. Not intentionally, but still . . . it was her fight, not his. He had no right to tell her what to do.

He winced to think of how much a challenge his words must have sounded. If she threw herself behind a dangerous plan now, he'd only have himself to blame and—

Something poked his knee. He scowled. "Tata, put down your cane."

She sniffed. "I asked you three times what this woman is like, but you did not answer. Is she so boring that you have nothing to say about her?"

"She is not boring. She is . . . frustrating."

"And?"

"She will not listen to a word I or anyone else tells her."

"So she is proud, then."

"Too proud for her own good. Worse, she refuses to follow the dictates of common sense, even when it comes to her own safety."

Tata nodded as if she liked that particular trait. "Like a Romany. We, too, are stubborn and proud, and perhaps not always so good at listening to advice of those who know better." She leaned back in her chair, her black gaze never leaving his face. "Tell me more." She waved her hand, her rings sparkling in the dim room.

Murian never wore jewelry. She must have sold it. His jaw tightened. "She lives for one thing: to win Rowallen back for her people."

"Who are these people?"

"The servants and others who were displaced when the earl took the castle. When Loudan demanded they leave, she took them into the woods, to some crofters' huts where they would be safe and could live without interference from the earl."

"He interferes, does he?"

"He punishes anyone who helps them."

"That *vash*."

"So he is. Her people are loyal to her and the late lord. To Loudan, that is treason."

Tata pursed her lips as if considering something. Finally, she inclined her head as if conferring a great privilege. "I will meet your woman. Bring her here."

"She is not my woman. She's no one's." *For now.* His blood roared in protest at his thoughts, but he refused to flinch away. "She is trying to find her husband's journal, for it holds the truth of what happened the night he died, before the fight. It could prove Rowallen does not belong to the earl."

Tata's dark eyes lit with interest. "So this journal is here, in this castle."

"She believes so, *da*. Whenever she can sneak into the castle, she searches for it—or she did until Loudan realized what she was doing and increased the guard."

"He fears she will find it, then." Tata pursed her lips. "Her motives are commendable."

"They would be if she'd show some reason in the way she goes about it. She risks her neck as if it were replaceable." And it wasn't. There would never be another Murian. There would never be another woman who would intrigue him as she did, tie his heart into knots and drive him mad with wanting.

Suddenly impatient, he stood and took the few steps to the window, leaning his fisted hands on each side of the windowsill and looking out with unseeing eyes. *Bloody hell, what am I to do?* But there was nothing for it. She was who she was, with her own dreams and responsibilities that tied her to Rowallen as firmly as his responsibilities and family tied him to Oxenburg.

It was impossible. Neither of them could step onto

another path without betraying all they held dear. By not doing so, they were forced into betraying each other.

He straightened and rammed his fists into his coat pocket, wishing he could release his tension with a good fight. What was he doing, staying here at the castle, when he could be—if not with her, then at least near her? Time was slipping away even as he breathed.

He should go to her now. He'd have his horse brought around and—

A movement in the drive below caught his eye and he leaned forward. There, by the front doors, were Orlov, Golovin, and Demidor. They'd just dismounted; two groomsmen were leading their mounts to the stables.

Why are they returning so early? It is not yet dark.

Orlov nodded at something Demidor said, then entered the castle.

Max leaned to one side and looked east, where the woods encircled the manicured lawn. There, almost invisible unless one knew to look for it, the wagon lumbered behind the trees that circled to the back of the property. From there, it would be hidden behind the partially dismantled barn, out of sight and ready for use when they needed it again.

Something must have happened that they returned so soon. He turned. "I must go."

"Why? What did you see?"

"Nothing that need concern you." He crossed to her chair and placed a kiss to her paper-thin cheek. "I will come to your room and escort you to dinner at eight." He headed for the door.

He was halfway across the room when she called out, "If you care for this girl, you must marry her."

He stiffened and slowly turned around. "It is not so easy, Tata."

"Isn't it? Have you asked her?"

"It is more complicated than that."

"Why?"

"For many reasons. We have responsibilities, both of us."

"Pah! If you care for her, you will find a way around that."

"That is not all." Max shook his head. "She has been a widow once; I will not make her one again."

"People die all the time, and not just in war."

"*Da*, but sometimes, the waiting can be as difficult as a death."

"You are not a rash general. You fight when you can win, and you do not sacrifice lives like chess pawns; it is why Oxenburg is in such a strong position. Our army, she is not big, but she is strong and smart. I've heard your father tell others how respected you are, how feared our army is, and how few deaths we experience compared to our enemies."

"But there is always at least one death. And one day, it will be mine. It only takes one bullet. I have seen it over and over."

"So you will just give up this gift that has been given to you, this love?"

"I never said I loved anyone."

"You said it, though not in those words. You do not give up happiness for anything else. But knowing you will one day be in danger does not mean you must live as if you've already died. Look at your men! They marry."

"They have not seen what I have. They do not carry the news to the loved ones, see the despair, watch the light die from the eyes of women who know they will never love again, see the pain of little boys who thought their father could walk on water and would never be killed." He shook his head. "I would die myself before I subjected Murian to that."

Tata Natasha's expression softened. "Maksim, women have been living with men being fools for as long as there have been men and women." She pointed a thin finger at him. "Listen, and listen well. You do not get to choose with whom, or when, or even how you fall in love. Those things are in the hands of a higher power. And it does not happen to everyone—nor often. Love is precious, Maksim. Precious. When this gift from the fates drops before you, you *cannot* walk away from it. Whether you marry this woman for one day or a hundred years, it will be worth whatever cost comes with it."

Max wished he believed her. Wished he hadn't seen what he'd seen, didn't know what he knew. He shook his head. "I cannot do that to her, Tata."

She scowled. "You are a fool, Max. A fool!"

He managed a smile. "I must go. I will see you at eight." He bowed and then walked out the door, ignoring her huff of frustration.

Max found Orlov leaning against the wall just outside the door, his arms crossed. He pushed himself upright when he saw Max.

"You are back early," Max said.

"When we left this morning, I sent Pahlen to await the courier. I had a feeling today would be the day."

At least one thing was going well. "You were right, eh?"

"*Da*. A packet arrived. He's to bring it to us here."

"Good." Max walked down the hall, Orlov falling in beside him.

After a moment, Orlov cleared his throat. "Pardon me, General, but I could not help but overhear your conversation with Her Grace."

Max stopped to face his sergeant. "She is busy involving herself in what does not concern her. Do not make the same mistake."

Orlov spread his hands before him. "I did not mean to overhear, but your grandmother's voice carries."

"Like the screech of a crow."

Orlov gave Max a searching look. "There is wisdom to be found in the beaks of crows."

Max grimaced. "You agree with her."

"It has grown obvious to us all you've come to care for Lady Murian."

"She has already been a widow once. I would not have her be one again."

"Because you think she will be like Henrietta." Orlov shook his head. "When Fedorovich died, a bit of all of us went to the grave with him."

"More for Henrietta than any of us. You did not see her face when I told her Dimitri was not coming back. You did not see her prostrate herself over his dead body, nor refuse to leave his side until she fainted from lack of sleep and hunger." Max rubbed his forehead where it was beginning to ache. "I would not have that for Murian."

"You wouldn't. Henrietta is my sister, and I know her far better than you. Perhaps even better than Dimitri did." Orlov shrugged. "Lady Murian is not Henrietta. My sister was never strong. I warned Fedorovich of this before he wed her, but he would not listen. Later, she had Artur and suffered horribly through the birth. It almost crushed her. Dimitri began to see what I meant and, while he never regretted his decision, for he loved her, he knew she was not as strong as she should be. That she would not survive without him, not well. It weighed upon him, and he worried about his son— which is why he told me that if he ever fell in battle, I was to take her and Artur into my house." Orlov hesitated. "I know you feel responsible that Henrietta attempted to kill herself, but it was not a surprise to those of us who knew her."

"Dimitri is fortunate you were there for her. He . . . he was like a brother to us all."

"And yet we did not crumple like a heap of ashes when he died. And do not tell me that is because we are men: my Katrina would never behave as Henrietta has. She has suffered losses, too, some as dear and close as Henrietta's, but not once has she folded into a limp rag. If anything, those losses made her stronger."

"She is a good woman, is Katrina."

"So is Lady Murian. She is a warrior, that one. As strong as steel."

Max heard the admiration in Orlov's voice. "She is."

"So you need not worry about her so much." Orlov smiled. "Katrina teases me that if I am ever killed in battle, she will find a new husband, one younger and wealthier. One who will give our sons better horses."

Max frowned. "I wouldn't laugh at that."

Orlov chuckled. "Neither would I, if I planned on allowing it to happen. But I do not." His expression grew serious. "I fight harder because of my Katrina. I want to return to her, and that makes me stronger. I fight to keep her safe, to keep our children safe."

"And if you died?"

"Then she would weep, as I would if she died. And she would be deeply sad, but not forever. Not like Henrietta. Katrina is strong and brave, and eventually, she would find another man."

"And this does not bother you?"

"To think I would not be the man to stand beside her? *Da*, it bothers me. But not as much as being the man who left when I could have been with her, protecting her, loving her and being loved by her. I would not miss that for a thousand victories."

"General!" Golovin hurried up, Demidor and Pahlen behind him. "You said you'd wish these right away." Golovin handed Max two packets.

Max examined the packets, surprised at the smaller of the two. He recognized the scrawl from a scrap of paper he'd received not long ago. Between Orlov's words and this letter, a slow smile grew.

Perhaps, just perhaps, things might turn his way after all.

"There is more." Demidor elbowed Pahlen forward.

The older man reddened. "Pardon me, General, but, ah . . . it is possible I have some information that might be of interest to you."

"About?"

"Lady Murian."

Max slipped the letters into his pocket. "Tell me."

"I will, because you know my loyalty, but . . ." He winced. "I promised not to tell anyone, especially you."

"You promised whom?"

Pahlen's sheepish look answered him.

"Ah," Max said. "The charming Widow MacCrae."

Pahlen flushed. "She is a lovely woman, General."

"Indeed. So she let something slip, and you promised not to reveal this information, yet you think I should know."

He nodded miserably. "But I cannot tell. I promised. So . . . Golovin and I were thinking, perhaps someone could *guess* the information. Then I could keep my promise."

Max crossed his arms and rocked back on his heels. "Ah! Very good."

"We will need a clue," Orlov stated. "Something to begin with."

"We already know it's about Lady Murian," Max said. "Let me begin. She has decided to ignore my request that she not act against Loudan until Lord Spencer returned."

Pahlen nodded eagerly. "*Da*, that is part of it. But there is more."

"Hmm." Orlov bit his lip. "Is she to hold up another coach then, in an attempt to draw away the guards?"

Pahlen hesitated, but then shook his head.

Orlov looked disappointed. "I was sure that was it."

"*Nyet*," Max said. "Murian's well aware that Loudan is onto that particular trick." He eyed Pahlen. "Lady Murian is not using her old tricks to draw the guards, so perhaps she has found a new one. One she has not yet tried?"

"*Da!*" Pahlen could not have looked more relieved. "*Bozhy moj*, I did not think you could guess it so quickly."

"What sort of distraction is she planning?" Orlov asked.

"She won't tell, so Leslie had no more information, only that Lady Murian and Ian had their heads together and something was afoot."

Max shot a look at Pahlen. "She is not planning this anytime soon, is she? This evening, perhaps?"

"Not this evening, *nyet*. Leslie, I mean Widow MacCrae, seemed to think it was still in the planning stages."

"I cannot believe Lady Murian did not consult us," Orlov said, his brows low.

"I can," Max said. "We were unsuccessful in getting her into the castle and have offered no new solutions, so she has found one herself."

"But there is a traitor in her camp," Golovin pointed out.

"Information leaked, but we don't know how. It could have been an innocent remark, overheard by the wrong person."

"Or it could be a traitor," Orlov repeated stubbornly.

"She doesn't know. Wouldn't she be worried the traitor might inform Loudan and put her and her people in jeopardy once again?"

"She does not believe the traitor is one of her own," Pahlen said. "She thinks it might have been one of us."

"*What?*" Orlov exclaimed. "None of us would do such a thing."

"So I told Widow MacCrae," Pahlen said. "It is not our way to behave in such an underhanded fashion. However"—he winced—"she was very certain it was not their way, either."

"The Scots have a temper, do they not?" Max put his hand on Pahlen's shoulder. "Thank you for your efforts. You did well, bringing this to my attention."

"What will you do?" Orlov asked.

"Another visit to Lady Murian is in order, so that I might discover what she is up to." The thought sent his spirits soaring, and it was in a regretful tone that he added, "But it will have to wait until tomorrow. First I must see to these missives, and we must be present for dinner. I assume the courier waits?"

"*Da*," Pahlen said. "Raeff is keeping him company until you are ready."

"Tell them they will not wait long. Orlov, you will assist me as I write the replies. There is a matter or two we should discuss. Golovin, would you be so kind as to escort my grandmother to her room? She's in the sitting room at the end of the hall."

Golovin looked at the sitting room as if it contained a wild dog, but he gulped and nodded. "*Da*, General."

"She's frailer than she looks." Max walked toward the staircase, his men dispersing as he walked. He paused at the stairs to say over his shoulder, "And Golovin?"

"*Da*, General?"

"Whatever happens, do not let her turn you into a goat."

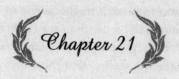

Chapter 21

Murian folded the foolscap in half and leaned back in her chair. "We are set, then."

"Aye, I suppose." Ian watched as she twisted the paper into a screw and then hid it in a sugar bowl that hadn't seen anything but scrap paper in over a year. "'Tis a bit risky. If it fails, Loudan will crow, fer he'll ha' proof we're committin' a crime."

"I know." She played with the sugar bowl lid, tracing the delicate roses in the pattern. "Are you sure, Ian? Last night, you seemed to think—"

"Och, lass, I told ye I dinna mean it. I was just cold and wet and frustrated."

"It is risky. If Loudan catches us, he will have us arrested. It could put your uncle the constable in a difficult place."

"Aye. There's naught he could do if there are witnesses. We willna leave him a choice."

"Then we willna get caught," she said lightly, though her stomach hurt with thoughts of what-ifs. She pushed the sugar bowl away. "Only you and I will know the plan this time, Ian. It's safer."

"Aye, lassie." Ian sighed. "Fer the record, I think 'twas one of the prince's men who let something slip."

She wanted to think it might be one of Max's men, too, for it pained her more than she could say to think one of her own people might betray her. But she couldn't shake the feeling that the worst was indeed the truth. *But who?*

She'd been at odds with herself since their failed raid, especially after her passionate night with Max. Just thinking of that night made her shiver, and her body's betrayal infuriated her. *He is leaving soon. He couldn't wait to remind me of that, to push me away.*

She shoved a curl aside, suddenly irritated with everything. "We must find this traitor. Today, while the prince's men were working, I found myself wondering about each and every one of them. Which is why no one else is to know anything until it's about to happen, when it's too late to pass on any details of our plan."

A regretful look darkened Ian's face. "I was sure 'twas Will at first, bu' no more."

"My heart tells me 'tis not him."

"I'm inclined to agree wi' ye. He had harsh words fer me last night, words I deserved." Ian hesitated, then added, "He's becoming a man, 'tis true."

Murian sent him a look from under her lashes. "I wonder why he's had such a difficult time with it."

"Lass, if ye only knew."

"I *would* know, if you'd but tell me. There's a secret there, one you've made certain I wouldna find oot."

Ian flushed. "'Tis no' a story fer tender ears."

"I'm no hothouse rose. I'm a Scottish thistle, strong

and hardy, and able to grow upon rock—and I want to know this secret about Will."

Ian sighed. "Bloody hell, ye're determined, aren't ye? I suppose 'tis time." He rubbed his chin, as if trying to decide where to begin. Finally, he said, "Ye knew his mither was a housekeeper?"

"Aye."

"She came to work right after Lord Robert's mither died, and she was a breath of fresh air during those dark times. She worked fer several years, and died when Will was born. The old lord took the lad under his wing and raised him as a brother to Lord Robert. They were inseparable, and many thought they *were* brothers." Ian cast a cautious glance at Murian. "They said tha' fer a reason, lass."

She blinked. "Are you saying . . . Will is Robert's half-brother?"

Ian nodded. "Born on the wrong side of the blanket."

"I had no idea! Although now that I think about it, they have the same color hair and eyes." She shook her head. "Robert once told me he and Will were close as children, before Robert inherited his title."

"Aye. They ne'er got along after tha'. Will was jealous and Robert was a bit too fond of his new title, a common mistake fer a lad, but Will wouldna stop fuming long enou' fer the two to patch things oop."

She frowned. "I wonder why Robert never told me this?"

"Mayhap he thought 'twas no' a topic fer a lady's ears." Ian grimaced. "Will had it rough, he did, the other children in the castle teasin' him aboot his lack of a father. Things weren't so bad when the old lord was alive, fer he stood oop fer the lad, but afterward . . ." Ian shook his head in regret. "I should be nicer to the lad, bu' he's so mouthy."

"You just said he's growing up."

"And mayhap so am I." Ian pushed back his chair. "Speakin' of which, I'd better get back to work. I've stone to break and it will no' break itself." He arose and gathered his cloak.

"Ian?"

He paused, his hand on the door latch.

"Thank you for trusting in me one more time."

He flushed. "I'm sorry fer wha' I said, lassie. I was angry and dinna mean it—"

"Yes, you did mean it." She met his gaze directly.

He rubbed his cheek. "Some of it, mayhap. Bu' mostly I was scared since we'd almost gotten caught."

"I know," she said quietly. "And you may be right; I may be chasing a unicorn. So I've decided something. If this new plan doesna work—" She splayed her hands on her knees and forced her stiff lips into a smile, though her heart fought the words. "I'll stop trying to find the journal and will wait for Spencer to return. Meanwhile, we'll stay here, and make our village the best village in all of Scotland."

Ian brightened and came to kiss her on the top of her head. "All will be well, lass. I promise."

She nodded, fighting tears. "Of course."

Ian awkwardly patted her shoulder and then left, softly closing the door behind him.

She crossed her arms on the table and rested her

head on them. It seemed as if the weight of the world sat upon her. She'd never felt so alone. Part of it was the deep fear that Ian and Max were right; that she was a fool to chase after evidence she didn't know for certain even existed. Yet she was sure, in her heart of hearts, that Robert's journal held answers. She could only pray they were the ones she hoped for.

But what if this doesn't work? What if the traitor again tells Loudan we are coming? What then?

She waited, but no answers came. Nothing but the silence of her cottage, and the faint murmur of the village.

She found her gaze resting upon her bed. The loneliness that had sat upon her heart swelled again, and she forced herself to turn away, although it wasn't as easy to quell her memories.

These last two days had been so very, very hard. The first day, Max had returned with the men, and it had been as if nothing had happened. Except that her heart tore a little more every time she caught sight of his broad shoulders, or the flash of his smile. As much as she tried not to watch him, her eyes were drawn to him over and over, each sight a slash to her composure. She knew he felt the same, too. He might not care for her as she had come to care for him, but he was attracted to her still, shown by the way his gaze followed her as often as hers followed him.

She took some comfort in that, even though it made her long for more. She'd been both relieved and depressed beyond measure when he hadn't returned the next day. While she told herself over and over that it was best for them both, she couldn't forget the taste of him, the feel of his roughened fingertips as they swept over her, the scent of leather and soap that lingered in his hair. If she closed her eyes now, she could see him before her, as vivid in memory as he was in person. The thought seared her. He would leave Rowallen soon and never return. *As he must. Just as I must stay here.*

It was better that she deal with her village and her people on her own, in her own way. She'd done so for the last year and longer. She didn't need the complication of someone else, especially a bossy, six-foot-two someone else who was far too used to doing things *his* way.

And yet, she couldn't stop the hollowness of her heart at the thought. In a few brief weeks, Max had reminded her of what it felt like to be a part of something close and intimate; the magic of waking up in someone's arms, the loneliness when those arms were suddenly no longer there.

Tears welled and she angrily dashed them away, unwilling to let her thoughts overcome her. She would help Ian break some rock. Swinging a heavy hammer would be good for her angst-ridden soul. She hurried to find her cape and had just wrapped her muffler about her neck when she heard a shout, followed by another.

Frowning, she threw her cape about her shoulder and opened the door. Coming down the forest path astride the largest bay she had ever seen, and dressed head to toe in unrelenting black, rode Max's tiny Gypsy grandmother. Riding in front of her was Golovin, looking embarrassed and terrified.

Ian, standing beside a large stone he'd fetched from

the stream, watched, surprised. On seeing Murian in her doorway, he came to stand beside her as their guests entered the village.

"Tha' is a big horse fer sich a wee woman." Ian's voice held a note of admiration as the grand duchess rode closer.

"I was just thinking 'twas a wee horse for such a large woman."

Seeing Golovin's expression, Ian said thoughtfully, "Ye may ha' the right of it, lassie."

"She certainly rides well." The duchess didn't seem to direct the animal at all, yet even though it was obviously a high-strung animal, it walked sedately down the path between the cottages without the least hesitation.

The villagers were alerted now, and stood in doorways and hung out windows, watching the tiny woman ride down their street. Suddenly the door to Widow Brodie's cottage flung open. Her five small boys ran out, followed by their mother, who stalked right up to the path, where she whipped out a crucifix and held it before her.

Her Grace pulled her horse to and eyed Widow Brodie with an icy stare.

Murian hurried up the street, Ian hard on her heels.

He murmured to Murian, "She's only sayin' wha' the rest of us are thinkin', lassie."

Murian reached the widow. "Widow Brodie! What are you doing? Her Grace has just come for a visit!"

"Tha' is no' duchess, Lady Murian. She's a witch. Ye've heard the whispers."

Widow Reeves stuck her head out of the window of her cottage. "She threatened to turn us all into frogs when we held oop her coach. Remember?"

"Or was it goats?" Ian asked, pursing his lips.

Golovin sent a cautious look at the duchess, and then leaned down to whisper loudly, "It was goats. They are her favorite thing."

The grand duchess fixed her gaze on Murian. "Lady Murian, I take it." The black eyes swept up and down Murian and, judging from the curl of the old woman's lip, apparently found her wanting.

Murian stiffened, her chin lifting. "Aye, Your Grace."

"I thought so. I have come to speak to you."

"Oh? About what?"

"If you'll invite me to tea, I may tell you. You do have tea, don't you?"

"Of course."

"Then I will visit you." She looked over her shoulder. "Golovin, I am done riding."

The huge soldier hurried to dismount, throwing his reins over a gate and then coming to the duchess's horse. He lifted her carefully to the ground as if she were made of china, unstrapped a gold-handled cane from her saddle, and handed it to her.

"Walk the horse. I will not be long." She hobbled to Murian. "Well? Which of these hovels is yours?"

Murian bit her tongue. "This way, Your Grace." *Hovel, indeed!* She led the way to her cottage, fighting the urge to reply in kind.

Reaching her cottage, she opened the door. "If you'll take a seat, I'll make your tea."

The duchess walked in, her brows rising as she noted the fine furnishings. "Well. This is a surprise."

"Not to me."

She flashed Murian an appreciative look, walked to the closest chair and ran her hand over the mahogany arm. "I take it you stole this from the castle."

"You canna steal what you already own."

"True." Her Grace felt the cushions on each chair, finally selecting a seat close to the fire. She sat, arranging her shawl and skirts about her. "Hurry up with that tea. I am thirsty from my ride."

"Of course." Murian hid her grimace and set about heating water for the tea. While she waited she pulled out cups and small plates, opening a packet of sweet biscuits Widow Reeves's sister had brought on her last visit. As she moved, she was aware the duchess's gaze followed her every move. *What on earth can she want?*

She supposed she'd find out soon enough. Murian placed the biscuits on the plates and filled the teapot with the boiling water so it could brew.

The duchess peered at the biscuits and poked about, finally selecting one.

Murian did the same.

"I suppose you wonder why I have come," the duchess said.

"I was wondering, aye." Murian tasted the biscuit. It was crumbly and sweetly almond flavored, and she savored the bite.

Her Grace sniffed at her biscuit and then tried it. "Mm. Not bad." The duchess took another bite. After a moment, she said, "I came to ask you why you chase my grandson so."

Murian almost choked on her biscuit. "I beg your pardon?"

"I have seen this before. Many women chase my grandsons, and I will tell you what I tell all of them: you waste your time. I have come to help you understand that."

"Your Grace, I'm not doing any such thing."

The duchess puffed out her lips. "That, I do not believe."

"In order for me to chase a man, I'd have to wish to catch him. I have no interest in Max—"

The duchess raised her brows.

Murian's face heated. "—His Highness. Not at all."

The dark eyes locked on Murian's face. "He is very wealthy."

Murian poured tea into the two cups and handed one to Her Grace. "How fortunate for him."

"He is a powerful man, the general of a vast army."

"I'm sure he is an excellent commander."

"He is also very handsome. All of my grandsons are."

He was all of that—handsome, powerful, wealthy— but it didn't touch his true qualities. He was funny, with a dry wit that made her chuckle. He was intelligent, too, and he never bored her. They'd talked for hours while working on various projects in the village, and she'd been surprised and pleased with the breadth of his knowledge.

But more than that, under his blunt and rough warrior exterior, he'd proven himself to be kind. Her heart ached anew.

"I have no doubt he'll be a wonderful husband to some lucky princess one day. But not for me." Murian took a sip of tea to loosen her throat. "There are many handsome men in this world, Your Grace. One day, I shall find one willing to stay here and share what I hold so dear."

She meant the words to sound calm and confident, but she couldn't help the waver in her voice at the end of her sentence. What she held dear were her people, Rowallen, and now a tall, handsome, scarred warrior prince with a propensity for barking orders. She found herself looking into her tea, and it felt as if her heart were at the bottom.

The duchess muttered something under her breath, reaching out to place her hand over Murian's. "It hurts, *da*? Love can tear the heart as easily as it warms it."

The unexpected sympathy was too much. Murian barely managed a smile before she snatched up her napkin and dabbed at her eyes. "It doesna matter. We are not meant to be. We—" She closed her lips over a sob.

Her Grace sighed. "That grandson of mine. Sometimes I think I should hit him over the head with my cane and knock some sense into his thick skull. It would be easier for us all."

"He doesn't lack for sense. He's quite right; he and I met at the wrong time."

"Humph. Tell me about your village, the people here."

Glad to be talking about something other than Max,

Murian obliged, at first only mentioning the important items, such as how they fared despite Loudan's attempts to force them to leave, and the ways they'd kept his men from finding their sanctuary. She told of the day she'd returned to Rowallen to find Robert dead and the household in shambles from Loudan's threats, and how she'd brought them all here for safety.

The duchess cackled when Murian told of taking all the furniture, but grew more serious when discussing how Loudan had increased the guards after catching Will in the castle, and how now they feared there was a traitor in their midst.

Murian also described Max's arrival in their village and all the work he and his men had done, how kind he'd been to her and the others, and how he had provided the much-needed wood from Loudan's own barn—which earned another laugh from the duchess—and how Murian didn't know what they'd have done without them. Somehow, in the midst of that, she found herself also telling the duchess about Widow MacDonald's temper, and Widow Brodie's struggles with five rambunctious sons, how Will was recently becoming the man she'd always thought he would be, and how Widow MacCrae and Pahlen were showing distinct signs of falling in love.

"Do you think she will go with him to Oxenburg?"

"Or he might stay with her here," Murian countered. "I dinna know. They have the freedom to choose."

The duchess took a pensive sip of her tea, eyeing Murian. "You are not what I expected. I thought I'd find a frivolous girl, one given to foolishness."

"Foolishness?"

"*Da*, you are involved in some wild scheme to retrieve your castle and lands."

"I dinna scheme, Your Grace. I plan."

The old woman's eyes twinkled. "By holding up carriages. Thus 'foolishness' is an appropriate term."

Murian had to smile. "Perhaps there is a wee bit of foolishness in my blood."

"Good. Do not lose it. It will save you from growing bored when you grow old. Ah, you have had adventures! How I envy you that." Her Grace selected yet another biscuit. "I have had these excellent biscuits before; I know I have."

"Have you eaten at Lady MacLure's? Her cook is the Widow Reeves's sister, so she visits us often and brings us her latest efforts."

"*Nyet.* I've never been off Rowallen lands until now, so I must have had them there— Ah! That was it. A week or so ago, they were served at tea. I commented on them then, too. Lady MacLure must have supplied them to the castle's kitchen."

"Why would Lady MacLure have her cook supply Rowallen?"

"She's been serving as Loudan's hostess. Did you not know?" At the shake of Murian's head, the duchess added, "She has, and she's been quite elegant about it, too, which is fortunate, for Loudan's housekeeper was dismal. I assume the menus now fall under Lady MacLure's purview, for they're much improved."

About to dunk her biscuit in her tea, Murian stopped. "Wait. When did this happen?"

"Over the last week, sometime. She and her husband seem miserable, so Loudan must have blackmailed them into it in some way. They give his affairs some legitimacy, and bring in the local gentry. You cannot lord it over people if they will not accept your invitations, so he is reduced to bribing them with food, drink, entertainment, and a respectable hostess."

Murian put down her cup, her mind racing. "Widow Reeves is very close to her sister."

The duchess didn't look impressed. "So?"

"So it wouldna be unusual for her to tell her sister about our plans here, in the village. And Widow Reeves has mentioned before how closely her sister works with Lady MacLure on the menus and such. So during these meetings, 'tis possible Widow Reeves's sister revealed a bit more than she should have."

The duchess put down her teacup, too, her eyes bright. "And then Lady MacLure repeated what she heard, which is how Loudan found out. So . . . your traitor is not a traitor after all, but a gossip."

"That must be it!" Murian sat back, so relieved she laughed. "I'm so glad you came today! That sort of traitor is easily dealt with."

The duchess tugged her shawl about her shoulders, looking pleased as well. "We would scheme well together, you and I. Perhaps . . ." She tilted her head to one side, looking like a wee black crow. "Perhaps we should do so right now."

"To what purpose?"

"To bring Loudan to his knees. He still has my tiara." She muttered something that Murian was fairly certain was a curse. After a moment, the duchess picked up a biscuit and waved it. "If only we could poison him."

"I'm not proud of it, but I've thought so many times. But I want justice, and that would not provide it."

The shrewd black eyes locked on Murian. "If we find this journal of your husband's, it is still possible your claim will be proven false."

"It is possible, but I must at least try. My people love Rowallen; it was their home. Some of them were born there."

"Then we must find this journal *and* my tiara, you and I. We must get to Loudan's bedchamber and search it." The duchess and Murian were silent a moment, each lost in her own thoughts.

Suddenly the duchess stiffened. "*Bozhy moj*, why not?"

Murian leaned closer. "You have an idea?"

"Of course I have an idea," she said testily. "I'm a Romany. It will require my help, but we should be able to get you to the earl's bedchamber."

"You will help us?"

"Why not? I've nothing better to do. But we may need a diversion, something to draw out the guards."

"I can help provide, although it would still leave the servants."

The duchess smirked. "The regular servants would never question a grand duchess. You will leave them to me."

Murian had to smile. "You are right; they wouldn't. Your Grace, I canna thank you enough."

"Thank me when we've found the tiara and journal."

"I will. We must plan this carefully. There will be

a dark moon in two days, which would give us some protection."

"Moon? I do not stay up so late. *Nyet*, we go now, in the daylight. They will never suspect it, so surprise will be on our side. Can you make this diversion happen today? Now?"

"I—I suppose so, but . . . Your Grace, if we go in the daylight, we will be seen."

The duchess smiled, a twinkle in her black eyes. "*Da*, I plan to make certain we are. Come. Call in your assistants. We will need all the help we can get."

Chapter 22

At Max's call, Orlov entered the bedchamber. "The letters are on their way, and I requested two horses be saddled and brought around."

"Good." Max finished tugging on his riding boots.

"I'm glad you decided to see Lady Murian today, after all."

"If we leave now, we should be back in time for dinner." It would be a short visit, but at least he would see her. It had been almost two days since the last time he'd laid eyes upon her, and now he had a reason to seek her out, to ask her about the information Pahlen had shared.

But that was an excuse, and he knew it. The truth was, he missed her. Missed her with a deep ache that made him restless and lonely, even when talking with his own men.

He caught Orlov's amused gaze and forced himself to ignore it. "It's important we find out what Lady Murian has planned as soon as possible."

Orlov pursed his lips as if considering this, a politely disbelieving expression on his face. "Very important. We should not wait a day."

"If we go straight there and back, we will be able to return in time for dinner."

Orlov sent a doubting glance at the clock. "Of course, General."

"I won't speak with Lady Murian long. A few minutes, fifteen at most."

Orlov inclined his head, though his eyebrows rose.

Max stood and picked up his coat. "You don't think we'll be back in time."

"I ordered lanterns, just in case."

"I see. I suppose you also don't think she'll tell us what she's planning."

Orlov lifted his hands.

Normally so much naysaying would be tiresome, but Max merely slapped Orlov on the back. "I will prove you wrong—if not on all three counts, then at least on one."

They left the castle and were soon on their way. Max set his horse to an easy trot down the drive, Orlov to his right. The sun had indeed come out. The unpredictability of Scottish weather fascinated Max. It was possible to experience as many as three seasons in one day.

When they reached the trail they slowed the horses to a walk. Though the late-afternoon sun was slowly sinking, there was still plenty of light for the ride. At least for the ride there. Orlov had been smart to order the lanterns tied to the side of their mounts; it would grow dark in the forest before the sun set.

Max wondered if Orlov had been as right about Murian. Would she share her new plan? And would he blame her if she didn't?

He'd made a mull of this entire business, and she deserved better. He'd been trying to do the noble thing, to give her what he imagined was the freedom to live a better life. But Orlov's words had made Max question that. He had no desire to abandon Murian, to leave her alone for no reason. Bloody hell—he wanted to protect her for the rest of his life, to keep her by his side and challenge anyone who dared harm her.

But she was not some pet to be caged, simply because it gave him peace of mind. She was her own person, this Murian of the forest, a fey and beautiful woman who was stronger than any man he knew. And he had no wish to leave her now, or ever.

Which was what he *should* have told her when he'd so baldly and unemotionally announced he must leave soon. That he'd said it right after a wildly passionate night made his error all the worse. He was just beginning to realize that there were many similarities between love and war, and timing was everything. He'd taken a special moment and turned it into far less than it should have been. He'd hurt her.

He couldn't take those words back, but he could apologize. And then, if she'd listen, he'd explain himself. Whether Murian shared her plans with him or not, he would at least try to repair some of the damage he had caused. This time he would tell her more—that he hated leaving her. That he'd never wanted a woman as badly as he wanted her. That he thought about her constantly but could find no way to solve the gaps in their destinies. That he loved her but could not promise her the "forever" she deserved.

As they went into the darkened pathway his spirits followed, growing heavier. He longed to see her so badly he could taste it, yet the thought of leaving her—

Max's horse lifted its nose and snorted, prancing a bit. As Max brought the horse back under control, he caught the faint scent of smoke. He looked back at Orlov. "Do you smell that?"

"Aye." Orlov peered over their heads, turning his horse in a slow circle. "I wonder where—General, there."

Max followed Orlov's gesture to where a plume of black smoke suddenly appeared above the break in the trees, billowing into the blue sky and then disappearing. "Rowallen?"

Orlov nodded. "Perhaps we won't be late for dinner after all."

Max whirled his mount and hied it down the path, Orlov following. *Murian, what have you done?*

*W*hen Max and Orlov emerged from the forest, Rowallen looked like a kicked-over anthill. People poured out of every door, some carrying buckets, others with empty hands, there to gawk. It took no time to find the reason for the disturbance. One of the outbuildings near the main barn was on fire, flames shooting from the windows, thick black smoke billowing.

Max rode past an old farm wagon that blocked the main door of Rowallen, a wagon he'd seen in Murian's village only a few days ago. The two large farm horses watched the mayhem with disinterested gazes.

Max jumped down from his horse. A footman who'd

been standing on the top step peered longingly at the servants milling about, reluctantly came to take Max's horse.

Orlov called to another footman, who was gawking at the fire from the other side of the drive. The footman took the horse and tied it to an iron ring embedded in the castle wall for just such a purpose.

Max climbed the steps to the castle as Orlov fell in beside him, the footman following. They paused on the top step. "At least it's not the main barn, where the horses are." *Very good, Murian. Well planned.*

"Aye, my lor'," the footman replied. "Tha' building is used fer storage. There's feed in there, and ropes and sich, bu' no animals."

"There's also oil fer the lamps," the other footman added, as he joined them. "A fire like tha' will burn fer a long while."

"That explains the black smoke," Orlov said.

"Aye. 'Tis so hot, no one can get close enou' to pour water on it. We'll ha' to wait fer it to cool afore we can put it oot."

Orlov peeled off his gloves. "It looks as if every person in the castle is there. I suppose this means dinner will be late."

"It wouldna surprise me, me lord."

Max sent Orlov a look. *Well, well. My lovely Murian not only dispersed the guards, but many of the servants as well.* They made their way into the castle, the footmen following.

Max handed them his coat and gloves and then strode to the grand stairs, Orlov behind him.

"I hope Her Grace is no' too shook up fra' her accident," one of the footmen called after him.

Max froze. Slowly, he turned. "Her Grace? I thought she was napping in her room."

The footmen exchanged uneasy glances. "I dinna know aboot tha'," the footman replied. "But a short time ago, she went fer a ride, she did."

"Aye," added the other footman. "Wi' one of your men."

Golovin. "What happened? Was she injured?"

"She's no' the one as got injured. Bu' she was upset, and I dinna blame her. It must ha' been horrible, a child runnin' oot of the woods and right into her path like tha'. 'Twas fortunate a farmer happened by to carry the child here."

"A farmer?"

"Aye, the largest mon I've e'er seen." The footman shook his head. "A giant."

Ian. "This child that was struck by the horse. The grand duchess brought her here?"

"'Twas no' a she, bu' a he. A tall lad, it was."

The other footman nodded. "They're oopstairs now, waitin' on the doctor, although it may be an hour or more before he comes. The fire broke oot just as they arrived, and there was no one to send fer help."

"I will stop by and see to Her Grace, then. Thank you for letting me know."

"Aye, Your Highness."

Max hurried up the stairs.

Behind him, Orlov murmured, "So the grand duchess convinced Golovin to take her to visit Lady Murian."

"Aye," Max said grimly.

"I take it we are not going to Her Grace's bedchamber."

"Why would we? We know where she is."

They went straight to Loudan's bedchamber. Normally guards were stationed to each side, but this afternoon the hallway was empty.

"Bloody brilliant," Orlov said, looking impressed.

"*If* they've as good of a way out of the house as in." Max knocked. "Open the door!"

The door cracked open and Tata's eye appeared in the slit. She looked him up, then down, and then back up. "Are you alone?"

"Orlov is with me."

"And the guards?"

"They are still gone, though they'll return soon."

She opened the door and waved them in with her cane. "Hurry!"

Max entered the bedchamber.

Golovin stood behind the door, his sword drawn, ready to support the grand duchess. Seeing Max and Orlov, he flushed and sheathed his sword.

"Don't," Max said shortly. "You may need it before we are done." He looked about the room. Will was hurriedly going through the drawers of a desk. The young man nodded at him and continued with his task. Past him, Murian's booted feet stuck out from under the bed, while Ian peered behind a huge wardrobe.

Orlov gave Golovin a disgusted look. "You had one task, Golovin. One."

Golovin looked ill. "I know."

"You were to see Her Grace to her bedchamber to take a nap. That is all. And what did you do? You rode with her into the woods, brought back thieves, set a barn afire—

"That wasn't me that set the fire, but Widow Reeves and Widow MacCrae." Golovin brightened. "They did a good job!"

"As distractions go, it was beautifully done. But it does not excuse you from your actions. You put Her Grace in danger," Orlov charged.

"Golovin did no such thing." Max crossed the room to where Murian was under the bed, admiring the shape of her legs outlined by her breeches. "No one needs to put my grandmother in danger. She does it all by herself."

"I like an adventure," Tata Natasha said from where she'd stationed herself at the window, looking out. "It keeps the blood running. But this— Pah! This is not danger. One day, I will tell you of the time your grandfather and I found ourselves afoul of an entire battalion of the tsar's men. *That* was danger."

"If this has to do with you and Grandfather stealing anything, please do not share your story," Max said.

Tata Natasha shrugged and didn't say another word.

Max looked at Ian. "How did you pass Lady Murian off as an injured lad?"

Murian's muffled voice came from under the bed. "It was harder than we expected."

"Aye, it took a bit of work on Her Grace's part to make tha' happen." Ian put his shoulder to the wardrobe and shoved it from the wall. "Lady Murian is a mite tall to be a child. We ha' her wrapped in a blanket, bu' one of the footmen commented upon her height. Fortunately Her Grace was able to point oot tha' one of her grandsons was six foot at the age of twelve. Tha' did the trick."

"It made learning to ride a joy," Max said drily.

Murian wiggled her way out from under the bed, then rolled over and looked up at him. Dust coated her breeches and coat, a smudge graced one of her cheeks, while a cobweb hung from her braid where it was pinned about her head in a tight circle. Yet the second their eyes met, it was as if the previous few days had never happened.

He'd never been so happy to see anyone. And from the warm glow in her eyes, she felt the same.

He reached down and pulled her to her feet, sliding his arm about her and holding her to him. All of the things he'd wanted to say to her slipped away, and all he could do was kiss her. They hadn't time for more than a quick, hard kiss, but it was enough for now.

Ian flushed and looked away, muttering under his breath.

Max grinned. "Your pet giant doesn't like me."

Soft and pliant in his arms, she smiled. "Och, neither do I, but if I must put up with a frustrating foreign prince, it may as well be you."

Tata Natasha limped to another window and peeked out a crack in the curtain, her cane thumping as she went. "The heat of the fire has lessened some. There's a bucket line from the well to the building. It won't be long now before they've put it out."

She looked at Max. "You're tall. See those sconces on the wall by the fireplace? You can reach them. Check if they move and open a secret door."

"A secret door?"

"'Tis a castle; one never knows. Murian, see if there's aught in that trunk against the foot of the bed."

Max gave Murian a swift kiss on her forehead and then moved to the sconces. Ian knocked on the wardrobe, looking for a false back.

Max examined the sconces. "I take it you've found nothing so far."

"Will discovered a hidden cubbyhole in the desk; there was naught in it but pen nibs."

"Which wa' disappointing," Will said.

Orlov left Golovin guarding the door. "Where shall I look?"

"Check the trim work of these windows," Tata ordered without pause. "Perhaps there is a piece of wood, a decoration that will remove to disclose a secret pocket of some sort."

"The sconces don't move." Max walked to a large dressing table that sat to one side of the fireplace. "Have you looked here?"

"*Da*. There are no hidden drawers, no false bottoms in the drawers, no nothing."

He opened a drawer, noticing a neat array of neckcloths to one side, silk kerchiefs to the other. He pulled the drawer free and dumped them all on the floor.

Tata scowled. "We have already *looked* there. Ian, check the marble table by the doorway."

Ian crossed to the table and peered at it.

Max dumped the other drawers empty and, finding nothing, went to the wardrobe, which was the next piece of furniture in the room. He opened the doors.

"Ian's already checked that, too," Tata Natasha said sharply.

"It will not hurt to look again." Hanging inside were numerous hunting jackets, dinner coats, and pressed breeches, while a row of shiny boots lined the wardrobe floor. He took the coats out, one at a time, shook them out, and then dropped them to the bottom of the wardrobe.

"Ye're wastin' yer time," Ian said. "The earl would ne'er hide something in so obvious a place as a pocket."

Max ignored him and removed a stack of starched shirts. Lastly, he picked up the boots and flipped them over.

As he turned over the fifth boot, something sparkly dropped from it, hit the floor with a loud *ping*, and then rolled in a circle.

Everyone stared.

"I believe I just found the Oxenburg crown." He picked it up and examined it, glad to see no damage had come from the fall.

Tata Natasha could not have been stiffer. "He had our royal crown hidden in a *boot*?"

"Apparently so. With so many guards, maybe he didn't feel the need to hide it that well."

"Did the fall hurt your crown?" Murian asked from where she was digging in the trunk.

"Not that I can see." He hefted it. "Bloody hell, that's heavy."

Tata came to take it from him. She leaned her cane against the bed and then wiped the crown with the edge of her shawl. "When you wear it too long, it gives the headache."

"I imagine so." Max checked the final boots but found nothing more.

Tata stuck the crown on her head, pausing to admire herself in a mirror.

"Tata!"

"It is my last chance. Start looking for that journal. We've not much time." She returned to the window, her cane thumping with each step. "The fire is contained. People are returning to the castle. We must hurry."

Will closed the last drawer on the desk. "Where else should I look?"

"The small tables by the bed." Murian slid a glance at Max, and then added, "Be sure you do not just look for secret compartments, but other places, too. Obvious places."

Will did as he was told.

All was silent as they each hurriedly raced through potential hiding spaces.

Outside, a noise arose. Tata announced, "Loudan is by the drive, yelling at the guards. I think he noticed they left the castle unprotected."

"Which means they will return to their posts soon," Max said grimly. "We must leave."

"We canna." Murian shut the trunk and stood. "I know it's in here. Robert kept it in this room, so it *has* to be here."

Max saw the desperation in her eyes. "Murian, we cannot stay. You know that."

"There are footsteps coming up the staircase." Golo-vin gripped his sword. "Many."

Orlov hurried to the door and threw it open. "This way!"

Murian plopped her fisted hands on her hips. "I'm not leaving."

"Murian, it's not safe," Max warned.

"I canna walk away from this opportunity."

"I'll stay wi' Lady Murian." Will left the small tables and came to stand beside her. "Ye've stayed wi' us fer the last year, and I know 'twas no' easy. The least I can do is stay wi' ye when ye need it."

Ian let out his breath in a huge puff. "Bloody 'ell, tha' means I must stay, too. Oh weel, 'tis no' often I get a chance to piss off his lordship in such a fashion."

Murian choked on a laugh, and even Max had to shake his head. But the rumbling outside was growing closer.

Bloody hell, what should he do? The soldier in him warned that they would be trapped if they stayed, but another part of him urged him to do this for her, to take a chance and find the blasted journal. She'd been look-ing for it so very, very long.

He looked at her and found her heart in her eyes. And she was in his heart. "We stay."

Orlov winced but nodded. He closed the door with a regretful sigh.

Max turned to Ian. "Help me move the wardrobe in front of the door."

The two hurried to do so, the heavy wood scraping on the floor.

"Continue searching," Tata Natasha ordered. "The quicker we find that blasted journal, the better."

Murian and Will hurried to do just that, Will pulling the mattresses from the bed while Murian searched through the shelves, shaking each book and then stacking it on the floor.

The doorknob rattled. And then rattled again. "Who's in there?"

"Tasha!" Murian whispered.

Max raised his brows. Not many were allowed to address his grandmother so, but Tata Natasha didn't look the least surprised.

"You must come out now!" the stern voice ordered through the door.

Murian whispered to Tata Natasha, "Answer him." A faint smile curved her mouth. "Make him regret it."

Tata Natasha barked a short laugh, and then she made her way to the door. In her most imperious voice, she called out, "Who is there?"

During the ensuing silence, they continued their search.

Finally, the same deep voice replied through the door, "Yer Grace?"

"Who else? What do you want? Who are you?"

"I beg yer pardon, bu' I'm Cap'n David MacNoor. Ye are trespassin' in his lordship's chamber."

"His lordship's chamber? Don't be ridiculous! This is my bedchamber, you bloody fool."

A muttering arose at this, and then Captain MacNoor answered, "I'm sorry, Yer Grace, bu' tha' is Lord Loudan's bedchamber, no' yers."

"How do you know?" she demanded. "It looks like mine. There's a bed and a dresser, several, in fact, and two chairs by the fire and—"

"Yer Grace, ye were in the green bedchamber. Lord Loudan's bedchamber is red."

"Really? Let me look."

Murian grabbed another row of books and shook them open.

"Wha' next?" Will whispered to Murian. "There's naught in the mattresses."

"Move the carpets and see if there's aught here," Murian ordered. "Mayhap there's a trapdoor."

He hurried to roll up the carpets.

Outside, the guard cleared his throat in what he obviously thought was a stern manner. "Yer Grace, I ha' been standin' guard on this chamber fer nigh on four weeks. This is Lord Loudan's bedchamber. I'd bet me son's head on it."

"Oh." Tata Natasha leaned on her cane. "Mayhap I'm mistaken, then. The bedchambers in these old castles, they all look alike."

"Aye, Yer Grace. Can ye open the door, please? I'll be glad to escort ye to yer own chamber."

"That would be fine, except I happen to be nude."

Silence stretched on the other side of the door. "I beg yer pardon, Yer Grace. Did ye . . . did ye jus' say ye were n—n—"

"Of course I'm nude! How else am I to take a bath?"

"Ye're bathin'? Bu' . . . is there water?"

"No, and there's no tub, either! Someone is supposed to send both. I've been waiting here, in the

nude, for a very long time. I hope I have not caught
a cold."

"Ah. Nay. I dinna. I—ah. Yer Grace, if ye'll hold one
moment, I'll fetch Lord Loudan and he can— One moment, Yer Grace."

The sound of his footsteps running down the hall
made Tata Natasha snicker. "That will keep them for a
few moments, at least." She turned and limped across
the floor, to where Will had rolled back the rug. "While
they fetch Loudan, I'll look in the—" Her cane, thumping with her steps, hit a board that echoed.

For a long second, they all looked at one another.

Tata thumped her cane again, the hollow sound
even more pronounced.

"I knew it!" Murian stood, her heart racing, her
palms damp. "That must be it."

"So it must. But why here?" Natasha asked. "In the
middle of everything?"

Murian looked around the room, remembering how
it once was. "It's where the settee used to be, for it faced
the fire. It is light and easy to move."

Max was already on his knees examining the boards.
"I need a knife."

Murian came to look over his shoulder.

Orlov hurried up to place a knife hilt-first into Max's
hand.

Using the tip, Max pried up a board. And there,
wrapped in a faded red piece of velvet, was a leather
journal.

Chapter 23

Murian splayed her hand over the familiar leather cover, the supple leather cool under her fingertips. She started to open it, but Max stopped her.

"We must leave while the guards are gone."

"I know a way oot," Will said. "Doon the back stairs. Ye can hide at the bottom while I fetch the wagon and sneak us away."

"Come." Max had Golovin and Orlov move the wardrobe, then they all hurried out to the landing, leaving the sadly mussed room behind.

They could hear men speaking, and then footsteps up the main stairway.

"This way." Will led them down the hall, away from the main portion of the castle. They went down first one hallway and then another, twisting and turning, and Max was glad they'd brought Will.

He finally stopped before a door that had been cleverly cut into the wall. "These are cut throughout the castle and serve as servants' passages." He opened the door and led them down a narrow, dark staircase. "When I was a wee one, me mither used to bring me oop and down this way to visit the lord, so we were ne'er seen on the grand staircase."

"I feel as if I'm in a novel," Tata Natasha announced, a gleeful tone in her voice.

They turned a corner and were just about to go down another flight of stairs, when a door could be heard opening, light suddenly shining up the stairwell.

Max held up his hand and everyone froze in place. They could hear two men talking.

Will leaned close and whispered. "They said someone has been sent to guard the bottom door. We canna get oot tha' way."

Max nodded. "We'll have to go back into the main part of the castle. What floor are we on now?"

"The third."

"My bedchamber is on that floor. We'll go there until we can figure another way out."

Will nodded and led the way to the next landing. Max moved ahead and carefully opened the door. Hearing nothing, he stepped out and glanced down the hallway. Seeing that the way was clear, he gestured them all to follow. They swiftly reached his bedchamber.

Everyone filed in, Orlov closing the door and locking it.

Tata Natasha looked around. "Your bedchamber is larger than mine!"

"I'm a prince." He turned to his men. "Move that large table in front of the door. It will at least slow them down. Will, hang this"—he pulled a kerchief from his pocket—"on the latch of the front window."

"Which one?"

"It won't matter. My men will see it and know to come."

Tata Natasha took a chair by the fireplace and bounced upon the cushion. "You have better furniture, too. The settee in my bedchamber is like a rock."

Murian sat in a chair across from the duchess, the journal held to her as if it were a shield.

Ian rubbed his neck. "Wha' do we do now?"

"Now we wait. My men will come eventually, and we will do what we must to get everyone out of here safely."

Will picked up a lamp and lit it, and then brought it to Murian.

She smiled. "Thank you." She carefully opened the journal, and the familiar writing made her voice thicken with emotion. "Every evening, Robert would write in this book. I can see the lamplight flickering over his hair as he scratched out a few lines." Her throat tightened, though she had to smile. He'd been so young, so full of hopes and dreams. "The last time I saw him, he was so busy scribbling in this that he barely said goodbye. At the time, I was only going to be gone two days, so neither of us thought it a momentous occasion."

"Robert loved ye, miss," Ian added softly. "More tha' anyone."

Max's gaze traveled over her face. "You miss him, and yet you smile."

"What else would she do?" Tata Natasha asked sharply. "They were married, and he died. I was married and my husband died." She looked directly at Max. "Sad as it is, it happens all the time."

Murian agreed. "Life is not always fair, is it? 'Tis just a sad fact. Robert was a wonderful part of my youth. We grew oop together, in a way. We were so young. . . ." She laughed ruefully. "'Tis a wonder we managed to be wed so happily."

She paged through the journal. "I'll always miss him. But as time passes, so does the pain. Now those memories are like an old friend, and they make me smile. We were fortunate to have what time we did." She turned to the back of the journal and as she did so, two letters slipped from the book and fell to the floor. She picked them up.

"From Robert?" Max asked.

"Nay. These two are in French. They must be from his mother's family."

Max's gaze fixed on the letters. "Robert's mother was French?"

"Aye. She died in childbirth, so Robert ne'er knew her. He married me right after his father died. After we'd been married a short time, Robert began receiving letters like those."

"From his mother's family?"

"Aye. He said his father had kept them from contacting him, but once Robert inherited the title, they'd realized his father was gone and they began corresponding with him."

"And the other piece of paper?" Max nodded to the folded sheet of parchment she held in her hand.

She opened it. "It looked like a marriage license, signed by the old earl. But the name . . . it's not Robert's mother's. I dina know— Och!" Her eyes widened, and she looked at Will. "I believe this belongs to you." She held it out to him.

With a hand that trembled, he took the heavy paper and looked at it.

"Wha' is it?" Ian asked quietly.

Will lowered the paper, his face pale, his eyes wet with unshed tears. "I ha' a father after all."

"The old earl?"

"He married my mither. He ne'er told me tha', but . . ." Will sniffed. "I think I knew. He was always kind to me."

Max noted that Murian had paused in reading the journal. He came to stand by her. "What have you found?"

She tapped the journal. "Here it is: December fourteenth. When Loudan's party arrived."

Max watched as she bent her head and started to read, her brows knitting as her eyes traveled rapidly over the pages.

He glanced at the two forgotten letters she'd placed on the table at her elbow. "May I look at these?"

Murian, already lost in the words dancing before her eyes, didn't look up. "Of course."

"Ye read French, do ye?" Ian said.

"*Da.*" Max unfolded the missive.

As he did so, Murian read her late husband's last words. She read slowly at first, hearing the words in Robert's voice. But then, as the words began to ring in her head, she read faster and faster, until she no longer heard Robert's voice, but her own.

The words swam before her. Finally, she reached the bottom of the last page. She lowered the journal and stared at the ink as it seemed to move and collide, new words forming in front of her astonished eyes.

"Well?" Natasha asked impatiently. "What's it say? Was there a duel at all? Or did Loudan murder him, as you suspected?"

Murian shook her head, unable to think clearly enough to speak.

"Lass?" Ian bent to see her face. "Wha' is it?"

Beside him, Max refolded one of the French missives, a shadow in his eyes.

"Och, Lady Murian!" Will said. "Wha' does Lord Robert's journal say?"

She took a shuddering breath. "Loudan was telling the truth. There was a duel."

Ian grimaced. "Bloody hell! I was afraid of tha'."

"But there was no card game," Murian added. "And it was not Loudan who challenged Robert. 'Twas Robert who challenged Loudan."

"So wha' was the duel o'er then?" Ian asked.

"Over these." Max lifted the letters.

Murian's gaze locked on them, her stomach aching and tight. She nodded. "Robert knew Loudan before we wed. He never told me that."

"He dinna tell you a lot of things," Ian said.

"Apparently so. Loudan is the one who put Robert in touch with his French relatives."

"Loudan?" Ian said, astounded.

"Aye. Loudan somehow knew Robert's grandmother,

saying he'd met her before the war, and how she'd spoken fondly of Robert's mother and had wished to know her grandson but the old laird hadna allowed it."

"When did Loudan tell Lord Robert tha'?" Ian asked. "I certainly ne'er saw him."

"He always visited with a large group of men who hunted together."

"Ah. Tha' explains it, then. There were always hunting parties stoppin' by to rest their mounts and ask fer refreshments. Lord Robert ne'er turned them away."

"He wouldna," Murian agreed. "On these visits, Loudan convinced Robert to write to his grandmother. Loudan had Robert dictate, and then the earl translated it into French and wrote the letters."

"Which Lord Robert then franked and sent," Max said.

Orlov frowned. "I don't understand. Were the letters not to Lord Robert's grandmother?"

"They were, but Loudan always included a letter to his friends, which he tucked inside of Robert's."

Murian nodded. "Robert writes that his grandmother was a frail, elderly woman who was so happy to hear from him that he was determined to keep the connection, even though it was illegal to correspond with the French because of the war."

"Good for him," Tasha announced.

"Loudan knew ways to get letters in and out of France, and he helped Robert. For a while, all was well. Robert would write letters to his grandmother, and Loudan would translate them for him on his way through, and would read the responses when they came. And every time, Loudan insisted on putting in a note from himself, saying it was mere courtesy."

"But it was more," Max said. "Much more."

Murian nodded. "Robert was too trusting, perhaps, but he wasna a fool. He soon realized something wasna right, so one time, after Loudan had given him a note to include in a letter to his grandmother, Robert first took the missive to the vicar in Inverness, a man fluent in French. The vicar translated it, and Robert was devastated. Loudan was corresponding with the enemy, sending troop locations and times, things Loudan had gleaned from his brother, Spencer. And the earl was using Robert's grandmother as a courier, too, endangering her as well.

"The next time the earl came to translate a letter, Robert informed Loudan he was going to tell Spencer everything. But Loudan was ready. He pointed out that Robert had franked all the letters. He convinced Robert that Spencer would think *him* the traitor and not Loudan. That he would lose everything, Rowallen and me, too." She traced her fingers over the words written in the journal. "Robert feared he would be sent to the gallows and I would be put oot into the cold."

Ian shook his head. "So the puir lad challenged Loudan to a duel."

"Aye," Murian replied. "And was killed. I daresay once that had happened, Loudan saw his chance to acquire the estate, so he made up the story aboot the card game, convinced his friends to swear false testimony, and took his claim to Edinburgh."

There was a long silence.

Orlov nodded to the letters in Max's hands. "Your brother was right."

Murian turned to Max. "Your brother?"

He met her gaze firmly. "My brother, Nik, has his fingers in many pies. He is forever looking for secrets. He found evidence that information about the troops was being filtered to the French. The battle where my friend Fedorovich died was caused by a surprise attack that could only have come from a leak of information."

"Spencer was involved in that battle?"

"We fought side by side, he and I. We were both almost killed."

Murian paled a little at that. "Loudan would have benefited greatly, had Spencer been killed in battle."

"Which is why Nik was certain Loudan was involved."

Murian nodded. "So that is why you are here."

"I thought you came to help me!" Natasha said, looking furious.

"As if you tell me everything *you* do!" Max exclaimed.

"I never keep secrets."

"Oh? Then why did you invite yourself to a card game with Loudan if you were not privy to Nik's thoughts about the earl?"

She sniffed. "I might have heard him mention his concerns."

"And so you acted on your own and used the Oxenburg crown as bait."

She patted the crown where it still rested on her

head. "He could not resist it. I thought I could get him drunk and find out what Nik wished to know. Sadly, it did not work out the way I'd wished." She scowled. "I've never met an earl more able to drink."

Max shook his head and then turned back to Murian. "Well? What do we do now?"

"Spencer must be told, if we can find out where he is. In the meantime . . ." Murian turned to Will. "Though Robert was brave in his dealings with Loudan, he was not always the best of men. After his father's death, he found that marriage license among the estate's papers and realized you were his brother. He withheld that information from you and there was no noble motive behind it." She placed her hand on the journal. "He didn't wish to share his fortune, or Rowallen. That was wrong of him, and I would have told him so, if I'd known."

Will flushed. "Me lady, dinna think poorly on Master Robert. 'Twould be a difficult thing to share, the castle ye were told ye'd inherit. He would ha' come around—I truly believe it. And had he spoken to me, I'd ha' told him I'd no wish to claim anything. Bu' I would ha' been proud to ha' him fer a brother."

Ian sniffed and slapped Will on the shoulder. "There's a guid lad."

Murian smiled and closed the journal.

"There's something I don't understand," Orlov said. "I can understand why Loudan wished to own Rowallen—it's a lovely castle, and the lands are rich with game. But why did he throw out the servants?"

"I daresay he wasna sure who Robert had confided

in," Ian said. "'Twas safer to get rid of the lot of us than to wonder which of us might slit his throat whilst he slept."

"Tha' bastard got away with far more than murder," Will declared.

"He might have, except for these." Max held up the letters. "These are two of the missives written by Loudan, in his own hand. Robert kept them in his journal, and I think it was for a reason." Max looked at Murian. "He feared he might not win the duel. He knew that, with these, you could clear his name, if need be. This is more than enough to convict the earl, and it's why Loudan didn't wish you to find the journal. He feared these letters might be hidden with it."

Ian cursed gruffly. "A fool, tha' boy, challenging the earl to a duel. A romantic, too, always thinkin' things would turn out well simply because they should."

Murian saw the hurt in Ian's eyes and she arose and put her arm about his broad shoulders. "He believed in what was right. In many ways, he dinna die in vain. We can take care of the earl now. At least we have that and can—"

A commotion sounded outside.

"Speaking of the devil," Tata Natasha announced.

As soon as she said the words, a heavy knock was heard upon the door. "Open this door or I'll have it broken down," Loudan said harshly. "And Your Grace, do not tell me you are *en dishabille*. I know who is with you and you would never do such a thing in front of your grandson, Lady Murian, her protector Ian Beagin, and those other fools." Loudan paused, letting his words soak in, and then he repeated, "Now open this door!"

There was a rustle of voices, as if the guards outside the doorway had grown in rank.

Orlov pursed his lips. "Golovin, what do you think? Twenty? Thirty?"

"No more than thirty. The hall will not hold more."

They listened closely. Over the muttering, they heard Loudan issuing low instructions, and then footsteps as guards moved into position on either side of the door.

Orlov eyed the door before he said to Max, "This reminds me of Paris."

"Ah, yes." Max considered it. "It is worth a try. We will need to move the table."

"Aye. We'll have to open the door wide." They went toward the door.

Ian jumped in front of them. "Wait! Wha' are ye doing?"

Max bit back a sigh. "Move. We are going to allow the earl to enter."

"He'll ha' us all killed!"

Orlov poofed. "He's only one man."

"And his guards? Ye dinna think they willna push their way inside as soon as the door is open?"

"They'll try," Golovin answered. "And we may have to knock a few heads. But in order to get through the number of guards that bloody fool has lodged inside this castle, we'll need a hostage."

"And who better than the earl himself?" Orlov asked.

"A good brawl and a hostage," Tata Natasha said with approval. "That is good for the digestion. Tonight, we will eat like Vikings!"

Murian blinked. What did that even mean?

Ian shook his head. "Ye're puttin' the lass at risk. I willna ha' it."

Max scowled. "You don't have a say in this."

Ian puffed up and Murian hastily added, "Ian, think a moment! We're locked in a room in the middle of a castle, surrounded by guards led by the man who killed my husband. I dinna think it can get worse. Let the prince and his men do what they do best: fight. We'll help them and—"

"Here now!" Loudan raised his voice. "You have until the count of ten, and then my men will knock down this door!"

"Fine, then." Ian cracked his knuckles. "In fer a penny, in fer a pound. Lass, take the grand duchess and get behind the bed."

"*One!*" Loudan yelled.

"Pah! Do we look like dishrags to you?" The grand duchess lifted her cane. "Get out of our way and let us have at them!"

"*Two!*"

"If things go well, no one will have to do much of anything." Max turned to Will. "Since they will not hide as they've been asked, watch over Lady Murian and my grandmother."

Will moved between them and the door.

"*Three!*"

"Orlov, you and Ian help move the table. Golovin, you know what to do."

"*Four!*"

"*Da*, General." Golovin sheathed his sword and went to the fireplace, where he hefted the fire iron judiciously.

"*Five!*"

Golovin returned to his position flat against the wall to one side of the door, the tire iron held like a cricket bat.

"*Six!*"

With the table safely out of the way, Orlov and Max stood in front of the door. Max said, "Ian, when we give you the signal, open the door wide, but do not let it go."

"*Seven!*"

Max said, "Once we have the earl, you must close it quickly."

As Ian went to the door, Orlov warned, "You'll have to put your shoulder into it. They'll all be pushing, trying to get in."

"*Eight!*"

Max said, "Ready? Now!"

"*Ni—*"

Ian yanked the door open.

The earl stood slightly back from the door, two of his guards before him, their weapons drawn.

They took a step forward.

Golovin swung the tire iron directly across the doorway, hitting the two guards across their faces, the taller one taking the hit to his nose, the shorter one to his forehead.

They fell to the floor like logs, their weapons clanging with them.

Before the earl could move or new guards push in front of him, Max grabbed the earl by the neckcloth and yanked him inside. "Shut the door!"

Ian pushed it shut as the guards rushed toward them, leaping over their fallen comrades. One guard managed to get his arm inside the door, but Golovin smacked it with the fire iron and, with a cry, it was withdrawn.

With his shoulder to the panel, Ian lowered his head and shoved the door closed.

Golovin latched it as Max threw the earl into a chair.

Loudan clutched at his neck, struggling for breath, glaring all the while.

Someone banged on the door. "Open this now or we will shoot through it!"

"And kill the earl, who is directly in the line of fire?" Tata Natasha yelled back. "If you kill him, he will not be able to pay you for a long time. Perhaps ever."

A muttering arose.

"Leave the hallway and go downstairs to await instructions," she ordered, as if she were the general and not Max. "You will not force the door open, nor plan any tricks, or we will be forced to kill the earl, cut out his heart, and eat it."

Still panting, Loudan's eyes widened, while outside the door, a horrified silence reigned.

Max sighed. "Tata Natasha, must you do that? People already think you a witch."

She shrugged. "It amuses me." She tapped her cane

on the floor near Loudan's feet. "You. Do something useful. Tell them to go."

Loudan looked at the tiara on her head and a sneer curled his lips. "I will tell them nothing, you Gypsy dirt—"

Tata's cane smacked his knee.

"*OWWWWW!*"

She smacked it again, getting one of his knuckles with it.

"*Stop! Please stop!*"

The guards outside the door grew deathly silent as Loudan whimpered loudly, cupping his knee with one hand, while he tucked the other under his arm and rocked back and forth.

Tata said loudly to the guards outside the door, "Are you still there? You've been told to leave."

They heard the clanking of arms as the guards moved away.

After a moment, Demidor's voice sounded outside the door. "General, Raeff and I are here. We will guard the door and make sure no one comes."

"Very good. And Pahlen?"

"He escorted the courier, but should return at any moment."

"Very good." Max turned back to Loudan, who was now slumped in his chair. "Well. Here we are."

The earl scowled. "How dare you enter my home!"

"'Tis *our* home, not yours," Murian said icily. "We found the journal, and we know what you did. You'll be hanged as a traitor, and Rowallen will be returned to those who love her."

Loudan paled. "Where was it? I looked everywhere for that blasted thing?"

"Does it matter?" Murian asked. She held up the journal. "We have this, and some of the letters you wrote."

Loudan's lips thinned. "You cannot prove those letters are mine. I have many friends in Edinburgh. Your case will be dismissed before you even arrive."

"We'll see aboot that. I'll also tell Spencer what you've done. He will see to it that you pay for your errors."

Loudan smirked. "Mayhap you should write to him, as you've been trying to do this last year and some."

"I know you've intercepted those letters. I dinna know how, but when Spencer returns, he will listen to me."

"*If* my brother returns from war." The thought seemed to reassure the earl, for he managed an ugly, cold smile. "Which I doubt will happen."

Murian's heart tightened. "You wouldna harm your own brother."

"My half-brother," Loudan corrected her. "And he's done much to harm me. When our father was on his deathbed, he told Spencer I was to have half the estates and fortune."

"Aye—when he *died*. Spencer told me as much when I lived with him."

Loudan's face reddened. "Why the hell should I have to wait for that? And then my bloodthirsty brother became embued with patrotic fervor. It is not cheap to provide for an entire army, so to fund himself and his troops, he began to sell estates. He sold every bloody one and left me with nothing."

"They weren't yours, but his," Murian said. "He loves his country."

Loudan laughed. "He loves *his* cause. *His* glory. *His* bloody title, and bloody medals, and bloody awards. People think him a demigod, and he drinks it in as if it were his due! They say the crown will reinstate his lost estates and fortune. And it might happen; he always knew how to come out on top. You think him a hero, but I know him for the petty tyrant he is."

"You said he would not come back," Max said. "Why wouldn't he?"

Murian caught Loudan's smirk and a sick weight sank in her stomach. "What have you done?"

Loudan shrugged. "My brother is not as smart as he thinks. I've had people near him this whole time—*my* people. People who will do as *I* wish, as *I* say. And I have told them it would be best if he didn't return from war."

A noise sounded outside: the trample of horses, the creek of a coach.

Tata Natasha went to the window. "It is a carriage, surrounded by guards. Many, many guards, all in uniform." She looked at Max. "Did you do this?"

Murian saw a smile flicker over Max's face, and for some reason, her fears fled. "Perhaps," he said.

"Who is it?" she asked.

"I don't know," Natasha said, as cries arose outside, followed by the clang of swords. "But the guards have no qualms taking on the earl's men. There is a fight and—" She scowled. "It is already over. Loudan's men are putting down their weapons. I suppose I cannot blame them. They are outnumbered." She squinted at the coach. "What an interesting crest. A golden lion eating a baby. That is quite formidable—"

Murian was on her feet, racing for the door. "'Tis Spencer! He's returned!"

Chapter 24

Murian stood on the back terrace of Rowallen, the wind swirling her cape as she watched the sun setting over the lawn.

The door behind her opened and she knew by her shiver who it was.

Max came to stand behind her, close enough that if she leaned back only a little, she would touch him. So much had happened over the last few hours. Too much to comprehend. Spencer had indeed returned, bringing his soldiers and taking back Rowallen.

Max's arms slipped about her, his chin resting against her temple. Warm, and strong, he offered not a word but stood silently, waiting.

Breaking the silence, she said, "Rowallen is finally free from Loudan's grasp."

"*Da*. It is about time."

"And now it is Will's, or it will be once the marriage license is authenticated. It is sad the old laird felt he had to hide his marriage to his housekeeper. I think his people would have been forgiving."

"Aye, but the neighboring nobility might not have been."

"Probably not." She sighed. "'Tis a pity."

"*Da*. Spencer has already sent men to the parish church to check the veracity of the license. We will know soon." Max's breath warmed her temple. "What if it is real, *dorogaya moya*? What, then?"

"It changes nothing. If he is the new master, then I will help him run the castle. He was never raised to that position and he will need guidance."

"So you are not upset the castle is not yours?"

"Not at all." She was surprised at that, but all she could dredge up was a faint regret that she hadn't known the truth sooner. "It was never about the castle, Max. It was about the people. They deserved their home back."

His arms tightened about her. Finally, after a long silence, he said, "I hoped that was the truth of the matter, but I was not certain."

She leaned into him and rested her head on his shoulder. "How is Spencer?"

"Still furious. He has spoken with Loudan."

"And?"

"The earl is now chained in the dungeon and Spencer has sent for the constable." Max looked down at her. "I did not know your castle had a dungeon."

"Loudan is the first guest in over a century. His visit is overdue."

Max rubbed his cheek on her hair.

She sighed. It felt so right when he touched her.

Comfortable and yet thrilling, at one and the same time. He melted her heart and warmed her soul. God, she would miss him when he left. She turned slightly to burrow her head in the crook of his neck, her chest aching with her thoughts.

He held her closer and she inhaled his scent, of leather and soap, and rubbed her cheek on his wool coat. Finally, she lifted her face to his. "I dinna know what I'll do wi'oot you."

He smiled and slid the back of his fingers over her cheek. "We have to talk about that. But first, Spencer waits for us in the dining hall. I'm to bring you there."

"You should have told me right away."

"Perhaps." His smile turned wry. "I could not give up this chance to hold you."

She nodded, but made no move to leave. They had so few of these moments left. Her throat tightened.

He didn't move, either, simply holding her, his heartbeat under her ear steady and strong. "I will miss you," she whispered.

His arms tightened about her and he pressed a kiss to her forehead.

She closed her eyes, tears welling. She knew she couldn't stay in his arms without weeping, so she forced a smile and stepped away from him. "We should join Spencer." She turned and went inside, Max following.

He didn't say a word as they walked, and she wished he would. She knew he cared for her. Perhaps not as much as she cared for him, but she'd seen it in his eyes, felt it in his embrace.

When they reached the dining hall, Max leaned

past her to open the door. Thoroughly miserable, she walked in.

And came to a halt.

The room was set for tea, cups and saucers at the ready, trays of tarts and cakes arranged in a neat line.

At the head of the room stood Spencer, tall and golden haired, and looking every bit the lion king of his coat of arms. He was filling Tata Natasha's glass with whiskey. Behind him stood Will, now dressed in borrowed clothes a bit too large but more befitting his station, Ian at his side.

Ian nodded to her, and then smiled as her gaze went to the others in the room. "We're all here, lassie."

Widow Reeves grinned. "Lord Spencer came fer us, he did, and brought us all back to the castle."

Widow Brodie stood by the windows, her sons lined up behind her, one of them secretly reaching behind her to taste the icing on one of the teacakes. "Ye did it, lassie!" Widow Brodie said. "Ye vanquished the earl!"

Widow MacCrae, Pahlen at one side, her daughter at her other, smiled shyly. "His Grace says ye were brave. We've been tellin' him how much tha' is true."

The other widows nodded.

Murian smiled mistily. They were her friends, her family. And she loved them all.

"Och, no tears! Come!" Spencer said, his voice loud and booming as always. "We've libations and much to discuss."

She made her way to his side, where he bent and kissed her cheek. "I hear you've been busy since I left."

"I wrote and told you all about it, but you dinna respond."

"Aye, there was a snake in my grass, one I dinna know aboot until the general here sent me a missive." Spencer slapped Max on the shoulder. "I owe much to this man."

Murian looked questioningly at Max.

He shrugged. "You said your letters were not reaching the duke. I was fairly certain a missive from a Prince of Oxenburg might make it past Loudan's lackey, whoever he was."

"So he wrote me," Spencer said, "and a long and involved letter it was—like a novel, filled with intrigue and danger, and a maiden in distress." He chuckled, though there was a sharpness to his gaze when he looked at Murian. "There was also a part about Robin Hood. I shall ask you more aboot that later."

Tata Natasha snorted. "She still owes me four chickens."

"So you were able to find the traitor in your midst after the prince's letter?" Murian asked.

"Only two of my aides touch my mail, so it took very little to find the culprit. After some ah, persuasion, he admitted all. We searched his belongings and found letters from my brother, as well as a vial of poison."

She couldn't hold back a gasp. "Your own brother!"

Spencer's gaze grew shadowed. "It was a bitter pill, but he was always weak. Father worried about him, and with reason. He was easily led astray and wont to think of himself as short-changed."

"And now?"

"He will face his crimes in court. Meanwhile, I owe much to you, Murian, both for alerting the prince and for taking care of Robert's people after his death. Rowallen is in your debt, as am I."

"I'm glad to see her back in the proper hands."

Spencer began, "Ah. Yes. About that—"

Max slipped an arm about Murian's waist. "Murian is already well aware the castle will go to Will."

Spencer looked relieved. "I'm glad to hear it. There is an entail on the castle and lands, so the castle would have never gone to you, as the widow, but to the next male in line for the title, which is Will. The records at the parish church have confirmed it."

She turned a smile on Will. "I canna think of anyone who would love the castle more."

Will flushed. "I'm shaken, me lady. Bu'—" His expression grew fierce. "I can promise ye tha' no one will take better care of her."

Ian slapped Will on the shoulder. "Tha' is the way to step oop."

Spencer agreed. "With the marriage license now proven, and Robert's journal as evidence, we should have no problems filing Will's claim." The duke turned to Will and began expounding on a number of improvements that could be made right away, leaving the young man with a stunned look upon his face.

Murian watched, though Max noted that her smile did not reach her eyes. He alone knew how much this latest turn cost her. How much pride she'd swallowed to give up her claim on a castle she'd fought for in such a fierce and determined manner. Though, as she'd said, it wasn't the castle that held her heart.

He'd never wanted to kiss her more.

Tata Natasha took a healthy sip of her whiskey. "It is for the better, Lady Murian. You do not belong here, but with my grandson. Tell him you love him and settle this once and for all, for I wish to eat cake."

"Tata!" Max snapped. "That is not how this will happen."

"How what will happen?" Murian asked, turning her clear silver gaze his way.

Blast it, I wished to do this in private, but . . . He looked at the people around them, all of whom were now staring at them expectantly. *Perhaps now is the best time, after all.*

He turned back to Murian. "Murian, when Spencer realized all you'd done for Rowallen and her people, he thought to offer you another estate—one he will receive for his service in the war."

"There are several, I've been told," Spencer said. "The crown will be very generous and you may have your pick."

"My own estate?"

"Aye, lass," Spencer said. "Bigger and better than Rowallen Castle, too."

"Nay." Murian shook her head. "I dinna want another estate." Her gaze flickered past Spencer, back to the widows and their children. "I belong with my people."

Max took her hand, the warmth immediately drawing her gaze to his.

She'd never seen such an expression upon his face. It was hope, and worry, and uncertainty . . . "What is it?"

"I was hoping you would say you didn't want another estate."

She blinked up at him. "Why?"

Widow Reeves chuckled. "Duke Spencer is no' the only one who came fer us in the forest. The prince came, too, and he asked us to marry him *wi'* ye!"

"*What?*"

Max muttered, "That's not—bloody hell—this is *not* how I wished this to happen!"

"But 'tis true," Widow MacCrae said, sneaking a peek at Pahlen, who beamed back. "The prince asked us all to come wit' ye to Oxenburg, and be yer family there as we've been yer family here. We're to all ha' our own houses, wi' gardens and such, and I'm to be the new housekeeper, I am."

"I'm yer new cook," Widow Reeves said.

Widow Brodie couldn't have looked happier. "And I'm to help with the cows and chickens and goats. Widow MacThune is to ha' her own lacemaking shop, and Widow Grier's to be yer laundress, and—"

"But we can't," Murian replied. "What about Will? Who will help him?"

"Ye can leave tha' to me," Ian said. "I'm too old to be traipsin' across the world." He put his arm about Will. "I'll be here to help Will, and we'll ha' the duke's assistance, too."

"Many of my men are through with war," Spencer

said. "They'll need a place to call their own, too. Neither Rowallen nor Will will lack assistance."

Max took Murian's hand and tugged her around so that she faced him. She didn't know what to say or what to do. "You've been busy," she said.

"Too much so, if you ask me!" Tata Natasha said, holding out her glass for Spencer to refill. "Can we have cake now? I'm starving!"

"Not yet," Spencer said. "But soon."

"Ignore her," Max ordered Murian. "Ignore them all, and listen to me. Just this once." He kissed her fingers, his lips warm, his gaze never leaving hers. "I know you've given everything for this estate and these people. If I thought moving this castle to Oxenburg would bring you to me, I would move it rock by rock with my bare hands.

"But it dawned on me that you do not love the castle at all. You love these people who made Rowallen your home. So I asked them to help me win you. To help me avoid the saddest day of my life, which would be one in which I do not see you, cannot hold you, cannot be with you. I love you, Murian. I love you more every time I see you."

He took a deep breath, and added, "But you should know that I am a soldier. I cannot change that. And I cannot promise you forever. But I can promise I will love you as long as I am breathing, and more."

She looked into his eyes and saw his love, felt it in her own heart as if he'd placed it there. And looking past him, she saw her people and his, his grandmother and Spencer, Will and Ian, all of them silently urging her to accept his love.

They didn't need to make such an effort.

She returned her gaze to his. "I suppose I should pack."

For a long second, he merely stared at her. Then he swept her into his arms and spun her around, kissing her until she was dizzy.

"Finally!" Tata Natasha said. "*Now* we can have cake!"

Epilogue

Oxenburg

Carriages lined the street near the wharf where *The Tempest* was moored. She was a proud ship, a ruddy clipper that took a large crew. Max had taken Murian to sea for their honeymoon. After four months of wedding preparation, which had been both too long of a time and too short, they'd had a quiet wedding. Quiet, that is, by royal standards. By Max's standards, it had been agonizingly formal. Though Oxenburg custom dictated that the bride and groom should not visit one another alone until after the wedding, someone—he suspected Tata Natasha—had obligingly placed Murian in a guest room on the second floor. Therefore he was never placed in danger when climbing the trellis into her room each night.

The second he'd seen Murian coming down the aisle dressed in her wedding gown decorated with silver thread, though, he'd forgotten every complaint he'd had about the too-long wait. God, he loved her. And now she was his, and he was hers.

After the wedding they'd spent six glorious weeks

traveling the ocean, visiting faraway ports and luxuriating in each other's company. They'd have sailed longer, but he was needed at home. Though Napoleon had been captured and the war declared over, there were still loose ends that needed tying up.

He smiled down at Murian now, noting how the sun had brought out the freckles on her nose. Had they not been in public, he'd have kissed it, tracing a line between her freckles and—

But there would be time enough for that later. They were home now and soon they'd go to his favorite house, where Murian's people awaited them.

He could not get Murian home fast enough.

"General!" Orlov strode forward. "The coach awaits."

"Good." Max grinned. "Orlov, I hear we are to depart for France."

"In three weeks' time."

"Very well." Max watched as Murian arranged a stack of bandboxes so that some of her new purchases would be near the top. Dressed in the latest fashions, her silk gown teased by the sea winds, she looked healthy and happy, though she'd been plagued with seasickness these last few weeks. "How long will we be gone?" he asked Orlov.

Orlov followed Max's gaze to Murian and smiled. "Two months, no more."

"Good. And our men?"

"They have been notified and will be ready."

He grasped Orlov's shoulder. "It is good to be home, my friend."

"It is good to have you home. Lady Murian's people have readied the house. Katrina is jealous you are to have such a cook."

"Widow Reeves is worth her weight in gold."

"Indeed. I will have your luggage loaded, General. Welcome home." Orlov inclined his head and made his way to where Murian stood with her bandboxes.

Max caught sight of a large man dressed in fine clothes striding down the wharf, a red cloak whipping about his shoulders.

"Alexsey!" Max hugged his brother, smacking him on the shoulders as hard as he could by way of greeting. "I didn't expect to see you here."

"I had to come," Alexsey said simply.

"You wear your court dress. You have been with our father and mother?"

Alexsey's smile faltered. "Actually, I was—"

"Alexsey!" Murian joined them, and Alexsey's grin returned and he swept her into a hug.

"Unhand my wife," Max ordered.

"I will, once I've kissed her." Alexsey kissed Murian's cheek. "Bronwyn sends her regards."

"She didn't come with you?" Murian asked.

"*Nyet*." Alexsey couldn't keep the pride from his face. "Her condition makes travel difficult."

"Her condition?" Max repeated blankly.

"*Alexsey!*" Murian gave an excited hop and then threw her arms about her brother-in-law. "We didn't know! Why didn't you tell us? All those boring letters from the both of you and neither of you said a word!"

Alexsey laughed. "We wished to surprise you."

"We are surprised," Max said. "I'll wager Tata Natasha is ecstatic."

Alexsey's smile dimmed. "That is why I am here." He looked around and then stepped forward to say in a lowered voice, "Tata Natasha has disappeared."

"Disappeared? From her home?"

"*Nyet.* She was traveling through Scotland on her way back from visiting Wulf and Lily."

Wulf was their youngest brother, and he'd lately been spending time with his wife's family and their friend, the Duchess of Roxburghe.

Murian frowned. "Why was Tata Natasha visiting Wulf?"

"Lily has not been well, so Tata Natasha went to offer her help. Whatever she did for Lily seemed to work, for Wulf says she's better. But then Tata Natasha left, and we've had no word for three weeks."

"Bloody hell. I should go over there—"

"There's no need. Nik was in London; he's traveling north as we speak. He'll find her."

Max nodded, relieved. "I didn't know Nik was in London."

Alexsey didn't look pleased. "Neither did I until this happened. Our brother has become far too secretive."

"Aye. I think so, too."

Murian slipped her hand into the crook of his arm. "I wonder if Tata Natasha will be found staying in the home of a spirited single Scottish lass?"

"I don't know," Max said. "She is far more frail than she seems. She shouldn't be traveling at all."

Murian hid a smile, for she suspected Max was the only member of his family to believe such a thing. Seeing his worried face, she squeezed his arm. "I suppose the only way we can keep Tata Natasha at home is to have as many great-grandchildren as possible."

Max smiled. "That would help."

"Thankfully, Bronwyn and I have that task well under control."

There was a silence. Max's gaze locked upon her lips, as if he could see the words she'd just spoken.

Then Alexsey gave a huge whoop, while Max swooped her up and buried his face in her neck. She hugged him back, laughing softly as he held her aloft.

When he slid her back to her feet, he pressed a fervent kiss to her forehead. "How long have you known?"

"For two weeks."

"And you're certain?"

"Very certain. That's why I've been sick every morning." She curled her nose. "I am so glad to be off that ship!"

He cupped her face between his hands. "And I'm so glad I have you here, with me." He pressed a kiss to her lips, soft and gentle, a promise in the caress.

She kissed him back, content and pleased, and he slipped a protective arm about her shoulders as they turned to walk to the carriage.

She smiled happily. This was love. They shared and encouraged. They teased and sometimes argued. Such was the way with people of passion. But whatever happened, she knew where she belonged: with Max and her loved ones.

She tucked her arm about him and hurried him to the carriage, grinning when he chuckled at her impatience. "Come, Max. Let's go home."

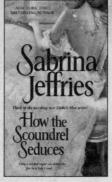